The Worst
Duke in
London

AMALIE HOWARD

A Taming of the Dukes
NOVEL

FOREVER

NEW YORK   BOSTON

Forever
Hachette Book Group
1290 Avenue of the Americas, New York, NY 10104
read-forever.com
@readforeverpub

First Edition: September 2024

Forever is an imprint of Grand Central Publishing. The Forever name and logo are registered trademarks of Hachette Book Group, Inc.

The publisher is not responsible for websites (or their content) that are not owned by the publisher.

The Hachette Speakers Bureau provides a wide range of authors for speaking events. To find out more, go to hachettespeakersbureau.com or email HachetteSpeakers@hbgusa.com.

Forever books may be purchased in bulk for business, educational, or promotional use. For information, please contact your local bookseller or the Hachette Book Group Special Markets Department at special.markets@hbgusa.com.

Ball of yarn art by Taylor Navis

Library of Congress Cataloging-in-Publication Data

Names: Howard, Amalie, author.
Title: The worst duke in London / Amalie Howard.
Description: First edition. | New York : Forever, 2024. | Series: Taming of the dukes novel ; 3
Identifiers: LCCN 2024001371 | ISBN 9781538737781 (trade paperback) | ISBN 9781538737804 (e-book)
Subjects: LCGFT: Romance fiction. | Novels.
Classification: LCC PS3608.O89695 W67 2024 | DDC 813/.6—dc23 /eng/20240119
LC record available at https://lccn.loc.gov/2024001371

ISBN: 9781538737781 (trade paperback), 9781538737804 (ebook)

Printed in the United States of America

LSC

Printing 1, 2024

FALL IN LOVE WITH
AMALIE HOWARD!

"Amalie Howard's books sit at the crossroads of history and herstory—Victorian romance, but with a dollop of strong women who take charge of their destinies...and as a result, who rescue the men in their orbit. Refreshing, steamy, and stocked with characters you don't normally get to see in the genre—her books are a must-read for me."

—Jodi Picoult, #1 *New York Times* bestselling author

"Amalie Howard tells a story with self-assured style, wit, and energy...her writing sparkles!"

—Lisa Kleypas, #1 *New York Times* bestselling author

"The fresh voice historical romance needs right now....I will read every word she writes."

—Kerrigan Byrne, *USA Today* bestselling author

NEVER MET A DUKE LIKE YOU

"[A] page-turning Victorian romance...Howard's admirable and progressive protagonists and *Clueless*-inspired plot are sure to have readers charmed."

—*Publishers Weekly*

Always Be My Duchess

"A dreamy summer romance designed to sweep you up into a world of ballerinas, hunky dukes, cheeky girl gangs, and delicious sex scenes. Light on angst and heavy on charm, it's a feel-good read of the highest order."

—*Entertainment Weekly*

"The story slayed me from page one."

—*Paste* magazine

"Howard creates great characters and dialogue...A real treat."

—*Library Journal*

"Howard's lyrical writing enlivens her bright, empathetic characters and her sharp eye on their class and cultural disparities only enhances their romance. Readers will be riveted."

—*Publishers Weekly*

"Fabulous writing...such a delicious escape. Utterly delightful!"

—Eloisa James, *New York Times* bestselling author

ALSO BY AMALIE HOWARD

Always Be My Duchess

Never Met a Duke Like You

CONTENT GUIDANCE

The discussion of animal welfare as well as some off-page maltreatment are part of an underlying plot thread in this novel. Some animals are in dangerous on-page situations, requiring rescue, though none are harmed. Abandonment by a parent as well as the death/murder of a family member are mentioned in dialogue. Some drug use, including morphine and cocaine-laced wine, is discussed. There is discussion of a consensual sex agreement as well as a visit to a sex club. Period-specific terms such as *harlot*, *trollop*, and *light-skirts* are used, and I have tried my best to keep these both authentic and sex-positive within context. Intimate scenes are described on page. Some offensive language is used in the narration as well as in dialogue.

For my friend Katie, a true Hellfire Kitty:
fun, fierce, feisty, and will always have bail money

CHAPTER ONE

Lady Evangeline Raine adored the country. Unlike London, Chichester was clean, the air was not heavy with fog, and it was completely free of gentlemen on the prowl for an heiress with a large dowry. After her previous disastrous seasons, crammed to the brim with silver-tongued fortune hunters, the last she could definitely do without. At one-and-twenty, she'd had quite enough of sly suitors and their fickle promises.

But while going to town was the least of her priorities, it was unfortunately her younger sister's greatest wish. And what Viola wanted, Viola usually got—in fact, it was the reason her sister had been living in France with their aunt Justine for the past two years. She'd been desperate to go to Paris—she was obsessed with fashion—and their father hadn't been in any frame of mind to argue. That, and the fact that the earl simply had been at his wit's end after his wife took off for parts unknown a handful of years ago.

The Countess of Oberton had simply disappeared.

She'd left a letter.

Evangeline had read it but taken great pains to hide it from her younger sister. Viola had been an irrepressible thirteen-year-old and Evangeline barely sixteen. The countess had wanted to be free of the tethers of marriage and motherhood—she'd been betrothed too young, hadn't had a chance to live, wasn't happy…along with a handful of more selfish excuses. Considering how much Viola adored their mother, Effie had wanted to protect her sister from a wounded heart. What kind of woman hied off without a qualm in the world, leaving two adolescent daughters behind?

Men weren't the only ones with fickle hearts, it seemed, which was why it stood to reason that people should guard themselves against love's crooked arrow. At least, that was what Evangeline believed.

"Honestly, Effie, I do not understand why you have to be so *dull*," Viola grumbled over breakfast. "I haven't even had anything that counts for a season. At least you've had yours, and now, I'm practically already on the shelf, facing a future alone and decrepit."

"Don't be dramatic." Evangeline bit her lip to stop herself from saying more—saying *worse*—that her sister was an overindulged brat who should hardly complain about her rather privileged circumstances. It was no secret that Aunt Justine had spoiled her rotten. Horribly so. Case in point, Viola did not like being told no.

"Perhaps you should wait another year," Evangeline said calmly. "You're barely eighteen. The season and all its considerable fripperies won't go away, never fear."

"This is insufferable," Viola wailed.

"Living in wealth and comfort on a four-thousand-hectare estate is insufferable to you?" Evangeline murmured, noticing their father lifting his newspaper even higher as though erecting a barricade against the incoming storm.

"Papa!" Viola screeched.

"Your sister is right, perhaps it's best to wait another year." The Earl of Oberton cherished both of his daughters dearly, but Evangeline suspected he saw how much like oil and water they had become, especially in the two years they'd been apart.

Evangeline lifted her brows in challenge. "I *am* right. A season is simply a grandiose affair to pander to the men of the aristocracy."

"Spare me your patronizing scolding, Effie," Viola shot back. "Not everyone wants to succumb to ennui as you seem so comfortable doing. Although you have your animal shack and your fur-loving diversions, and I have nothing."

"The *shelter* is a home for lost and starving animals. It is not a diversion or a shack," she replied. "Those poor creatures are in danger of dying without proper food and care."

"Can't you be a Good Samaritan in town? There are hungry dogs there, too."

Evangeline *could*...but it was London. She'd rather douse herself in horse piss than ever set foot there. And besides, the local shelter home for animals was her passion, and it was wholly hers. She could not abandon it. Those poor, defenseless animals needed her, and she needed them.

Slipping a piece of crispy bacon from her plate, she fed it to the mutt of mixed breed that lay at her feet. Lucky had been found abandoned, sickly, and left for dead on a country road, but she'd quickly become her devoted companion.

"No. I loathe London."

"You loathe anything fun," Viola grumbled.

Evangeline shot her pouting sister a glance. Viola's thick, golden-brown curls bounced as she shook her head, her bright blue eyes flashing with temper. She was lovely, even in the throes of her childish sulk, and genuinely kind when it suited her. And she had a sensible mind, though she rarely chose to use it. In Viola's own words, why would she have need of cleverness when her looks got her what she wanted easily enough?

In their aristocratic set, that logic was true. A pretty face backed by a generous dowry always trumped acumen or wit. Viola got the lion's share of beauty and charm from their mother, while Evangeline was blessed with a keen intellect and their father's much-too-soft heart, which she buried under layers of aloofness. She was as unique of face as she was in character, and neither of those had served her well in her own three miserable failed seasons.

Only a few years younger, Viola was molded from an entirely different cloth. Unlike Evangeline, she lived for revelries, parties, and obsequious gentlemen. She'd insisted on attending every country assembly within reasonable distance, no matter how small, and had garnered three excellent offers of marriage over the past few months. So she didn't actually *need* a season to form a match. She craved the pageantry of an official coming-out.

And one bachelor in particular.

Lord Huntington, who had found out about Viola's return and made his interest clear, was a pompous arse who held himself in glorious regard. He was a dandy through and through, but nevertheless a favored son of the aristocracy. Set to inherit an enormous fortune and a marquessate, he was a catch by all accounts, except Evangeline's. It didn't matter that he was shallower than a muddy pond at the height of summer or fancied his reflection more than he could ever hope to esteem another. The man was an utter knave...and one who needed to keep a far step away from her sister.

None of his obnoxious qualities signified to Viola, however, whose lips were set in a flat, white, stubborn line. "Papa, I am ready to wed and wish to secure a husband. May we *please* go to London for the season? Lord Huntington has—"

The earl wrinkled his brow, his gaze darting to Evangeline. "Perhaps it won't be too much trouble if—"

"Trust me," Evangeline interrupted sharply, dismay at what was certain to come next out of her father's mouth. "That man is so in love with himself, he'll hardly notice if you aren't there."

Viola shot her a withering look. "He intends to court me."

Heart sinking, Evangeline gritted her teeth. Of course he did. Viola was vivacious and beautiful, exactly the prize a braggart like Huntington would covet. If she warned Viola to stay away, she would undoubtedly do the opposite. "Along with three-quarters of London's debutants, I'm sure."

Her sister's glare could incinerate the table. "You're just jealous that Lord Huntington never looked twice at you, Effie dear. Or shall I say, Lady Ghast—"

"That is *enough*, Viola," the earl cautioned from where he'd once more ducked down behind his newspaper.

It hurt, that barb, but Evangeline kept her expression composed, even as Viola's pretty face crumpled in instant shame. "That was truly awful of me, Effie. I apologize."

Evangeline gave a placid nod and calmly buttered her toast as the hated memory rose to taunt her. During her very first season, she'd scoffed at something Huntington had said to the rest of his fawning toadies, and he had not taken it well. Granted, she probably should have stayed silent, but she hadn't, and that had been the first of many proverbial nails in her coffin.

"These suffragists are a scourge and a disgrace," a self-aggrandizing Huntington had declared. "Politics is no business for females. A woman's place is at home, and her vote is the same as her father's or her husband's. I will decide what's best for any wife of mine or what opinion she should have."

"That would make you a rather gifted ventriloquist," Evangeline had blurted out before she could stop herself . . . in front of *everyone*.

His reaction had been thespian. "I beg your pardon?"

Evangeline's cheeks had boiled. Silly, *silly*, ungovernable *mouth*! In for a penny, in for a pound then. She'd lifted her chin and opted for tongue-in-cheek humor. "Shall you think for her, too, my lord? This mute marionette wife of yours?"

"Women, like children, should be seen and not heard." His narrowed, scornful gaze had raked her person, letting her know exactly what he'd thought of her. "Though in your unlucky case, *not* seen and *not* heard would be preferable."

The bald insult was made worse when their avid audience started twittering, and only then had Evangeline realized what her unruly opinion and the offense against *this* particular gentleman would cost her. "I only meant we . . ." She'd cleared her throat, ears aflame with mortification. "That is, women, have their own minds and their own voices."

Lord Huntington had sneered at her down the length of his perfect, patrician nose, a condescending jeer twisting his full lips. "I suppose for someone like you, it could only be a choice between being a spinster or a suffragist."

"Someone like *me*?" she'd echoed amid the murmur of cruel laughter.

"A frigid corpse of a wallflower. Shall we add *specter* in there for good measure?" That glittering, spiteful gaze had speared her, eyes settling on her distinctively pale hair and even paler skin. "One better suited to a crypt, Lady Ghastly."

Lady Ghastly.

The awful moniker had cut deeply. Her best friend, Vesper, now the Duchess of Greydon, had told her that the gossip would die down when the ton found something new to talk about, but the dreadful and ugly nickname had stuck.

Not only for one season but also for the other two that followed.

Since then, Evangeline had inured herself to the pain of hearing the nasty nickname, though not from her own sister. It hurt. *Terribly.*

Breakfast resumed in silence, the tension so thick she could slather her cold toast with it. Evangeline could feel Viola's pleading glances, but she refused to look up until the meal was nearly done.

Baxter, their longtime butler, entered the room. "I beg your pardon, my lord, but Lord Huntington has arrived and is asking whether you are at home to callers."

As if the foul sobriquet had summoned its equally foul master.

So *that* was what the morning's diatribe was about. Evangeline did look at Viola then, but the younger girl was focusing all of her beseeching attention on their father, who had lowered his paper. He frowned at her over his spectacles. "Was this your doing, Viola?"

Her sister's lower lip trembled, and Evangeline held back an eye roll at Viola's predictable theatrics. "I didn't tell him to come right this minute, Papa."

"Very well, since he has interrupted our breakfast, send him in here."

Evangeline smoothed her wrinkled, fur-covered skirts, though it didn't matter what Lord Huntington thought of her. Not anymore. He had made his opinion of her rather clear. When he entered the room, Evangeline could almost hear the celestial horns heralding his illustrious presence.

She and Viola stood to greet Huntington and then retook their seats.

"Huntington," their father said, folding his newssheets. "To what do we owe your visit?"

"Lord Oberton," he said, giving a courtly bow. "Lady Evangeline, Lady Viola." For a second, Evangeline sighed in relief that he hadn't called her by that cruel nickname, but she did not miss the tiny smirk that crossed his lips, as if he knew she'd been expecting it, the despicable cad. "My apologies for calling so early and interrupting your breakfast, but I'm off to London shortly."

The earl arched a brow. "Well, get on with it then."

Evangeline bit her lip to keep from snorting at Huntington's miffed expression. "I was wondering if I may call on Lady Viola in London, my lord."

"We've no plans to go to London."

Viola made a noise in her throat, her eyes filling with tears. "Papa, *please*."

He let out an aggrieved sigh, his eyes darting to Evangeline, whose spine froze in alarm at the resigned expression on his face. Surely, he wouldn't give in to such a false display!

As the earl reached for his reading glasses and began cleaning them with a cloth, Effie felt her heart tumble to her feet. Cleaning his spectacles was his tell whenever he was about to concede…especially to Viola.

It was some kind of guilt, Evangeline knew, for sending her off to France after Mama's disappearance. He'd done so gratefully without so much as an argument when he hadn't been able to cope with parenting a rambunctious daughter who looked too much like her mother, and Viola had become adept at taking advantage of their father's misplaced culpability. New gowns? No expense was spared. A new pianoforte? Why not a harp as well?

Paris? Of course, why not go for two years instead of two months?

Evangeline felt guilt, too. After all, it was also partially her fault that Viola had been sent away to live with their aunt in France three years after their mother had left. Perhaps if Evangeline had been a more capable older sister and not caught up in her own woes, Viola might have fared better in England. She could not change the past, however, and making up for it now when she could, just like their father did, was the only alternative.

The earl cleared his throat, and Evangeline's heart sank. "The only way my younger daughter will be in London for the season is if her elder sister decides to accompany her. You may find a gentleman of your own there, Effie."

"I won't," Evangeline said followed by the sound of Viola's unladylike shriek of despair. "I don't wish to marry, Papa. It's been three seasons already, and I only agreed to go to town the last time for my friends."

"That's not fair!" Viola complained. "What about *my* season? She just wants to stay here like a dried-up old prune."

The earl stood without meeting Evangeline's furious gaze. How could he spring something like this on her—he knew very well how she felt about the whole marriage mart farce. "That's my final say on the matter." He glanced at their visitor. "Good day, Huntington."

After Lord Huntington left with a strange, purposeful glint in his eyes, Evangeline gulped her now cold tea, the old feelings of distress coming back to plague her. While she tried not to care about gossip, being ostracized by the entire ton had left its mark—a mark she worked valiantly to erase by shoring herself up with a small circle of trusted friends and the shelter animals that needed her. If she attended balls at all in previous seasons, it was always on her own terms, and certainly *not* to attract a husband.

"Papa, please, I cannot," she said, chest tight.

He looked disconsolate, running a hand through his thinning hair. "Effie, I wouldn't ask this of you if I didn't need your help."

"Surely we can get a suitable chaperone for Viola. Hire a companion. Anyone!"

"There is more at stake here, Evangeline, for you as well," he said. "Who will look after you when I'm gone?"

She clenched her teeth. "Give me my dowry and I shall look after myself. I don't need a husband to command my every move."

The earl rose and came over to place a hand on her shoulder, making no attempt to hide the guilt written all over him—she knew he did not want to be the bad father, but she didn't want to be the scapegoat either. "I'll leave it to you then, Effie."

Dear God, the pressure of those words.

The fight drained out of her, but the despair remained as he shuffled from the room.

Her sister's tears fell in earnest now. "Do this for me, Effie, please," Viola begged.

Evangeline swallowed hard, dread climbing into her throat at the thought of enduring another interminable season as poor Lady Ghastly, even for Viola's sake. Her heart felt like it was being stampeded, crushed beneath the weight of the ostracism and ridicule she thought she'd moved past and long overcome.

Like most aristocratic young women, she'd once dreamed of

marriage and a family, of succeeding where her own mother had failed, but her dreams had died when her prospects had dwindled to the dregs of society. A fitting match for the so-decreed bottom of the barrel.

But Evangeline would rather be alone than with someone who held no real esteem for her or who only wanted her inheritance. She did not want to be her mother…marrying for the wrong reasons and hurting those she was supposed to care for because she was resentful.

Sometimes, a person's dreams had to change, even if stupidly impossible hope lingered that someone might love her one day. Such hope was a recipe for heartache and disaster.

Evangeline shook her head. "Don't ask this of me, Viola. I *can't*."

CHAPTER TWO

Lord Gage Croft, the rather impoverished Duke of Vale, drank a toast of Ceylon tea to the final of his personal fortune, currently earmarked to pay off his dead brother's final remaining vowel. The Croft men were known for their love of drinking and gambling, from gaming halls to cockfighting to anything in between. No prize was too small, no wager too big. They were notorious for their brand of boldness. Their utter daring.

Their *folly*.

The vice was in their blood. And anyone who could bleed his late father and brother dry had tried... and had mostly succeeded. Fake ventures, loans, illegal races, prizefights, absurd wagers—the schemes added up to an obscene amount, one that had nearly ruined the ducal name.

Anything that wasn't entailed had been sold to pay off the accrued mountain of debts, down to the last pair of candlesticks in the ancestral estate. Everything of value had been put up for auction—heirlooms, art, furniture, even clothing. The only things Gage hadn't sold were the family portraits, a few necessary items, and his bed.

A man needed somewhere to sleep, after all.

Thanks to his Scottish mother, Gage had stayed away from the gaming halls, seeing what it had done to his father and grandfather, but he scratched that bone-deep itch—the thrill-seeking curse of the men in his family—in other ways. The same rush that plagued them was the same one that had driven him to bare-knuckle boxing.

A younger Gage had loved the primal buzz of it, of giving in to the feeling of pitting his body and his fists against the odds, and the high of being named champion, the scent of sweat and blood thick in the air. It was still a compulsion, he knew, an *addiction*. He craved the excitement like an opium eater and gorged himself on it whenever the need arose. But he never wagered or played any stakes. Strenuous physical activity like boxing—and later on, caber tossing—had kept his head clear.

But then, in a sudden and awful twist of fate, his brother Asher died in a curricle race gone wrong, and the dukedom had become Gage's reality. A reality he resented, but was now his nonetheless. He was responsible for dozens of tenants, staff, and servants, all of whom were suffering from unpaid wages on his family's account, not to mention living off lands that were fallow and quite barren.

He had to make things right. Then, perhaps, once that was done, his life could finally go back to what it had been in Scotland. Calm, steady, predictable. No temptations and no irredeemable vices. A trustworthy steward would be more than capable of managing the estate in his place.

Cracking his scarred, thickened knuckles, Gage blew out a breath as he glanced at his somber solicitor. Mr. Boone had worked for Gage's family for years, and Lord knew how much money he probably owed the man. Perhaps *he* might be amenable to overseeing the ducal lands, if Gage offered him a persuasive enough raise. Not that he had the funds for that at the moment. One hurdle at a time.

"So the accounts are in the clear?" Gage asked.

"The remaining balances were the last of it, Your Grace."

"And you?"

The solicitor nodded. "I have been compensated in arrears as well, Your Grace, including the rest of your staff and the remaining servants. Thank you."

Gage bit back another sigh. Said household was down to a meager few—barely enough to toe the boundaries of respectability for a duke. His house may be empty, and his coffers scraped to the absolute bottoms, but he was out of debt, barring one outstanding gambling vowel owed to a society fop by his late brother. A debt that was now his to bear…on top of an estate that still required an enormous amount of upkeep and a leaking roof that needed replacing.

Boone cleared his throat. "Do you plan to be in London for the season, Your Grace?"

As if he could afford a fucking season. Gage glanced down at the frayed cuffs on his coat and the abraded wear of his boots. "No."

"Pardon my impudence, Your Grace, but perhaps you should consider it," Boone suggested. "A wealthy wife could be an excellent option for a peer in your position."

Gage couldn't quite curb his derisive response. "And which highborn lady in your estimation, Mr. Boone, would fancy the penniless Duke of Vale and move to the wilds of Scotland?" The man blanched, but Gage waved an arm. "Trust me, I'm aware of what the gossip rags say."

The half-Scottish *Destitute Duke* with his pugilist hands and rough edges was much too uncouth to be welcomed in pretty London ballrooms. He was in fact quite unkindly ranked the worst duke in London by the *Times*. A lady would have to be desperate to want him. In fact, he might have to pay *her* a dowry.

Gage let out a dark chuckle at that last thought. "One day, I'll wed a bonny Scottish lass, Boone. In the meantime, I'll find a way to settle Asher's debt and pay for the remaining repairs on the estate. There are some railway investments I'm looking into as well as some shipping ventures. Real ones, not the absurd, sham schemes that my brother and father fell prey to. If that fails, I can always field a fight or two for the prize money." The solicitor balked, and Gage laughed. "Sorry, old man, that was in poor taste. No gambling, I swear. You don't have to worry about me taking unnecessary risks like Asher or my father did."

After Boone took his leave, Gage ran a hand through his thick tangle of hair. He needed a haircut and a shave. He was starting to resemble one of the shaggy red roan Shetland ponies in his paddock that he'd brought in to sell for extra coin. His brother's old valet had retired due to his fading eyesight, and without money to replace him, Gage had just managed to make do over the past few months.

"Jenkins," he called out, and waited for the young footman turned butler to come to the study door. "Do you know how to cut hair?"

"Not unless you wish to lose an eye, Your Grace."

Gage blinked. Was looking presentable worth losing an eye? He was seriously deliberating the question when sharp, booted footsteps echoing noisily in the empty foyer snagged his attention. He frowned, wondering why whoever it was hadn't been announced and then realizing that he'd summoned Jenkins from his post.

"See who that is, will you?" he told him. He wasn't expecting any visitors, not that many came to Vale Ridge Park these days, unless it was to either purchase his family's heirlooms for pennies on the pound or buy the occasional head of livestock.

Or to collect monies owed.

Gage frowned. He smoothed a hand through his sweaty matted hair, attempting some semblance of civility, and straightened his threadbare coat. The few days' growth of thick copper stubble gracing his cheeks and jaw would have to stay. When Jenkins ushered his visitor into the study, Gage's gut tightened.

Lord Evan Huntington, the owner of his brother's last vowel, stood scowling in the doorway. He'd come to collect his two thousand pounds, no doubt. A bloody fortune. Why his brother owed such an exorbitant amount to Huntington, Gage did not know, but the loan had been the straw that had broken the camel's back. That fatal curricle race had been Asher's last-ditch effort to cancel out the debt. He'd bet on himself and lost.

"I told you, I'll get you your money," Gage bit out without preamble once the butler had shut the door. "You gave me six months to repay what my brother owed you."

The man's nose lifted in a haughty gesture. "You look like you were dragged and trampled by a wild horse, Vale."

"Did you come all the way here to compliment me?"

"I have a wager for you," Huntington said, ignoring the sarcasm.

Gage's eyes narrowed. "I don't gamble."

"Call it a gentleman's agreement then. Do this one thing for me, and your brother's debt—*your* debt—will be forgiven."

He stared at the man with suspicion. Huntington was filthy rich, but what *one thing* could possibly equate to two thousand pounds? It had to be illegal, whatever it was, and Gage might be desperate, but he wasn't a fool.

"Not interested," he said.

Huntington cleared his throat, spreading his pristinely gloved hands wide as he perched on the edge of the desk, the only seating option since the rest of the furniture that once filled Gage's study had been sold.

"Goodness, it's like a mausoleum in here, Vale. Did you sell every piece of furniture you own?"

"I kept the desk as a memento. I'll thank you not to sit on it." Devil take it, Gage wanted to punch Huntington in his supercilious mouth. "If there isn't anything else, I do have a busy afternoon."

"Hear me out, Vale," Huntington cajoled, pushing off the desk. "It's worth it, I promise you."

Obviously, he wasn't going to get rid of the man until he said his piece, so Gage nodded, folding his arms over his chest and sighing. "Go on."

"Do you know the Raine sisters? The Earl of Oberton's daughters."

In Chichester, everyone knew of the Raines. Oberton was a decent man, one of the few good peers, in his estimation, but Gage had had little opportunity of late to cross paths with either the earl or his family. He'd spent the last month working on the deteriorating portions of the estate with toil, elbow grease, and no small amount of patience. He hadn't had the time to be social and, in truth, hadn't wanted to be.

A forgotten memory of two girls skipping in the creek that bordered their neighboring estates filled his head. Both had haloes of pale hair; one was plump and pretty, and the other was thin with sharp, foxlike features. He and Asher had seen them from time to time, but the gap in their ages meant they hadn't been in the same circles.

"No, I wouldn't say I know them," he replied.

Huntington sent him a patronizing nod. "Of course not. Well, I intend to set my cap for Lady Viola, the younger of the two. However, her father has stated that she will not be in London for me to court, unless her older sister goes to town as well."

Gage frowned. "And why is that my concern?"

"I need *you* to convince the older sister to go to London."

"Convince her how?" he growled.

Huntington spread his palms wide. "Woo her, seduce her, tell her she's pretty. Whatever you do to get women to capitulate. Lie, if you have to."

Gage opened his mouth and closed it. Surely, he could not have heard right—Huntington wanted him to play some kind of Lothario? He squinted at the man, searching his eyes for signs of cloudiness or confusion. "Are you in your cups, Huntington?"

"Stop staring at me as if I'm daft. I'm quite serious," he snapped. "Simply get her to go to London for the season, and I'll erase your debt."

Gage flinched, fist curling at the reminder of his inherited obligation. "I have no plans to go to London."

"Then make some." Huntington stood, adjusting his pristine lace cuffs. "Think of it, Vale. Two thousand pounds gone just like that. All for one little favor."

A favor that would cost him funds he did not have. The season was *expensive*. Not to mention annoying and exhausting.

"Perhaps you did not hear me, Huntington. I am not fit for town." Gage drew a hand down his worn, stained clothing with a pointed glance. "You are well aware I have no money to pursue any-one, much less a lady of quality. Furthermore, I can barely afford to keep myself in last decade's style, much less this season's fashions. I will not be made a laughingstock to help you get your prick wet."

"Watch your tongue. I intend to marry the girl," Huntington shot back, nostrils flaring in outrage.

"Congratulations."

The man stalked toward him, oozing arrogance as if it was only a matter of time before Gage agreed to his asinine plan. "I'll pay for it all," Huntington declared, his eyes gleaming. "New togs, boots, a carriage, whatever you need. No expense spared."

It sounded much too good to be true, and offers like this usually were. Gage's brows drew together, a thought occurring to him. "Is something amiss with the lass? I've been in Scotland for a decade and a half, if you recall."

"Not exactly, no." Huntington hesitated, lips thinning. "Other than the typical lineage and acceptable upbringing, she might be...a bit unusual in looks. Unremarkable, really. A spinster prone to nattering on about animal welfare and whatnot. She'll be an easy conquest."

Gage blew out a breath. Nothing in Huntington's description sounded alarming, unless *unremarkable* meant something else entirely. Uniqueness of face did not bother him, nor did a love of animals.

He cleared his throat, bringing himself back to the business at hand. "So, if I have this right, you wish for me to falsely woo a spinster so that you can court her sister, and for this task, you will forgive my brother's entire debt and pay all my expenses for the forthcoming season in London?"

"Expenses *within reason*," Huntington amended quickly.

The man was harebrained. But if the offer was real, there was no question, Gage would have to do it. He could not afford to let his pride or morals get in the way of *finally* being out of the red. Then he could wash his hands of this place, hire Boone to be steward, and go back home.

"How long do you expect this farce to go on?"

"Get her to London and keep her there long enough for me to win the sister, and I will do the rest." Huntington's expression was smug. "As soon as my offer for Lady Viola is accepted by the earl, consider the debt paid in full."

That sounded much too dependent on Huntington for Gage's liking—what if the fop failed in his suit? That wasn't something in Gage's control. He narrowed his eyes. "I will convince her to go to London and keep her occupied for a month, that's the agreement."

"A month?" Huntington spluttered. "I need two, at least."

"Surely you have better faith in your abilities than that?" Gage scoffed, watching the man turn red at the snide insinuation that his skill with women was lacking. "Six weeks. I will require the agreement in writing and access to an account."

Huntington conceded with a gnash of his teeth. "Fine. You shall have both."

Something tugged at Gage's conscience…a warning, perhaps, that this was just another kind of wager in disguise. Another *bet*. He shrugged it away. This was opportunity, and he would be a fool to walk away. Not when two thousand pounds was at stake.

"Very well, you have yourself a deal."

A satisfied grin crossed Huntington's face as he shook his hand and then walked to the door. He paused. "One more thing, Vale."

Of course there was. "What's that?" he asked, gut clenching uneasily.

"Lady Viola can never know about this."

Gage nodded. "Naturally."

He raked a calloused palm over his face. It mightn't be bare-knuckle boxing, but anticipation coursed through his veins all the same. Poor, on-the-shelf, unremarkable Lady Evangeline Raine wouldn't know what hit her, and maybe, just maybe, she might actually thank him for it.

After all, what highborn female didn't like a bit of attention?

Chapter Three

"Oh, come here, you sweet little buttercup," Evangeline crooned to the fluff ball of a kitten. Its fur was so soft, despite being matted in some areas. Her heart melted as the tiny feline gave a pitiable mew. "Shall I call you Buttercup then? Do you approve?"

The kitten had been rescued along with its four brothers and sisters from a nearby alley and brought to Evangeline's shelter by a good neighbor, which made her happy for two reasons. One, any animal rescue was a miracle, and two, people clearly *valued* her animal foundling home. She had managed to lease the small set of rooms at the far end of the village from her good friend William Dawson, the local veterinarian, who owned the building.

It was because of his generosity that she could follow her passion.

Her thoughts drifted back to her father's coldhearted edict and Viola's disappointment at Evangeline's reticence to go to London for the season. She didn't want to be courted or to open doors she'd already firmly closed. A woman didn't *need* to be married to be happy. At least, Evangeline didn't. She had her own space, she employed one helper, and she couldn't be more content. In truth, who needed marriage when one had loving animals and a higher purpose?

"Why are you frowning so fiercely at the poor thing?" Vesper, the newly minted Duchess of Greydon, asked. "Is it ill?"

"No, I was thinking about something else. They're all healthy, I think."

The kittens appeared to be about nine or ten weeks old, and though they were despairingly thin, they were sprightly and alive. There'd been no sign of their mother when they were found. Evangeline frowned. No cat would abandon her young, so she must have been caught by a fox or some other predator. That made her hug her precious little orphan tighter.

"Goodness, Effie, you're getting orange fur all over your gown," Vesper said, wrinkling her nose.

She cuddled the kitten under her chin and nuzzled kisses to its fuzzy head. "It's just a dress. Feel how soft she is, Vesper."

Vesper stretched out a tentative finger and then drew it away with a narrowed gaze. "What if that mangy little thing has fleas or it's rabid?"

"A few fleas won't kill you. And she's not rabid," Evangeline said, and chuckled at her friend. "Look how sweet she is. Cat was a rescue too, and I didn't steer you wrong with her, did I?"

Cat. That was the exceedingly uninventive name that her friend had come up with for the kitten that Evangeline had gifted her a while ago. Vesper pursed her lips. "That's different. You didn't find Cat in an abandoned alley. How do you know it's a she anyway?"

"Not an alley, but a barn. All my animals are rescued." Evangeline flipped the kitten to her back and peered at her soft white underbelly. "And last I checked, this one is female because she doesn't have a...er...penis."

A distinctly male throat cleared from behind them, making both women jump. Evangeline felt a blush scorch her cheeks as she glanced past Vesper to the man towering behind her. Gracious, what atrocious timing! She sniffed—the word had been appropriate to describe the male anatomy—but it was hardly proper in polite, *mixed* company. Still, she would not apologize for being pedagogic, even if her flaming face proclaimed otherwise.

"May I help you, sir?" she asked, gently depositing the kitten back to the floor. The stranger was a man of means, as she could discern from his smartly cut clothing. Those broad shoulders would require a private tailor. Perhaps he'd come to donate funds.

Evangeline rose to greet him and sucked in a breath. Good lord, he was huge. She was ridiculously rangy for a woman, yet he still loomed several inches over her. Hair the color of dark, polished copper curled into a wide brow over deep-set green eyes. His clean-shaven face was all hard angles and harsh rugged lines, except for his mouth, which looked full and inviting and…remarkably kissable.

Goodness, where had *that* thought come from?

Her pulse thrummed in her veins. *Stop thinking about kissing!*

"I'm looking for Lady Evangeline," he said in a voice so deep it made her skin tingle. Was that a hint of a Scottish burr? "Is she here?"

Vesper made a humming noise in her throat as she pretended to inspect the rambunctious kitten who'd jumped off her lap and darted a few feet away. Evangeline blinked. Why was he looking for *her*? She tempered the urge to smooth her hair, which she knew was a mess from the boisterous kittens who'd used her braid as a chew toy. She could feel the wispy strands glued to her cheeks and then remembered that Vesper had said something about her dress being coated in fur.

Evangeline bit back a groan. Of course when a gentleman of

obvious means dropped in at the shelter, she *would* be a rather sweaty, fur-covered hot mess, but there was nothing that could be done for it. The rescue home was funded through her own resources as well as charitable donations, and if he was a philanthropist who had seen her pamphlet and intended to contribute funds, her appearance would not matter. She hoped.

"Who may I say is asking?" she asked primly.

"The Duke of Vale."

Vesper's eyes grew wide and her hand fluttered up to her throat, her startled gaze flicking back to Evangeline. "Your Grace," she murmured, rising to dip into a curtsy.

Evangeline blinked and fumbled through a curtsy of her own that resembled more of an awkward squat than anything remotely refined. Hadn't she read in the newssheets a year or so ago that the Duke of Vale had died in a tragic carriage accident? She hadn't known him well even though their estates shared a border—the family had not spent much time at their ancestral seat, preferring to live closer to London. If she recalled correctly, the parents had been estranged and the two young children were shipped off to Scotland with their mother.

The ducal title would have passed to the younger brother. Was this him, and if so, why would he be looking for her?

"Congratulations on your nuptials, Your Grace," he said to Vesper with a short bow. "My mother mentioned seeing news of your wedding in the papers. I am an old friend of your brother's. How is the earl these days?"

Vesper smiled and canted her head. "Thank you. Lushing is well."

"Good to hear," he said and then turned to her next. "Lady Evangeline, I presume?"

She pressed her lips together and nodded, even though a part of her wanted to deny it for some ungodly reason. "You found me."

"Ah, how wonderful." He beamed so brightly and so widely she could almost see his back molars. A person smiled like that only when they wanted something, not when they intended to *give* something. Evangeline narrowed her eyes. If he hadn't come to make a donation, what on earth *did* he want? And why did his smile suddenly remind her of a wolf from a children's fairy tale?

Suspicious, she peered down the length of her nose at him. "How can I help you?"

An odd, nonplussed look crossed his face, as if he hadn't quite expected her flat, chilly reply. Evangeline supposed she could have been a bit more gracious and included his honorific, but something about his manner seemed too…obsequious. "I'm looking for a companion for a friend's daughter. Something small and not too troublesome. Like a fish."

"A fish?" she echoed. "Sir, this is a foundling home for lost and starving animals, not a pet shop."

He cocked his head, studying her with that deep green gaze that made her think of forest-wet leaves after a rainstorm, though why she would even draw such a comparison was peculiar. The man had green eyes, the end; there was no need to wax poetic on their extraordinary color. "Are you saying that fish are not deserving of assistance or rescue?"

"Well, they might be, I suppose, but not *here*," she replied with some confusion.

"That seems rather selective. Shouldn't lost or compromised fish be included?"

Evangeline couldn't quite tell if he was being serious or not, but most people of her set tended to mock her passions and her efforts toward the causes she championed. Her lips flattened. "Should they be in need of rescue, then certainly, sir," she replied, a rising edge to her tone. "However, at the moment, we currently have five kittens, four dogs, two rabbits, a goat, an owl, a three-legged lamb, and one surly hedgehog with a penchant for pricking. But might I direct you to the pond behind the neighboring field, where you might find the fish you seek?"

Surprising her, he chuckled, and she felt a bolt of electricity travel through her at the sound. Gracious, what an odd reaction! Distressed, she crossed her arms over her chest.

"Noted, my lady," the duke said, that unctuous, too-bright smile appearing again. If she didn't know better—and she *did* know better—Evangeline would think he was attempting to charm her. But there was no reason for some strange man, a duke no less, to seek her out for a bloody fish. So what then was his true purpose?

"Is that all, Your Grace?" she asked. "We are rather busy arranging for the adoption of our rescues from *serious* patrons."

Amusement bloomed in that bottle-green gaze. "I am quite serious and can be convinced. What does adopting a kitten entail?"

Vesper was watching them both intently, her blue eyes wide. Evangeline shot her a look that broke her friend out of her unusual spell.

"Heavens, look at the time! I must be off. Greydon is expecting me back at the manse. Effie, may I have a word before I leave?" With another curtsy to Lord Vale, Vesper took Evangeline's hand and led her toward the door. In a lowered voice she said, "Are you truly so opposed to going to London? It's my first birthday ball as Aspen's duchess. I need you there. Please come."

"You have Laila, Nève, and Briar."

She pouted sadly. "Yes, but the Hellfire Kitties are not complete without you."

Evangeline bit back a snort. The unique nickname had grown on all of them, even Laila, though their friend would deny it to her last breath. Evangeline spared a glance at Vale, who seemed entranced by the litter of kittens. "Vesper, darling, you know how I feel about London, or I would. And besides, I have nothing fashionable to wear. I would be an embarrassment."

"Nonsense, it's weeks away. Surely you can commission a gown in that time." Vesper's gaze shifted to Lord Vale, who was now being batted by the tiny kitten he'd lifted in one enormous hand. Evangeline followed her stare and bit her lips to keep from smirking as her friend went on. "Please say you'll think about it?"

"First Viola and now you. Neither of you seems to consider my feelings on the matter."

"I do, of course I do. You managed last year in London, and even seemed to enjoy yourself." She joined their hands. "Please, Effie. It would mean the world to me."

Evangeline stared down at their linked palms. "Huntington intends to court Viola. That's why this is different. You know what happened with him."

Vesper's eyes widened with empathy. "I do, but if you keep letting that ferret turd hold such power over you, Effie, he'll always win."

"But Viola—"

"Is a smart girl and will see him for who he is." She squeezed their palms. "Eventually, Huntington will show his true colors. People like him always do. Besides, I'll be there, and if you're truly worried about that horse's arse doing anything untoward, the girls will intervene. Hellfire Kitties for life, remember?"

Evangeline huffed a small laugh. That was comforting, at least.

Vesper, Laila, and Briar, and more recently, Nève, were her closest confidantes. At least they knew who she was, and they had made it easy to avoid Huntington and his toxic set. Maybe Vesper was right. The few events she'd attended during the last season hadn't been so terrible with them at her side.

She sighed. "Fine, I'll think about it."

"That's all I ask."

After Vesper took her leave, a furious volley of mews reached her ears, and Evangeline turned only to clap her hands to her mouth in a fit of laughter. The utterly astonished Duke of Vale was covered in kittens. Two clung to his trouser legs while a third hung onto his coat sleeve for dear life, the fourth was held by its scruff in his hands, and the fifth, Buttercup, was valiantly climbing his lapel to his shoulder like the queen of the castle. Evangeline's nose burned from trying to stanch the giggles.

"They're swarming," he whispered, his mouth barely opening as though he were afraid to move. She snorted and the suffocating tightness in her chest from a minute ago suddenly loosened. A clear green stare met hers. "I prefer not to be climbed like a tree."

"Here," she said, rushing to his side. "Let me help."

With careful fingers, she detached three of the adventurous kittens one by one, extracting their tiny claws and popping the little miscreants back into a box, where they would not get into trouble. Though she couldn't blame them…the Duke of Vale was rather climbable. Evangeline pushed that ludicrous notion *far* out of her head.

She buttoned her lips, took firm hold of her untoward urges, and retrieved another kitten. Buttercup she saved for last, though she had gamely climbed around the duke's nape and was cheerfully batting a loose auburn-brown tendril hanging over his collar. The curl caught the light and gleamed like molten copper for a moment.

"She likes hair," Evangeline said in a breathy voice that hardly sounded like her own. "Hold still and I shall attempt to detach her before she sinks those nails into you. They haven't been clipped."

"I don't mind being scratched," he said, and something in his tone made her eyes dart to his. The green depths had darkened, and for a moment, she wondered if she was overstepping by standing so close or misunderstanding the suggestive nature of his reply. Good God, was he flirting with her, after all? That made no sense—she was not a lady whom gentlemen went out of their way to charm, or at least she hadn't been since Huntington had deemed her Lady Ghastly.

She cleared her throat and tore her gaze from his.

"You will if the scratches get infected," she said. "The kittens might also have parasites, and they haven't been checked yet."

He lifted a brow. "Checked?"

"By the local veterinarian, Mr. Dawson. He'll have a look to make sure they are healthy and haven't got worms, fleas, or any infections themselves. They're quite feral, as you might have guessed."

Feral and deviously clever. Clearly, Buttercup did not want to give up her lofty perch atop the wonderful mountain that was her prize. *Who could blame her?* Huffing an impatient breath, Evangeline reached around the duke's arm, but every time she got close to the little ball of mischief, Buttercup danced out of reach as if it were a playful game.

"Come here, you naughty kitty!"

Moving stealthily, Evangeline crept one arm up as slowly as possible so as not to startle the little ginger troublemaker. It struck her notice again how tall and wide the duke was...and how well those broad and clearly powerful shoulders tapered into a narrow waist, as evidenced by the snug fit of the coat he wore. She bit her lip, unwilling to peruse any lower, though she was precariously close to his trim hips as she reached up onto her tiptoes.

"Goodness, Lady Effie, what on earth are you doing?" her helper, Hannah, bellowed. Her loud exclamation followed by a massive clatter of falling trays made the kitten hiss and leap into the air, her little spine curving upward as she toppled off the duke's shoulder. Lucky, Evangeline's rescue pup, who had been hot on Hannah's heels, darted into the room and made a beeline straight for them.

"Lucky, no!" Evangeline shrieked, ignoring Hannah's slew of muttered curses. "Hannah, fetch the dog! I'll catch the kitten."

Evangeline pitched forward and missed, crashing into a wall of stone. It wasn't stone, of course, because he was a man of flesh and blood, but gracious, the duke had to be made of granite or some such. Instinct made her scrabbling fingers snatch at his waist to stop her ungainly tumble as her skirts got caught in the scuffle.

His rigid body went even more rigid, a grunt leaving his lips at her unexpected and categorically ill-timed handful. Right at his deuced crotch...a location much, *much* lower than his waist.

Oh. Dear. God.

"I beg your pardon!" Snatching her burning palm away, Evangeline lost both her breath and her balance as her skirts became hopelessly tangled. How she'd ended up mauling a duke while collapsing in an undignified heap of fabric and flailing limbs was anyone's guess. Horrified, muffled snorting giggles erupted from her, even as Vale's large frame twisted like an enormously graceful feline himself, his right hand steadying her and his left hand managing to catch Buttercup mid-fall.

"I've got you, little one," he rasped, his face so close to hers that she could feel his warm breath feathering her cheek. That over-bright smile from earlier had hardly had any effect, but his tender, gruff whisper to the kitten had her chest clenching. Once Evangeline had found her feet, Vale released her and bent to lower the wriggling menace to the box with its four siblings.

Good God, she'd grabbed the man's *groin*! His unforgettably *full* groin. Face on fire, she didn't dare look at him. Pulling away, she fixed her eyes on Hannah—a much safer option than the duke who had successfully caught a whining Lucky—and grimaced. "Bested by a puffball," she muttered. "I suppose that round goes to Buttercup, doesn't it?"

Alas, she was distracted by the duke's beautiful mouth pulling into a wicked grin that did unconscionable things to her heart rate. "Buttercup?"

"The kitten, though perhaps Beasty might be better." Good lord, even her voice was affected, emerging in an airless whisper.

"Thank goodness you weren't hurt, Lady Effie," Hannah said after locking Lucky in the next room and returning to gather the feeding dishes she had dropped. Her curious gaze darted to the duke, who had remained at Evangeline's side before she disappeared into the kitchen.

"Who's Effie?" he asked, the low rumble nearly making her leap out of her skin.

"Oh, that's me. I mean, it's a family nickname."

"Much like Buttercup, that name doesn't suit you either," he murmured.

Evangeline stared up at him. "What would suit me then?"

"Your given name. Evangeline." That Scots burr deepened to caress each syllable of her name. Dear God, she never wanted to be called Effie ever again. She renounced it forthwith! "*That* name reminds me of a powerful fairy queen from the caves of the Schiehallion mountain deep in the Highlands. Effie is too flat for someone like you."

He sounded sincere, but there was no mistaking the glint in his eyes. Was he making fun? Or did he truly hold her in such high esteem? Heavens, one would think she was as vapid as Viola when it came to compliments, the way she was going all melty inside because a man had likened her to a *fairy queen*. Then again, that was a far step from a ghastly specter!

She *should* be preening.

She might in private. Much, much later.

He smiled, a bit less bright than the first few, but something about it still felt off. *Why* was he trying so hard to compliment her? Of course it was quite possible she was misinterpreting him altogether. After all, it'd been quite some time since any gentleman had been interested in her beyond what her dowry could afford him.

Was that it? Was it her dowry he was after?

Just then Hannah returned, announcing the arrival of the veterinarian, and Evangeline had no chance to further ponder the duke's motive. She'd known William Dawson for years, and besides being a wonderful doctor to animals, he'd been a steadfast childhood friend.

Evangeline greeted him warmly. "How lovely of you to come so quickly."

"My pleasure," William said, blue gaze lit with his usual affability. For the hundredth time, Evangeline wished for her sister to open her eyes and see what was right in front of her—a kind man who held her in the highest esteem. But alas, Viola was utterly obtuse.

She dragged William over to the litter of cats. "Aren't they precious? They were found in the alley next to the haberdasher's. You know the one?"

"I do. Please tell me you did not go in there yourself," William scolded, stooping down to inspect the closest kitten. "It's foul, practically a latrine."

"Fine, I won't tell you." He lifted a knowing brow. Crouching beside him, Evangeline bit her lip, feeling Vale's eyes on her. After the babies had been dropped off, she had to see if the kittens' mother had truly abandoned them. The alley had been worse than foul, but an animal's life was more important than a clean hemline or her olfactory senses.

"Effie." His tone was laced with exasperation.

She rolled her eyes. "*William.*"

A throat cleared, hard green eyes spearing them as she and William glanced up in unison. "Do you address a lady so familiarly, sir?"

Stunned by the spike of venom in the duke's voice, Evangeline took in his rigid stance and the full lips that were now a hard, grim line and felt herself recoil with astonishment. What in the world had possessed him to react so?

"You should be addressed properly as Lady Evangeline," he ground out when she stared quizzically at him.

A frown pleated her brow. "I'm well aware of my honorific, Your Grace. I've given Mr. Dawson leave to address me thus."

William was a dear friend. He'd never once stepped out of line with her or given her any reason to question his honor. The doctor was a good man, and she would not let some self-important peer disparage their friendship. Or even worse, chastise *her* as if she were a child to be reprimanded for not toeing the line of etiquette!

"I am a lady, and one of sound mind and capable speech," she said evenly. "Don't presume, Your Grace, to tell me how to conduct myself. I am a grown woman and require neither your advice nor your approval."

"I beg your—"

She held up a hand. Surprise erupted in those emerald eyes, but she wasn't about to let any man, even a duke, ride roughshod over her, not *here*, not in the hard-won sanctuary that was hers alone. "No need. Perhaps you should leave, Your Grace."

Nostrils flaring, she straightened her spine and stared him down as he studied her in perplexed silence, a muscle flexing in that firm jaw. He looked upset, though it seemed to stem from frustration rather than anger. Evangeline was well aware that she might have crossed a line; however, backing down from a bully was never her forte, not since Huntington had dragged her through the mud in such a horrid, heartless manner.

"No, no, the duke is quite right." William stood, palms in the air between them as though seeking to thwart a war. "His Grace is correct. Please accept my sincere regrets, my lady."

"Nonsense, you have nothing to apologize for. I've given you leave to call me Effie." She said it with a degree of defiance—the nickname might be insipid, but *she* wasn't—and attempted to control her careening emotions. "That is my name, and I've given you permission to use it, William."

"As you wish," he mumbled, eyes darting between her and the duke, who was now staring at her with a look of intense calculation, as if she were some species of animal he did not recognize but intended to tame nonetheless. He'd learn she had claws and teeth, too, like all the others before him.

"Vale is a duke, you see," she explained. "Which means he likely has a stick of politesse lodged right up his—"

"My lady!" Hannah interrupted from behind them.

"Spine," she said, stifling a snort of pure amusement at Vale's expression. "I was going to say spine, Hannah dear."

See? This was why she would never be able to survive the marriage mart in London. She would be sure to horribly insult some proper gentleman, and the entire ton would riot. Evangeline almost laughed out loud at that. Perhaps that should be her angle—behave so badly that she would have to leave in blissful disgrace! She would never be a mincer of words. Women had voices, too, and they deserved to be heard, not silenced.

While this duke might be nice to look at, deep down, he was just like the rest of the nobility. Highbrow, arrogant, and brimming with his own privileged, male importance. She reined in the rest of her waning temper and smiled at William. "In any case, His Grace was just leaving. He's on the hunt for a special kind of lost fish."

Vale's eyes narrowed at her jab, but he tilted his head. "In hindsight, you're right about the fish. But this visit has been rather enlightening. I do hope to see you again, Lady Evangeline."

She did not miss the rumble of that blush-worthy burr over her name, and her pulse kicked as though a gauntlet had just been dropped between them, just as a truly wicked grin transformed the duke's beautiful mouth into a weapon of utter ruination. Resisting the intensity of that smile was pointless. She'd have a stern word to her good sense later.

For now, Evangeline hiked her chin.

"Sadly, I don't feel the same. Good day, sir," she said pertly, wondering briefly if she'd gone too far in her dismissal when his cheeks darkened and his eyes flashed with the promise of...*something*. Retribution?

With any luck, she'd never see the man again.

CHAPTER FOUR

That could have gone better, Gage supposed.

Either he was losing his touch, or he had sorely miscalculated his charm. Not that he was any kind of Casanova—far from it!—but he was competent enough with most reasonably minded women, which, clearly, Evangeline Raine was not. The termagant had practically kicked him out of her bloody shelter. Him, a duke! The audacity! And yet, he admired her more for it.

She was delightfully direct.

But what was most concerning, however, was that from the sound of the snatches of conversation with the Duchess of Greydon he'd shamelessly overheard, the lady did not seem to esteem London or the season in the least, which would certainly interfere with his plans. He wasn't that fond of town himself, but what had happened in London to make *her* despise it so?

Perhaps it was that very directness that had not suited the empty-headed aristocrats of the ton. But if she was truly opposed to London, then his strategy would have to take some finessing, or he could kiss Huntington's deal goodbye. Furthermore, he'd done himself no favors by chiding her on etiquette like a fool.

Gage cursed under his breath. He was off to a spectacular start.

Notwithstanding being climbed by a devious quintet of kittens,

Gage had felt strangely charged for the better part of his visit, a feeling that had intensified the minute Lady Evangeline's innocent palm had grabbed a handful of his nether regions. His interest had deflated somewhat when William Dawson had arrived, the intimacy between him and the lady impossible to ignore. The whisper of possessiveness Gage had felt had been unwelcome as hell. He had no claim on Evangeline Raine, none whatsoever.

She was simply a means to an end…a very much-needed end.

And yet, he'd wanted to beat Dawson to a pulp.

Either Huntington was blind, or he simply did not know beauty when he saw it. Then again, Lady Evangeline Raine was far from conventional ideals. Hers was a razor-edged sort of beauty, in the way of wolves or hawks, one that might not come without its share of danger.

With all that silk-spun, flaxen hair escaping her braid and framing her face in a gossamer cloud, as well as those angular but starkly arresting features, she'd resembled a creature that wasn't of this realm. He hadn't been far off the mark with his overly mawkish sentiments about her name. Thank God he'd been saved from spouting more nonsense by Dawson's arrival.

As much as her face was all sharp, finely honed angles, her figure was also lithe and long—quite unlike his usual preference for an abundance of curves—but his body didn't seem to care. Her eyes were huge and a pale grayish blue, the color of a Scottish loch in the middle of a winter storm. The Scots loved stories of their woodland sìth, and he was certain if she wandered one of the dells in the Highlands, she'd be mistaken for one.

And he'd been wrong about her being easy; she was going to be a challenge. Although he could already see his advantage. The thorny fairy queen of Chichester may have dismissed him, but she'd been attracted to him as well, despite her clear efforts to conceal that fact. Her fair complexion hid nothing, and those changeling eyes of hers had gone from the palest shade of blue to the silvery gray of an icy morning in the space of a few scattered heartbeats.

In her anger, she'd been magnificent, all cold fire and wintry fury. What would she be like in the throes of passion? He imagined her then, lips parted, elegant throat on display, a crimson blush diffusing through that soft skin...

Hell and damnation.

With a glance back at the shelter house he'd just left, Gage buried those thoughts and raked a hand through his neatly trimmed locks and walked toward his waiting carriage. Both his new valet and the stylish coach were thanks to Huntington's generosity. He couldn't very well call on the lady in rags and on foot, could he?

Terrible first impressions aside, Gage needed to rethink his approach. That striking head of hers housed an equally impressive tongue, one that she was not afraid to use, as evidenced in her swift and unsympathetic setdown. She was no wilting miss at all.

Why did he feel *relief* at that?

He likely has a stick of politesse lodged right up his... Arse, she'd been about to say arse. Gage shook his head, a reluctant grin curling his lips.

"Did you convince her?" Nearing the corner of the main promenade, he halted mid-stride at the voice to find Lord Huntington lurking near Pilar's Emporium, a shop fancied by all the local ladies.

"It has barely been a fortnight, Huntington. I'm a man, not a miracle worker." He lifted a cool brow. "Or did you expect me to toss the lady over my shoulder and cart her off to London?"

The man's lips tightened as an arrogant gaze swept him. "I see you've not wasted any time in putting my money to use on clothing, however."

Gage smiled. "Thank you, yes. Your man of business was rather helpful."

"Time is of the essence, Vale," Huntington snapped. "I'm not paying you to strut around Chichester like a peacock on display. Get the lady to agree to London."

Gage resisted the urge to punch the pretentious fop in his teeth. "She'll be at the Duchess of Greydon's birthday ball."

It was a daring boast, and one he wasn't entirely sure he could pull off given the frosty temperament of the lady in question. Still, it would get Huntington off his back for now.

A feminine and utterly contrived gasp interrupted them as a beautiful girl exited the shop, trailed by her lady's maid. "Oh, Lord Huntington, I didn't expect to run into you. How lovely! Alice, come quickly, perhaps his lordship will generously agree to escort us home."

The resemblance in the lady's face was enough for Gage to realize who she was: his quarry's younger sister, Lady Viola. He could see why Huntington was interested in her. With her golden-brown curls and huge blue eyes, she was a stunning girl. But while Lady Viola's beauty was soft and welcoming, her sister's was its opposite; one was a perfect sunny day, and the other, a fierce storm that promised splendor with a healthy side of frostbite.

"Oh, I do beg your pardon," the young woman said, her eyes drifting toward him and then falling away with demure perfection. Gage rather missed the direct stare of her elder sister. "I am intruding on your conversation, my lord."

"Of course you are not, Lady Viola," Huntington said with a courtly bow, his saccharine tone making Gage want to vomit. "My business here is finished."

Gage tipped his hat to Huntington and grinned. "Well, I must be off. Skirts to snare, virgins to seduce, and all that."

This time, Lady Viola's gasp of surprise was real. Gage's grin deepened as Huntington frowned before taking the lady's arm and steering her swiftly away as though he half expected Gage to blurt out the entire scheme. He wouldn't, of course, but just because Huntington was paying him didn't mean he *owned* him. The man was a pompous, overblown windy-wallet.

Watching them head back the way he'd come, Gage narrowed his eyes in thought, cursing himself for declaring that he would have Lady Evangeline at the most anticipated ball of the season. His quarry was astute, and her wit was sharper than the dagger he carried in his boot. It was evident that she wasn't the type to be led to water...or be told what to do. And worse, she categorically seemed to loathe London.

It would be difficult, but not impossible.

A reluctant smile tugged at his lips as he recalled her fierce defense of her life choices and her complete aversion to propriety. She didn't like rules. Well, neither did he.

The season would begin in three weeks, which meant he had less than that to get her to change her mind. An arrogant part of him had expected her to swoon and simper the minute he'd sauntered into that odd little sanctuary, much like the ladies of his youth. Instead, she'd thrown him out on his ear.

But then, he should have known that she would be different.

Before arriving at the shelter, he'd called in at Oberton Hall, only to be informed by the housekeeper that Lady Evangeline was *working*.

Needless to say, he'd been intrigued.

Gage couldn't recall the last aristocratic lady of his acquaintance who worked. Besides his own mother, though she was an anomaly. Lady Catriona Croft was a Highland warrior disguised as a duchess, and no woman he'd ever met had her measure. One day he'd find a lady of equal worth to introduce to her. She had never pressured him to marry, despite Gage being twenty-eight and yet unwed. Instead, she'd encouraged him to cut his own path.

She would not approve of *this*, however.

Toying with the heartstrings of a woman as a ploy was not how his formidable mother had raised him. But if he was careful, no one would get hurt. He would get Lady Evangeline to London, they would enjoy each other's company at a ball or two for six short weeks, and after that, he'd bow out. Simple.

Besides, it was obvious that she needed him to get over her antipathy to London. She was the daughter of a British earl, after all, and marriage was her duty. Even if he were the worst duke in London, he still had *some* influence. His attention would undoubtedly spark more; men thrived on competition. Looking at it that way, he was *helping* her.

But first, he needed ideas on how to woo the most recalcitrant spinster in England.

And he knew just the person to aid him.

"Where to, Your Grace?" the coachman asked when he arrived at his elegant, borrowed conveyance.

"Worthing, to the Earl of Lushing," he said.

He'd heard from his new valet, Pierre, who was excellent with a pair of scissors and well-versed on local gossip, that the Duke of Greydon and his duchess were visiting her brother on their way to London for the season.

Gage had met Lushing over a bloodied boxing ring in Edinburgh, when the earl had bet on him in the face of terrible odds. Gage had won the fight by the skin of his teeth, earning Lushing a massive windfall, and they'd been fast friends ever since. Rumor had it that his old mate had opened a club, Lethe—aptly named after the Greek river of oblivion—in an interesting part of London, but Gage had yet to see it.

He caught a glimpse of lavender-gray skirts as the carriage rolled slowly toward the shelter home, and recognized they belonged to Lady Evangeline. Gage watched as she thanked William Dawson and then smiled in salutation at the couple strolling toward her. Lady Viola greeted her sister, the sound of her laughter like bells on the wind.

As if sensing his perusal, Lady Evangeline half turned as the carriage ambled past, her pale silvery-blue gaze fastening on the coach window. She couldn't see him inside, of course, but he felt the visceral weight of her stare through the wood and iron as if her bare fingers had grazed his skin. His ducal crest was emblazoned on the coach door, and her face pinched slightly before the expression was smoothed away by indifference.

Difficult, not impossible, he reminded himself.

He would see her again, once he got some answers from Lushing. He couldn't afford to screw this up. He needed to shore up his estates, pay off this last debt, and fuck off back to Scotland. And to do that, he needed *her*.

Two hours later, an efficient butler ushered him into Lushing's richly appointed study, where Gage admired the gold and mahogany accents and the heavy French furniture. His booted feet sank into the plush carpets while his eyes took in the framed art on the walls. He imagined that Vale Ridge Park might have been as impressive once upon a time, but even when he was a boy, nice things hadn't lasted in his home. Possessions were always being sold and art replaced with cheaper items or forgeries until there'd been nothing of value left at all.

Now that Huntington had offered him a way to cancel Asher's debt, Gage could use the thousand quid he'd put aside from the sale of a portion of his land in Scotland for critical repairs. Any heirs of his would have a future to be proud of, not one that left them poor and insolvent.

If his efforts with Lady Evangeline came to fruition, that was…

"Vale, this is a nice surprise," the earl called out as he entered the room. Lushing was a handsome man in his late twenties and one of the few peers Gage did not wish to pummel into the ground.

"I need a favor," he said without preamble.

The earl cracked a smile and topped up his glass from a decanter of whisky that stood on a small table. He settled himself in a comfortable chair near the fireplace and indicated for Gage to take the one opposite. "Good God, man, I haven't seen you in seven years, and you won't even buy me dinner first?"

"You can afford to buy your own dinner."

"True. Drink?" Lushing chuckled, lifting his tumbler.

Gage shook his head and settled his large frame into the armchair with a shake of his head. "No, thank you. I'm off the swill. What do you know about the Earl of Oberton's daughters?"

"Which one?"

"Both, I suppose."

A smirk slid across the earl's lips, his eyes sparkling with amusement. "Planning to dust off your dancing slippers, Vale? I thought you abhorred the season and hoped to avoid it at all costs. If I recall, you once told me that you'd rather guillotine yourself than be pursued by hoity-toity English debutants looking for the latest wealthiest stud in the stable. Decided to put yourself through some paces and join the rest of our brothers lost to perpetual wedlock?"

The image of Lady Evangeline putting him through said paces, that long, lean body of hers hovering confidently over his, made Gage's mind go blank for a second.

"I'm thinking about it," he finally managed.

The earl stared at him. "You're serious. *You* intend to look for a wife?"

"Maybe. It's complicated," Gage replied, discomfited at the small prevarication. He did intend to look for one eventually... in Scotland. "What can you tell me about the Raines? The elder one, in particular."

Lushing's eyes narrowed, his face falling. "If you don't mean to marry, what is your intention? My sister is quite fond of Effie."

The sound of her nickname on the earl's lips did something strange to Gage. "I'm simply considering prospects," he clarified to Lushing. "Don't get your petticoats in a twist."

The earl gave him a guarded look but conceded. "Effie is a bit of an odd duck. Their mother left the roost a handful of years ago, some scandal that was swept under the rug. Seems like she might have eloped with an artist. A few years after that, the younger one was sent away to France to live with an aunt and only returned at the turn of the New Year. That didn't stop the offers from coming immediately in, so if it's Lady Viola you're after, you'll have healthy competition."

"And Lady Evangeline?" he asked. "She wasn't sent to France with her sister?"

"No. She was raised here and has had a few seasons with Vesper but hasn't received any tenders of marriage." The earl gave a slow lift of one shoulder, brow creased in thought.

"Why?" Gage asked.

Lushing blew out an exhale and stared at his drink as though searching for the right words. "She's...rather unconventional at best, but she's a kind girl with a deep heart. She can be outspoken at times, but some of our dinner discussions about the pitfalls of Parliament have been the most lively I've ever had. She's as smart as a steel trap."

Gage had already discerned that on his own, though that didn't explain why she'd had no offers. A clever brain wasn't a deterrent in his book. "Do you know why she seems so determined to stay away from London?"

"She didn't have an easy time of it during her first season," Lushing said and frowned.

Gage leaned forward with interest. "How so?"

The earl's mouth twisted with unusual rancor, his always pleasant mien absent. He seemed to weigh his words once more. "She ran afoul of a gutless prick."

"Who?"

"Huntington." When Gage's mouth slackened, Lushing nodded

with a snort. "She called him a gifted ventriloquist for inserting his own bigoted words into his future wife's mouth. Needless to say, he did not take well to the rather clever insult and gave her the unfortunate moniker of Lady Ghastly on account of it. Sadly, the name stuck, and she became the laughingstock of the ton. My sister was one of her few champions. In her second season, Effie made the wallflowers look desirable when she became a defiant pariah." Lushing gave a fond chuckle and shook his head. "I still recall the pamphlets she distributed during Huntington's own ball to save lost and starving dogs. She refused to be cowed by his vitriol and became the symbol of the type of female no aristocratic gentleman *should* want, according to him." His mouth twisted. "He made her an outcast."

Shunned for standing up to a bully? Gage frowned.

Huntington was bloody full of himself, but he was also the type of pompous aristocrat who would not take kindly to being shown up, especially by a woman. He also had more influence than Gage thought, if he could destroy a woman's entire future for no valid reason but a bruised ego. His frown deepened. There had to be more to it.

"Did he ever court her?" Jilted men could be cruel.

"Not that I recall." He tapped a finger to his chin. "She was much too smart for him. Effie was quite the conundrum, quiet and strong of mind, though Vesper later told me that much of her shyness fell away when she no longer sought to impress the ton. She refused to quake and cower." *Good for her*, Gage thought as the earl drained his glass and refilled it. "Despite my sister's wishes, the lady most likely won't be in London for much of the season, so even with the competition, I do hope it's the younger one you're considering. Effie is quite opposed to marriage."

Lost in thought, Gage nodded absently, tapping his fingers on the polished armrest as he considered the information. That would suit him fine. He didn't want to marry either. He only needed to convince her to go to London for six weeks to meet the terms of the agreement he'd made. But how?

His mind was whirling. Clearly, she was immune to being charmed or wooed, or perhaps it was just that he'd bungled both beautifully. So what did she care most about? Her friends and her shelter animals, obviously, but how could either of those help him penetrate her defenses?

"I'd be careful with Huntington, too," Lushing went on. "It's no secret that he intends to court Lady Viola. He's been to Chichester from Crawley a dozen times over the winter months already. Half the ton is in his pocket, and the younger set is so afraid of incurring his displeasure they won't cross him." Lushing's face flashed with dislike once more. "He's a nasty piece of work and not to be trusted."

"I'm aware," Gage said, discomfort burning at the thought of the deal in place, and the fact that he would play a part in bringing such a cad back into Evangeline's orbit, but he had no choice. "I'm still repaying Asher's vowel to Huntington," Gage said bitterly. "The interest alone is exorbitant. My fool brother agreed to the terms without even reading them."

"Can I help pay it off?" Lushing offered, but Gage was already shaking his head. The earl had sunk enough of his own money into Asher's schemes, and Gage's pride would not allow him to accept his friend's generosity.

"I have a plan," Gage said.

The earl slumped back with a sigh. "It's my fault. I cut him off

after that last scheme at Tattersall's when he attempted to rob Peter
to pay Paul in hopes of settling his debts," he said with regret. "If
I'd loaned him more money, maybe he wouldn't have gotten in so
deep—"

Gage shook his head, cutting him off. "My brother made his
choices. He bought that Arabian pair with money he didn't have.
He *chose* to wager all our unentailed property and sell off everything that wasn't nailed down. He *chose* to get into that curricle
himself. Cutting him off was the only thing you could have done.
He'd have dragged you down with him. Why do you think my
mother kept me in Scotland after the duke sent for his heir? She
didn't want me following in my father's or my brother's footsteps."

Choice.

It made men who they were.

"Did it help?" Lushing asked.

"She saved my life." Gage swallowed the knot in his throat. Ini-
tially, he'd resented his mother for taking him away to Scotland,
but later on, he'd realized leaving England had been for the best.
Without her, he would have turned out just like Asher and their
father, and followed the same path to self-destruction.

"You were lucky then." The earl cleared his throat and exhaled a
harsh breath. "Do you believe the rumors? That the bolts on Asher's carriage had been tampered with?"

Gage sucked in air. He'd heard the same, but there'd never been
any proof.

The Metropolitan Police had deemed his brother's death a
tragic accident, but for all Asher's flaws, he was meticulous and
loved horses. The idea that he'd not inspected his carriage and
team before the race was hard to believe. Yet accidents did happen,

especially in racing, but loosened bolts were a serious accusation. "I don't know," he replied finally. "Do you?"

"The fact that Huntington goaded Asher into doing double or quit with the curricle race never sat well with me."

"Double or quit?" Gage echoed, his stomach churning. He hadn't heard that.

The earl flattened his lips. "Huntington desperately needed that money Asher owed him, and he didn't have the funds to cover his own losses, so he badgered him into the race."

Gage frowned. "Wait, *Huntington* had money problems?"

"Still does. He's a preening peacock of a spendthrift." Lushing sipped his drink. "Why would he bet *against* Asher, who had bested that course dozens of times, unless he was certain that your brother was going to lose?"

And he'd made a bloody fortune from it, Gage knew. "So you suspect he had a hand in fixing the race?" he asked quietly. "Was Huntington competing, do you know?"

Lushing shook his head. "No. A craven hector like that would never put his own neck on the line."

They fell into silence, preoccupied with their own thoughts. Even if it hadn't been an accident, chasing down answers wouldn't bring his brother back. Asher had been dead a full year now. Gage had to look ahead . . . to the future. To *his* future.

"So London for the season then?" Lushing asked, breaking the silence, and when Gage nodded, the earl sat forward with forced cheer. "Good, at least it will be entertaining to watch you, cap in hand, posturing for a bride."

Given the earl's earlier protectiveness of Evangeline, Gage suspected that if Lushing knew the truth, he might not be so eager.

One could argue that what Gage was doing with Evangeline was in poor taste. He was planning to *use* her, after all. But reason and logic warred inside him. She could make the choice not to see him or go to London. He would not force her, but that didn't mean he wouldn't do everything in his power to convince her. He simply had to find the right motivator.

"I'm not setting my cap for anyone," he said. "I'm only having a look. It's not like any Englishwoman accustomed to a life of leisure and luxury in the ton will be itching to move to Scotland."

"There are plenty of mothers and their daughters who will salivate at the thought of a coronet," Lushing said with a devilish grin. "Should you announce you're on the hunt for a duchess, you'll have your pick of the crop. A look will turn into a betrothal, mark my words."

"Hardly," Gage said. "Didn't you read the *Times*? I'm the poorest, most dreadful duke in London."

Lushing made a scoffing noise. "You're a duke, Vale. You could be as poor as a church mouse waving a sword in a bloody tartan in the middle of Mayfair and these matchmaking mothers would still fawn at your coattails."

Gage hoped not—he had one goal, and that was *one* spinster to snare.

CHAPTER FIVE

The rain had fallen in white sheets over the hills at Oberton Hall. Evangeline adored rainstorms. They meant renewal, new flowers and new shoots, and rich-smelling earth. They saw the sky washed, the air made fresh, and rushing brooks overflowing with bubbling songs. There was no other joy like a brisk walk through the fields and gardens after a storm had passed through, and nothing Evangeline liked more.

Which explained her current predicament.

Distracted by a baby raven that had fallen out of its nest on her walk, she'd lifted a heavy and drenched Lucky into her arms and navigated a treacherous patch of mud to reach the creature, only to get firmly stuck bang smack in the middle of the muck. It was also her rotten luck that it was right at the start of the long drive leading up to the main house, which meant any help was a good mile or two away. She could scream her lungs out and no one would hear her.

Evangeline grasped the wriggling, soaked dog in her arms and glanced down with a wince. Well, this wasn't a *little* mud. It seemed to be a sinkhole or some such. Lucky gave a sharp yelp— *she* wanted nothing more than to jump down and roll around in the mess, but from the way Evangeline's boots were sinking, she didn't think Lucky would enjoy swimming. Or drowning. This was sludge and it was sticky.

Lucky's overexcited motions made Evangeline sink deeper in the mud as she tried to calm twenty pounds of squirming dog. "Don't worry, dearest. If it comes to life or death, I'll simply toss you to safety."

In other better news, the baby bird had somehow flown off, so that was one good thing. Now, she just needed to save herself and her dog. But the more she struggled to lift her leg, the more she sank. The higher the mud rose—it was clear up to her ankles now—the more apparent it became that it stank. Not like rich earth at all, but like fermented horse dung.

Evangeline let out a few hysterical snickers. "Serves you right that you're stuck in shit. Good Lord, where's a shovel when you need one?"

Her chortles grew until her sides were aching. She turned into a gigglemug when she was nervous—another oddity that *never* served her well in public—but it wasn't until the snicker-snorts came that she'd have to worry. For now, her sanity hadn't completely mutinied.

"What shall we do, Lucky?" The dog stared at her with trusting brown eyes and licked her chin as though she had all the faith in the world of her mistress rescuing them. "I hate to say it, but we seem to be up shit's creek, wee lassie!"

Why on earth was she speaking in Scots? She blinked. Could it be because of a certain giant gentleman with the faintest of burrs? She wondered whether the Duke of Vale sounded more so when he was in the Highlands. Devil take it, why was she thinking about *him* when she was stuck in man-eating muck? The maniacal puffs of laughter erupted anew. The snorts were definitely en route.

Stop braying and think, woman!

In a fit of frustration, she yanked her leg hard, and with a loud squelching sound, her foot came loose...without its boot. Peering over Lucky's bedraggled fur, she cringed at the brown color leaching up her sodden skirts. She couldn't see beneath them. Balancing precariously on her hidden leg, she attempted to feel for harder ground, but everywhere she stuck her stockinged toe, the wet earth sucked at it like a hungry mouth.

Evangeline let out a frustrated howl, startling poor Lucky, who tumbled into the mud. She grabbed the dog quickly before she could sink. Gracious, could their predicament get any worse? At this rate, they'd both be consumed before dinner. A faint crunching sound like wheels over gravel met her ears, and she swung around. Her heart soared and sank in the same giddy exhalation. There *was* a carriage coming up the drive, but it was one she instantly recognized.

Be grateful. At least you'll be rescued.

And maybe you're mistaken about that crest.

But no, as the coach drew closer, her initial assumption had been correct. Damn and blast! The crest on the side was indeed a ducal one—it was the same coach she'd seen outside of the shelter—when the Duke of Decorum himself had criticized her conduct. Of anyone who could have visited Oberton Hall, why, oh why couldn't it have been a farmer or a local merchant, or even her father?

She'd settle for a scolding from the earl over being caught in such a fix by a man who made her feel like she was on the edge of a bottomless crevasse and about to tumble to her doom. A stupidly handsome face didn't excuse an irritating and cocksure manner. She'd had enough of dictatorial men. Dictatorial *dukes*. Irritation swelled in her stomach as well as a strange, excited fluttering as the coach drew closer.

"Oh, behave, you silly sausage," she snapped to herself and then bit her lip as Lucky gave a small whine at her acerbic tone. "Not you, sweeting."

Her bloody sole was beginning to ache from balancing on it. Gingerly, she placed down her bootless foot and gasped as it sank deep, throwing her off-kilter. The carriage rolled to a stop, the coachman giving her the oddest look before jumping down. Perhaps it was just the one man. Maybe the carriage was empty, and he was here alone because sometimes coachmen borrowed their employers' conveyances. Her ponderings were absurd, of course, because the door opened and the irksome duke she hoped never to see again emerged.

It didn't help that he looked utterly gorgeous, those singular dark coppery locks gilded with tones of garnet in the overcast daylight. Evangeline wondered idly whether his hair was as thick and silky as it looked. Whether his chest hair, if he had any—she'd seen a smooth-chested farmer or two in the height of summer—would be the same. *Was* he hairy?

She blushed hotly and cursed her arbitrary brain. Dear God, which cod's head of a girl thought about a gentleman's body hair while stuck in a mudhole? He looked entirely too perfect, standing there in a pair of snug fawn-colored trousers...while she was stuck in a sinkhole and resembled a drowned piglet. Not that she needed to impress him. Or notice the well-fitting fabric stretching over thick, muscular thighs.

Those would definitely be hairy.

Focus, for mercy's sake!

"Good afternoon, Your Grace," she called out in a faux cheery greeting. "Lovely day for a drive, isn't it? If a bit damp and muddy in parts." A half-demented giggle followed, earning her another alarmed look from the duke's coachman. Evangeline pinned her lips, but she could feel the hysterical mirth bubbling up like a geyser about to explode.

"Indeed," the duke said, squatting a safe distance away, bright green eyes taking in the muddy expanse. His stare landed on Lucky, widening for a second. "What is that?"

"My dog," she replied defensively. Surely he would recognize Lucky from the shelter? Then again, the duke had been pounced upon by kittens.

She knew what he saw—Lucky was part bulldog, part miniature trawler spaniel, and had inherited the lesser qualities of both—which made her a brown-and-white, squat-of-face, thick-bodied, short-legged mongrel, and in a word, homely. But she was smart and calm in temperament, unless provoked. Possibly why the two of them got on so well. "Don't be cruel. She's a rescue. She wasn't wanted and had been thrown away."

"I meant she resembles a wee mud monster. Lucky, if I'm not mistaken? She looks heavy." Vale smiled, his eyes crinkling, but another emotion glittered in their clear depths, one that she did not want to think on too deeply. It had the sheen of admiration, and she would not fall into that ready trap again! She did not care what the Duke of Vale thought of her.

She shifted the sturdy dog to the other arm, and couldn't help noticing that the duke's eyes were the color of clovers today, and then cursed herself in the same breath. Heavens, was she going to now catalog his eye color? What was next? His broad brow? Or the gentle breeze teasing those garnet strands into his bold cheekbones?

Or his lips…

Goodness, they were a hedonist's dream, sculpted to perfection, even pursed in thought as they were now, the corner of the bottom one momentarily tugged between his teeth. The upper formed a dissolute heart, the lower dipping into a sensuous half curve that made her mind stutter to an undignified halt.

"Can you help, or are you going to crouch there all day and stare?" she snapped, peeved at herself for being so unusually concupiscent.

"You seem to have…er…gotten yourself in a pickle," he said.

"A shit pickle, Monsieur Obvious," she muttered. A corner of that lip kicked up as the coachman gave a hurried cough that sounded like a laugh. Heavens, her tongue was ungovernable when she didn't have the wherewithal to keep it corralled. Evangeline's cheeks flared hot, but she was beyond caring. "There's a hole here. It must have been worsened with the water flow from the creek. As you can perhaps discern, I am well and truly stuck."

Lucky started barking again as if she sensed rescue was imminent, and Evangeline struggled to keep holding the wriggling creature *and* her balance. The dog was starting to feel like a lead weight in her arms. "Enough, Lucky!"

The animal's panicked whine spurred the duke into action.

"Douglas, go get help," Vale instructed the coachman, standing to toss his hat, gloves, and walking stick into the carriage. "As well as ropes, planks, anything we can use. And be careful on the road in case there are more of these. Wouldn't want to get a stuck wheel."

"Yes, Your Grace."

After the young coachman did as bid, Evangeline watched as the duke removed his coat, trying not to be distracted by the flex of the ropy muscles in his arms and the way the seams of his shirt were stretched to their limits. Thick thighs...thick arms. He was thick everywhere, it seemed. Her ears burned hot, and she kept her lips firmly buttoned, lest she give *those* sentiments away. Her brain was broken. It had to be. No one could possibly have such debauched thoughts while stuck in such a dire situation. Or perhaps it only made her more desperate...

She'd die a virgin, after all.

Evangeline held back an unwelcome snort as the duke spread the expensive fabric on the muddy ground between them. "Your coat!" she exclaimed.

He shrugged. "It can be replaced. You, my lady, however, are much more important."

Warmth slicked through her at his words. No, no, *no*. He was simply being nice. Gallant. Dukes, even arrogant, domineering ones, were known for that. *Aren't they?* The only dukes of her acquaintance were friends of her father who were old and rheumy and could hardly remember their own names. Then again, Vesper's husband wasn't so bad. Nève had married a duke as well, though he was rather fractious.

Evangeline's eyes narrowed in suspicion. *Why* was Vale being so charming and solicitous? Men complimented women only when they coveted something, and right now, buried in mud as she was, she was at his mercy. *Oh, come off it, Effie. Surely you won't look a gift horse in the mouth?*

No, because her besotted brain had other plans for said gift horse's mouth.

And it didn't involve talking.

Good gracious! It had to be the mud: carnivorous sludge that made people feel lewd things. It definitely had some kind of poison in it. Mind-altering mud. *Lusty* mud. A storm of snickers surged in her chest, forcing her to pin her lips to keep them at bay.

This was simply attraction, nothing more. It happened to all animals, and humans, at their most basic level, were just that. However, unlike an animal, she could exercise her will. And. She. Did. Not. Want. This. Man.

Lies.

Evangeline peeked up at him again, breath catching as he rolled up his shirtsleeves to reveal veiny, muscled arms covered in a—*sod her life*—dusting of bronze hair. Her mouth dried. Good God, she couldn't win, could she? Cool mud squelched into the hem of her underclothes just above the ribbons of her stockings. Against her overheated skin, it was a small reprieve.

He cleared his throat. "Here's what we will do. Heft the dog onto the coat first, and I'll drag it to safety."

It took her a minute to realize that pretty mouth was shaping words, and she let out an unseemly huff when her brain caught up. "I beg your pardon?"

"Toss the dog to the coat. Carefully."

With a sniff toward him—as if she wouldn't be careful with her sweet girl—Evangeline hitched Lucky closer to her chest and kissed her wet muddy head. "Don't be afraid, sweeting. The duke will save you." She glanced up at Vale. "Don't make any sudden movements. She doesn't like...er...males."

One slash of an auburn brow lifted. Her eyes met his, daring him to say what he was thinking. Like dog, like mistress, or something equally clever. Lucky had been found cowering on the side of a busy road, and when her footman had attempted to retrieve the animal, the dog had gone wild with fear. She'd been docile for Evangeline, however. Lucky never showed hostility toward her or her sister but had trembled and growled at the butler and the earl. Lucky's fear of males had lessened over the years, but she was still skittish around those she did not know.

With a harsh breath, Evangeline launched a heavy and wriggly Lucky toward the coat, her arms burning from the effort. Lucky hadn't made it that far, given Evangeline's quivering muscles, but it was enough to get her to safety.

Evangeline watched, her heart quailing, as the duke carefully drew the coat back toward him. Lucky, for her part, continued cowering, but the minute she was within reach of the duke, she growled and snapped at his hand.

"Enough, pup," he said in a low, commanding voice. "Calm down or you'll land yourself back in the mud. Don't worry, I've got you."

Evangeline stared as her persnickety pet gave a tiny whine and rolled over onto her back, exposing her mud-covered belly. That little hussy! Though Evangeline didn't blame the dog. At the sound of the duke's velvet command, *she* wanted to roll over.

"She hates everyone," Evangeline blurted in astonishment.

He lifted one shoulder. "Kittens and dogs like me, apparently. And on the rare occasion, beautiful damsels trapped in muddy bogs."

Did she hallucinate or did he just call her *beautiful*? "I'm not a dam...oh no!" Something must have shifted beneath her, because the ground slackened enough to threaten her already precarious balance. Her luck had just gone from worse to catastrophic…and she was slipping and about to eat a face full of mud.

The duke set Lucky on firm ground and spread the now filthy, soiled coat back upon the earth. "Don't move, my lady."

"Can't fight gravity." Evangeline gasped, just as the thickened loam that kept her in place suddenly gurgled and released. At the precarious shift, her arms windmilled and her body tilted in slow motion. Instead of going forward, she went back. Smelly, muddy water sucked greedily at her hips, soaking instantly through to her skin as she hit the sludge with a wet smack. She could feel wetness seeping down her neck and into the gaps of her bodice.

With an emphatic curse, Vale lowered himself down to his coat, stretching one long arm out over the edges of the sinkhole, where watery mud was undulating from her fall. "Can you reach my hand?" She strained toward him, barely skimming the tips of his fingers with hers. "A bit more. Come on, lass, you can do it."

But she couldn't. The counterpull of the sticky mud made her feel as if her arm were wrenching out of its socket. "Ballocks. I can't move."

This time, at the expletive, the duke did smile. "Say it louder and stretch as hard as you can."

She blinked. Had the mud confused him as well? "Say what louder?"

"Ballocks."

Hot cheeked, Evangeline frowned. "I didn't…" But the duke only appeared to be amused instead of scandalized. "I do beg your pardon, Your Grace."

"Stop apologizing and say it, Evangeline," he said, inching forward along his coat.

Her eyes widened at her given name on his tongue—the sultry, commanding cadence of it making her quite useless knees quake. God above, she was as bad as Lucky! If she were able, she probably would have shown him her belly, too, and shamelessly begged for a rub. Heat sluiced through her.

Oh, sod it!

"Ballocks!" she screamed and propelled her upper body forward at the same time. It was enough to get her slick, mud-covered palm into his. Long fingers curled about hers and crept up her arm. Her breath caught in her throat as the edge of his coat started to get swallowed by the muck, his elbows starting to sink as well. "Vale, please don't let go."

A penetrating green stare anchored hers. "Never."

CHAPTER SIX

Gage had her now. He wouldn't let go, but he could feel his elbows digging in to the softened earth. He wouldn't be surprised if the hole was some part of an underground offshoot of the overflowing creek. The rain had been constant over the past few days, and a few of his own pastures had flooded. Rain was good for crops, but too much of it could be disastrous.

He'd been on his way back from visiting his own tenant farms when he'd decided to call in on the Earl of Oberton to see if he had any ideas about irrigation. The earl's estate was thriving and didn't seem to have suffered as much damage as his fields had. It wasn't until he'd seen Lady Evangeline that he realized he'd also been hoping to see *her*.

Though finding her wallowing in a mud swamp hadn't quite been what he'd been thinking.

But it was a welcome opportunity to win her over, and he wouldn't waste it.

Shimmying forward an inch, Gage slid his hand over her slender wrist, putting most of his weight into his hips so that he didn't pitch forward and end up in the same predicament.

"Hold on," he said. "I'm going to guide you toward me."

She let out a shuddering breath as she closed brown-splattered, ice-cold fingers around his forearm. Gage's gaze jerked to her face. He hadn't noticed before, but the edges of her shell-pink lips were beginning to turn blue and her teeth were clenched tightly together. He could feel the cold damp seeping up from the wet ground beneath him, and a beat of worry pulsed through him. How long had she been stuck there before he'd come along?

"What were you doing?" he asked, inching forward again in a precarious balancing act, his core muscles burning as he fought to keep his lower half glued to the harder ground. "To end up here?"

"I saw a raven fall out of its nest."

His brows went up. "Where?"

"It was in that tree over there. It flew away."

Gage gave a mock grimace. "And abandoned you? How dare it be so ungrateful?"

"If I waited for the animals I rescue to thank me, I would be here a very long time." She gave a small shrug. "But even so, I'd much rather their mute ingratitude than dealing with those who have tongues and use them for sport to wound others."

The toneless edge in her voice told him much more than the words themselves. "Surely not all people are so badly behaved."

"No," she agreed after a moment. "Not all of them."

"All right, hold tight, but let your body go limp as though you're floating in a lake," he instructed her. "I won't let you go, I promise. Trust me."

He saw her eyes flicker for a moment before her pale, gilt-tipped eyelashes fluttered down and then she gave a short, decisive nod.

Pivoting his hips, Gage started inching backward. It was hard, grueling work, but with every sliver of ground he gained, her body crept forward. The trick was to keep consistent movement. With a squelching sound as though the earth were unwilling to release its hard-won prize, she came loose, offering just enough leverage for him to get his hands under her arms.

With a tremendous heave, he pulled her free, and they tumbled back to safety in a muddy heap. Gasping for air, she rolled to her side next to him as they both stared up at the blue-patched sky, breaths coming in stuttered pants. A barking, wet bundle of fur leaped on them. Lucky was obviously thrilled that her mistress was safe.

"Oof," he huffed when the dog jumped onto his midsection to get to her.

"Goodness, that was an adventure," she said with a breathless laugh as the dog hopped up to cover her face in licks. "Wasn't it, my sweet girl? We have a duke to thank." She glanced at him. "I'm not sure what might have become of us if you weren't here."

"You're both welcome."

Smiling, Gage stared at the dog. It truly was an odd-looking thing—likely the result of chance or a cross-breeding situation gone wrong. Trust the lady to love something that most others would deem unlovable. Lady Evangeline draped herself in thorns, but now, he caught a glimpse of that tender heart Lushing had said hid beneath that truculent exterior. It fascinated him.

She fascinated him.

"I've lost my walking boots," she lamented. "They were my only pair."

Still panting from exertion, Gage propped himself up onto one elbow, peering down at her. She was covered in brownish-gray mud and yet still made something inside of him tighten. It was concern, that was all. He swung his gaze down her dirty clothes, and sure enough, the points of her dainty toes wriggled within her befouled, soiled stockings. He frowned. "Your *only* pair?"

"I direct all of my pin money to the shelter. One pair was enough for me. Until now, that is." She stared morosely at the mudhole that had greedily devoured her boots, a stoic smile limning her lips. "No use crying over spilled milk, however. I shall simply have to borrow a pair from Viola. She has dozens. Her feet are smaller than mine, so they'll pinch a bit, but a little pain is better than an animal going hungry, isn't it?"

Her pale eyes glittered with purpose, and good God, Gage suddenly wanted to bottle some of that passion. How was she even real? She'd been stuck in mud for who knew how long, lost her boots, and still had the wherewithal to smile and think about her bloody strays. He stood and held out a hand, and before she could attempt to stand on her own, he swept her up into his arms.

"What are you doing?" she squeaked.

"You have no shoes," he pointed out. "It's a long way to the house, and I fear that Douglas, my coachman, might have gotten stuck."

"You cannot carry me all that way."

"You weigh hardly anything, and you're half frozen to death. I insist."

She firmed her blue-tinged lips into a mulish expression, eyes gleaming with what looked like unshed tears. "And *I* insist on walking, Your Grace."

Surprised at the intense reply, Gage stopped and gazed down at her. He didn't pretend to know or understand why she would insist on such a thing or why she suddenly seemed on the verge of tears after such fortitude earlier, but it wasn't his place to assume he knew better. He would not force her to accept his assistance against her will. Still, there was no way she could go barefoot without injury.

He exhaled, sat her down, and then proceeded to kick off his own pair of boots. "If you insist on walking, then you'll wear mine."

Glossy eyes widened as she swung a hand over his. "Vale, stop." She glared at him. "I won't take your boots, you vexing man. Will you cease this foolishness if I let you carry me then?"

"It's your choice, my lady. Boots." He extended his arms. "Or these."

"Very well, arms, though that's not much of a choice," she grumbled when he swept her up once more, sliding one arm beneath her cold, damp knees and the other behind her back. "Who gives away his bloody boots?"

Gage was pleased. Even though she was covered in mud, wet, and smelled like a pigpen, he savored the satisfying shape of her in his arms. And besides, he couldn't have gotten his new boots off without the help of his valet anyway—it took the strength of two men to pry them free.

"I'm heavy," she muttered after a while. "I'm not a waif."

"To me, you are," he said.

"You are rather enormous." She pursed her lips, staring at a point on his cravat, color flooding the tops of her cheeks. "I can almost imagine you throwing cabers around somewhere in the Highlands." A curious frown pleated her blond brows. "Are you a Highlander?"

"Yes." A rumble of laughter left him, even as his biceps gave an involuntary, prideful flex. "I hold the record in my mother's clan for best toss."

"That doesn't surprise me," she murmured and then worried her bottom lip. "I'm sorry about your coat. It's ruined."

"I'll add it to the favors you owe me. That's two coats now."

An indignant gaze lifted to meet his, and Gage bit back his grin. It was astonishing how her expressive eyes went from silvery gray to ice blue in a heartbeat. They were a mirror to her emotions; grayish when she was hurt or angry, bluer when calm, silver when heated.

She glared. "That was the kittens' fault, not mine!"

"They're your monsters, aren't they? Feline destruction happened on your watch."

"And who said anything about favors? I never agreed on any such thing." Those jutting cheekbones of hers flushed, and he let her stew for a moment, knowing her just nature would not let his help go unrewarded. "Fine," she grumbled eventually. "One favor, but only for the second coat. The first coat is what happens when you venture into a den of feral kittens of your own foolish will."

He hid his pleasure. "Very well."

"What kind of favor did you have in mind?" she asked, eyes narrowing with distrust.

"Nothing wicked, trust me." He couldn't keep the rasp from his voice.

The bit of muslin in his arms dropped her eyes, but not before he caught the slightest burn of reciprocal interest in them. If his own muscles weren't currently absorbed with the effort of carrying them uphill, he was certain other parts of him would have been at full roaring attention.

Thankfully, they were met halfway up the road by the earl's

coach and several of his men, his own coachman among them. "Cracked a wheel, Your Grace," Douglas admitted sheepishly.

"I gathered so when you didn't return quickly." Gage canted his chin. "You weren't hurt?"

"No, Your Grace," Douglas replied. "And the wheel is being repaired as we speak."

"Good man."

Within minutes they were driven up to the house, whereupon Lady Evangeline and her canine companion were whisked away by a bevy of maids and Gage was escorted to a cheery salon, despite his missing coat and disheveled, mud-covered appearance. He was offered a hot cup of tea by the housekeeper, which he accepted gratefully, but did not sit. He didn't want to soil the furniture.

"It seems I am in your debt, Your Grace," Lord Oberton said, shuffling into the room with the assistance of a cane.

"Anyone would have done the same, my lord."

The earl shook his head with a slanted glance at the mud drying on Gage's waistcoat. "Not everyone would have gone to the ends you did. I thank you. If there's ever any service I can provide, please do not hesitate to ask."

"Truly, it was no hardship, but you are welcome." He set down his empty teacup.

"May I offer you something stronger?" Oberton asked. "Whisky, brandy, port?"

Gage shook his head. "Tea is perfect, thank you. Is Lady Evangeline all right? The mud was quite cold with the river runoff, so I hope she does not catch a chill."

"She seems to be in good spirits, given the circumstances." The earl let out a rueful laugh. "If you ever have children, Your Grace,

I pray you don't have daughters like mine. Every gray hair on my head is because of those two. If it isn't Effie's misadventures, it's Viola's constant intrigues and flirtations." He shook his head. "How my eldest managed to find and get stuck in a sinkhole, I have no idea."

"She explained that she meant to rescue a raven."

The earl's eyes gave a fond twinkle. "Of course she did. Ever since she was little, she couldn't bear the thought of any creature suffering. I shall have to send men to backfill that area. It does tend to get marshy after a big storm. Something to do with the type of soil."

Gage was reminded of why he'd come in the first place.

He cleared his throat. "As a matter of fact, Lord Oberton, I was actually on my way here to ask you about your fallow pastures and how you manage drainage. Mine are quite submerged, you see, while yours seem to be protected."

Oberton nodded. "It's a system of brick-lined barrages, clay pipes, and headworks that act as valves on each of the channels between the fields. So it sends the water when it's needed, and redirects it around the pasture, if there's too much."

"Ingenious," Gage said.

"Effie's doing."

He blinked. "I beg your pardon?"

"It's her design." The earl's shoulders lifted in a proud shrug. "When she's not with her animals and her charities, she spends her time ensconced in the library, poring over manuals and civil engineering books. For fun, she claims. Much of the improvements at Oberton Hall, including the ones on the estate, are my daughter's doing."

"What have I done now?" the object of their conversation interjected.

Turning toward her voice, Gage froze. Her face was still pink from a recent bath, and she was clad in a clean blue muslin dress shot through with silver that matched her eyes. Pale, damp hair, pinned away from her face, hung in a loose sheet down her back. She looked no worse for wear after her valiant fight with a mud pit. In fact, she quite took his breath.

"Field irrigation," he answered in a rush. "Lord Oberton said it was your idea."

Her cheeks flushed as her gaze panned from the earl back to him. "Papa is exaggerating. I just suggested the design based on some simple research. Anyone could have done it."

Gage frowned. Was she embarrassed? She should be shouting her brilliance from the rooftops. Then again, if she were a man, she probably would have. Women in their world were held to different standards. Not in his mind, however—as he'd learned watching his mother be laird of a castle, handle hundreds of clan disputes, and negotiate dozens of political agreements, intelligence wasn't a factor of one's sex.

"Well, it's bloody genius." His gaze flicked to the earl. "Apologies, my lord."

"Don't on my account, I completely agree," Oberton said.

He bowed. "Thank you for the tea. Lady Evangeline, I hope you stay clear of mud traps in the future."

"I've learned my lesson, thank you, Your Grace," she said with a small nod.

Something glinted in her eyes as she stared at him, a thawing and a bit of goodwill, perhaps. It wasn't much, but it was there.

Gage nodded back, but for some reason, when he should have felt elated at the victory, he felt guilt instead.

The earl's gaze swung between the two of them, intrigue clear on his face, and Gage squashed down his discomfort. He had no wish to lead her father on as well as to his intentions, but it was obvious that the man loved his daughter and hoped to see her situated. What father wouldn't? His guilt only sharpened.

He blinked and shoved the emotion away. He needed to remember what was at stake here. The lady might be splendid and smart in equal measure, but this was his life hanging in the balance.

Becoming intrigued by her would be a mistake...no matter how fascinating she was.

CHAPTER SEVEN

Why, oh why had she agreed to this wretched outing?

Under her breath, Evangeline cursed herself, the Fates, and anything else she could, as she sipped sickeningly warm ratafia and watched Viola flirt with Lord Huntington across the room.

Surely, it was culpability that had brought her here.

The thought of the upcoming season in London might turn Evangeline's stomach, but she could put up with a harmless country assembly or two if it would make her sister happy. And Viola certainly *looked* happy. Even among the group of local gentry in Chichester, she stood out like a fresh flower in a barren field.

Evangeline's own gown itched abysmally at the neckline—or that could be from Beasty Buttercup's fur—she'd stopped at the shelter to check on the kittens before directing her coachman to the local civic ballroom at the town hall. Reaching up a discreet finger, she scratched at the offending spot, not that anyone would see. She was currently ensconced behind the biggest potted fern she could find and intended to stay there as long as she could.

"Goodness, Effie, hiding already?"

"Gah!" She nearly screeched at the voice in her ear, her heart stampeding like a herd of elephants. "Vesper, you scared the spit out of me! And I'm not *hiding*. I'm simply saving people from bleeding out willy-nilly from the blunt hammer of my tongue. It's rather altruistic of me to stay out of the way, I'd say. You know how terrified of me they all are."

"They are *not*," her friend said, plopping down in the chair beside her in a sea of aqua tulle. The color was shockingly bright, but it complemented Vesper's blond hair and rosy complexion. Unfortunately for Evangeline, it was very eye-catching, and she loved her clever, *quiet* little nook. With any luck, she'd have only an hour or two to go before Viola had had her fill of dancing and flirting.

"Lady Harriet ran the other way when she saw me arrive," Evangeline said dryly. "And Lord Filbert paled to the color of ash when I complimented his cravat. Conversation withers when I appear. Ladies shudder and gentlemen gird their loins."

Vesper rolled her eyes. "You are being histrionic on purpose. No one girds anything."

"They should." She grinned and waggled her fingers. "I'll cast my devious spell over them all and make them dance until their naughty bits fall off."

Her friend snorted. "I think you secretly love this dreadful reputation you've constructed, Effie dear. If they truly knew you as I do, they might not be so unfriendly. You have to let people in sometime."

"Why? I have you, the girls, and William as well, and Viola, too, when she's not being a brat. That's quite enough people for me."

"You can't wed any of us," she pointed out and then thought for a moment. "Well, you *could* marry Mr. Dawson."

"Bite your tongue. That would be like marrying my brother. And besides, he's quite besotted with Viola, and you know I don't intend to wed." She gnawed on her lower lip, a latent shiver chasing down her spine at the memory of hard muscles and a warm mountain hearth scent that made her mouth water. "However, of late, I've decided I might be convinced to procure a lover to discover the, er, ins and outs of copulation."

Vesper knew her well enough not to take that bait, though her cheeks pinkened and she let out a choked cough. *She* clearly knew what copulation entailed, being married herself, but the normally flippant and vociferous Vesper had been surprisingly closemouthed on the details of her marriage with her studious paleontologist duke.

Not that Evangeline blamed her…some things were too private to share. That didn't mean she hadn't gone scouring the library on her own, however, and devoured a rather enlightening handful of wicked novels on the subject, including several erotic vignettes by their resident expert on the subject herself, Briar. Her friend's short stories had been eye-opening to say the least, but Evangeline had never had any actual interest in sexual congress.

At least not until…

She put *that* thought right where it belonged. Her designs on a lover had emphatically, categorically, unequivocally nothing to do with *him*.

"I didn't expect to see you here," Vesper said, thankfully changing the subject and steering Evangeline away from any more forceful adverbs to the contrary. "You abhor these things."

Evangeline's mouth quirked with an unwelcome burst of conscience, considering Vesper's own request for her birthday ball in London. "Viola does not, and she shouldn't have to suffer my failings."

"*Failings?*" her loyal friend shot back. "What that man did to you, that entire set of toad-faced ratbags, was unconscionable. They tormented you, Effie, for no reason at all but for sport. They are responsible for their behavior, not you."

Vesper's impassioned speech drew her attention, and Evangeline noticed her friend's deeply flushed cheeks and overbright eyes. "Heavens, Your Disgrace, are you in your cups?"

The duchess gave an unrepentant grin and tapped her reticule. "In the flask is more apropos."

"What's in there?" Evangeline asked with interest.

Vesper removed a small silver receptacle. "I stole it from Jasper's study. Want a sip? I bet it beats that sad swill you're drinking."

Under cover of the dense fern, Evangeline accepted the palm-sized flask and took a bracing sip, eyes smarting as the Earl of Lushing's potent and clearly expensive brandy nearly went down the wrong way. Instant heat bloomed in the back of her throat and into her belly. She wasn't much of a drinker, apart from the occasional glass of champagne or revolting ratafia, but a little liquid courage never hurt anyone.

"That is potent," she gasped after another bracing sip, handing the flask back to Vesper.

"My brother always has the good stuff."

They stared at the dancers getting ready for a polka, including her sister and Huntington, and Evangeline wrinkled her nose. "Where's Greydon?"

"He's off talking to Jasper and Vale."

The duke was here? Evangeline felt her heart kick up a notch within her breast. Or perhaps that was the heady effect of the very excellent brandy. Hunching down, she swallowed past the expanding knot in her throat, her eyes scanning the dancers, looking for that distinctive head of copper-bronzed hair. Notwithstanding hair color, he would stand out by virtue of his size alone. The man was a mountain whom kittens liked to climb.

A grin broke over her lips.

"What is that smile for, or better yet, *whom* is it for?" Vesper demanded, perceptive blue eyes widening and then narrowing. "Wait one deuced minute. Is that for *Vale*? Effie Raine, you sneaky little minx, you fancy him! I knew there was a moment between the two of you at the shelter!"

"Keep your voice down," she hissed back. "And no, I don't fancy the duke at all. He's brash and unpolished and takes far too many liberties."

Vesper's eyes nearly fell out of her head. "*Liberties?* Do tell."

"There's nothing to tell. Forget I said anything."

But her friend was like a hungry dog with a bone. "Don't think you can lie to me, you scamp. I know every tic and tell of yours, and right now, you won't even look me in the eye and your nostrils are flaring like a bull about to hunt down a red rag."

Evangeline snickered. "They are not."

"Are too. Like a lady bull about to go full tilt."

"There are no such things as lady bulls."

Vesper sniffed. "Then there should be."

"Right, those would be called cows," Evangeline replied wryly.

The polka was now in full swing, and she couldn't help the fond smile at the sight of her sister's glowing countenance as she swirled in front of them with a new partner who wasn't Huntington, thank goodness, and completed the deft turns and complicated patterns. Despite her troublesome interest in the man, Viola deserved a season. Evangeline just wished their father hadn't put the burden on *her* to attend.

Being at peace with a hurtful event didn't diminish the memory of it.

Evangeline could not help her unusual looks or the fact that she often spoke without thinking. When she had an opinion of worth, she gave it. It was a side effect of learning, she supposed. All that knowledge had to go somewhere. A beat of warmth pulsed through her as she recalled the unguarded admiration on Vale's face as her father had spoken of her aqueduct design. *He* hadn't acted as though she were some kind of repulsive anomaly for using the brain she was born with.

Honestly, the design wasn't a stretch of ingenuity. She'd simply recommended a canal system that others had already been using for centuries in other parts of the world like India. England wasn't a monolith, even though it acted like it. Still, the duke hadn't looked at her as though she were an abomination for having a mind of her own. Unlike Huntington and his awful set, who had ridiculed her for daring to voice an opinion.

Evangeline scowled at the gentleman in question, who was watching her little sister from the periphery like a hungry hawk on the hunt. She grimaced. Evangeline truly hoped that Viola's infatuation was fleeting. Suddenly, the notion of shepherding her sister away from Huntington sank in, and Evangeline tapped her chin with her fan. There might be some merit to going to London, after all, where handsome, eligible gentlemen would be available in droves, and Huntington would be besieged by rivals. That vision alone buoyed Evangeline's spirits.

"Viola looks so happy, doesn't she?"

Her friend made a disagreeable noise in her throat. "Too bad she has her sights set on such a colossal dandyprat of a man."

Evangeline snickered. "You're not wrong about Lord Cunting-ton."

Vesper burst into raucous giggles at Evangeline's inventive nick-name for the cad. "Doesn't your veterinarian friend have a tendre for her?"

"Yes, and Viola's oblivious. She wants more than what he can offer." Evangeline shook her head. "Whatever that means."

Vesper sipped from her flask again. "What's wrong with want-ing more? You did once. You dreamed of finding someone whom you could spend the rest of your life with."

"That was different." Evangeline's brow pleated. "I was…young and idealistic."

"And she is, too."

Guilt rushed through her anew. The season didn't seem so insur-mountable when the alternative of Viola ending up with Hunting-ton was so much worse.

The duchess straightened suddenly, patting her cheeks and smoothing her impeccable coiffure. Evangeline followed Vesper's stare to the gentleman who had claimed her friend's attention with a single crook of his finger and a smirk. Vesper blushed and primped some more.

"It appears that Greydon is summoning me. Do I look foxed?"

Evangeline begrudged Vesper those thick, glossy blond ringlets that would stay put in a hurricane. Her own hair was like gossamer spiderwebs that would hinder any attempt to pin it down. Right now, she was certain there were flyaway wisps all around her face and nape, and she hadn't moved since she'd arrived. "No, you look lovely as always."

When Vesper left to join her handsome husband in a Viennese

waltz, Evangeline felt a sharp pulse of envy. Not the ugly kind, the wistful kind. She'd long resigned herself to being unwed and alone, but seeing her dearest friend so blissfully happy made her feel like something was missing in her own life. Esteem. Affection. *Love.* All those things she'd once craved, to Vesper's point. Then again, she supposed that was what kittens and puppies were for.

They loved unconditionally.

The lump in her throat swelled, and she almost wished for another bracing nip of Vesper's brandy. Or perhaps that was what was making her more dispirited than usual. Liquor had a way of doing that—lifting you up and then hurtling you down when you least expected it.

Evangeline gnawed her lip, peering around the fronds to the clock on the far wall. Midnight. Perhaps she could leave. Viola would get home safely. This was Chichester, after all, and not London. But as she watched her sister in the current embrace of Lord Huntington, her spine prickled. She could never leave her sister alone...not with a man like him. Vesper was right—he was arguably worse than a turd—but her sister was headstrong. Telling Viola she could not have something because it was rotten to the core would only make her want it more.

Perhaps she could endure another hour...for Viola's sake.

At least she was safe behind her fern.

But then the fragrance of warm hearths filled her nostrils, and she knew who had breached her haven even before she turned. Only the Duke of Vale smelled like a combination of her favorite things—fresh, crisp air after a rainstorm, a blazing fire in the grate, and the faintest scent of dark melted chocolate. Her chest squeezed, pulse hammering and lungs tightening, a sense of raw awareness skimming over her skin.

A rolling burr layered with gravel skated over her. "Dance with me, Evangeline."

Gage had watched her hiding out behind that fern like an other-worldly, mystical nymph. He had sought her out instantly, as if he were a planet bound to her sun, lost to her gravity, and when he'd finally seen her, something inside of him had settled into place. He'd arrived late after an issue with his tenants and their flooded wheat crops, but the minute he'd set foot inside the ballroom, he'd sensed that she was there. His skin had tightened, and his nerves had leaped with awareness.

It was curious. And alarming.

In the past handful of days, Gage had longed for a sight of her, found himself riding past her shelter home, hoping for a glimpse of that shining hair and incandescent smile with an armful of cats, dogs, or ravens, or whichever stray she'd rescued that day. He was fast becoming obsessed.

It's for the agreement, he'd told himself.

Earlier, he had pretended to listen to what the Duke of Greydon and Lushing had been saying, but he'd been distracted, wondering what she had been thinking or saying to the Duchess of Greydon. And now here he was unable to resist asking her to dance…and using her given name like a boor. But the desire to seek her out had been like an insistent beat in his head, humming in tune with his own heartbeat, driving him toward her like a beating drum.

Ice-blue eyes lifted to his, a wash of color spreading across her pale cheeks. That slender throat of hers worked, showing that she was not as serene as she'd appeared from afar. A smile curved one side of his lips as he noticed the tuft of orange fluff caught in the modest neckline of her bosom. Buttercup, that sneaky little fiend, had been tucked there against her pearlescent skin.

Gage's blood ran hot.

Was it possible to be jealous of a kitten?

"Pardon me," he rasped, and lowered his hand to pluck at the unruly bit of fuzz.

Her breath hitched when his gloved knuckles grazed the plump flesh at the edge of her bodice, more rosy color painting her collarbones and décolletage. Gage marveled at whether the berry hue quickly spreading over her porcelain skin would be the same color as her nipples. Would they be taut beneath her dress? How would they taste? His mouth flooded with water even as the soft scent of lilies with a hint of spice curled into his nostrils.

"Oh," she whispered, and Gage realized with dismay that he'd been leering at her breasts like a lust-filled lecher, hand frozen in midair as though about to pluck a deliciously ripe fruit from its vine. He snatched his hand back and curled it into a fist.

With a grunt, he cleared his throat and swallowed, offering the small tuft as evidence that he wasn't a complete scoundrel. "Apologies, my lady. You had a bit of fur there."

"Beasty Buttercup," she said, pupils blowing wide, melting away the icy blue. Was that because of desire, or had she taken offense to his outrageous liberty with her person? Aware of the many people in the ballroom and the accompanying wagging tongues, Gage was grateful for the cover of the fern.

"How *is* Beasty?" he asked.

"Healthy. Rambunctious. Naughty in the extreme." Her lips curled. "She has already ruined three dresses, one embroidered chair, and despoiled poor Hannah's favorite shoe."

"Despoiled?"

She bit her lip, eyes alight with mirth, and his cock twitched. "Defecated in it. Hannah has threatened to toss her back into the alley and let her learn the rules of survival."

Gage chuckled. The strains of a waltz filled the room as more couples took the places of the ones leaving to refresh themselves. Greydon and his wife had disappeared from the ballroom. It didn't surprise Gage one bit. In the moments he'd been conversing with the duke, the man had hardly taken his eyes off his wife, who had been glued to her friend's side. Perhaps such possessiveness was contagious, because he had the sudden need to do the same. To whisk Evangeline away.

But that wasn't the goal here.

His only goal was to convince her to go to London.

"So will you dance, or will you cut me down with your refusal?" he asked.

A small frown pleated her brow. "You were serious?"

"Why wouldn't I be?" he countered.

The rounded slope of her shoulder lifted, drawing his eye to the elegant line of her nape. "There are many other debutants and suitable ladies in attendance, Your Grace. Dancing with someone like me will not earn you any favor. Trust me, your efforts will be better served elsewhere, lest you be unfairly doomed with the spectral, cursed touch of Lady Ghastly."

"I don't like that designation," he said bluntly, taking her hand and placing it over his arm to lead them toward the ballroom floor.

To his surprise, she let him. Gage already knew that Lady Evangeline was not one easily led. His pride thrilled at the concession. "Please don't call yourself that again."

A startled gaze met his, a deprecating smile crossing her lips as though she did not believe he meant it. "Does it offend your ducal honor, Your Grace?"

"It should offend any man's honor." He lowered his voice as he settled them into place. "I mean it, Lady Evangeline. Do not give power to something that mean-spirited...or it will forever haunt you. Trust me, I know about the power of painful designations."

She stared up at him with mild surprise. "You do?"

"Don't you think I know half the guests here call me the Destitute Duke behind my back?"

"How terribly unimaginative," she said in a droll tone, though something fierce glinted in her eyes. Something *protective*. "Lady Ghastly trumps that by a mile. I win, Your Grace."

"Is this a competition of undesirable names?" he shot back. "Duke of Empty Coffers and Lady of Winter and Ice."

A smile twitched to life. "Ah, I see you have lost the point of the game, sir. The second is neither ugly nor undesirable. You're poor and I'm plain, that's how the plot works."

"You could never be plain."

She peered at him askance, her mouth going tight as if she doubted him. The flash of stark desolation in her eyes followed by her words confirmed his suspicion. "You needn't flatter me, Your Grace. I'm already here and I will dance with you. No need to oversell it."

"Tell me you don't believe those idiots," he demanded in a low, furious voice.

"But they're right. I am ghastly and frigid and off-putting. I'm no gentleman's perfect prize, and I have long made my peace with that."

"Beauty is bought by judgment of the eye," he said. "And *my* judgment says otherwise."

"You're quite the proficient flirt. Do they teach you such empty flattery in the wilds of the Highlands?" Sarcasm gilded the edge of her words.

"It's not empty if it's true."

Her mouth thinned more. "Then it seems that we are a match made in hogs' heaven, aren't we, Your Grace? The spinster and the supplicant."

"I'm certain I can perform exceptionally well on my knees." Gage took immense pleasure at the look of shock rolling across her face followed by a heated spark of interest, those flattened lips parting on a silent gasp.

Blazing eyes met his, her pupils so huge, the blue was barely a ring, but she tossed her head. "If you're trying to rattle me with whatever tactics men use in a lackluster attempt at seduction, it will not work. I am immune to such nonsense."

The wild look in her eyes suggested otherwise, however.

It was obvious she was still wary of him, but Gage was sure that if he kept chipping at her defenses, he might eventually make some headway. Rome wasn't built in a day, after all.

Once the music began, Gage moved her effortlessly into the first roll and turn. He fought not to notice the slender curve of her waist, or the soft pressure of her gloved fingertips on his shoulder. It was a losing effort. After their rousing verbal sparring, Gage wanted to crush her to him . . . to say to hell with the requisite twelve inches of distance and feel every delectable part of her pressed against every part of him—breasts to his chest, hips hitched beneath his.

Hell.

Gage cleared his throat and focused on how poor he actually was. The reality was always sobering. "To your earlier designation, admittedly, my coffers have seen better days, but money does not define who I am."

"You are a duke, Your Grace."

He grunted. "I'm a man first."

An insightful gaze speared him, and Gage regretted saying that. She wasn't like other women, who took things at face value or pretended to listen and didn't hear a word. Evangeline paid attention and that made her quite dangerous. That hardworking brain of hers was never idle for long.

His poverty might not define him, but the lack of fortune challenged him in other ways. It allowed men like Huntington to feel they held some sort of leverage over him. To some degree, that was true. He owed payment on Asher's gambling debt. But that didn't mean Huntington had power over how he chose to see himself. At the thought of the man and his bargain, the building pressure in his groin decreased.

Thank fuck.

Something of his thoughts must have been transparent in his face, because his partner smiled brightly, her changeling eyes turning back to a more placid blue. "I hate to prick your bubble, Your Grace, I've only ever heard the name Daredevil Duke associated with the Croft name, though I cannot recall where."

Phantom pain bled through his chest. Asher had worn that mantle with pride, pushing the limits whenever and wherever he could. "That was my brother," he said. "They called him that. He ran with a fast set."

"Ah yes, that's where I saw that nickname. I read about the accident in the papers." Gentle fingers flexed on his shoulder through another twirl. "I'm so sorry for your loss."

"Thank you."

The accident. His lungs compressed as Gage's eyes searched the throng for Huntington, finding him near the refreshments table, privileged entitlement stamped all over him. His sullen stare was fastened to Lady Viola, who was dancing with another gentleman. With a start, Gage recognized the veterinarian from the shelter, William Dawson, when the couple came into view. Huntington's fists were clenched, and he looked like a child deprived of his favorite confection.

That did not bode well for the doctor.

"Your sister seems taken with Lord Huntington," he remarked.

"Yes." Her tone was resigned. "Mr. Dawson is a much better fit, but he's the third son of a viscount. Huntington is in line for a very solvent marquessate, and my sister has lofty goals of marrying well."

"Doesn't every lady?"

"The *well* in that is defined differently by each lady, Your Grace," she said, glaring at him as if he'd said the wrong thing. Again…

"Did I offend you, Lady Evangeline?" he asked.

She laughed deprecatingly. "No, I am continually astounded by how shallow men think women are. Some might wish for fortune, and others for titles or position. But quite a few wish for companionship and affection, though both are rare in aristocratic marriages."

"And you? What do you wish for?" he asked with genuine curiosity.

The music came to an end and she curtsied, shutters descending over her eyes. "There's only one thing I wish for, and that is my sister's happiness."

Evangeline pressed a hand to her trembling stomach as she settled onto a settee in the retiring room. Her true wish had been on the tip of her tongue: *I wish for you to take me to a private room and demonstrate your skill on your knees.*

It was a scandalous wish. Men could presume to be so bold with their carnal desires, but women were shamed for theirs. How would he have reacted had she told the truth? Ordered him to pleasure her? Evangeline had never felt such a liquid rush of desire, licking along her veins and incinerating everything in its path when he'd so wickedly teased her after she'd called him a supplicant. Now the word would never be associated with anything else but lust.

From. One. Dratted. Dance.

But the minute his huge palm had gripped her waist on the ballroom floor, she'd been unable to think or function. All she could imagine was that hand slipping up her ribs to her breast or down her hip and lower still. In truth, she had been *desperate* for more of his touch...even if she couldn't quite work out what he wanted from her. The attraction was clear, of course, and seemed quite mutual, though the duke's motives remained murky.

But by God, his physicality overwhelmed her every good sense.

She ran a hand down the column of her neck and suppressed a delicious quiver.

Despite her lack of experience, Evangeline was no stranger to pleasures of the flesh. Self-fulfilled pleasure, that was. Years ago, she'd been thoroughly educated when she'd blazed through a racy private journal written by an actual French courtesan, and more recently, thanks to Briar's secret hobby, romance novels with heroines seeking their own pleasure weren't in short supply. But Evangeline had never felt such bone-shaking need as she had during the entirety of that waltz.

She'd had to fight to keep her knees locked and her own hands from wandering the expanse of that deliciously broad chest. What would it be like to feel that huge frame of his crushing hers? *Nude.* A heated blush filled her already scorched cheeks, and Evangeline gratefully accepted a cooling cloth from one of the attending maids. She was surprised her skin didn't sizzle at the contact.

"Effie dearest, are you well? You look quite ill." Her sister collapsed in a heap of pink organza beside her. Even flushed and sweaty, Viola was the picture of health and beauty, while Evangeline was sure that she looked like she was overcome with fever.

"I'm fine. A bit hot."

The understatement of the century.

"It is rather warm in the ballroom," Viola said with a cheerful sigh. "I've danced every single dance. My feet are aching. I was happy to see that you came out from your fern to dance with the duke. How was it?"

"It's not *my* fern."

Viola giggled and poked her with an elbow. "By now, you and that fern are practically betrothed, sister dear. I do hope you haven't let it make any untoward advances. I've been told that ferns can be quite forward, touching you when you least expect it with their wandering fronds. You better hope you don't end up with little frond-haired babes."

Evangeline couldn't help it, she burst out laughing. It was good to see Viola happy. This version of her was much more preferable than the alternative. "You are quite ridiculous. And yes, I did accept His Grace's invitation to dance. It was—" *Incredible. Divine. Euphoric.* "Satisfactory."

"*Satisfactory?* Good Lord, Effie. Your fern has truly ruined you for other men." Viola gave her a long-suffering look. "A waltz should be titillating, heart-pounding, *thrilling*. It should make you feel like you're flying, that you're about to burst out of your skin on the next twirl."

Viola's adjectives were much better than hers. Evangeline shot her a circumspect look. "Did you feel that way with Mr. Dawson or Lord Huntington?" she asked tartly.

Viola stilled for a moment, but then rolled her eyes with a false, shrill laugh. "Why, Lord Huntington, of course. I danced with William as a favor. He looked rather lonely there by himself. Think of it as my good deed for the week. You should probably dance with him as well, Effie. Honestly, you two would make a good match. You're always together and I've seen the way he looks at you."

God above, her sister was utterly oblivious.

"With forbearance or resignation at bringing him another animal to treat for free?" she replied sardonically.

"No, silly. With fondness and a great affection."

"Because we are *friends*, Viola."

"Friends can make good spouses."

Evangeline huffed a laugh. "Trust me, William does not want

me. His heart is well and truly owned by another, if only she'd open her pretty eyes and realize it."

Whether it was by design or not, her sister ignored her comment and rose to straighten her dress and fix the pins in her hair. She had lovely tresses, the hue a deep gold-brown, unlike Evangeline's own colorless white-blond strands. And Viola's stayed put, unlike her fairy floss. She raised a self-conscious hand to her fluffy coiffure and winced.

"Here, let me," Viola said, deftly smoothing and repinning the sides of Evangeline's flyaway hair. "Mama always used to say your hair could never hold pins or a curl. It's as slippery as corn silk. There, that's much better."

"More like spider silk," Evangeline muttered. "Thank you."

Viola fixed her own perfect curls with a deft touch and blew a kiss at her reflection before winking at Evangeline. "See? I knew you could have fun if you only gave it a chance. London will be much the same. The two of us together for a season. Wouldn't that be wonderful, Effie?"

It was rather excellent manipulation, but Evangeline wasn't immune to the sweetness of her sister's sentiments, even if they proved to be false. She'd missed two years of Viola's life...and this felt special. The onslaught of emotion only compounded her earlier thoughts of getting her sister away from Huntington before she became thoroughly distracted by the Duke of Vale. "Yes, it would be."

Viola's eyes brightened. "Then you'll go? To London?"

"The notion is growing on me," Effie admitted with a smile.

The squeal that left her sister could shatter glass as she threw her arms around Evangeline, and for a moment, she let herself savor the feel of her sister's embrace. It had been so long since Viola had hugged her or vice versa. Squabbles and petty disagreements didn't leave much room for affection, but at the end of the day, those things didn't matter.

After Viola left the retiring room with another ungodly squeal, Evangeline slouched against the velvet squabs of the settee. Well, in better news, the inconvenient bloom of arousal had finally disappeared, replaced with her usual pragmatism and common sense. The first order of business was … to avoid the object of her unfortunate and ill-fated lust. That dreadful pining was simply not *on*.

She was a steadfast spinster.

You're one-and-twenty, hardly on the shelf.

She had a plan for an independent future, sans husband.

But you could be a duchess. Think of the independence then.

She was an educated, self-sufficient woman with a shelter to manage.

Who could make excellent use of those hard muscles and that luscious mouth.

Her thighs shuddered as an indecent lick of heat swept between them. Sometimes, she hated her own brain. With a sigh, Evangeline lifted another damp cloth to her brow, wishing she could stick it between her legs instead. That part of her clearly needed a thorough cooling.

Maybe London *wasn't* such a bad idea for her as well. While she couldn't have the Duke of Vale, for obvious reasons, perhaps a suitable distraction of comparable virility would do.

There were clubs like the Earl of Lushing's Lethe, which might serve her needs. Evangeline had heard rumors of Vesper's brother's leanings when it came to the underground club that he managed—one that catered to vice in all forms.

During her second season, she and Vesper had snuck into Lethe once for an underground boxing match. It had been like attending a theater production with finely dressed aristocrats, flowing libations, and women of the demimonde dressed in scantily clad costumes mingling with the guests. Utterly shocking! But the show stealer had been the ring at its center—the complete incongruity of a boxing ring in the middle of a fashionable party. Unfortunately, she and Vesper had been caught by Lushing before they could see the actual fight, which Evangeline had been looking forward to.

But more specifically, there were also parts of the social club that catered to fulfilling the sensual desires of both their male and female membership, no holds barred. Briar had alluded to that scandalous bit of gossip a while ago, though how she knew of such a thing remained a mystery. Evangeline put it down to the fact that Briar was practically obsessed with the earl even though she swore to high heaven she wasn't. Perhaps Briar would have more insight on how Evangeline could secure an invitation to one of those parties.

A single evening of pleasure would be an excellent reward.

CHAPTER EIGHT

"I require confirmation, Vale." Huntington's face was pulled into a displeased sneer. "Do I need to remind you of what is on the table here? We're a few weeks away from the season's most anticipated ball."

"I've told you," Gage replied without looking up from his task. "They will be there."

Huntington's eyes fell to the paint staining Gage's hands as he finished the last coat on the newly repaired columns gracing the sprawling entrance. "Don't you have servants to do that for you?"

"A little hard work never hurt anyone."

"Unlike you, I do not seek to lower myself by performing menial labor when I can pay someone to do it for me. Much like how I'm compensating you to do something that needs doing, *Duke.*"

Gage gritted his teeth at the overt insult in the address. Yes, Huntington was exactly the sort to get others to do all the hard work for him. Gage couldn't wait until he didn't have to see the man's scornful face, lording his brother's vowels over him like a hangman's noose. He would clear the debt, and then he would find out whether the rotter had anything to do with what really happened to Asher. If so, there'd be hell to pay.

"Anything else, Huntington?"

The man scowled. "So, do I have your word, and should I make preparations?"

"I said as much. Now scurry along."

"Careful, Vale," Huntington said in a low snarl. "You might possess the title of duke, but don't forget that I am the most powerful man in London. It won't serve to insult me."

Based on what he'd learned from Lushing, Huntington's so-called power might be an exaggeration, but in spite of Gage's deep desire to take the cocky bastard down a peg or two, he forestalled himself. Eliminating Asher's debt wasn't worth the gratification.

Gage didn't bother to form a reply, staring Huntington down like they were facing each other at dawn. Or standing toe to toe in a blood-spattered boxing ring. His lips curled back from his teeth in a mockery of a smile. He'd give anything for the latter, if only to watch Huntington piss his pants.

Within seconds, the other man's shoulders sagged at the pure aggression in Gage's stance. "Don't fail me, Vale," he snapped.

The *or else* wasn't subtle. Then again, nothing about the arrogant prick was subtle.

After Huntington left, Gage ran a hand through his hair, uncaring that his fingers were wet with paint. He still had to convince Evangeline to go to London, but he was more confident in his ability to do so after their dance. There had been an encouraging... progression.

He hadn't seen her in the days following the country assembly, but he'd been busy with estate repairs and being fitted for a full wardrobe that he had little patience for. But that didn't mean he hadn't thought about her. The memory of how she felt in his arms had dominated his hours, and what he was lacking in experience,

he certainly made up for in imagination. His nights had been...
interminable.

The fit of her body against his combined with the look in her
eyes had almost unmanned him. When he'd asked what she wished
for, her expressive gaze hinted at untold wants and hidden desires.
He'd seen those pretty eyes flash from ice blue to molten silver, bolts
of hot color cresting along her high cheekbones.

What he would have given to be privy to *those* thoughts.

But in the space of the next breath, she'd tamped down every
single one of those emotions with the ease of a seasoned card sharp
being dealt a new hand at the gaming tables. Lady Evangeline was
also a master at concealing her true sentiments, it seemed.

A throat cleared from behind him. "Goodness, this is rather a
far cry from what the outside was before. A coat of paint can work
wonders."

It was as though his very thoughts had summoned her.

Gage caught his breath, feeling as though he'd been punched in
the gut. He was conscious of his paint-splattered shirtsleeves and
hoary waistcoat, but his appearance could not be helped. She, on the
other hand, looked every inch the earl's daughter, wearing a smart
but worn riding habit with a deep wine-colored velvet jacket over
striped cotton skirts that were buttoned up to one side. A jaunty,
slightly battered plumed hat with a ribbon chin strap hid her moon-
kissed hair.

"Lady Evangeline," he croaked, remembering his manners.
He wiped his hands on his trousers and gave a short, cursory bow.
"What brings you to Vale Ridge Park?"

The groom hovering behind her stepped forward to hand over
a parcel. Unwrapping it, she held out a roll of documents to him

along with several books. "I thought I would deliver these personally. They're some irrigation plans. It should help with your challenges in the fields when it rains."

Gage blinked at her in surprise. "Thank you, that's very thoughtful of you."

"It's a small thing," she said, a faint blush brightening her cheekbones. "The books were lying around, and it was no hardship to draw the diagrams."

Draw them? He reached for one of the rolled pieces of parchment. It was a drawing of his field, complete with scaled representations, detailing the channels that needed to be dug and the barricade that would have to be constructed. The lines were impeccably drawn, her handwriting neat and precise. "You did this for me?"

That blush on her cheeks deepened. "It was nothing."

"This is astonishing."

"Yes, it seems I surprise a lot of people," she said in a quiet, guarded tone. "Most in our set don't expect a woman's brain to be able to handle anything but needlepoint or the occasional pianoforte performance. Our brains are just as proficient as any man's, given the opportunity."

"You misunderstand me, lass. I meant it as a sincere compliment."

It was true. He was more than impressed. Her gaze bored into his, as though she was expecting some kind of trick in his reply. What had made her so disbelieving of genuine praise? Gage kept his face blank, showing nothing of his inner thoughts. Perhaps she had been belittled for her efforts before, though he couldn't fathom who would be so parochial.

"Do you have time right now?" she asked, shielding her gaze once more. "If I'm not interrupting, that is. We could take a ride out to the fields, and I could show you where I envisioned the work to be done. It won't take long."

Gage nodded. He was genuinely interested in her ideas, but it was also an opportunity to convince her to go to London. One he couldn't waste. "Give me a moment to get changed."

"You're fine as you are, Your Grace."

Most ladies would have sniffed and demanded he change into proper garments. In loose shirtsleeves and worn breeches, he wasn't dressed for polite company, after all. But then again, Evangeline wasn't like anyone he'd ever met.

He hid his smile and nodded, grabbing hold of a coat that Jenkins held out without comment, before accompanying her down to his stables, where he saw two horses had been hitched to a nearby post.

"I could have sworn that a woman like you would ride astride," he remarked, calling for his own stallion to be saddled. "And be fitted in men's fashion for such."

A pale brow arched. "A woman like me?"

"One who flaunts her irreverent disregard for the rules of polite society."

Those ice-blue eyes narrowed, offense flaring in their depths, as she directed a glance to the young groom who stood some distance away, before coming back to him. "Are you mocking me, Your Grace?"

"Does it feel like I'm mocking you, my lady?"

He could sense rather than see her spine snap straight at his silky reply. God, it gave him such sinful pleasure to tease her. Lushing had called her thoughtful and quiet, but for some reason, she was the exact opposite in Gage's company. He liked that. He liked that she fired up with him.

Her eyes were pure ice. "Yes, I do believe you are being provocative for reasons known only to you."

"It was simply an honest observation," he said, watching as she stalked toward her mount, with a near violent toss of her head. He did not hide his smile this time since she could not see it, but waited with bated breath for her reply.

"I do not flout the rules, Your Grace. I simply believe that some of them are much too antiquated and discriminatory toward my sex. Why shouldn't a woman ride astride? Catherine the Great did it. In the Middle Ages and Renaissance periods, women did so until it fell out of favor because such a thing was thought to compromise a lady's modesty. How insufferable! That our only virtue and value rests between our legs. Honestly, it's a wonder most women's hips and knees aren't in a permanent state of dislocation from being seated thus on a hundred stone of horseflesh." She let out a loud snort, face red from passion. "And men consider us the weaker sex? If it wouldn't hurt the horse, I'd challenge you or any male to ride in a sidesaddle for half a mile. You would not last two minutes."

"You are rather intense, do you know?" His cheeks were aching from the force of his delight at drawing her out. "Remind me never to dagger the dragon again, my lady."

"There's no crime against intensity, only unfair criticism because insufferable men feel that women should be seen and not heard. And I am *not* a dragon."

He let out a guffaw. "But you are, aren't you? With me, anyway. All fire, brimstone, and belching embers. In my company, you like being able to say what you please, let those erudite opinions of yours fly while knowing none of it will shock me. Knowing that I, in fact, might *enjoy* hearing your exceptional views."

He saw the apple of her cheek lift where she stood hidden by her horse, though she did not confirm his assertion. After adjusting the fastenings on her skirts and climbing nimbly into the stirrup— which was not a sidesaddle, he belatedly noticed—she speared him an arch look. Gage fought not to gawk as one slender booted leg, clad in a fitted pair of *men's breeches* visible beneath the split in her skirts, was agilely thrown over the horse's back.

She arched a brow at his gratified expression. "As far as my preferences in wardrobe, which once more should not concern you whatsoever, I was attempting to be fully covered while riding astride and not scandalize your poor ducal sensibilities."

"Scandalize away," he said, mounting his own horse and riding up to her. "And besides, I much prefer the true Lady Evangeline. The one who sips on brandy while hidden behind ferns, and the one who speaks her mind when it matters."

"I do not…" She pinned her lips and exhaled. "Hide behind ferns."

"Or swearing a blue streak and yelling *ballocks* at sinkholes."

Her porcelain cheeks burned. "*You* made me say that word!"

"Oh, is that the story you're sticking with?" Gage let out an amused laugh. "You and I both know, Lady Evangeline, that there isn't a soul on this earth who can force you to do something or say something you do not wish to do or say. And before you get your very resourceful skirts into a froth, that, too, was meant as a genuine compliment."

Pale eyes met his, holding his stare for an interminable moment before she broke the connection. "Shall we go, Your Grace? Unless you plan to stay here and pontificate my merits all day, in which case I will offer my regrets and leave you to it."

Gage barked out a laugh. Dear God, she was adorably salty.

With a scowl at his amusement and an expert touch, she tugged on the reins, setting her mount off in a gallop down the driveway. Guiding his own stallion forward with a wide grin that he could not banish for the life of him, Gage followed.

Evangeline was already in a fine froth.

Indeed everything inside of her was *frothing*.

Her blood, her curiosity, her completely indecorous passions.

God, the man was entirely too vexing! She had come here in person only because it was the right thing to do. And perhaps she'd needed to convince herself that the intensity of what she'd felt during their dance had been because of the brandy she'd drunk or being caught up in the waltz, and not because of any *true* attraction between them.

She'd been dead wrong on both counts.

Because the attraction fairly sizzled with heat.

And the moment she'd set eyes on him, the conflagration had blazed. Her breath had shriveled in her lungs, every nerve in her body vibrating to life, no stolen sips of brandy to be blamed.

Evangeline couldn't decide which version of him she preferred— the put-together duke, or this primal, earthly version of him in sweaty, worn shirtsleeves that was so deeply tantalizing…so wholly *delicious* that she had to bite her lip to keep from groaning in pure appreciation. Even with the flecks of paint speckling his copper hair and the trickle of sweat meandering down the tanned column of his scandalously bare throat, he was delectable.

Gulping, she clenched her fists over Ares's reins and refused to look behind to see whether the duke was following, though she could hear the pounding hooves of his mount as well as her groom's. While a compliment on her beauty might make her scoff, this kind of esteem felt sincere because it was rather specific to her. To her *skills*. Vale was applauding her mind, and it was... wonderful. A flicker of warmth gathered in her chest, which she quickly extinguished.

What was the duke's aim here? Men like Vale, *dukes* like him in their shared circles, did not esteem misfits like her, much less encourage them in their polemic and usually unwelcome opinions. Was Vale being facetious then when he claimed to enjoy her opinions? Her disdain for the vagaries of the ton? Her impassioned, unapologetic views when it came to the female sex and traditional roles of women? Her scandalous riding habit?

Something didn't feel right, and she was determined to find out what it was.

Soon, they reached the hillock that divided their properties, where she had a clear view of her fertile, well-drained fields, as well as his still-sodden and muddy pastures. Evangeline stiffened as he pulled up beside her, much closer than necessary. If her horse shifted an inch to the side, her knee would brush against his.

"Over there," she said breathlessly, pointing to the top of the field, handing him a small nautical telescope that she pulled from her saddlebag. "The buttress should be built there so that gravity does the work when you need it. See on our fields how the aqueducts are constructed? It eases the drainage so the ground doesn't turn into a swampy marsh."

"That's bloody brilliant," he said, peering through the glass.

"It has been effective on this type of soil."

"Genius."

She flushed with pleasure at the respect she heard in his voice. He was so close that Evangeline could smell the musk of his sweat cooling on his skin. Out of the corner of her eye, she sought out that glistening swath of flesh visible beneath his open shirt, inhaling a meager lungful of air when his Adam's apple bobbed on a swallow. Heaven knew why the sight of *that* made an ungodly shiver chase over her. How was a man's throat arousing? Evangeline turned her attention back to the fields.

She felt his eyes drift over her person.

"I see you found another pair of boots," he said.

"These are Viola's," she said. "I cannot justify the expense for a few moments of discomfort."

"More than a few moments," he remarked.

"It's of no consequence."

His horse shifted sideways, and suddenly, Evangeline was excruciatingly conscious of the heat of his leg, even through her riding skirts. A sliver of distance separated them, and yet, every part of her body tightened with *yearning*. What was this indescribable surge? It was as though she would settle only if he touched her ... if they finally connected and *she* pushed her knee into his.

Folly, that was what it was!

She lifted a shoulder in a shrug and nudged her horse a few paces away, where she could ease some air into her contracted lungs. The need churning beneath her skin lessened, but only slightly. She scanned the rest of the pastures and then jerked back as something caught her eye in the distance. "Goodness, is that smoke?"

"Where?" the duke asked, craning his neck toward where a thin plume of black soot was spiraling into the air.

"Do you see it? The east end of your property. What's over there?"

"An old barn, if I recall."

She whirled Ares around. "Well, it's on fire."

With both the duke and her groom on her heels, she swiftly reached the small dilapidated shack, which was absolutely on fire though it was reduced, thank goodness, by the dampness of the wood after the recent rain. But it was the sound of panicked bleating that made Evangeline's heart quail. She was only a few lengths ahead of Vale, but there was no time to be lost. The roof could come crashing down at any moment.

Evangeline dismounted and detached the skirts of her riding habit with a deft movement of her wrist. It was an ingenious design by the very talented Laila that offered the modesty her set demanded but allowed her the economy of movement beneath.

"What do you think you are doing?" Vale demanded as he reined his horse to a stop.

She gave him a blank stare. "What does it look like?"

"You cannot think to go any closer. It's much too dangerous. Step back before you get burned or worse."

Evangeline recoiled at the curt command. "It's too wet to burn properly, and besides, there's a terrified animal in there. Can't you hear it? A lamb, from the sounds of it. If we don't help it, it will die."

The duke leaped off his horse and stalked to where she stood, frowning at the gaping entrance where a door used to be. He seemed to be trying to determine the safest point of entry. Just then the sound of an animal in distress rent the air, more desperate than before. The poor creature must be trapped or confused, if it could not escape. She stepped forward, only to have a large hand clamp around her upper arm, stalling her. "Don't."

Evangeline glared at him. "Let go of me."

A growl rumbled from his chest. "You are *not* going in there."

"Who do you think you are?" she growled back.

He leveled her with a cool look, green eyes snapping with ire. "The owner of this property, and there's no way in hell you are going anywhere near that death trap."

More pitiful bleating reached her ears. Gritting her teeth, Evangeline wondered whether she could yank her arm out of the duke's grasp and make a run for it. As if he suspected her plans, Vale's grip tightened, not painfully, but enough so that she knew she would not easily escape him. "Please." She resorted to begging. "It will die if we don't do something, Vale."

A conflicted green stare met hers, filled with worry and compassion, but then he sighed and nodded. "Do not move," he said. "I'm serious, Evangeline. Promise me."

"I promise I will stay right here," she said, but crossed her index and middle fingers behind her back, hoping for God's forgiveness for the small lie. If he needed help or things took a turn for the worse, there was no way she wasn't going in after him.

Vale glanced at the groom, who also wore a resigned and long-suffering look on his face that Evangeline recognized. Philip was more than aware of the scrapes she often found herself in. This was not so far out of the ordinary.

"You there," the duke said. "Make sure she does not follow. Restrain her if necessary."

Evangeline gasped her outrage, but Philip nodded. "Yes, Your Grace."

"Bloody lamb," he muttered and turned to her, sparks in those clover-green eyes that promised something...exactly what she did not know, but that look stole the breath from her lungs. "You owe me, leannan."

Evangeline had no idea what *leannan* meant, but the mere graveled sound of the word poured over her like molten waves of heat, making her nipples tauten as if they were in complete understanding of its meaning. She swallowed hard and bit her lip.

Philip moved to her side after the duke disappeared into the smoking structure, his huge frame barely clearing the collapsed entrance. She glared at the groom. "Don't even think about it, Philip. May I remind you who pays your wages."

"He's a duke, my lady."

"Yes, yes. I'm well aware that His Grace has astronomical powers, and the wrath of the heavens will come crashing down should he ever be disobeyed."

The sound of more terrified bleating came from the shed, drowning out her caustic reply, and a creaking, groaning noise filled the air. The structure was about to collapse!

"Vale! Hurry!" she yelled out. There was no response from the duke, even as a terrifying crash boomed and one wall of the barn buckled inward. "Your Grace!"

Damn and blast, something had gone wrong. She could feel it. She had to go in.

"Philip, go back to the residence and get help."

"But, my lady," he protested, eyes wide with fear. "You cannot go in there. It's too dangerous. The whole thing could come down at any moment."

She gritted her teeth. "Then we have no time to waste. Go now!"

Before he could stop her, she retrieved her discarded skirts and wrapped them around the lower half of her face, and plunged into the barn. It was dark, and the thick bands of smoke made her eyes water. Heat seared her skin from where the blaze ate at the load-bearing posts. She didn't dare look up for fear of what could come tumbling down.

The panicked bleats had ceased, but she was more worried about the man who'd gone in for them. "Vale, where are you?"

There was no answer, but the creaking of the wood above grew stronger as bright orange-red embers fell from the roof. Her heart thundered in her chest, knowing that the eaves could topple at any moment.

"Vale!"

Venturing deeper into the shadowy depths, she could feel the smoke penetrating and smothering her lungs through the fabric covering her nose and mouth. "Devil take it, you blockheaded, arrogant sack of rocks, answer me, or I swear to God I will turn around and leave you here!"

She could barely see, the smoke was so thick. Suddenly, an enormous form materialized in front of her, struggling to hold three soot-covered lambs tucked under each arm. Three!

"Don't you ever listen, woman?" he croaked, shoving the smallest of the lambs into her arms. "Here, take it, and quick, go before we're both crushed or die of smoke inhalation."

They rushed out, just in time, as the entire barn made an ugly grinding sound and crumpled inward. They both collapsed onto the grassy earth, coughing hard. When she'd caught her breath, Evangeline released the limp but still alive lamb from her arms as he did the same.

"There were *three* of them. You saved them!"

He shot her a furious glare. "I told you to stay put."

"You weren't answering me," she said, refusing to cower. "I sent Philip for help. What was I to do? Wait and watch that thing cave in on you?"

"Yes," he bit out, voice a raw rasp. "Exactly that."

She set her jaw. "You said it yourself—no one tells me what I can or can't do. Not even you, the all-powerful, all-everything, omniscient duke who is clearly too big for *his* boots."

The sarcasm was a mistake. She saw it in the flare of those darkening green eyes, a half of a heartbeat before he leaned in with purpose, his lips halting a hairsbreadth away. Goodness, was he going to kiss her?

Evangeline startled, her lips parting in invitation, chin tilting up, before she could grasp hold of herself, and he didn't hesitate as his mouth closed the distance to hers, his tongue sweeping in to torture hers with a punishing, velvet swipe that had her mind reeling.

He stank of soot and ash, but beneath it, the taste of him emerged like the most wicked of flavors. Rich, delicious, *intoxicating*. Heavens, she'd never felt anything like this kiss—the abrasion of his stubble, the sleek slide of his tongue, the scrape of his teeth— all the sensations coalescing into unadulterated need.

As if in agreement, a thick arm banded about her waist and yanked her into his lap, making her sharply aware of every hard inch of his body. And he was hard *everywhere*. His chest, his legs, his groin. Breath ebbed from her as her core pulsed with desire.

She wanted *more*.

Evangeline fisted her hands in his ruined coat, dragging herself to her knees and straddling his hips as she savaged his mouth, kissing him back as feverishly as he was kissing her. It was hungry. It was raw. It was *real*. Vale groaned into her mouth when she chased his tongue with hers, sucking, nibbling, and taking what she wanted without an ounce of shame. She might regret it later, but for now, all she wanted was to embrace the storm and drown herself in the pleasure he offered.

With one last punishing nip to her bottom lip, the duke pulled away from her, eyes like shards of brilliant jade. "Good then. As long as we're clear."

Bemused, Evangeline's brows pleated. "On what?"

"That I am superior in all things. And my boots are like the rest of me. Big."

Good Lord, the sheer arrogance of him.

"I only said that to feed your poor fragile male ego," she said with a sniff, reaching for the fraying threads of her composure.

The duke's mouth—swollen and red, she noted with a pulse of pure gratification—twitched as he sat up and stared morosely at his singed, tattered clothing. There were ragged holes in the elbows and black soot stains all over the white fabric of his shirt. Evangeline bit back a horrified snicker at his baleful expression.

"This is the third coat I've ruined in your company," he remarked. "I'm starting to think that it would be a fine idea to not wear anything I do not wish to lose in your destructive presence. Because what will be next after this poor shirt? My trousers?"

Evangeline fought the wild rush of snorts building. "Then you will not be fit for proper company, Your Grace, especially if you are nude."

"Precisely. And I promise you, I will not be held responsible for any ruined sensibilities from lascivious ogling. You will be the sole one to blame."

Evangeline's mouth fell open, even as the deep sound of his rumbling laughter at her thunderstruck expression filled the air. Good God, the mouth on him. Not to mention the vanity. It didn't even take a second before her own giggle-snorts came, hot on the heels of his easy chuckles, but for once in her life, Evangeline did not bother to stifle them.

It was either give in to her emotions or give voice to the catastrophic realization that after *that* kiss, her own sensibilities might be in grave, *grave* danger.

CHAPTER NINE

Lord knew that Gage was holding on to his composure by a thread—being alone with her, even out in the open, was too much of a temptation. Not now, when he knew how divine she tasted and how good she felt in his arms. He kept his distance for both their sakes until her groom returned with help from the manse.

When the meager handful of Gage's servants arrived on the hill, armed with buckets of water from the nearby stream that cut through the lower part of the property, it was already much too late for what was left of the barn. Gage led them to douse the earth around the structure so the blaze would not spread. And then, they could only watch the fire burn itself out, which thankfully didn't take long. Dark plumes of smoke curled into the sky, lessening in intensity, until only wisps remained.

But despite the arduous work of soaking the perimeter, Gage was consumed with thoughts of the willful hoyden who didn't give a hoot about her own safety or for listening to instructions, nor did she seem the least bit affected by the kiss that had hurtled them both into stupidity. He hadn't meant to kiss her, but once she'd given her consent and his lips had touched hers, nothing could have torn him away.

Hell, the *taste* of her. Tart and fresh, like sweet mulled wine.

He preferred to abstain from spirits, and yet, he could have drunk from her forever.

Even now, he watched as she peered through the tiny portion of the barn that still remained standing, and made a sound of satisfaction before scooping up some furry creature from a corner of the unburnt but crumbled beams. To his alarm, upon further inspection, it was a very plump and well-fed rodent.

Still a bit muddled from the smoke as well as the unexpectedly ardent kiss, Gage stared at her when she carefully put the mangy thing into one of her saddlebags. "That's a rat," he pointed out.

"I am aware."

"It's a *rat.*"

She peered at him as though she was worried that he had been hit by a falling beam and was confused. "I can see it's a rat, Vale," she replied slowly as if speaking to a young child. "But just like the lambs, it requires care as well."

"They're pests. Those things will survive anywhere. It doesn't need your help."

That diamond bright gaze turned mulish. "Well, I say it does."

With a wince, Gage rubbed his throbbing jaw and shook his head. What kind of highborn woman saved rats? Most of them would clutch their skirts and run screaming. She'd be lucky if her little shelter didn't end up with an infestation of the rodents within the week.

The rat wasn't even the last of it. She ordered Philip to search for more wounded. The groom didn't even blink at the request, which made Gage wonder how often she collected injured creatures. *Very* often, it seemed. By the time Gage sent the servants who had valiantly come to help back to their duties at the manse, she'd also collected what looked like a fox kit that must have been abandoned in a den under the south side of the ruined building.

He watched as she cradled the baby fox to her breast, crooning softly. Once more, as it had with the kitten, the pulse of envy took him by surprise. He frowned at his reaction. That *wasn't* envy…it was concern that she might be mauled by a wild animal, even one so little.

"Don't hold it too closely," he warned her. "That kit could be diseased or covered in vermin."

She scoffed at him. "He's not, and besides, I'm wearing gloves. Look how scared he is. They're usually born in burrows in the spring. His mother must have been desperate to get her babies to safety, and somehow he got left behind. Or perhaps he was the only survivor."

"How do you know it's a he?"

Pale blond eyebrows winged skyward, a sly smile tugging on one corner of her wide lips. They were not overtly full, but something about the voluptuous width of them drove him wild. "The usual way, Your Grace. Do you require an instruction in anatomy?"

"Are you offering your services, my lady? I do believe you might have been educating the Duchess of Greydon in such matters when I visited your shelter." He met her smirk with one of his own, and to his utter delight, she didn't back down. Instead, she favored him with a quiet stare, something like mischief flashing in those eyes as she, too, recalled the event in question and the hushed descriptor she'd used.

"You poor, untutored thing," she said primly, gaze glinting with impish humor. "Good gracious, it is rather sad that you have come so far in life, Your Grace, without such rudimentary knowledge of your own body. A travesty to be sure." She shot him a look dripping in over-the-top sympathy. "You see, the male sexual reproductive organ is called a penis, though there are many other names, like prick, truncheon, rod, tallywag—"

The groom who had been walking toward them with a small bucket for the fox kit gave an about-face and made a choked noise, cheeks going red. Only Philip's mortified spluttering stalled her mid-lesson, but Gage found himself wickedly eager for her to continue. The sound of such uncouth words falling from *those* lush, aristocratic lips was unbearably suggestive. She might have looked like a demure angel, but she had the tongue of a sybarite.

He wanted that tongue in his mouth . . . on his *body*.

And he'd never craved something so viscerally. Until now.

"You are a menace, Lady Evangeline," he said, chuckling under his breath as she sauntered back to her horse with her impromptu menagerie adorning her person and in tow.

She shot him an arch look over her shoulder. "Only to those in dire need of menacing, Your Grace."

He was quite certain that menacing had absolutely nothing to do with kissing, but his brain was too far gone to listen. He was in dire, dire need.

Blinking stars out of his vision, Gage scowled at the Earl of Lushing, who was wearing an infuriatingly smug expression. Gage swallowed and tasted the metallic hint of blood before running his tongue inside his mouth to check for anything loose. No slack teeth though his jaw ached. Normally, no one could get the drop on him in the ring, but he'd been distracted.

Distracted enough to almost get himself knocked the hell out.

By *Lushing*.

The earl boxed for sport, never for competition as Gage had, and while he was competent with his fists and his footwork, there was no way he should have been able to land such a blow. Not without Gage seeing him coming from a mile away. But nearing the end of their friendly bout, Lushing had gotten in a wallop to the side of his chin that had near crashed his head around.

All because of that fucking kiss.

Although, admittedly, Gage had more on his mind than just the softest pair of lips in England. One of the western walls of the manse had simply given up the ghost. Luckily that part of the castle had been empty, so no one had been hurt, but the funds needed for repair were beyond measure.

Fulfilling his agreement with Huntington was now essential if he had any hope in hell of keeping the bloody ducal seat habitable. He supposed he could marry a wealthy heiress, as his solicitor Boone had suggested, which was an option for many impoverished peers. But marrying an English heiress meant staying in London.

And that was not an option.

Neither was letting Lushing get in another lucky shot. For days, Gage hadn't been able to work or focus, his mind too preoccupied with trying to figure out a solution. He had the savings from the Scottish property he'd sold, which would help with repairs, but it wasn't nearly enough.

He'd thought a round of boxing would center his head and ground his emotions. And it had succeeded in putting his financial problems and the kiss with Evangeline from his mind at the start, but in a moment of weakness—of pure lust, to be fair—she had resurfaced like a bad rash. One he couldn't help wanting to scratch.

Evangeline Raine was a mystery, one that he did not have the time nor the wherewithal to unravel. But by God, the lass captivated him. And *that* was what had made him falter in the ring, allowing his opponent's fist to collide with his face. Trust Lushing to take full advantage of the moment to land a right hook that had rattled his skull.

"So tell me, Vale, what was that look for?" the earl asked, unwrapping his gloves and moving to murmur to a footman who hovered just outside the room. "If I had to guess, I'd say a pretty piece of muslin had just flitted across your thoughts. Who is she?"

More like a pretty piece of razor-edged lace.

And Evangeline wouldn't *flit* . . . the lass would strut and leave terror in her wake.

"No one," he said, cupping his jaw and wincing. Lushing's lucky wallop was going to leave a hell of a bruise. "Where'd you learn that move?"

Lushing grinned and gave him a wink. "If I recall, that's the one-two combination you used in your last fight in Edinburgh when you knocked your opponent on his arse in the first round. I might not be a champion like you, but I'm a quick study." A footman entered with a tray containing a decanter and two glasses.

Pouring himself a whisky, the earl shot Gage a sidelong glance before handing him the second glass that was already filled with water. "If you're serious about London, would you be interested in an exhibition fight at Lethe? Could be worth your while with all the toffs back in town."

The offer was . . . provocative. It could be the solution to all his money problems. No, no, no. That was a slippery slope and one he knew he couldn't be on.

"You know I don't gamble."

Lushing nodded, peering at him over the rim of his glass. "I know. You would not be betting. You'd be the main attraction. I'd be the one betting and winning."

"I see how it is," Gage grumbled. "I'm a milch cow to you now?"

"Well, not if you're going to get distracted. Then I'd have to bet against you, and that would be much too risky for me. On that note, don't think I've not noticed how you evaded my question about said distraction."

"I didn't evade the question, I said, *no one*."

"Didn't you say you were having a look this season?" The earl shot him a sly look and lifted his glass. "To distractions named *No One* then."

He refused to be baited into a confession. Instead, he tossed back his water in a few gulps, watching as Lushing did the same with his liquor, his ruddy face twisting at the burn.

Gage could not afford to lose sight of his immediate, more pressing goals.

> *Settle Asher's debt.*
> *Fix the manse walls and roof.*
> *Take care of his tenants.*

Being bewitched by a beautiful, icy, sultry-tongued siren beyond the limits of the agreement with Huntington to get the lady to London for six weeks was not ideal, even if hitherto untried parts of him now had other ideas. Then again, why shouldn't he take advantage of a mutual interest? She was clearly attracted to him as well.

Gage hissed out a breath. *You know why, fool.* A blue-blooded daughter of an earl came with strings—*wedding strings*—which meant he would have to bury those kinds of needs, no matter how much she tempted him. No woman was worth staying in England for, not even a blue-eyed minx with a saucy mouth and the sweetest kisses this side of Hadrian's Wall.

Well then. He'd simply have to keep his cock on a leash while keeping her in London for a month and a half. Many aristocrats explored courtships during the season—even platonic ones. He could do that for six weeks. *It's a drop in the bucket*, he told himself. Gage felt a sharp twinge of guilt. What if she thought his interest was genuine? Would she be hurt? The idea didn't sit well with him at all, considering he was walking a fine line between obligation and obliquity.

"Speaking of the season, any luck with the Raines?" Lushing asked.

Gage blinked at the question, considering his current train of thought. "What do you mean?"

"A fortnight ago, you asked me about them, remember? And then you danced with Effie at the assembly. What was that about? Trying to find ways to get the sister by way of the spinster?" He stretched his arms over his chest and shook his head. "It's a good strategy, but I can tell you that there's nothing in Viola's head but rainbows and ribbons. And I'm not being cruel. It's the truth from my sister's own lips. Just let the chit talk about herself—she'll tell you how wonderful she is, sure enough."

Wrong chit, though Gage did not correct him.

Because the woman he was lusting after did not have rainbows and ribbons in her brain. No, she had blades and barbed wire beneath a keen wit that could reduce any accomplished gentleman to a babbling milksop. "I'm not worried," he said to Lushing.

"There's stiff competition," the earl said with a cunning grin. "Will you be at Huntington's house party this weekend? I've heard rumors that he's throwing it in your future bride's honor. And, of course, to mark his territory before the season gets away in London. Perhaps you should do some marking of your own or at least get some practice in. Sow some oats for once."

"No, and you know I'm not like that," Gage said mildly. Not that he was opposed to other people sowing their wild oats; that just wasn't him. When he'd told Lushing years ago, the earl had been surprised but had never thought any less of him for it.

"You should really come to Lethe," the earl said sagely, brows rising. "I've a lovely friend who would be delighted to cure your condition."

Gage laughed. "It's not a condition, it's a choice."

"I suppose Lady Viola would appreciate such a firm stance when it comes to the marriage bed, considering you'll be on even footing vis-à-vis mutual deflowering."

Something in Gage's belly curled at the idea of wedding—and bedding—Viola. "It's not her."

"What do you mean?"

"I'm not interested in Lady Viola."

Lushing blinked as the quiet admission sank in. "Wait. Surely you don't mean you're after *Effie*?"

"Why is that so hard to believe? She's not unpleasant in looks. She can carry a step, play a passable tune, I imagine, hold a proper conversation, and she's the daughter of an earl."

A troubled look brewing, Lushing opened his mouth and closed it, and then repeated the action. Instead of telling him he looked like a fish out of water, Gage arched a brow with a questioning look on his face and waited him out.

The earl scrubbed at his chin, face going ruddy. "Vale, look... never mind."

"Just spit it out."

Lushing sobered, finding his words. "As much as I've come to esteem Effie myself, she's very set in her ways. She wants what she wants, and that's to manage her shelter and to stay in Chichester."

Guilt dug at Gage. She was devoted to those animals, and yet, he was determined to drag her into this farce all to placate Huntington. Before, when she'd just been an unknown target for a brief, fake courtship, making the agreement had been easy. Though now, Gage felt uneasy. He didn't want to hurt Evangeline. He didn't want to be the one to erase the laughter and the light from those expressive eyes.

"She won't leave England?" he asked, and then wanted to kick himself. Of course she wouldn't. Her life was here. Just as his was in Scotland.

"No. Why are you so hell-bent on pursuing her?" Lushing asked suddenly with a narrowed stare as if something else had occurred to him. "Weren't you always opposed to the idea of marriage to an English bird? But now suddenly, you're interested in wedlock with an inaccessible spinster in your sights. It makes no sense. Don't you want to go back to Scotland?"

"Minds can change," he prevaricated. "Perhaps England is growing on me."

Lushing shook his head, suspicion welling in his gaze. "Like a second head on my arse. Something's rotten in Chichester, and I'll get to the bottom of it, mark my words."

"You sound like a thespian scoundrel."

He looked delighted. "Did I? Capital! And I didn't even have to do my villain laugh." Still grinning, he reached for the discarded boxing gloves. "How's your face? Ready for round two, or do you need to get some ice on your contusion?"

Gage rolled his neck. "You're going to regret that."

The weather in Crawley was unbearably humid. Why, oh why had Evangeline agreed to this?

Oh, of course, because her younger sister was exceptionally gifted at turning on the tears like a faucet. Viola should have been destined for the stage instead of born as the daughter of an earl.

"Please, Evangeline," she'd begged, her pretty face distraught. "I know I've been asking a lot of you, but please, let me have this. It's a party in my honor! You know Papa won't let me go without you. Don't be beastly, *please*."

The heart-wrenching sobs had started then, and idle admiration had flicked through Evangeline at how delicate and dainty her sister looked with her luminous eyes and her cheeks fetchingly pink and damp. Her sister's sniffles were sweet and adorable, if sniffles could ever be called so. When Evangeline cried, there were splotches and snot, and not an ounce of daintiness in sight. And when she sobbed, it was painfully loud, enough to frighten the animals in her care.

"Stop weeping, you know I'll do it for you." Evangeline had

given in with a resigned sigh. "But don't expect me to stay more than an hour or two. And we are *not* staying overnight!"

Viola had flung her arms around her and squeezed tight. "Thank you, Effie. Thank you! You won't regret it, I promise."

And now, here she was...*thoroughly* regretting her current life choices.

Evangeline blew a discreet breath toward her sweaty bodice as she descended from the carriage in a gown that felt like sodden blankets draped over her person. She was not made to endure weather like this. Even her hair felt the same, like wet thread clinging to her skin wherever the unruly strands managed to escape the braids that ran over her crown.

Viola looked over her shoulder and smiled. Of course, *she* looked as fresh as a daisy. "Thank you for doing this, Effie."

Evangeline tamped her irritation down. She couldn't very well be waspish after such sweet sincerity, and Viola was quite earnest... especially after she'd gotten her way. "You're welcome."

Viola smiled and turned around, her gaze scanning the crowd, and Evangeline felt a beat of unease, knowing who her sister was looking for. "Viola?"

"Yes?"

Her words tripped over themselves. "Be careful with Huntington."

Viola's eyes narrowed to blue pinpricks, all trace of her earlier sweetness fading away, her mouth turning down. "I'm not a child for you to fret over, Effie."

"I didn't say you were." She pinned her lips, sorry that she'd said anything at all. Viola was going to do whatever Viola wanted to do. "Just watch yourself with him."

"Huntington's perfectly harmless." Huffing a breath, her sister rolled her eyes. "Do try to have fun, Effie, if you can allow yourself to relax for half a sorry minute. Don't concern yourself with me. I'm not one of your sad little strays."

And then Viola was off. Within moments, she was surrounded by admirers, including their host, Lord Huntington himself, whose unctuous face made Evangeline want to kick it. He only coveted Viola because she would most likely be named the jewel of the forthcoming season. But deep down, self-centered men like Huntington only cared about themselves.

Evangeline tugged at the muslin bodice of her gown, the embroidered roses there starting to pill and fray from her constant manhandling. It was hot, but she was also on edge. She had more important things to be doing than sipping champagne on a lawn or playing cricket or croquet, or whichever sport was de rigueur at this absurd lawn party.

She should be at the shelter making sure the animals that she and the Duke of Vale had rescued from the barn had proper nutrition and care. Speaking of that redheaded giant, where was he? This was exactly the kind of bride buffet that would draw any gentleman's attention, especially an unattached duke. Though *was* he on the hunt for a wife?

She wrinkled her nose. Vale had certainly been charming enough with her, not to mention kissed her utterly senseless, but that didn't mean he was interested in wedlock. And if he were, that wasn't any of her business, was it? But the thought of him sharing those heart-stopping kisses with another woman made her stomach twist and sour.

She'd thought of that kiss often enough over the past week—and the passion between them that had burned as hot as the fire they had narrowly escaped. It had awakened other feelings inside of her, and a wild desire to know more of his touch, to have more of those electrifying kisses, to know what his bare skin felt like...how it tasted. Which was absolutely *unacceptable*.

Vale was a duke who would want a proper duchess. Not a dalliance with a woman who had no intention of getting married. He didn't even truly seem like the *dallying* type. Though that kiss of his had spoken volumes...

She touched a pair of fingers to her lips.

"Hullo, pretty lady!" a voice said, two bodies bumping into her from each side so she could not escape.

"I do say, I'm surprised to see you here, Effie."

She glanced at Vesper and then at Briar, both gracing her with expectant looks. "Well, I am determined to protect Viola, now that she is obsessed with the most malignant fop of the ton." Her gaze narrowed on Briar. "Weren't you supposed to be in Bath?"

Briar nodded. "I was but Vesper wrote that she needed reinforcements to get you to London."

Evangeline shot the duchess a look, and her friend had the grace to look sheepish. "In my defense, I mailed that letter ages ago before we even spoke," Vesper said. "I knew you were going to be recalcitrant."

"That's a word for it," Evangeline muttered.

"But you're here," Vesper said. "At a house party of Lord Huntington's, your favorite nemesis no less."

She was well aware of the incongruity. The tiniest sliver of silver lining was that Huntington's estate in Crawley was a short carriage ride away from Chichester, which meant that she and Viola weren't overnighting guests. Thank her ever-loving stars. Evangeline did not know what she would have done if that man were sleeping under the same roof as her sister. Everyone knew that country house parties were renowned cesspits of depravity. A girl could find herself ruined without blinking, if she wasn't careful.

"I told you, I'm here to keep an eye on Viola." Evangeline huffed out a breath. "I'm the only one she has to chaperone her, even if she tries my patience on a good day. It's not her fault our mother left, nor should she have to pay the price because her own sister is a complete social pariah."

She felt rather than saw her friends' stares. "You're not a pariah," Vesper said loyally. "And you have us. Besides, even though you're quite committed to being a spinster and I positively respect your choices, what if love finds you when you least expect it? Look at me and Greydon. Who knew he would ever return to London from his travels? Or carry a tendre for me, of all people."

"Everyone did." Evangeline rolled her eyes. "You've always loved him. You just couldn't see past your own nose for a long time."

"Are you calling me conceited?" Vesper said with a huff.

Evangeline and Briar broke into cackles. "Do you even know yourself?" Briar teased.

Sniffing, Vesper waved them off. "One woman calls it conceit, another calls it confidence. Just you wait, Effie dear, your time will come."

"Don't you dare matchmake me, Vesper!" Evangeline warned, knowing her friend's infamous predilection for meddling.

"I won't have to. I have an inkling that love will put you on that smug little arse before you know it, and we shall see who has the last sodding laugh."

None in their small group were unfamiliar with Vesper's fondness for the vulgar tongue. She was part of the reason Evangeline had become so proficient herself.

"Well now, who is that husky specimen of ginger delight with your donkey's tail of a brother, Vesper?" Briar asked as two men on horseback thundered up the drive, and Evangeline knew without a doubt that she was speaking of Vale.

The duke's steed was massive—it had to be to carry the equally large man on its back—yet its rider descended with an agile ease. She'd never seen such a big man move with such lithe grace. Like a battle-honed warrior from another time.

Do. Not. Stare.

Evangeline couldn't help it; she ogled despite her own judgment. A frisson crept up her spine at the breadth of his shoulders, tapering to lean hips and long muscled legs. She had felt the strength of that body when he'd carried her, and his gentleness, too, when they'd danced and he'd held her as though she were something infinitely precious.

Her gaze slid up to his face...and hitched on that sculpted, serious mouth. Her own lips tingled in visceral memory of how those plush curves had hugged and caressed hers, and every single part of her went molten.

Dear God, why were her ears on fire? Why was *all of her* on fire?

There's no fire, you raging nick-ninny, only the flames of lust immolating your brain.

"That's the Duke of Vale," Vesper pronounced in a gleeful voice. "Honestly, I'm surprised Jasper even came. He loathes Huntington more than he loathes responsibility, so it must be on Vale's behalf."

Briar's eyes widened. "I thought the Duke of Vale died."

"The old one did. This is his little brother, and he's very much alive." Vesper's smile was so wide, Evangeline could see her back molars. She instantly wiped all expression from her face, but it was much too late—her bloody cheeks were so hot they could be a signal fire to the Continent for how crimson they had to be. Curse her transparent skin! "However, this duke, Briar my love, is our stalwart Effie's downfall."

"*Hardly*," Evangeline muttered. "He's a nuisance."

"A sultry-as-all-hell nuisance who's marching over here like a possessive Viking about to toss you over his shoulder and cart you back to his ship for plowing," Briar said out the side of her mouth. "Or perhaps take you to the ground and have his way with you right here."

"He's a Highlander, not a Viking, and no one's plowing anyone, you hussy," she bit out, ducking her head to hide her fiery blush. If not for that heated kiss they'd shared, the idea would not be so damned titillating. Or start a wicked rhythm between her legs. Evangeline did not want to be carted or taken. Or plowed.

Did she?

"Oooh, a *Highlander*, is he?" Briar teased relentlessly. "If you're lucky, he might show you what's under his kilt and impale you with his mighty sword!"

"Briar!"

Evangeline swallowed a horrified giggle and peered up through her lashes. Vale stopped only when he and Lushing were waylaid by other guests, but she could feel his gaze on her like a brand. Briar fanned herself and exchanged a look with an absurdly delighted Vesper. "Did the temperature just rise a million degrees?" Vesper asked. "That or everyone here might have just gotten with child. It's a close call, truly."

Evangeline rolled her eyes at her friend's antics and fought for calm...and coolness. "Don't you have your own duke to impale you somewhere?"

Vesper grinned. "I do, and if you play your cards right, you might, too."

The throb became indecent.

"I don't want a duke. I don't *want* a husband. I don't want any man."

It wasn't as though she were *lying*. Want and need were two very different things, not that she would make that admission to a soul. She wasn't that naïve or sheltered! Given her sizzling chemistry with the duke and the current dewy state of affairs beneath her skirts, it was patently obvious she was attracted to the man. Evangeline was not so completely ignorant as to what such copious dampness meant, which probably said a lot about her own lewd scruples.

Women weren't supposed to have needs or even acknowledge them, but thanks to Briar and the rest of her forward-thinking friends, Evangeline wasn't ignorant or ashamed of hers. She'd always taken matters into her own hands, so to speak, but now it didn't seem like that would be enough. She didn't simply want release, she wanted to experience what it would be like to be with a man. Without strings. Without complications.

Without the bonds of marriage that high society demanded.

She *could* certainly do that at Lethe with a stranger, but she could also approach someone she actually liked and esteemed. The question was...what was she willing to do to get what she wanted? Her stare trailed over the handsome copper-haired duke, her mouth fairly watering at the novel idea of using *him* to satisfy her carnal needs.

The thought was scandalous. Outrageous. Wicked in the extreme. And yet, the idea, once lodged, refused to be ignored.

Was it so wrong for a woman to seek out her own satisfaction? Men did it all the time. It was easy for them to separate sexual intercourse and intimacy. Women could do that, too. She'd already proved her brain and willpower could equal any man's. Why should this be any different? Would the duke even be amenable?

And why *him* out of every man in England?

The answer was instant. Despite their rocky start, the plain truth was…in addition to being wildly attracted to him, she felt safe with Vale. He had honor…his gentleness with the kittens and his care for Lucky had been early indicators. Lucky was always an excellent barometer of character. And the fact that he'd run into a burning barn to save those desperate lambs—all because Evangeline had asked him to—was evidence enough. While the idea of a sexual connection with no strings attached held its appeal, she still required a modicum of trust and perhaps mutual fondness for such an endeavor.

Lifting her chin, Evangeline turned toward the refreshments tent, not waiting to see if her infuriating friends followed. A cold drink would quench the surface fires, and then she would figure out a way to get what she wanted.

Without ruination, scandal, or unwanted wedlock.

CHAPTER TEN

What the devil was the Earl of Oberton's daughter doing in his bedchamber?

Sitting on his bloody *bed* like one of the prince's own courtesans. Though she wasn't dressed like a light-skirt, every prim inch of her buttoned up to the chin in royal-blue muslin.

However, it wasn't a stretch to imagine her unclothed, with that pale hair unbound, tumbling over creamy shoulders and that long elegant spine as she lay on her stomach with a come-hither look. His imagination had run wild ever since he'd seen her at Huntington's party last weekend, looking like a shining lily in a field of pastel rosebuds. To his dismay, he'd been besieged with introductions and requests for dances, and by the time he'd sought her out, she'd already left. He and Lushing had departed soon thereafter.

"You don't have much furniture, Your Grace," she pointed out, making him jump as if a phantom had spoken, considering his fantasies were now busy positioning her in every way known to man right here on this very bed. "Though I admit your mattress is quite comfortable. And large. I suppose it has to be to fit a man of your . . . size."

Holy *hell*.

Did his illicit fantasy just leer at him from head to toe and moisten her lips? What the deuce was happening? Closing his eyes,

Gage pinched himself in the side and winced, but she was still there when his lids rose. This was a dream. It had to be, because ladies of quality did not frequent the bedrooms of unmarried gentlemen, not unless they wanted a swift ride to the altar. He blinked. Was that her game...chasing a title?

If that was the case, it would make his financial problems a hell of a lot easier to overcome.

Would that be so bad?

He ignored that voice. Of course it would. He was not going to marry Evangeline Raine. Her life was here. Everything she knew was here. His was in Scotland.

"How did you get in here?" he rasped, staying safely enough away in the doorway.

She wiggled her limbs beneath her skirts, allowing him a brief glimpse of stockinged ankles. "People have these things called legs that get them from place to place. Some residences have multiple floors with a staircase. Said legs then marched me into this large room, whereupon I had to wait for your arrival. I became tired and I couldn't very well sit on the floor."

He didn't even have the forbearance to appreciate her sarcasm. Jenkins was stretched thin acting as a footman and butler, but where in the hell was Pierre? He was going to sack that wretched valet! No, he wasn't. Pierre had already proven his worth, and Gage was still down enough staff as it was, and nothing on earth would make him take Jenkins back. Gage had nearly lost an ear during a haircut.

"This is my bedchamber," he said stupidly.

She nodded. "It's spacious. Sparse. Suits you."

"Why are you here, Lady Evangeline?" he asked gruffly.

"I have a proposal for you." Crimson bled into her cheeks. She hadn't seemed bothered to be found propped upon his bed, but whatever was about to come out of that plush mouth of hers was making her blush.

"And you couldn't leave your card with the butler like an ordinary person?"

"I knocked and no one answered. The door was open, so I thought I would wait for you," she replied. "This proposal is of a sensitive nature."

Gage propped his body on the doorjamb and folded his arms across his chest. "Enough to invade a man's private bedchamber?"

But surprisingly, even as she blushed, her chin lifted. In defiance? With resolve? Despite himself, he was intrigued. In all their interactions, Lady Evangeline had been decisive, obstinate, and fiercely outspoken. She was intelligent, and clearly, once she had a plan of execution on something, she went after it. So the question was... what *did* she want now?

"Considering that parts of it might include this bed, then I see no misstep."

His jaw dropped to the floor. Surely he'd misheard. "I beg your pardon?"

"Will you close the door, Your Grace?"

It was comical, his reaction, their roles reversed as if he were the blushing maiden and she the scoundrel attempting to divest a shy virgin of his virtue. It wasn't *that* far off the mark. He fought the flush but could feel his own ears burn as a calculating smile drifted over those shell-pink lips. Gage half thought that he might still be dreaming.

"No, I cannot," he said through his teeth. "There's no one on this floor besides my valet, and we have your modesty to consider. The door stays open. In fact, we should withdraw to the study."

One arm rose in a dismissive gesture. "I'm not concerned."

"Not *concerned*? Are you that cavalier about your reputation, my lady? Might I remind you that you are unmarried and unchaperoned in a gentleman's company."

She stood then, her graceful form lifting off the bed in a fluid movement, and prowled like a lioness toward him. Gage's entire body tensed. There was a hint of a predatory air about her, and he wasn't sure he liked the sensation of being stalked. She stopped when she was within arm's length, her head tipping to the side.

God, what would she look like without any of that rigid control?

The ice maiden melted to nothing but need.

"Then I shall get straight to the point, Your Grace." Her voice was low. Low enough to scratch at places it shouldn't, but soft enough she would not be overheard by any wandering servants. Gilt-tipped lashes lifted, revealing eyes so crystalline he was momentarily stunned by the purity of their starlit hues. "I wish for you to deflower me."

Gage choked on his own spit. "To *what*?"

"Does *fuck* work better in this instance?"

His eyes goggled as his brain completely blanked. He had to be dreaming!

Wake up, amadan! He might be an idiot, but this was no fever dream. The floor was firm beneath his feet, and her clean, sweet scent of spring lilies had settled into his nostrils.

"Just the one time, or maybe twice, if required," she rushed out as he fought between his own good sense and the lust hammering his lower body. The latter was clearly winning.

"What about your future?" he asked dimly. "Marriage prospects. You're an earl's daughter. Shouldn't you save your, er, virtue for your husband?"

She snorted with a caustic roll of her eyes. "Do you mean my hymen? No, I don't intend to marry, so that isn't required. I am committed to a life of solitude." She sucked in a bracing breath even as he struggled to keep up with her cavalier use of scientific parts. "However, I *am* interested in exploring this connection between us."

Gage's brain felt like it was wading through honey. He was still stuck on the erotic invitation that had crossed her lips. "And you want *me* to...make love to you?"

Perhaps he was the puritan, because he could barely echo the choice verb she'd used earlier. That blush of hers was pure fire now, but the throaty huff that emerged from those plush lips twisted him into knots.

"There's no love about it—think of it as an agreement between two willing parties. Two friends, if you will. We are friends, aren't we, Vale?"

"We are," he said, completely taken aback by the turn of events. His uncooperative brain started to tick over. Perhaps he could use her proposal as a means of getting her to London, but the moment he thought it, something ugly and unpleasant curled in his chest. Gage shook his head. He didn't have the luxury of indulging in guilt. She'd come to him and she did not want anything beyond a physical connection—this was a damned windfall!

Then why the devil didn't it feel like one?

Another soft breath hissed out of her at his prolonged hesitation, drawing his gaze to her parted lips. Her tongue darted out to wet them, and his mind blanked again. "You do desire me, don't you, Your Grace? Our kiss proved that at least."

Gage couldn't breathe. Couldn't think. Didn't dare look down to his groin, even though he could feel the unwelcome tenting of his trousers as if it intended to answer her question.

"Lady Evangeline, this is…"

Senseless. Absurd. *Dangerous.*

The role reversal would have been comical at any other time—gentlemen petitioned ladies night and day for sexual favors without care for consequence—but this was different. This wasn't some brazen courtesan or horny widow. This was *Evangeline.* He might not agree with the sentiment, but a woman's virtue was an important measure of respectability in the eyes of the ton.

Footsteps echoed down the bare landing, and Gage stiffened as his single remaining maid dusted the empty alcoves that once held busts of his ancestors and valuable art. "This conversation, though it must be in private, cannot be here. I do not wish to ruin you, and gossip is something neither of us can control."

Her lips kicked into a mischievous grin, her voice a whispered brush against his senses. "I believe that is the whole point, Your Grace. *I* intend to be thoroughly ruined, based on mutual agreement, of course. And as I told you, I don't intend to wed, so the point is moot."

He took her elbow, and they exited the bedchamber as he steered her past the wide-eyed maid slash housekeeper, who fled in the opposite direction, and ushered his guest to the vacant study. Shame rose that he could not even offer her a seat other than the one behind his desk.

"Sit or stand, your preference," he told her.

To his surprise, she perched on the edge of the desk without any expression of contempt or discomfort. "I realize this is an unexpected request, Your Grace."

"Unexpected is the least of it," he muttered, raking a hand through his hair. Most of his brain was still stupidly stalled on the fact that she'd asked him to be her lover, but a smaller rational part considered the advantages. She wanted this. She wanted *him*. If he could convince her to carry out their dalliance in London, he could kill two birds with one stone—give her what she desired in town to the tune of at least six weeks, which in turn would fulfill the terms of the agreement with Huntington.

You're deceiving her.

Self-reproach rubbed him raw, and he scrubbed his palm over his face. He had nothing to feel guilty for. She had come to *him* with her proposal. What did it matter whether he agreed to the act here or in town? He hissed out a low curse. It *did* matter...because he wasn't being truthful with her about his own motivations. Lying by omission was still lying.

Watching him wrestle with his thoughts, she blew out a quick breath. "The crux of the matter is you desire me." Did he imagine it, or did her gaze slide discreetly to the crotch of his trousers? His arousal had diminished at the appearance of the maid upstairs, but it was by no means gone. "And...that feeling is returned. As inconvenient as it is, I believe we can both find some relief."

"Relief?"

"Sexual congress, Your Grace. With rules."

Gage blinked. Hearing her admit it so baldly threw him for a loop. "Rules?" he echoed, sounding like a deuced parrot.

"Yes," she explained. "The nature of our arrangement must be a secret for obvious reasons. While I do not care for the opinions of the ton, I'd rather not be vilified." She paused. "Or my sister be tarnished by association, since she does wish to make an excellent match."

Discomfort slammed through him, the attack of conscience staggering. What she spoke of was life-changing enough to give him pause. Considerable pause...because he did not want to hurt Evangeline. Perhaps if he told her the only way he'd agree was if they carried out their liaison in town, she would say no, considering how much she hated the place.

"Alas, I intend to leave for London," he said and cleared his dry throat. "Quite soon, so this probably will not—"

She smiled, interrupting him. "London, it is."

Gage balked, feeling a cold sweat peppering his spine, and shook his head at her earnest expression. God, what was he *doing*? Throwing a perfectly good opportunity away for what?

His fucking *conscience*?

His estate was run into the ground. His tenants were on the cusp of leaving for better pastures. The walls of the manse were in danger of crumbling down about his head. And if he failed to hold up his end of the deal with Huntington, he would have to repay Asher's vowel. So much was riding on this, but for some inane reason, he couldn't bring himself to agree.

He'd figure out another way.

There is no other way, you buffoon. Gage let out a harsh exhale.

Stop being so damned honorable, Asher would say. *They want you to fleece them, otherwise they wouldn't be here at the tables instead of at home with their families. Why not take advantage? They are unscrupulous, greedy, and dimwitted.*

Evangeline wasn't. No, she was clever and bright, and so fucking vulnerable right now with those limpid blue eyes and soft expression. Fuck, he couldn't do it. He swallowed hard and pressed his fists into his thighs.

"I don't think this is a good idea."

"Why not?" she asked. "You want me, I know you do. And this is a way for you to sate those desires. By mutual, emotion-free agreement. Isn't this how men do it?"

He huffed a low laugh. "I assure you that not all men are led by their pricks, my lady." She pinned her lips again in a nervous movement, lashes fluttering down. "Though indeed, it is a good many."

"So?" she asked.

A grunt left him, his usual way to avoid answering, but when she waited, he had no choice but to refuse. "As tempting as your offer is, I will have to respectfully decline."

Her face fell, but that pointy chin of hers lifted in the next breath as she pushed off the desk and curtsied. The aloof mask he was getting well accustomed to descended over her features, giving no hint to her true thoughts. "Very well, I understand. I cannot force a horse to come to water, and there are many other fish in the sea."

She swept past him, and he frowned. What did she mean by *that*?

"Wait? Fish?" Gage hustled after her and tugged her elbow to halt her retreat. The icy glare that speared him made him drop his hold.

"Yes, Your Grace," she said in an even tone. "Thank you for pointing out that you are not in possession of the only prick in existence. I bid you a lovely evening."

In a state of full-on confusion, Gage watched her as she marched up the hill between their estates, torn between running after her and standing his moral ground. The former was motivated by said very frustrated prick, which was more than willing to oblige her offer, while the latter was influenced by his somewhat more reasonable brain. Though in truth, said morals were hanging on by the skin of his teeth.

Be the better man, he told himself firmly.

If he repeated it enough times, perhaps it would stick.

"Nincompoop! Dunce! Silly, silly, *silly* girl."

Evangeline couldn't help flinging curses at herself as she charged across the fields. Her feet pinched in their too-small boots, her spirit stung from the burn of rejection, and arousal still coiled in her body just from being around the object of her inconvenient obsession.

Oh, he wanted her, too. *His* arousal had been evident, bunching his trousers and making her pulse gallop when she'd noticed it out of the corner of her eye. Her whole eye, if she was being honest. She'd wanted to drop to her knees—for instructive purposes, of course—and take a detailed study of its curve, its girth, its length.

He probably thought her a wanton already.

She *wasn't* wanton, though. She was simply a woman who knew what she wanted, and if she couldn't advocate for herself, then who would? Her body, like her mind, was hers to use as she saw fit. Even if a ridiculous significance was placed upon it by others in society.

Her cheeks burned as she recalled the look on the duke's face. She had taken him quite by surprise. Perhaps she'd overestimated *his* unconventional thinking. It appeared he was a proper English duke after all, even if he'd been raised in the Scottish Highlands, and had encouraged her to speak her mind and be herself.

Obviously, that did not include propositioning him for sexual congress.

She winced. It sounded rather crude in her head when she thought about it like that. But any arrangement between them would be neat and consensual. Boundaries would be set. It would just be coitus, without head or heart complications. No one would be hurt or have expectations.

Why couldn't life be simple? Human beings were the only creatures who copulated for pleasure as well as procreation. Since she was uninterested in the latter, why *shouldn't* she explore avenues to the former?

Because it's not done, that's why. You're a woman and you must be wholesome.

"Wholesome, my arse, it's a bloody double standard," she muttered, frowning when her boot sank into a marshy patch.

This area of Vale's fields reminded her of the muck she'd gotten stuck in with Lucky. It was no wonder the duke had come to her father for assistance. No crops would grow in these conditions. Soil that was wet wouldn't allow for enough air pockets for the roots of plants to flourish. They would drown, in essence. The duke needed to look at drainage in addition to irrigation, then figure out adding organic matter and a proper plowing.

Why was she obsessing about the man's dratted fields?

Her field needed a good plowing.

Dear God, now she was sounding like Briar.

A low snicker burst past her lips. Hadn't that been the point of the whole proposal? Obviously, he hadn't seen any worth in what she had offered. Evangeline wrinkled her nose, bypassing the marshy earth for more solid ground. Perhaps she could have thrown in some of her ideas and solutions on irrigation for good measure. The duke had seemed impressed with her designs.

I'll help you irrigate your fields if you irrigate me.

"Enough," she muttered. "He said no. Move on."

By the time she got back to her own estate, Evangeline had calmed enough to ignore the residual twinges of embarrassment. She had nothing to be embarrassed about. She'd made a perfectly reasonable offer, one she'd deemed mutually beneficial, and it had been rejected. People declined things all the time, and his refusal had no bearing on *her*. If he was too proper to accept her proposal in the spirit in which it was meant, that was on him.

Then why did she feel so bloody scorned?

For some reason, the Duke of Vale had made it sound like he refused her offer because he had to be in London. Was that because he'd have his pick of ladies there? Evangeline wasn't a diamond, after all, and she wasn't even offering marriage. She was offering something that a man could get anywhere. Damn and blast! Her cheeks burned anew with mortification. She was bemoaning the fact that she'd even asked.

Her body felt restless, the faint hum between her legs was no less diminished by the long walk back, and her mind spun with the sting of rejection, despite her steady words to the contrary. She wasn't a catch, not for any gentleman of the season. Of *any* season. But she hadn't misread Vale's interest. So *why* would he refuse a casual liaison? Didn't most men like sexual congress? Or was it that he didn't like *her*?

"Effie, have you given any more thought to London?" Viola

demanded as she walked in the front door, trapping her at the bottom of the stairs once she'd removed her cloak and bonnet, and handed both to the waiting footman.

"Not now, Viola," she ground out. She wasn't vexed with Viola, but in the dreadful frame of mind she was in, Evangeline would no doubt say something regrettable.

"But, Effie…"

Her fingers fisted. "If you continue to pester me, the answer will be no."

Viola's pretty face screwed up, her mouth twisting into a rancid moue. "Why must you be so wretched all the time? Can't you just be normal for once?"

"Normal is overprized."

Viola huffed. "Says the one who looks like she was dragged across a dirty field for miles. What did you do? Go for a swim in a pond? You're covered in muck and God knows what else."

"Which is why I would like to have a bath, if you would only let me pass." Evangeline blew out an irritated breath. "And it's called walking in fresh air. You should try it sometime."

"Just say yes, Effie," Viola wheedled, changing tactics and hurrying behind her. "It's one season, my *only* season before I wrinkle and wither away. All you have to do is show your face and leave. You wouldn't even have to stay in London."

"Might I remind you that you require a chaperone, Viola." Evangeline paused at her bedchamber door. "What is it about Huntington that you esteem so much?"

Viola pursed her lips. "He's the most eligible gentleman of our set. Being seen with him, coveted by him, makes me look good."

"That's shallow," Evangeline murmured.

"It's reality." Something flashed across her sister's face for an instant before it was gone, too quickly for Evangeline to decipher it. "I want to make a match, Effie. Get out of this house, out of the countryside, and if Lord Huntington is a means to that end, then so be it. I want to flirt, have fun, *fall in love*."

"With that cad?" she scoffed gently. "He's so head over heels in love with himself that there's no room for anyone else."

"Some men simply need guidance, Effie," Viola said. "Besides, there are other fish in the sea. It won't hurt to give him a little competition and let him enjoy the chase a little bit."

The words rattled her, only because Evangeline had *just* used a similar analogy herself. Not that she planned on going fishing, but she had wanted to retort with something clever after Vale's refusal. And besides, there was only one other *fish* she could stand to be around, and that was William Dawson...who was emphatically enamored of Viola.

"What about William?" she said to her sister. "He has been in love with you for years."

If it wasn't for the blush that crested Viola's cheeks, Evangeline would have thought her sister hadn't heard her. "What can he offer but a house down the road and a boring life stuck here in the country reeds?"

"Love, companionship, constancy?"

Viola's brows lifted. "And what would you know of those things, sister dear?"

"We're not talking about me. We're talking about you." Evangeline pushed open her bedroom door. "Sometimes, dreams change. Don't make a mistake that you can never come back from. Huntington is bad news."

"It's not about him, Effie. It's about *me*. I just want something more than this boring country existence."

Evangeline's emotions were all over the place after the episode with Vale, which was probably why she let out a belabored groan, her fingers clenching the doorknob at the sound of the sad, doleful sniff behind her. Guilt was quick to follow. She'd been prepared to go to London to get Vale into her bed but balked to accompany her sister for the season. It was selfish, and going would mean so much to Viola.

Would it truly be so bad?

With a sigh, she closed her eyes. "Very well," she said, glancing over her shoulder. "We'll go to London."

Viola opened her mouth and closed it, her eyes going wide with disbelief before she screamed with happiness. "Do you mean it, Effie? You won't regret this, I promise."

But as she closed the door behind her, Evangeline already did. No doubt her regrets would have regrets. She stripped off her clothing and stalked into her bathing chamber, locking it behind her. She was hot. She was bothered. There was only one thing she could do to take the edge off. The copper pipes in the combination of bathtub and shower beckoned. If she placed her body just so beneath the stream of water, knees straddling each side of the tub, relief could be had in a matter of moments.

London was going to take more than a few orgasms to be bearable.

She only hoped the plumbing at their residence in Mayfair could handle the brunt of her frustration.

CHAPTER ELEVEN

The Thames stank, but that was the price one paid to be in London. Smelly rivers, stuffy aristocrats, toadying crowds, garish ballrooms, and that was the least of it. Gage tugged on the cravat that strangled his neck, and peered through the dense throng, wishing he could escape. At least Chichester was bearable. It was nothing compared to the fresh, storm-kissed breezes of the Highlands, but he'd take the southern English countryside over London any day.

This, however, was torture.

And he was stuck here for six bloody weeks.

If Huntington hadn't called on him at Vale Ridge Park a week ago and clapped him on the back for a job well done, Gage would have never known about the Raine sisters going to London at all. That bit of news had taken him quite by surprise, given Lady Evangeline's feelings on the matter. Then again, she'd agreed quite readily when he'd used London as an excuse to deflect her outrageous proposal.

Gage had deliberated letting Huntington believe that he'd had a hand in Evangeline's decision, but it hadn't sat well with him. "I hate to disappoint, but the lady agreed to London of her own free will," he told him.

The man hadn't missed a beat, all slick smiles. "I don't care what's gotten her there. *Keep* her there. Six weeks, remember?"

He did remember. Just because she had decided to go to London didn't absolve him of his collusion. Notwithstanding her indecent proposal, he was still on the hook to make sure she stayed for the next month and a half. Unfortunately, Evangeline's sudden decision had also gotten him to thinking about other things, too. *Why* had she suddenly decided to go? Had it been his rejection of her scandalous offer? Was she now on the prowl for another more amenable gentleman to suit her needs? The thought had bothered him to no end.

And so the only option had been to confront her in London and save her from herself.

She doesn't need saving, you fool.

Nor did she care about her reputation.

That, he knew. But she did care about her sister, and should Evangeline fall into the clutches of an unscrupulous man, her younger sister would not be spared the malice of the ton.

And so he'd accompanied Lushing to his sister's ball, where they now stood, impersonating a pair of marble pillars on the side of the enormous room. He barely noticed the sumptuous decor of the lavish space, the large orchestra at the end, or the hundreds of people swirling past, dressed to the nines. His mind was consumed with finding one face.

"Good God, man," Lushing murmured, peering at him with an entirely too amused look. "One would think you were a chit at her first ball, wondering who will come to sign your dance card, the way you're scouring the crowd." He shook his head. "Don't worry, every unwed lady in London is here."

"I'm not looking for anyone," he snapped.

Lushing laughed. "Of course you're not."

"Who's he looking for?" the Duke of Montcroix interjected. Gage glanced over his shoulder, taking in the duke who had arrived with the beautiful French ballerina he'd married.

He willed Lushing to keep his mouth shut, but the irritating fop only grinned. "A certain neighbor of consequence might be in attendance."

Both the duke and the duchess perked up with interest, and Gage nearly groaned. It was a fact that gossip kept the lights burning in this town. "It is not like that."

"Then what's it like?" Lushing goaded. "You demand my tailor's name and his time, you rush to London like a man with his arse on fire, you wheedle an invitation to my sister's ball, and you're staring at the entrance hall like a beggar with his eye on a hot meal."

Gage had never wanted to punch the man more. When he said it like *that*, it did sound terribly desperate. Not that he was…he simply needed to make sure a certain bold, quarrelsome hellion did not make an irreversible mistake. He was merely being a good neighbor. A good *friend*.

His self-righteousness soured. Not that any kind of well-meaning friend would consider leading a person awry for their own personal gain. Then again, Gage hadn't influenced Evangeline into going to London—that had been her own doing. But he was still benefiting from the fact, so he felt complicit.

"May I inquire as to which young lady has caught your notice, Your Grace?" the Duchess of Montcroix asked. "Are we acquainted? Perhaps I can offer my assistance?"

Gage glared at Lushing, but the blasted man grinned wider,

eyes going comically round with roguishness. "Oh, what marvelous luck for you, Vale! Did you know that Her Grace is bosom friends with Lady Evangeline?"

"Effie?" the duchess said in surprise. "She's coming here tonight?" Gage frowned. Wouldn't she know if her friend would be in attendance? "I've only just returned from Paris and haven't had time to catch up with anyone." She poked her husband in the side. "Did you know Effie would be here, and didn't tell me?"

Montcroix shook his head and promptly scowled at Lushing. "Of course not, dearest."

"Effie loathes London," she explained. "Vesper had despaired of her attending tonight, so I'm surprised she agreed." Then, with the precise focus of a woman on a mission, she turned a spearing gaze on him. "You wish to court her?"

Gage cleared his throat. "The lady does not wish to be courted by anyone who doesn't have fur, fangs, or is in need of rescue."

The duchess let out a small laugh. "So you *have* met our Effie then?"

"We became acquainted at her shelter in Chichester, yes."

She shot him a circumspect look. "And she caught your interest there?"

"Geneviève, mon cœur, don't interrogate the man," Montcroix put in, but she silenced him with a graceful lift of her hand, and Gage nearly chuckled at the duke's miffed expression. He was obviously well accustomed to his wife's gestures, however, because he sealed his lips and took a sip of his drink.

"Tiens, it is *care*, not interrogation." Her eyes narrowed in a way that convinced Gage it was definitely the latter. Evangeline's friends were protective. Gage had already gathered that. He wondered what they would do if they knew of her audacious intentions to take a lover. "Effie also does not intend to wed. Has she told you that?"

But before he could reply, he felt something drift across his nape—the slightest sensation of his hairs lifting—and there she was. Gage's pulse sped up as he spotted her entering on the arm of her father, followed by a smug Lord Huntington and her sister, Viola.

He kept his focus on Evangeline, however, his greedy gaze devouring the fine, sharp features that had haunted him for a straight week. As if in defiance of the moniker she knew she would be facing, she was clad in pale silver. Gage bit back a grin. Dauntless to the last.

She held herself like the queen she was, peering down upon the lesser mortals who crowded beneath her. The half smile on her lips was just enough to convince everyone that she was in pleasant spirits, the light in her eyes just bright enough not to arouse concern. But he saw the strain in the rigid carriage of those proud, elegant shoulders—a sure sign of distress. Something inside of him ached to offer her comfort, even if she might refuse it.

Gage watched as she greeted the Duke and Duchess of Greydon, the hosts of the ball, before descending the staircase. It didn't escape his notice that other members of the ton gave her a wide berth, the women especially, whispering their poisonous gossip and twittering behind their fans. It did not matter—Evangeline Raine was above them all. So intent was his focus on her that he did not notice the scrutiny of the three people beside him until it was much too late.

"Never mind," the Duchess of Montcroix said with a toothy grin. "It's clear now."

"I beg your pardon?" he said, but she was gone, escorted to the ballroom floor by her husband in a flurry of emerald-hued skirts.

Gage frowned at Lushing, who shook his head and snorted into his own glass. "Do you wish me to procure you a fan for your cheeks, Vale? That's quite the blush on you."

"Fuck off."

Lushing clapped a hand to his chest. "Such language, sir. I am appalled!"

"Go away, Lushing," Gage bit out, forcing his stare not to return to Evangeline.

"Then you won't mind too much if I ask your lady to dance."

"She's not—" Gage felt his brows drawing together before his mind caught up with what Lushing intended as he cut a swift path to the Earl of Oberton. The bloody nerve. He was going to break Lushing's fingers knuckle by knuckle.

Gage bristled and watched as his friend bowed and brushed his lips over Evangeline's gloved hand. Something intensely possessive filled him, squeezing along the knots of his spine. What if *Lushing* offered to be her carnal tutor? Possessiveness wasn't the emotion swamping him then. It was pure, unmitigated jealousy.

He stormed over, bowed stiffly to Oberton, perhaps said something that could pass for a greeting, and then faced off against his gloating friend. *Ex*-friend, that scheming rat bastard.

Three pairs of brows rose in concert—though the lady's were accompanied by a sudden ferocious glint that meant he was in treacherous territory. Before turning on his heel and mumbling something about the refreshments room, the Earl of Oberton speared him with a knowing look that Gage would worry about later, and Lushing remained there leering.

"This dance is mine." Even to his own ears his voice sounded like a feral growl.

"Careful, mate," Lushing muttered from the side of his mouth. "You might splash your shoes."

The joke fell flat, though Gage knew how territorial he was behaving, when he had absolutely no right to be. He had no claim on Lady Evangeline, none whatsoever, but he could not curb his urge to make his mark so no one else could. It was beyond brutish, and yet he could not bring himself to care.

Pale blond eyebrows collided as that cool, silvery stare met his, lightning brewing in their depths. "I believe Lord Lushing has this dance, Your Grace."

His throat worked, teeth clenching, but thankfully, Lushing was not a complete good-for-nothing. The earl gave a pretty bow and grinned. "Alas, my lady, my deepest apologies, but my sister seems to be summoning me. Please do excuse me. I leave you in His Grace's capable hands."

The bastard actually had the audacity to wink before he left them.

"Shall we?" Gage asked.

Evangeline stared at him, wide lips pursed. "Are you actually asking me, or do you plan on dragging me along the floor by my hair like a scowling troglodyte?"

Was he scowling? And bloody hell, had she called him a *cave-dweller*? He blinked. By God, he'd completely lost his senses. Recalling the way he'd stalked over and roared like a lion whose pride had been invaded, he felt his neck heat at what he'd been reduced to in the moment. Suddenly, he was aware of the stares fluttering toward them as well as the new strain on her face.

He canted his head. "My apologies. Will you please permit me a dance, my lady?"

She paused but lifted a hand to his. "As you wish, Your Grace."

Evangeline most categorically did *not* want to dance with the over-bearing duke, but she had no choice. Declining now would draw even more notice.

Once again, she was the center of attention. *Unwelcome* attention. The Duke of Vale wasn't exactly hard to miss. No, she'd noticed the handsome mountain of a man the moment she'd entered the ballroom. *Felt* him, too, as if there were some invisible thread between them.

It was lust. Sexual attraction could feel like a tangible, magnetic pull. She'd read enough literature on the subject to know. And she had kissed him, been caged in those thick arms and ravished his mouth, which made the connection infinitely worse. Angst, sweaty palms, thudding pulse, obsessive yearning. It was a primal reaction, like any creature that went into heat. On top of that, she was in the middle of her courses, which made her heightened senses worse.

In hindsight, she should have cried off from the ball, cited the female malady that most ladies of her acquaintance usually did. But she'd always felt that menstruation was a natural part of life...and her courses had never stopped her from functioning as usual before. Then again, she hadn't accounted for the shocking increase in lust-ful feelings, especially down *there*. Evangeline squeezed her thighs together, cursing her sensitivity.

It took all she had not to combust when his large palm clasped about her waist and he drew her unbearably close. She gave a sharp inhale and breathed out. "I did not expect to see you here, Your Grace."

"You left me no choice, did you?"

She cleared her throat, not expecting that response nor the baleful look in his green eyes. "How so? I do not presume to control a duke's movements."

A ragged sigh escaped her as a thick thigh grazed hers on a sideways turn. She could feel his heat on every half step. She'd danced with him before at the assembly in Chichester, but this felt different. This dance was imbued with a charged erotic energy neither of them could elude or ignore. It was curious how any sexual discourse could cause such a disturbance between two people. Every measure became a tease, every turn a sensual torment.

He said no.

Yes, he had.

"You will not cast your nets elsewhere, Evangeline," he ground out, his words a rasped whisper against the shell of her ear. Everything inside of her responded to that gravelly, dominant tenor, but she threw her chin up, rebelling as she always did to such a tone. She answered to no man.

"Why should you make such a command? You refused my offer."

"It was untoward."

She twirled out of his arms, keeping her voice low. "I did not take you for a prude, Your Grace."

"And I did not take you to be so bold," he shot back.

"Why?" she whispered, stung. "Because I dare to admit what my body wants? That I have needs? That I dare to fulfill them? Men seek out female company all the time, and they don't get any harassment for it."

"Because they're men," he ground out. "And women don't—"

"Deserve pleasure?"

His fingers flexed at the back of her waist as he gaped at her, green eyes darkening to deep jade and his lips parting on air. "That's not what I meant."

"Then what *did* you mean?" She leveled him with a look, watching his expression bleed into utter confusion. "It's a double standard, is what it is. But none of that matters because it's a moot point. I have never needed a man or a partner to fulfill my needs. I only need myself."

When she lifted one palm and wiggled her fingers in an obvious motion, Evangeline took smug pleasure in the fact that he almost stumbled over his own two feet as her meaning sank in.

Pleasure was a gift.

And a well-read woman had a wealth of information at her fingertips.

Evangeline had expected the duke to flush. What she did not expect was for him to come to a complete standstill in the middle of the ballroom, the other dancers nearly crashing into them as he stared at her like the most fascinating creature he'd ever encountered.

"I've never met anyone like you," he murmured.

She swallowed. "Because I'm forthright?"

"Forthright, stubborn, dauntless, take your pick."

The music kept playing while couples whirled around them in a kaleidoscope of color, but Evangeline was mesmerized by the heated, intensely fixated look in his eyes. Those flecked greens held hers captive as much as the large hands splayed over her back, and suddenly, she was the one flushing, warmth twining up her spine and into her ears.

Aware of the censorious glances flicking their way, Evangeline cursed her brashness. She'd gone and done it now. She would earn herself some new and deserved nickname, Lady Unspeakable or some such. Even Viola's neck craned from where she was waltzing with Huntington.

Evangeline frowned as Huntington's gloved fingers lifted, forcibly turning Viola's face toward him, and she saw the shock on her sister's face before it was quickly masked. If the odious cad had no qualms about putting his hands on her sister like that in public, how would he behave behind closed doors? She vowed that she'd get Viola away from that man at the first opportunity, even if her sister seemed oblivious to his glaring faults.

Trapped in Vale's arms, Evangeline stuck a foot out, kicking the duke neatly in the shin. She winced at the pain that vibrated from her dancing slipper to her toes. "Your Grace, what are you doing?"

"Thinking," he rumbled.

She glowered up at him. "Can't you think *and* dance? You're making a scene."

"This particular thing requires every ounce of my brain."

She hissed between her teeth, unable to budge from his hold, her own embarrassment starting to take root as more and more people twittered. For once, the whispers were not at her expense. She wasn't sure whether to feel elated or upstaged by the redheaded lout.

"Honestly, what could possibly be so important to come to full stop in the middle of a dance? You're being rude, Vale."

He smiled slowly, the expression lighting those clover-green eyes with jeweled flames, his rugged features lifting and shaping into something both pleased and predatory. An incongruous combination that made an indecent shiver rumble through her. "I'm done now."

"Capital," she muttered. "Can you release me then?"

"No."

As if he hadn't just halted mid-waltz, he lifted her by the waist and twirled her like she weighed nothing, resuming the dance without any further missteps or hesitation. One would think he hadn't stopped for a full minute while the music played on. When they flawlessly rejoined the pattern of the other dancers, Evangeline cleared her throat and tilted her neck to peer up at him. "Are you going to explain what that was about, or will you leave me in the dark?"

He didn't answer for another few turns, but as the last measures of music drifted to a close, he paused, lifted her gloved hands, and bussed a kiss over her knuckles. With an unreadable look, the duke escorted her back to where her father was in conversation with the Duke of Greydon, and then bent, his warm breath skating over the sensitive whorls of her ear.

"About that offer in Chichester, I've changed my mind. I'd like you to choose me," he grated, that voice doing worse things than the gust of hot air on her skin. "Meet me in the folly to discuss your terms."

Mouth gaping, she stared after him as he cut a swift path through the guests, and lifted a hand to the rapidly fluttering pulse at the base of her throat. Did he...did he just agree to her proposal? Oh, dear God, she needed to sit or find a pillar to prop herself against because her legs were turning into the consistency of jelly. Evangeline gulped, her thoughts whirling at his rasped directive to meet him outside.

What *terms* did he intend to discuss?

Her throat contracted. Now that he had agreed, it felt much too real. She would have a lover, one who could be depended upon to be discreet and one who could be trusted to keep their liaison a secret. Underneath his gruff, rugged, uncouth exterior, Evangeline knew that the Duke of Vale had a noble heart. Not that she was interested in that specific organ...she was here for *other* parts of him. But a good heart meant he could be trusted to keep his end of the bargain. A good heart also meant he would not hurt her, at least not intentionally.

With a deep breath, she plucked a glass of champagne from a nearby footman and drained it. For courage.

She was going to need all the help she could get.

CHAPTER TWELVE

Gage paced near the entrance of the arbor and then swore at himself for even suggesting the blasted folly in the first place. Greydon had mentioned his duchess loved the thing, and Gage had thought it might offer them a measure of privacy. He didn't realize he'd have to navigate a deuced maze to get to it. But if he waited and strayed too close to the entrance, he risked being recognized.

On the way here, he'd already passed at least three couples. London parties during the season were infamous for the garden tryst. Women, men, dukes, scullery maids, couples, groups…they all indulged, given the opportunity. It was rather absurd how proper the ton pretended to be in ballrooms while they mocked the lines of decency beyond it. As if everyone didn't *know* who was fucking whom when they returned with tousled hair, rumpled clothes, and swollen lips.

In fact, he could have sworn he saw Huntington disappearing into a grove with a young woman who was decidedly *not* Lady Viola. The man was the worst kind of rogue. Gage would have to find a way to keep Huntington away from Viola, for her own good as well as for Evangeline's sake. His agreement was for a period of time, not arranging a match.

Gage raked a hand through his hair for the fifth time and

palmed the back of his neck. What if Evangeline didn't come? Or changed her mind? Which was entirely within her right and would probably be best for all involved. As the minutes marched on, a sour ache expanded in his belly. Was that *disappointment* he felt?

He was truly a fool to have yielded to her proposal, but the thought of her giving those rare, hard-won smiles to someone else dug under his skin like nothing else. Evangeline Raine was an uncommon gem, an opal in a sea of diamonds. He was stunned that none of the idiot gentlemen of the ton had realized that. But he was the one she'd trusted enough to ask, and he would be the one to give her whatever she desired.

She needn't know that he genuinely enjoyed her company. That he wanted to spend more time with her, not because of the arrangement with Huntington hanging over his head like a noose, but because of the kindhearted, unique woman she was. The truth would be a problem only if it came to light, which it wouldn't. There was no reason for Evangeline to be aware of his plans or the deal he'd made. Gage ignored the sharp spike of guilt. He'd agreed to do it . . . but that was before he'd known her.

If he hoped to remain amicable, somehow, he would have to come clean.

Hearing the soft murmur of voices followed by a giggle, Gage pressed deeper into the hedgerows and winced as the prickly branches poked into his flesh. Easing through, he navigated the narrow circular pathways toward the center. He got stuck three times before figuring out the pattern. Eventually, he found himself in a narrow little grove with a pretty wooden pagoda. Boughs of wild flowering vines covered the beams. A statue of Aphrodite, surrounded by a wide decorative stone bench, faced him from the center of the copse.

Fate, it seemed, had a fickle sense of humor.

Blowing a lock of hair from his brow, he leaned back and peered up at the goddess of pleasure, desire, and passion with an amused groan. She had to be laughing at him. God, the irony of this particular statue gracing the place he'd asked Evangeline to meet was nearly too much. A whisper of sensation chased over his nape, and he turned.

"You do realize you could have spoken to me inside the residence, Your Grace, like a normal gent." That low, mellifluous voice of hers was equal parts temptation and reprimand, reminding him of the speech he'd given her when she'd been in his bedroom.

Gage turned to face her, his breath catching at how even more ethereal she was in the dappled moonlight. Silver and shadow speckled her face, making her seem like a dreamy illusion instead of a flesh-and-blood woman. He forced his brain to cooperate, opting for humor to defuse the sudden tension coiling inside of him.

"And risk someone overhearing?" He gasped with mock outrage. "I think not. Besides, I have my virtue to protect. I wouldn't want anyone getting the wrong idea about me."

She snorted softly. "Wrong idea?"

"That I'm flirtatious."

Full lips twitched as those moon-bright eyes glowed with laughter. "So you decided to wander into a maze with an unmarried, desirous female who might be intent on stealing every ounce of your virtue instead? That doesn't seem very sensible, sir."

He fluttered his eyelashes, pleased that she was playing along.

"Should I be concerned that your intentions are wicked then, my lady?"

Her slow smirk wore teeth, the kind that promised a bit of pain with any pleasure, and Gage felt his body lurch. Fuck if that sultry look didn't bring his blood to lava. "Oh, Your Grace, but they are, make no mistake about that."

The puckish reversal in their roles fired him up to no end. She embodied the seductive libertine, and he, the shy ingenue. And for whatever reason known only to her, she'd chosen to expose that hidden, playful, and deliciously wicked side of herself to *him*.

He liked it far more than he should.

She strolled toward him, silver skirts swishing. "You wanted to discuss terms?"

Reality intruded like a dousing of cold water. He nodded. "First, are you certain this is what you want?"

"I wouldn't have said so if I wasn't."

"And what if you intend to marry later on? What if you find a husband?"

"I won't." She sniffed and took a seat beside him on the stone bench. "And should I be cherished any less because I've been for a tumble in the sheets? Women don't fault men for their sexual experience. In fact, they are grateful for it. Why should any future husband hold me in contempt for walking a path that men have trodden for centuries? Surely, I'm worth more than my maiden-hood, Your Grace."

Gage swallowed hard at her matter-of-fact tone. "You are, but that isn't the way the ton works."

"Trust me, Vale, I'm well aware of the unreasonable ideals women are held to in aristocratic society." She sighed and waved an emphatic arm. "A woman must be lovely, chaste, and, most of all, quiet. She must never speak. She must never express an opinion or demonstrate that she has a working brain. She must be biddable, docile, and obedient."

"Is that who you are?" he teased, knowing fully well she wasn't.

She stared at him for a protracted moment. Her fingers clenched and unclenched the fan held in a loose grip on her lap, belying her firm resolve. "If you haven't learned by now, I do not have a passive bone in my body, Your Grace."

Gage grinned. He was hard-pressed to keep himself still. "Since you are in charge here, why don't we start with your expectations?"

She took a moment to consider her response. "What I require, Your Grace, are lessons. I gather you have some experience in the matters at hand. I wish to learn, and I wish to explore at my leisure. I want to experience everything I've read in books." The corner of her lip kicked up into a grin when his eyebrows quirked in confusion. "Erotic books. Medical tomes. Scientific study. I might be chaste in society's eyes, Duke, but I am the most educated ingenue in England. I've read everything on the subject, though, as you can well imagine, reading something and having empirical knowledge are two vastly different things."

He stalled on her cryptic words. "Educated? How so?"

Evangeline's cheeks rose in one of those rare half smiles. "Do you require another anatomy lesson, Your Grace?"

"I suppose I must," he replied easily.

"By default, a virgin is a maiden of intact chastity, one whose sheath has not been broken by a man's penis, but penetration means different things to people." She quirked her lips and shrugged. "What if two women come together? According to such a definition, then they are still virgins, even though the act of copulation has undoubtedly occurred. If a lady ruptures this so-called barrier while riding a horse, does that mean she is unchaste or has been penetrated by a gust of air?" Despite her logical reasoning, she blushed, face darkening in the moonlight, her grip hard on her fan. "Furthermore, what if penetration happens and a woman is alone, pleasuring herself with the assistance of an... instrument, what then?"

She broke off then as if her quick, erudite tongue had done enough damage.

And it had.

Gage's poor brain was spinning. He fought to keep his face calm, but the idea of the last, of her using some sort of sexual tool, had both his mind and libido galloping. *Had* she? *How* had she? An image of her lying on soft sheets, pale blond hair splayed over the pillows, those elegant fingers lodged between her thighs, nearly undid him.

He drew in a tight breath, fighting to cool his blood, only to have her unique scent of lilies, spicy and floral, pervading his space. It was a bloody miracle his voice emerged at its usual pitch. "How long do you expect this undertaking to be, and how do you hope to execute the plan?"

She gave a shrug, tension draining from her stiff shoulders as if she'd expected him to stand, rebuke her for her words, and walk away. Her slender throat worked. "Perhaps a week or two, and I was hoping you could make the arrangements for where we could meet."

Gage nodded, stomach sinking, though he couldn't discern if it was disappointment he felt at the short time frame, or simply his own nerves. "There is a club. Lethe. It's owned by Lushing, so you would have to be careful not to be recognized, but we won't be disturbed there. I'll send you the details."

"I'm familiar with the place. Briar's mentioned it once or twice," she added hastily at his raised eyebrows, her beautiful face angling up to him. "Thank you, Vale."

He gave her a wry smile. "My given name is Gage, and don't thank me yet. This might well be utter foppery on both our parts."

Gage. It suited him. Strong, singular, and solid.

Evangeline let out a tight exhale through her teeth even as she fought against the heated jolt his words elicited. "When we're alone then," she agreed. "And you may call me—"

"Evangeline," he put in before she could offer up her nickname. In truth, she loved the way his sultry rasp sounded over the four syllables of her name. The way he said them in his rumbling drawl made her feel as though a feather were being stroked down her bare spine. Somehow, she couldn't imagine *Effie* coming anywhere close to making her feel the same way.

Effie was responsible and focused. Evangeline seemed dauntless and daring.

Effie was drawn in shades of charcoal pencil, while Evangeline was painted in bold splashes of color.

She glanced around the small but elaborate folly. It wasn't completely hidden, but private enough that no one would come upon them without showing themselves first. She knew from experience that this garden had pockets of such groves all over its perimeter. She'd ambled past others while trying to find the duke and had been lucky to catch sight of his towering frame just as he'd slipped through the first hedgerow.

He remained quiet in the gloom, indistinct strains of music

reaching them from the ballroom. A faint breeze teased through the hedges and kissed her hot cheeks. The silence between them should have felt awkward, especially given the nature of the conversation that preceded it, but it didn't. Still, she felt the need to say something.

She turned her face toward him at the same time that he pivoted on the bench, his knee colliding with hers. Inches separated them—*charged* inches—and Evangeline caught her breath, eyes tracing his defined features. They seemed harsher in the darkness. Bold nose. Broad brow. Slashing jaw. All hard, uncompromising lines, except for the sinful curve of his lips.

"What does *leannan* mean?" she asked.

He hissed out the exhale. "It's a silly endearment in Gaelic."

The way he'd said it hadn't sounded silly, but rather a sensual promise given under the cover of darkness. Her core clenched at the recollection. Or perhaps that was her imagination again, taking the leaps it craved despite reality. She wanted him to say it in a voice brought low by need.

"Vale?" she asked. "Why did you change your mind?"

"Would you have found someone else?" he countered.

Oh.

Her heart fell a little. So that was behind his reversal. He might not truly want her, but he didn't want anyone else to have her either. What did that say about him? *Nothing*, her mind supplied. Because what did it say about *her* for suggesting such an outrageous agreement in the first place? Most men of her acquaintance were competitive and possessive. His reasoning should not surprise her.

This was an experiment of her making. Nothing more and nothing less. The Duke of Vale was simply a partner in an empirical, physical study. What led him to agree was of no import. She was in control. In charge. If she'd learned anything from each of the Hellfire Kitties about female confidence when it came to pleasure, this was her show, and what she got out of it was for *her*.

Without stopping to consider her insecurities, Evangeline hefted her skirts, stood, and pivoted to straddle him in one swift movement, her crinoline quite crushed between them. His gasp was loud, eclipsing hers.

"What are you doing?" he bit out, eyes widening comically, though his palms went to her hips to anchor her in place and keep her from tipping backward.

Perching upon him thus, like the most skilled of courtesans, felt frightening, but brave and oddly freeing. She'd never done anything so brazen in all her life. And yet, here she was…climbing a duke. Beasty Buttercup had nothing on her!

Biting back a snicker, Evangeline nibbled her lip and met his paralyzed stare directly. "Testing out the merchandise," she said. "What does it look like?"

"Here?" His reply was strangled.

"Trust me, outside of the duke and duchess, no one even knows about this folly. I was surprised you did, considering it is at the center of a maze."

"But what if someone comes upon us?"

She let out a breath, moving her hands to his nape. "Then someone does." She stared at him, surprised by the discomfort she read in his expression. The duke looked almost nervous. Evangeline frowned. What did *he* have to be nervous about? "Don't tell me you've never done this before?"

He shook his head. "I have not."

"Had carnal relations outside?"

"Or at all, actually."

Gaping, Evangeline reared back, the jerky motion making him grip her sides to keep her from falling. How on God's green earth was such a handsome specimen like the Duke of Vale untried? He was half-Scot. Didn't they run around the Highlands bare-arsed beneath their tartans, seducing lasses with dozens of orgasms and proclaiming their chest-pounding virility to the heavens? Perhaps she was being unjust by eroticizing him so.

But Vale...he was...

She glanced at him—hooded eyes, indecent lips, and huge, muscled body—and her mouth went unspeakably dry. He was built for sin.

"How is that?" she croaked.

One shoulder shifted upward. "The opportunity never came up. When I was younger, my mother was strict when it came to young women visiting the keep, and I was focused on my studies. It's not some puritanical reason, if that's what you're thinking."

Evangeline frowned. "There were no buxom young maids to be found in your castle?"

He let out a huff. "Do you take me for that sort of man? I would never compromise a servant from such a position of power."

She bit her lip. No, he did not strike her as the type of lord to corner a maid belowstairs, even though many aristocrats took such liberties without batting an eye. "I find it hard to believe that ladies weren't throwing themselves at you."

"They did." He gave a noncommittal shrug. "I was not interested. Life simply did not allow for romantic entanglements, and I did not wish to be entrapped by a mistake as my mother had been, so abstinence was preferable."

"Your mother was compromised?" she asked.

"She and my father were wed over the anvil the minute my grandparents learned of her pregnancy with Asher. My father, though a duke, was little better than a scapegrace with a crumbling estate and a weakness for beautiful, trusting women." His face went hard. "It was not the match her parents wanted, and after years of watching him break his vows under the influence of drink, and wager everything they owned down to the last pair of candlesticks, I swore to never be anything like him."

"You don't wish to save yourself for someone special?" she asked quietly, still stunned by his admission. Vale's chastity changed everything. She didn't want to make him go through with their arrangement if this was something precious to him. Her chest clenched, making it hard to breathe, and for some reason, her eyes stung.

"No, it was never about saving myself," he said. "There's simply been no one I wanted enough." A large hand crept behind her nape as he drew her face toward his, eyes glinting in the shadowed moonlight. Evangeline wished she could read his expressions, discern his thoughts, but the darkness made it difficult. That muscle in his cheek was still drumming, his lush mouth tight. "Until now."

Oh. Warmth dripped through her veins like honey.

Before she could reply, the duke's mouth stole hers, palm creeping around to her chin to angle it just so, as he held her in place, one hand at her left hip, the other on her jaw. When his tongue sought entry, she gave it, relishing in the hot, silken feel of him. She matched him stroke for stroke, mapping him as he was mapping her, reveling in his strength, his sensual mastery.

He might be a virgin, but he kissed like a rake.

Evangeline was a quick study herself, savoring the groan that tore from the depths of his chest when she licked up against the roof of his mouth and sucked on his bottom lip. Straddling him as she was, her thighs tightened deliciously over his and she could feel *everything*—the heat between them, the tremors of his straining muscles. As the kiss went on, she felt him thicken beneath her, even through the monthly cloth padding that rubbed indecently against her core. The heat of his length was like a delicious brand between her legs, and her hips gave an unconscious roll that had them both gasping.

Vale pulled away, and she stared at his passion-blown pupils and swollen mouth. "How was that?" he rasped.

She didn't understand the question. "How was what?"

"You said you wanted to sample the merchandise. Did I pass muster?"

Evangeline couldn't help it, she laughed. "It sounds much more vulgar when you say it like that." She leaned in to snatch a quick peck from his smiling lips. "But I do believe I shall require some more demonstration, Your Grace. I'm not yet quite convinced."

He grinned as he gathered her close. "As you wish, lass."

Chapter Thirteen

A day later, Gage could still taste the sweetness of Evangeline's warm lips, feel her thighs bracketing him and the sensual weight of her that had imprinted on his body. Devil take it, the kissing had been sublime—hot and sweet with just the right hint of ferocity.

He had been stunned into stupidity when she'd climbed over him at first. Flushing, he cursed his prim, starchy reaction for the thousandth time. He might be a virgin, but he wasn't a prude! There *had* been women in Dunalastair, ones he'd kissed and fondled. He wasn't a stone statue without needs—he'd simply been pragmatic and careful.

In truth, the only thing he hadn't done was the act itself. He wasn't a greenhorn, and yet her impulsive move had taken Gage by surprise. After all, what highborn young woman threw herself onto the lap of an unsuspecting gentleman and joked about testing the merchandise?

The kind intent on seduction, his mind supplied.

She had been bold in the maze, but only enough for a few more exploratory kisses. The threat of discovery was too great, and neither of them wanted to end their dalliance before it had even begun. Their agreement would include a private experiment of mutual satisfaction. One that was purely physical in which intercourse would be a foregone conclusion, a definitive performance with no emotional ties or empty promises.

There were no games with Evangeline, only a frankness and sincerity that he appreciated. Some might feel threatened by a woman speaking her mind, but he was not one of them, and he liked that fact that she'd wanted this for herself. She invigorated him. *Inflamed* him.

He'd never been a man much driven by base emotions, at least not around women. He controlled his urges—they did not control him—but around *her*, he was finding that his usual methods were severely lacking in efficacy.

As it was, he'd had to visit Lushing's London boxing ring last evening after the ball just to put his humors back to rights, and *that* had taken several hours. Even weak and physically spent, he'd still returned home and taken himself in hand in the bath. And now, it seemed he couldn't go a single second without seeing her again. With a muttered curse, Gage shook his head. He had to pull himself together instead of behaving like a desperate novice.

Gage was blessedly saved from his spiraling—and lustful—thoughts by Pierre, who had arrived with his laundered and pressed clothing for the evening.

He frowned at the valet. "Are you certain this green waistcoat isn't too bright?"

Pierre reared back in affront. "Bite your tongue, Your Grace. That green matches your irises exactly. Do you know how much trouble I went through to source that exact color? You don't even appreciate me."

Gage hid his grin. Obnoxious wasn't the least of the quirky valet's qualities. He was melodramatic, too. But he was rather good at his job, and the green was quite an excellent match.

"Don't get your underclothes in a twist, Pierre," Gage said, raising his hands. "And thank you. It's a fine color."

Dressed in his debonair set of evening clothing—thanks to Pierre and to Lushing's outstanding personal tailor—Gage eyed his reflection with approval before dismissing the valet. On the way out, he stopped in his study to glance at the sheaf of papers on his desk. Though he delighted in needling Huntington with expenses, Gage wasn't a complete spendthrift. He did not require paintings on every wall in his domicile or thick carpets on every floor. But now that he was in London, impressions had to be maintained, so the foyer, drawing room, dining room, and small ballroom had been elegantly furnished for callers, although the rest of the rooms in the manor remained bare.

Any extra funds went to the man he had employed to stay on Huntington's heels.

The reports thus far had been sparse, but Gage was convinced that Huntington would slip up eventually. As he'd stated, he'd never gotten his hands dirty. He paid others to do his work for him, and Gage suspected the man might have someone on his payroll who would be willing to talk for a price and expose the truth about Asher.

Tonight Huntington was expected to be at his social club before attending the opera, and Gage had intended to keep an eye on him there. But he suddenly had no interest in going to White's. His blood churned, restless, as he drummed his fingers on the desk.

"Your Grace," his butler said after knocking quietly on the study door.

Gathering the papers, Gage glanced up. "Yes, Jenkins?"

"A message has been delivered. The courier says he must await your reply."

Gage blinked. Was it his man with something new to report on
Huntington? Excitement fired in his blood, but as he opened the
folded square on the salver, a different kind of thrill grew. The note
was written in a distinctly feminine hand.

> *I find myself in need of company.*
> *Will you oblige me? ~E*

There was no signature beyond the initial, but there was an
address, which he recognized as the Earl of Oberton's London residence in Mayfair. She was playing with fire, inviting him to her
father's home, but she wasn't one for half measures. She also wasn't
foolish, which meant she had to be alone.

Smiling, he reached for a sheet of parchment and his quill, writing his reply with decisive strokes. A quote by Horace would not go
amiss.

> *Yes, but remember, he who is greedy is always in*
> *want. ~V*

Gage folded the paper, put his waxed seal on it, and retrieved
a copper from his coin purse. "Give this to the lad." Gage handed
him the note. "And I do not require my coach this evening. I fancy
a bit of air."

"Very well, Your Grace."

Out of an abundance of caution, Gage took a hackney and then
walked the remaining distance to Oberton's address. It wasn't that
far from his own home, but he was on the outskirts of the fashionable district while she was at the center of it. Pulling the brim of

his hat low, he kept to the shadows. It was hard for a man of his size to hide, especially when the streets were busy with well-heeled evening revelers spilling out of the well-lit residences, but he tried anyway.

He paused at the end of Oberton's street, glancing up at the stairs to the entrance of the palatial residence. Did she expect him to come to the door? There were eyes everywhere, and tongues would wag should the Duke of Vale be spotted calling upon this particular address at this time of night. He *could* be visiting the earl, but gossip thrived on the sensational, and he had no intention of giving the rags something to print.

"Over here," a low voice called.

Eyebrows shooting upward, Gage turned toward a side gate barely visible in the shadows, where he could discern the outline of . . . someone. "Hullo," he said cautiously.

"Move, you dolt, before someone sees you!"

Now *that* sharp tongue he recognized. As he moved swiftly toward her, the dark alley swallowed them both up, the gate there opening on well-oiled hinges. "What the devil are you doing out here?" he demanded in a soft voice.

"Having a tea party," she shot back. "What do you think I am doing? Waiting for you."

He frowned. "How long have you been outside?"

"Hush!" She pressed a bare palm to his lips, and heat raced through him at the brusque touch. "Not long. You'll alert the servants, and I had a devil of a time convincing them to retire for the evening, considering I'm supposed to be ill."

He did not speak as she led him into the house via unlit corridors, stuffing him into a dark room when muted voices emerged from the vicinity of the kitchens. Once all was quiet, they crept along carpeted hallways and climbed two staircases, and then she shoved him into another room, this one dimly illuminated by the light of a single lamp. It was a bedchamber, he realized with a jolt. *Her* bedchamber. The turn of the lock kicked him into alertness.

"I've dismissed my lady's maid," she began as she moved past him. "I'm sure she's in the arms of her beau, one of the grooms, right at this moment." Evangeline peered at him. "Don't look so stiff. I won't bite, well, not unless you ask nicely."

He folded his arms and grunted. "I'm not stiff."

"Not yet anyway." Good God, that tongue of hers would be his undoing.

Her bottom lip disappeared between her teeth before it reemerged glistening. "I seem to recall a boast of your ability to perform on your knees, Your Grace. Shall we see if you're up to the task?"

Gage stared at her, breath hitching. He had, in fact, made such a boast. Evangeline's eyes gleamed, her color high. An eyebrow vaulted in challenge as she held his stare, her own chest rising on shortened breaths and the air charging with desire between them.

Well then, never let it be said he wasn't a man of action.

Gage grinned and bowed. "I am at your service, my lady."

Evangeline's ears were hot. In fact, her entire face felt as though it were immolating. Dear God. She had invited an unmarried *man* into her chambers.

And not just any man—the Duke of Vale. Large, elegantly assembled, and yet, encompassed by that charged air of savagery, as if a wild creature like him could not be contained in such urbane clothing. He would be better off in nothing but a kilt, those dark auburn locks tousled and untamed, a great sword strapped to his back, chest bare and glistening with sweat. She swallowed audibly at the image and then tore her gaze away, deluged with nerves.

Be confident.

She should be. A woman's body was *hers*, as was her mind and her heart. And this—inviting Vale here, taking charge of her own sensual needs—was what she desired, she reminded herself.

"Make yourself comfortable," she told the duke, watching Vale where he stood near the door. "We have two hours before the end of the opera, when my father and sister return. I should like us to get to know each other better. I want to see you."

"I'm right here." She bit her lip at his troubled expression. At times, he was so overbearing and dominant, like when he'd rescued her from the mudhole, and others, he was as soft as one of the kittens she had in her care.

Button it, Effie. He's not a kitten, nor is he soft.

No, the Duke of Vale was all imposing, hard man, and she wanted to *see* him.

Swallowing audibly at the lurch of her pulse, she approached him and then leaned back on the nearest armchair, gripping the top of the polished wood for strength. She gulped. "No, you misunderstand me, I wish to see you undressed. Unless you have...changed your mind."

A pair of russet brows shot upward, but he shook his head. "I have not."

Thank God.

The hat, gloves, and coat went first. Then his jacket, cravat, and a gem-bright green waistcoat that matched his eyes rather sublimely.

A white shirt remained tucked into his trousers as he knelt to remove his footwear. Evangeline's mouth went appallingly dry at the ripple of muscles in his back beneath the fine lawn, and her hand lifted to the pulse hammering in her throat. Heat raced through her, arousal an indecent flood between her thighs. When the shirt went, tugged over those straining shoulders, she held her breath, and then he straightened to his full height, fingers stalled on his waistband.

"More?" he asked, his voice low and deep now.

It took her a moment to realize he'd spoken. Her gaze shot up. A lock of hair dropped onto his brow, giving him a rakish air. Green eyes gleamed with desire, that troubled expression from earlier gone. Evangeline could barely focus her attention, struck dumb by the enormous expanse of chiseled flesh from his thick neck to the bulging pectorals and ridged abdominal muscles that arrowed down below.

Evangeline found her voice. "Yes, please. I wish to see all of you."

"What do I get in return?"

"You get to see all of me as well," she croaked when his fingers released the first of the buttons over his fly and more of those roped diagonal muscles came into view, including a narrow swatch of red-bronze hair below his navel. Unlike his chest hair, a lighter mix of bronze and reddish blond, this trail was much darker and led to…

Her brain fizzled completely at the enormous ridge there, practically holding his trousers in place. "Goodness, *are* you smuggling a caber in there?"

He barked a low laugh. "Dare to find out?"

"Yes. Now. All of it, Vale," she bit out, hands scrabbling for purchase against the chair. She wouldn't be surprised if her nails left gouges in the wood.

"So demanding."

"*Demanding* is a word men use for women they cannot control," she said. "I've already told you, Your Grace, I am not biddable by nature."

Those trousers hung precariously when he spread his hands wide. "How would you know? You haven't yet been to bed with a man. You might be as docile as a lamb."

She resented the suggestion. "Or a tiger with teeth and claws."

The duke smiled and let his clothing fall. "I look forward to the discovery."

But Evangeline could not form a retort for the life of her. The power of speech and rational thought had completely abandoned her. She'd seen pictures of men's genitals before in the tomes she'd studied, but nothing had prepared her for the reality that was Vale.

Godlike seemed too insignificant, though he could rival the marble sculptures of Zeus. Except for *there*. The duke was bloody enormous. Thick and veined, his phallus strained outward from its nest of dark red-brown hair. Even from where she stood, she could see a drop of fluid beaded at the tip. His testicles were tight spheres, resting at the apex of a pair of well-formed thighs. More moisture pooled in her own body at the erotic spectacle.

"Turn around," she commanded him in a shaky voice.

When he did, she closed her eyes and slumped against the chair. Hell, if he wasn't as perfect from the back as he was from the front. Tapered muscular back. Full, round buttocks. Bronze-furred, strong legs.

She opened her eyes and gasped. Vale had turned back around and closed the distance between them. He now stood inches away, towering over her and so close that she could feel the heat from his body. His very naked, very aroused body. *That* part of him bobbed dangerously close to her midsection.

"Am I to your satisfaction, lass?" he asked, his voice husky.

"Yes," she said in a breathless whisper.

His arms went around her, and she released her stranglehold on the top of the chair as she allowed him to turn her body away from him. Her mind caught up to what he was about only when he went to work on the buttons and then laces at her back. When the bodice gaped, she clutched it to her chest, feeling a sudden rush of embarrassment. What if she did not come up to snuff? She knew she wasn't the most voluptuous of women.

The blaze of heat behind her disappeared, and she glanced over her shoulder to see that Vale had folded his large body into the opposite armchair. "Now you," he said. "You started this. I want to see you, and I want to see what you do."

She blinked. "I beg your pardon? What I *do*?"

"Strip, get into that bed, and pleasure yourself, Evangeline. Give me a show."

The growled directive made her legs quiver, but turnabout was fair play. Trembling, she did as he asked, discarding her clothing piece by piece. She kept her eyes on his, watching the black of his pupils swallow up the green as more of her skin met the air. His hand stroked lazily along his length. God, it was indecent how wet she was beneath her chemise and drawers.

Undoing the tapes, she let the latter fall and tugged off the garment. She resisted the urge to cover her small breasts before bending clumsily to unroll her stockings. When she was completely nude, she climbed on to the bed, reveling in the hiss of breath from his direction and sat with her back against the pillows. "Now what?"

"Spread your legs," he bit out. "Touch yourself. Show me how you do it when you're alone. I've thought of nothing else since you said it."

Evangeline took courage from the sight of him stroking his own swollen flesh and let her fingers wander down over her breasts to her stomach to her pale blond maidenhair, which was indeed mortifyingly wet. Reluctantly, she let her knees inch apart to his shuddering intake of air. Emboldened by the raw lust on his strained face, she dragged a finger through her slick folds and then reached for the slim case in her beside drawer. If he wanted a show, he'd get one.

"What is that?" he asked in a voice that was more groan than words when she removed the cylindrical carved piece of jade from its velvet confines. It was nowhere near his size, of course, she noticed with a belated huff of amusement when she held it up for his examination.

"Why, it's a billy club, Your Grace. I keep it nearby to bludgeon intruders." His eyes widened, and she laughed at his wild expression as she drew it down between her breasts. "Are you ready? Shall we begin?"

Damn his wilting self-control, that little temptress was going to kill him.

His heart was going to explode, and he was going to die right here in this chair, cock in hand, for anyone to find, and there wasn't a deuced thing he could do about it. Notwithstanding those perfect lips inflaming him so, the sight of her—a sheltered noblewoman—dragging the dildo down her body like a seasoned courtesan was pure temptation. Watching her had to be one of the most erotic things he'd ever seen in his life, and all she'd done was wave the sodding thing and tease him about it.

That isn't all she's done.

There were no words in the English language to describe Evangeline Raine in the altogether. He'd been stunned mute by the torturous reveal of all that creamy skin, the perfect teardrops of her breasts topped by berry-pink nipples that had flooded his mouth with water, and the sparse thatch of silvery wisps at her groin framing the heart of her that had glistened with arousal, the sight of which had been eminently gratifying.

Sitting propped as she was with a secret smile on her lips, legs parted and instrument in hand, she was a queen on her throne, and he, her devoted supplicant.

"It's not quite as big as you are," she said, hot eyes watching him grip himself.

His fingers cinched, enough to make him wince. Gage didn't want this to end too quickly, and he was already close. His skin felt too tight, his muscles quivering from the strain of holding his release at bay. "Show me," he ordered in a guttural voice. "Put it inside."

A blush spread over her skin as she dragged the jade piece down the center of her, mouth parting on a gasp when the smooth tip reached her entrance. Gage held his breath as she inched the instrument into her wet passage, one hand going to her nipple. A breathy moan left her lips, eyes glued to his fingers as he matched her movements. When she pushed in, he stroked down, imagining what those soft, slick depths would feel like. Heaven. *Better.*

Gage bucked into his fist, thrusting his hips, and her eyes widened as she unconsciously mimicked him. "I'm already close," she whispered, after only a few strokes. He knew exactly how she felt—both of them caught on the hair trigger of arousal—the weeks of mutual attraction building up to *this*.

"Find your pleasure, Evangeline."

She worked herself harder, her thumb skating across the bead at the top of her sex. He'd never seen anything lovelier than her coming completely undone, a small shriek escaping her lips as her body went rigid and then quivered as her orgasm took over. He savored the sight and sound of her caught in the throes of it, and then he was grasped in the grip of his own, his hot release erupting over his fingers.

When his body had stopped shaking, he slumped back in the chair, only to let out a grunt at the sight of two cats near the window silently judging him with censorious eyes.

Gage cupped himself on instinct, cringing at his sticky hands, only to hear a smothered giggle from the direction of the bed. He glared at her, still looking indescribably lovely in the aftermath, though she'd draped the edge of the counterpane over her middle. "It's not funny," he bit out. "They were there the whole time? *Watching?*"

"They're just cats, Vale."

"Cats who can take your soul to hell with one look," he muttered. "And they've judged me, I can feel it."

"I don't think you have anything to worry about." Limpid eyes dipped to his covered groin and then skated away. "It's not their fault they were prick-merized."

He choked. "That is not a word."

"It should be. Do you prefer cock-notized? How about caber-tranced?"

"You are ridiculous." One giggle turned into two, and then she was overtaken by a delightful series of snorts. Gage couldn't help it, he chuckled as well, mostly at the sound of her uncontrollable mirth. "You are lovely."

"I'm a mess," she said and glanced down again to his cupped hands. "As are you."

"By my count, we do have some time left. Shall I draw you a bath, my lady?"

That unguarded smile of hers made her radiant. "Great minds *do* think alike."

Gage rose on unsteady feet. "I have one stipulation however."

"Yes?"

"No cats." He paused, eyes narrowing. "Or mice. Or birds or any living creature beyond the two of us." He made a show of peering around the room. "In fact, I'm surprised that Lucky isn't in here, sniffing at parts that shouldn't be sniffed. Where's the little mud monster anyway?"

"I put her in Viola's room."

He exhaled and darted another fulminating glance to the two felines, half expecting them to pounce. "Well, thank God for small mercies. But please, promise me."

She collapsed in snickers at his expression when he shuddered. "I promise, Your Grace, your virtue will be entirely safe from prying eyes, canines *and* felines included."

CHAPTER FOURTEEN

According to the missive delivered by messenger, the plain black coach would arrive at precisely midnight. Evangeline had been surprised to receive Vale's correspondence so soon, considering their scintillating interlude in her bedchamber only less than a handful of nights ago, but perhaps the duke was as eager to see her as she was to see him.

At night especially, Evangeline was consumed by dreams of the man. She couldn't get him out of her thoughts—the sight of that marvelous body unraveling to the tune of her own release played on repeat in her brain, leaving her hot and bothered by morning. And to think, he hadn't even touched her! All he'd done was watch, his eyes glued to her body as she'd pleasured herself.

Nonetheless, she'd attempted to keep herself busy with her own work, including scheduling a visit with the head of the committee managing the Temporary Home for Lost and Starving Dogs. Before her death, its founder, Mary Tealby, had been vehemently passionate about the plight of stray dogs in London, and Evangeline wanted to offer her assistance while she was in London. Indeed, Mrs. Tealby's work in London had inspired Evangeline to start her own sanctuary home in Chichester, though hers wasn't limited to dogs, but all animals.

To her surprise, Viola had asked to accompany her and William to the foundling home in Holloway and then on to the Royal Society for the Prevention of Cruelty to Animals meeting in Pall Mall. Viola was remarkably curious about Mrs. Tealby's work for someone who had shown little interest in Evangeline's shelter at home.

"Who is this Tealby woman again?" Viola asked as they climbed into William's fancy lacquered coach, blushing prettily as its owner offered her his palm. William had done quite well for himself with various railroad investments—but from her sister's wide eyes at the pristine seats and well-appointed interior, it seemed she did not realize just how wealthy he'd become. Even the four matching black horses shone. Evangeline lifted a brow at her old friend.

As he helped her enter the coach, he winked and whispered, "Had to prove somehow that the life of a veterinarian's wife isn't so humdrum."

Evangeline grinned. "Clever."

When she got settled next to a rather impressed Viola, she handed her sister a printed pamphlet from her reticule. "Sadly, she passed away two years ago, but Mary Tealby was a humanitarian and philanthropist who started a home simply for the purpose of keeping lost dogs until they could be reunited with their owners or find new homes. The shelter was originally in her scullery, but then she managed to secure some stables behind Hollingsworth Street, which is where we're going."

Evangeline couldn't keep the admiration from her voice. Interestingly enough, the intrepid woman had been divorced from her husband and quite independent before she died. She hadn't been wealthy and had depended on fundraising to help run the temporary home, but she'd still supported her animals with whatever money she had. Much of the upper class looked down their collective noses, influenced by the newssheets that her behavior—along with her divorced status—had been immoral and much too controversial.

A handful of years ago when Evangeline was just sixteen, she had been desperate to meet the woman and visit the shelter ever since she'd first read about her efforts in the newssheets, but sadly, Mary had become ill and died before Evangeline had been able to fulfill that dream. In recent years, however, she had gotten to know Mary's brother, Reverend Edward Bates, to whom Mary had bequeathed everything. He and Mary's friend Sarah Major were part of the committee of trustees who ran the shelter.

"It says here: funds urgently needed," Viola said, studying the pamphlet and wrinkling her nose. "Is it in danger of closing?"

Evangeline nodded. As she well knew, funding a shelter for animals was an uphill battle for support. The shelter had been viciously mocked by the *Times* as an indulgence, and by men who saw women of their ilk as overly sentimental or who said the plight of the poor was significantly more pressing. But Charles Dickens had come to his friend Mary's aid, praising her generosity and drive, and afterward Mary had been able to secure royal patronage from the queen, who was fond of dogs and rarely seen without one of her furry companions.

"Yes, shelters are often in precarious situations because they're run on charity. I've pledged some money to help," Evangeline said. "And Mr. Dawson of course is always quite generous when it comes to the welfare of animals, as you know."

William canted his head, blue eyes sparkling with their usual warmth. "Anything for the puppies."

Viola bit her lip, and Evangeline caught sight of her reddening cheeks. "I'd like to pledge some of my pin money as well."

Evangeline's eyebrows shot to her hairline. "You would?"

"I'm not completely heartless, Effie," Viola said with a wounded look. "I want to save the puppies, too."

"I think that's rather admirable, Lady Viola," William said.

Her sister sniffed. "Thank you, Mr. Dawson."

They arrived at the address for the converted mews and entered the building. The stalls built for horses in the shed were filled with dogs of all breeds and sizes, and Evangeline lost no time in surrounding herself with the dozens of animals around a water trough that were barking and howling with excitement at the visitors. A few scared growls also punctuated the barks and whines. Most of the animals looked healthy enough, although there were a few who were emaciated, and some quite sick. She saw William bring out his bag and immediately go over to the section that housed the animals in need of medical attention, with Viola in tow.

"Dogs always know whom to trust," a female voice said, and Evangeline looked up from where she sat on the floor with three dogs vying for her lap to see a woman with a kind but solemn face.

"Mrs. Major…" she stammered. "Gracious, what an honor. I was hoping to see you at the RSPCA meeting in Pall Mall."

"Please, call me Sarah." The woman smiled and knelt beside her, gathering one of the dogs to her. "You must be Lady Evangeline. I received your letter, and am delighted to meet you finally. Edward has been quite complimentary about you."

"He's too kind. What you've both done here is incredible," Evangeline said, blushing. "You're saving so many lives."

"They were lost, unwanted, or suffering," she said simply. "The biggest part of injustice is walking by without doing or even saying something about it."

Evangeline nodded. "Is that how it started for you?"

Sarah stroked a dog's patchy head. The poor thing was missing an ear. "When my friend Mary asked me to help a pup she found in the gutter, unfortunately, it died overnight. She vowed then never to pass by another dog again, and that she'd never turn away a dog that needed help. Her brother and I contributed however we could, and now, we are simply continuing Mary's work and her legacy."

"I feel similarly compelled to help any animals in need. My shelter in Chichester is small, but I do what I can."

"And that is always enough." Sarah patted her hand. "Stay as long as you like. The animals love a bit of company. Will I see you at the charity event later?"

"I wouldn't miss it."

Uncaring of her fine clothing, Evangeline had removed her gloves to help feed and even wash a few of the dogs. William offered his medical assistance as well, and to her utter shock, Viola did not let out one whimper of complaint. Her fine dress was streaked with dirt and covered in fur, and even as she assisted William with not-so-pleasant tasks like collecting soiled linen, her soft laughter could be heard throughout the stables.

Even after the quick stint to Pall Mall, despite being dirty and tired, her sister seemed happy. Evangeline couldn't help noticing that Viola had sat next to William in the coach on the return journey. "God, Effie, you should have seen Mr. Dawson. He saved that dog's life! It was barely breathing, and then, lo and behold, it cried and opened its eyes, looking directly at him with so much gratitude."

Goodness, was William blushing? He cleared his throat. "It's not as impressive as all that," he said.

"Stop being so humble. You were magnificent, William." Viola patted his chest and then snatched her hand away in mortification, her own cheeks going crimson, both at the touch and the informal address. Evangeline hid her smile behind her hand.

"Thank you, my lady. You were also a magnificent helper."

Watching them, Evangeline felt her heart swell. It might be new, this fledgling connection between them, but seeing it blossom before her eyes made something unfamiliar squeeze inside her chest. She might not have such a relationship with a gentleman, but anyone with sense could tell there was something there.

Evangeline swallowed as her thoughts veered to Vale…there was nothing remotely quixotic about them or their plans. But that was the whole point, wasn't it? A physical liaison completely free of romantic entanglements. But the knowledge that her best friend and her sister might come out of this season with a chance at true happiness and a possible love match made her sacrifice worth it.

It was nearly evening when William dropped them off at their residence, but she overheard them making plans to meet as soon as he returned from conducting some business he had back in Chichester.

As they removed their cloaks and bonnets in the foyer, Evangeline smiled at Viola. "So, you and Mr. Dawson seemed to get on tremendously."

"Effie!" Viola opened her mouth and snapped it shut, a furious flush overtaking her pale skin. Just when Evangeline thought Viola would dismiss her and flounce off, she let out a soft, dreamy sigh. "Goodness, Effie. He's not at all what I expected. He's smart and funny, and ever so kind. And he thinks I'm clever, too, with steady, capable hands, he said."

"Quite the compliment, coming from him," Evangeline said.

"I didn't know he was that rich," Viola blurted, and then blushed harder. "Not that it matters. Well, it *does*, I suppose, but I thought he was a poor animal doctor. I'm afraid I let that affect my judgment of him." Her voice went small. "Does that make me a bad person?"

Evangeline shook her head. "Not at all. We women must always be cognizant of the kind of lives we can secure for ourselves and our children through marriage. It's simply a practical consideration since we have no means of earning an income ourselves." She pulled her sister closer. "But when it comes to William specifically, Viola, he's a good man, and he'll treat you as you deserve, even if he doesn't have a title. And even if he was poor, you would still be loved. But only you can decide what it is you want in a husband."

"He makes me feel like I can accomplish anything," Viola whispered, her smile so wide, it shone. "And he asked me about my interests. About Paris and my love for fashion! I haven't spoken to anyone about those old dreams in months. He wants to hear everything I have to say."

"You *are* more," Evangeline said and tapped her sister's nose fondly. She, too, had forgotten how much her sister adored fashion. "You only need to realize that."

"Thank you for letting me come today, Effie. It meant a lot."

Heart full, Evangeline smiled. "You're welcome. It did for me, too."

The eventful day had hardly taken the edge off her nerves as Evangeline waited in the deserted courtyard outside the scullery door. Earlier, she'd had to place a cool cloth against her cheeks and taken a quick walk about the garden to settle her raging emotions. But the brisk round of exercise had done nothing to quiet her nerves. Or her fears.

Evangeline heard the stroke of midnight from a clock some- where inside the house just as a plain black coach ambled to a stop in front of the mews behind their residence. A liveried but silent coachman opened the door and set down the step with a short bow. Shivering with anticipation, Evangeline pulled the cloak tighter around herself, making sure that the depth of its cowl covered her face, and entered the coach.

Her distinctive white-blond hair was unique enough to be rec- ognized, and while she did not care about ruination when it came to herself, she still had Viola to think about. As such, she'd fitted a dark wig over her own tightly bound hair. Because God only knew what kind of party she was heading to, especially if it was hosted by the Earl of Lushing.

The carriage jolted, and she clasped her fingers together when her nerves fired again.

Vale's instructions had been simple: *Dress is whimsical, wait for the coach at the allotted time, and above all, do not be seen.*

The gown she'd chosen hadn't been too risqué—who knew what *whimsical* actually meant—but it was pretty and fancy enough to pass muster.

With a puff of airy laughter, Evangeline wondered what anyone from the ton would say to learn that an unwed lady of their ranks was on her way to a possible bawdy house to meet a gentleman for an illicit adventure. They'd likely label her a trollop or worse. Then again, she'd choose Lady Harlot over Lady Ghastly in a heartbeat—at least the choice to engage in a carnal liaison would have been all hers.

Evangeline let out a snort as the coach finally rolled to a smooth stop. Admittedly, she was still nervous, her stomach coiling in knots. Peering out the window, she did not immediately recognize the building or the vicinity. It was much too dark, but she could see shadowy forms milling farther down the street, which didn't do much to ease her trepidation. The coach seemed to have stopped in some kind of narrow alley. Had the duke planned the stop here? Or was she about to meet an untimely end to cutpurses?

A brisk rap on the door had her heart flying and lodging into her throat, a panicked hand flying to the humming pulse at her nape. But it was only Vale, also in a dark cloak and hat, peering into the coach and letting out a breath that sounded too much like one of surprise. She blinked. Had he not expected her to come?

"My lady," his deep voice rumbled.

"Your Grace," she murmured. It was only after she took his proffered hand and descended that the area became vaguely familiar. They were not at Lethe as she'd guessed they might be, but somewhere else in London's West End. Then again, it wasn't as though she frequented this part of town often. Perhaps the Earl of Lushing had branched out.

"Have you eaten?" Vale asked.

She nodded in answer, peering up at the nondescript brick exterior and the dank alley in which they stood. "Is this another of Lushing's clubs?"

"No, but I do owe him for this particular invitation."

Evangeline felt a whisper of panic. *She* might be open to her brazen scheme, but the idea of the brother of her best friend knowing what she was up to left her cold. Even Vesper, as much of a free spirit and breaker of the rules as she was, would not sanction what Evangeline was about to do.

"Does he know?" Her voice emerged as a breathless squeak.

"No, and don't worry, he will not be here tonight."

She exhaled, the tension in her lungs easing a marginal amount. "Won't we be recognized? And by we, I mean *me*."

"Even if you are, people pay handsomely for the privilege to attend one of these parties. They value their privacy and discretion above all things, even gossip. The venue might change but the clientele does not." Vale handed her a black invitation with a red seal that had only one word on it, written in a splash of red ink, *Bacchanal*. The cardstock looked expensive and exclusive. A thrill of anticipation spiraled through her. "You can also choose to wear a mask," he told her in a low voice.

Evangeline nodded. Yes, she definitely wanted a mask. The more anonymity the better. They entered a double-high foyer, which was rich, lush, and opulent. After the dank, narrow alleyway it was like walking into another world full of plush velvets, gilded railings, and polished wood. Evangeline gaped in awe. Part receiving salon, part lady's boudoir, it smacked of luxury and vice, making the tiny hairs on her arm rise in decadent anticipation.

What kind of depravity was she walking into?

The hum of conversation and music resonated from beyond a pair of towering velvet drapes that beckoned at the far end. After she'd donned a black lace domino that covered two-thirds of her face, Evangeline let Vale take her cloak and felt his eyes fall to her dark wig. A frown drew his brows together as if the sight of the disguise displeased him, but it was gone quickly.

"You look different with dark hair," he murmured when she lifted a brow.

She frowned. "You don't like it?"

"I like your hair the way it is."

Evangeline felt inordinately pleased at his words. "It's too recognizable a color."

"That's true," he agreed.

"What made you decide to bring me to an event like this?" she whispered when he took her arm and ushered her toward the mysterious drapes at the other end.

"It's a ladies' choice masque," he said. "I thought you would approve, and that it might give you comfort to be around like-minded females."

She peered at him. "*Ladies'* choice?"

The duke's smile was sin incarnate. "At this particular kind of soiree, the woman sets all the rules. Whom to approach, whom to talk to, whom to dance with. Every desire starts with her." He paused, his lip quirking. "With *you*."

It was a novel concept that had her mind reeling, and by the time the curtains were pulled apart by two very efficient and handsome footmen, Evangeline's breaths had reduced to short pants of excitement. When she entered, she gaped. Nothing in her wildest imagination had prepared her for the decadent tableau that spanned the enormous ballroom. At least not for the scene straight out of *A Midsummer Night's Dream* that greeted her. It felt as though she were walking onstage... into a forbidden, fantastical world.

Which she *was*... metaphorically and physically.

Towering marble columns painted to look like tree trunks were wrapped in gold and green silks with huge boughs of flowers hanging from the ceiling. Portraits of frolicking fauns, centaurs, and other mythological creatures adorned the walls. But the thing that stood out most was the guests. *Whimsical* was hardly the word to describe the diaphanous and gauzy fabrics that left little to the imagination.

One buxom woman was dressed in a gown made of strategically placed ivy and golden ribbons, like a seductive forest nymph. Evangeline felt her cheeks heat when the woman winked at her and licked her lips. Her own gown—a bloodred siren costume left over from Briar's annual harvest All Hallows' Eve party—though lovely, was modest in comparison. Low-cut and brazen in color, it had felt daring enough to wear tonight per the duke's sparse instructions, but Evangeline felt overdressed even *without* her petticoats.

"That is hardly whimsical wear, Your Grace," she chastised him in a soft whisper.

"Would you rather I'd written *licentious and titillating*?" He chuckled when she nodded instantly, eyes darting back to the half-naked woman. "She is a performer. The guests are less adventurous in their clothing choices."

When she looked, Evangeline realized that he was right. Most of the guests were dressed as she was, though a few of them wore outlandish costumes. She watched as a man in a donkey's head galloped past her with a raucous neigh on the heels of a saucy sprite. Another man's breeches were so low and tight, Evangeline swore she could see the ridged outline of his semi-erect manhood. She swallowed, her blood simmering at the unvarnished hedonism drifting from every corner.

The Duke of Vale peered down at her, a storm of *something* that resembled an inferno burning in those bottle-green eyes as if he could sense the shift inside of her. "So what next, my lady?"

She wanted what she'd always wanted: him on his knees and lifting her skirts with his teeth. That vision ferried an indelicate throb right to her already humming sex. Well, he was hers for the evening, wasn't he? She would not waste one second.

"Kiss me."

If purgatory was real, then Gage was neck-deep in it. But devil take him if an unguarded, confident Evangeline wasn't the most glorious thing he'd ever seen in his life. A queen coming into her own. Most ladies, if invited to a fete such as this, would have blushed and swooned.

But not her. No, she strutted. She preened. She *reveled*. And it wasn't by chance that everyone took notice of the new vixen prowling in their midst. No one could see her face under the domino, but Evangeline exuded a sensuality that was so powerful he could almost taste it.

And he wanted them all to know that she was his.

Blood hot, he bent, his lips finding hers with unerring accuracy. She parted hungrily for him, hands threading through his hair and tugging on the strands, tongue teasing his, sweeping his contours, dipping deep with light flicks that drove him mad. It was the sensuous ambiance, he knew. It flowed into the vein like opium... everything designed to make guests give in to their deepest, darkest carnal desires. She broke the kiss, panting.

"More of that later," she promised, eyes bright.

The husky vow made him want to devour those glistening, ruby lips, her flushed throat, the voluptuous expanse of rosy flesh brimming over her bodice. Gage felt his lungs squeeze. He'd seen those modest breasts completely uncovered, and yet the sight of them barely confined by the scarlet lace edging had him losing his breath.

He observed the rest of her in bold appreciation. The dress itself was sultry, clinging to her long, lithe frame in undulations of crimson silk. Her small waist led to gently flaring hips beneath tantalizing red panels that wafted between her legs with each step. She wore no bulky petticoats that he could determine, the shapely outline of her thighs and buttocks sending unseemly bolts of lust straight through him.

Fighting not to haul her into his arms, Gage stuck his hands into his pockets. This evening was hers, as it was to any woman within the walls. He'd never been to one of these parties before—they were more Lushing's preference—but the notion behind them was both revolutionary and brilliant. For the evening, women were the predominant sex. They ruled, their desires trumping all else, and the gentlemen in attendance had to obey or leave.

Though the host was anonymous, Gage had his suspicions. Lushing claimed it wasn't him, but Gage knew better. It was too much like the man himself…bold, unapologetic, and ingeniously progressive in its views of women. He huffed a laugh. An erotic party that gave women the upper hand in a puffed-up, pretentious society where they were ranked as lesser by default of their sex? Fucking brilliant.

"So how does this all work?" Evangeline murmured as they ambled toward the tables at the far end of the room. "Do I just go up to anyone and declare my intentions? Demand for a gentleman to be my plaything for the evening?"

Jealousy stung like a hive of hornets. Gage's throat knotted with the sudden realization that under the rules of the invitation, she was free to choose *any* gent she wanted. Though she'd come with him, women's choice meant women's *choice*. Frowning, he ignored the cold wash of dread that shot down his spine. "If that is your wish, yes."

Eyeing him, she gave a dramatic sigh. "Such a banquet of beautiful men. However will I decide on just one?" He stiffened, and her provocative laughter filled the air. "Goodness, Vale. I am only teasing."

"You're different tonight."

"Different how?" she asked and then touched her hair. "You mean my disguise."

"No," he said. "I've never seen you so...untrammeled."

She laughed again. "Perhaps I am one of those mysterious flowers that only come alive when the sun sets. Gardenia or evening primrose or some such."

"Queen of the night," he murmured.

"I beg your pardon?" she asked curiously, peering up at him.

Gage cleared his throat. "It's a night-blooming cactus."

She slanted him a mock-injured look. "Are you calling me prickly, sir?"

"If the shoe fits, lass." Amusement tumbled out of him when her eyes danced with answering merriment. "But no, the queen of the night's flowers only open one night per year. Perhaps this is your night to bloom."

"Perhaps indeed." She pointed to a nearby card table where the bet was clothing instead of coin. "Shall we play a spot of vingt-et-un? I've a hankering to see that starched cravat of yours loosened."

When she sat confidently in the chair across the opulent card table, the buds of her taut nipples were visible, her pert breasts pushed high by the corset she wore. But it was her eyes that demolished. They were hungry. *Ravenous.* Lady Evangeline Raine embodied the hunter.

And hell if *he* didn't want to be her prey.

Other men felt the same, by the heat of their gazes, but his newly nascent huntress wasn't bothered by them. Her curious stare absorbed the gaming tables edging the sides of the hall, and the scandalous state of undress of some of their participants.

"Do you know what you're in for?" Gage asked.

Guests at these parties played for clothing, secrets, and favors, not money. He wondered if she'd discerned that before suggesting the game. From her quiet inhale when a woman at the neighboring table removed the lace fichu from her neck, and the intrigued light in her eyes, she had. Gage smiled—if it was a thrill she sought, then she'd get it.

"Yes, I do. Sit, sir." When she arched a brow and patted the seat to her right, Gage found himself hesitating. A game or two would be harmless, and it wasn't as if they were playing for money. He cracked his fingers and sat with a lazy shrug. She wanted to see his cravat loosened? He would see her a pair of silk stockings. More, if he had his way.

Four hands later—down one coat, a diamond stickpin, and his deuced cravat—Gage realized too late that aloof, reserved, animal-loving Evangeline Raine was a bloody card sharp because, to his utter disappointment, not one item of clothing had left her person.

"You're good at this," he murmured.

"I'm good at many things." She peered up at him through gilt-tipped lashes and winked, her voice sliding over him like velvet.

His blood warmed. "You certainly are, vixen."

CHAPTER FIFTEEN

Vingt-et-un was proving to be highly entertaining.

Evangeline had never had so much fun in all her life, but the most gratifying thing of all was the disgruntled look on the Duke of Vale's face. That, and his state of undress, which she was taking more delight in than she probably should. His waistcoat was gone, revealing the bulging muscles beneath his shirtsleeves. The others at the table had lost various pieces of clothing as well, but she had eyes only for him.

While the others at the table were ruddy with an unending flow of liquor, the duke drank only water. Her opponents' drunkenness made it easier to keep track of the cards, but she had to be careful with Vale. He might be large and gruff, preferring grunts to actual words, which she believed he did on purpose to aggravate her, but those observant eyes took in everything.

"You, my lady," an older, shirtless gentleman across the table slurred. She blinked. Was that gold dust on his chest? How droll! "Are a sorceress."

Evangeline laughed, looking over her hand of cards. "Am I?"

"I cannot concentrate for the life of me," he grumbled.

The only other woman at the table—Persephone, she called herself—tittered beside him. She was a beautiful woman in a peacock-trimmed mask, black ringlets coming undone and bright splotches of color in her bronze cheeks from the wine she'd consumed. She lifted a hand to the older man's arm, which he caught and pressed to his lips. "I should think that's because you're a poor player, my love," she told him.

Oh. They were together. Or at least they might be in short order.

"My luck turned when she joined the table," the man complained.

Persephone winked at her. "Or perhaps you underestimated her skill." Her eyes flicked appreciatively to Vale. "I, for one, hope she continues to win. The view is rather nice from where I'm sitting." She leaned forward, offering the table a healthy look of the ample bosom threatening to spill from her dress. "You're that Scottish duke."

Like all the other gentlemen, Vale was maskless...and recognizable.

A lazy smile curled his plush lips. "*English* duke. Scottish mother."

"I see," Persephone crooned and touched her hand of cards to her mouth, eyelashes fluttering in a coquettish manner. "Well, I find you eminently fuckable, Your Grace."

Evangeline gaped. Goodness, were women here always so forward? At the woman's overt advances, a possessive instinct inside of her reared up in instant ire, but Vale just smiled. "That's nice of you to say."

"Nice is the last thing I am, but you'll find that I am as generous with praise as I am with my attentions," she drawled, teasing a fingertip over her décolletage and leaving no doubt to anyone at the table that she was talking about intimate acts.

To Vale's credit, his eyes didn't follow the woman's finger, his stare instead remaining fixed on Evangeline. Would Persephone change her mind about the man at her side and proposition Vale? *Could* he refuse under the terms of the evening if it was ladies' choice? She felt her brows furrow. She hadn't thought to ask Vale about consent at these parties, but fervently hoped it would apply, otherwise that would make the women just as bad as the men, if they simply took what they wanted.

Evangeline, at least, was secure in her knowledge that Vale *wanted* her to pursue him. Although admittedly she'd lost sight of that pursuit as she'd focused her energies on the card game.

But perhaps winning *wasn't* the idea here after all.

Evangeline glanced down at the three cards she held totaling twenty points and called for another card. With the count the way it was, she would go over. When she received a five, she lost for the first time that evening as Vale won with a paltry fifteen, one eyebrow raised as if he knew that she had lost on purpose. Watching him through lowered eyelashes, she held out one gloved arm.

"Will you do the honors, Your Grace?"

She couldn't help her small intake of breath when he flicked that piercing green stare over her, a feral heat moving in their depths. Everything and everyone around them disappeared when he took her hand in his, fingers skating up the length of her forearm to the first button near her elbow. Her pulse tripped as a fingernail grazed the tender strip of skin above the edge of the glove, the light scrape making her nipples pucker.

Evangeline sank her teeth into her bottom lip, breath hitching as the first mooring came loose, then the second and third. Her lungs shrank with each one. She could feel the attention of the others at the table as if the two of them were putting on a private show, but she could barely take them in. She was utterly preoccupied by those long, thick scarred knuckles—the contrast of his calloused palms with the fine kidskin of her glove mesmerizing. Vale's hands weren't delicate. They were rough and worn, hard and strong like the rest of him.

The rest of him…

Dear God, all she could think about then was his thickly hewn, naked body that had crowded her bedroom armchair. Heat blazed through her, a series of arrowed pulses striking her aching nipples and right into her throbbing, molten center. When the last button came loose, Evangeline bit her lip so hard she tasted blood, but even that tiny lash of pain did nothing to corral the intense pleasure brewing inside.

A smoldering pair of eyes collided with hers when Vale tugged the tip of each finger, and as the glove finally, inexorably, slid off, Evangeline felt her body seize and then release in a languid, undulant wave. Goodness, did she just…

No.

But, oh, so much yes.

Her lids fluttered shut as she rode out whatever it was that had just detonated in her body, a balmy bliss feathering across all her nerve endings. It was an orgasm, that much she knew, but unlike any she'd ever given herself. A warm grasp engulfed her hand, the sensuous rasp of skin making her relaxed muscles quiver anew.

"Well, that was enlightening," Persephone drawled from across the table, her voice thick with desire. "Your Grace, might I entreat—"

But Evangeline didn't give her a chance to finish, her fingers going tight around the duke's palm as she rose. "His Grace is taken for the evening," she interrupted, and then remembered her own thoughts on consent. "Unless, of course, he has changed his mind."

"I have not," came the instant gravelly answer.

When she finally met Vale's stare, the black of his pupils had almost swallowed up the green of his iris, blown out by lust as she was certain hers were.

"My loss," Persephone said without rancor, fanning herself. "Let me know if you fancy a bit of sharing. I'm open to a partner or three in the bedchamber."

"Not tonight," Evangeline murmured. *Not ever.*

The woman chuckled. "I don't blame you. If I were in your shoes, I would keep that one under lock and key for my own private entertainment. If he can do that with a look and a fistful of buttons, I'm envious of what awaits you."

Evangeline was suddenly of the same mind. Unable to look at Vale for fear that her carnal yearnings would be easily read, she cleared her throat and took her leave of the card table. Gathering his discarded belongings, the duke offered her his arm as they strolled in the direction of the refreshments room.

Despite her calm outer mien, her insides felt like lava. She was dreadfully in need of a cool drink, one that wasn't wine, or she would truly release her moral inhibitions and climb Vale like the sublimely sinful mountain he was. Right in front of everyone. She had a feeling that these particular guests, including Persephone, would approve of such a spectacle. Evangeline shivered, feeling that wicked throb resume between her thighs.

Without warning, Vale yanked her into a small alcove between two marble statues. Evangeline promptly lost her breath when his huge frame blanketed hers from the front, one palm gathering her wrists above her head as his body imprisoned hers against the wall.

"That was interesting," he growled in a tenor so low it rumbled through her bones. Evangeline's knees wobbled, knowing instantly he meant her orgasm. *That* was one word for it.

"Mortifying," she whispered.

"Magnificent," he countered. His fingers cupped her jaw, thumbs feathering over the skin beneath the edge of her lace mask. "You were a woman in her element. Fierce. Provocative. Undeniably sultry. Every single man in that room wanted you."

"Did you?"

He took her hand and guided it downward. Evangeline's eyes widened at the thick, huge, straining ridge she found there. "How did Persephone say it? 'Eminently fuckable,'" he drawled, and she giggled.

"I think this state of yours might be quite painful and require immediate attention," she said huskily. "Vale…I need…" Her fingers closed over the fabric of his trousers, gripping the rigid flesh beneath and making him groan. "I want to leave."

"Patience, leannan." Good heavens, that voice. That *word*. Though from the sound of the gravel in his tone, impatience was grinding him to bits, too. A muscle flexed in his jaw as though he was fighting for control not to have his wicked way with her. Why was he fighting? She *wanted* to be wicked. He pressed his forehead to hers as he gently shifted her palm back up to his chest, away from his hard sex. "No more."

"Why not?" she whispered. "I can help."

"I know you can, but if you continue to do that, I will be walking around with wet, sticky trousers." Hunched over her, he grunted.

"At the moment, I'm trying to think of the most dreadful things I can think of, *not* how good your hand felt."

Evangeline frowned in confusion, and then his meaning clicked about what he was trying to do—diminish his arousal. While she wanted nothing more than to stroke him to oblivion, it was his body. "I think my cats might have formed an attachment to you. My maid found your cravat in one of the cat beds the other morning."

A strangled noise resembling groaning laughter rumbled from his chest. "That is working, thank you."

"I had to tell the maid that it was my father's and then steal it from the laundry before anyone discovered that it wasn't his." She laughed softly. "My animal friends do seem to have a terrible habit of either destroying or pilfering your clothing."

"Incredibly suspect. I'm beginning to think they've been trained to do so."

She snickered. "Alas, our diabolical scheme of world domination via extorting naked dukes has been exposed! Whatever is this villainess to do?"

"World domination?"

"They are cats, Your Grace." She walked her fingers over his shoulder. "If they aren't plotting to take over the world, then what do you think they are doing?"

Her fingernails scratched at his arms in the imitation of claws, making him shudder.

"You are devious but effective, lass," he replied with a chuckle and then straightened, the tension easing from his bunched muscles. "Shall we find a drink and discuss alternate plans for domination?"

Evangeline's breath stuttered. "*World* domination."

"That's what I said."

That was, emphatically, *not* what he'd said, the tease!

When the duke handed her a full glass, she drank it without questioning what it was. Water, thankfully. Indecent fires and thirst temporarily quenched, she peered up at him, grasping at the first thing she could think of that wasn't sensual in nature. "Why don't you ever imbibe?"

"It dulls my wits," he replied easily. "My father and brother were habitual drunkards. I'm not a teetotaler, by any means. I enjoy the bite of a dram of fine whisky on a cold evening from time to time. My mother's distillery produces some of the best in Scotland."

"Do you miss it?" she asked at the hint of pride in his tone.

"Scotland or the whisky?" he replied with a smile.

Her pulse galloped. Good heavens, what was wrong with her? One quirk of those plush lips and her brain turned to mush. "The former."

"There are things I miss about it," the duke said, leading her toward a pair of doors that led to a narrow outdoor terrace. They weren't alone, but the cool air was welcome and refreshing. "I miss the wide-open hills, the people, the old keep, and even my mother, bloody tyrant that she is."

"What's she like?"

"Fierce and formidable with a spine of iron and a heart of gold." He gave a light shrug. "If she hadn't taken me back home to Scotland with her, I would have turned out just like my brother. He was with us for several years, but then my father insisted that his heir belonged in England with him. My mother could not refuse. Thankfully, he did not summon me. The rush of drinking and gambling would have been too much to resist, and I might have found myself at a similar end."

Those words were soft but bitter. There was a story there, but Evangeline didn't want to pry. When Vale turned her and pulled her against his chest, she had a perfect view of the backlit ballroom through the doors.

"I should love to visit one day," she said.

His chin came to rest on her crown. "Perhaps you will get that chance."

With you, she wanted to add, but that was a hollow wish. Their liaison was only meant to be temporary. And without emotional attachment.

The truth was, she should not be enjoying this—enjoying *him*—so much. While their physical draw was undeniable, she liked how easy it was to talk to him, too. For the first time in her life, Evangeline did not feel spoken down to or belittled by a gentleman who wasn't her father. She was well aware that she was treated like a leper because of Huntington's influence, but not all men were like his set. Her friends' husbands seemed to be cut from a different cloth, as was Vale.

But you're not looking for a husband, remember?

She bit her lip hard. No, she was out for a lover. Muddling that with warm emotions and fantasies of happily ever after was a recipe for disaster. Evangeline *knew* that. No feelings, no strings, no heartbreak. That was the whole purpose of carving out this kind of agreement.

Exhaling, she twisted her arm and reached between their bodies to find what she was looking for. There. Not quite as hard as before, but something to work with.

"What are you doing?" Vale rasped when she boldly fingered his manhood.

"Do you want me to stop?" she asked.

He swelled in her palm and pressed his body closer. "No."

Evangeline smiled. "Very well then. A little wet fabric never killed anyone."

She was going to kill *him*, that was the plain truth.

Gage groaned into her hair as he went from half-mast to full sail in the time it took for her fingers to find purchase. They were lodged well enough into the shadows that no one could see what she was doing, not that it would matter if they did. This kind of party favored the voyeurs and the sybarites.

He glanced through the terrace window toward the lewd dance currently playing out in the ballroom. Gage spotted Persephone, the brunette from their card table, draped over the older gentleman who had bemoaned Evangeline's card skill. Neither of them wore much at all, nor were they making any effort to conceal their desire for each other.

However, while Gage wanted Evangeline to be free to explore her adventurous side, he did not want her to suffer for it, if her identity was exposed. But then he couldn't think much more on anything when a firm palm slid up his length in a breath-snatching slide. He hissed as her fingers rounded the tip of him, and then had to lean all his weight on the stone balustrade when she gently circled his sensitive crown.

"Damnation, Evangeline," he groaned through his teeth, nuzzling the shell of her ear.

"Am I doing it right?" came her breathless whisper.

A huff of laughter left him. "Any touch of yours is right."

She continued to work him in endless, maddening strokes and circles, the light touches driving him crazy. He needed her to grasp him harder, but the excruciating torture of the drawn-out pleasure was worth keeping his lips pinned, and he wanted to last. Unable to keep his own hands still, he let them drift down the silky sides of her waist. When he got to the flare of her hips, instead of the mass of crinoline, he felt firm womanly flesh. The sharp inhale of breath tempted him to skim lower, tracing her outer thighs.

Desperate to confirm what he already knew, Gage tugged at her satin skirts, fingers creeping down as he greedily lifted the fabric of her hem. He opened his stance and reached under, letting the scarlet lengths drop to pool over his wrist. One fingertip wandered up to the lace edge of a stocking, tracing it from the outer part of her thigh to the inner.

Hell if she wasn't wearing drawers beneath her chemise either! Images of her sprawled out on her bed assaulted him, visions of that rosy pink flesh on wanton display while her fingers pleasured her beautiful body. He had watched, but he hadn't touched. Was her skin as soft as it had looked, supple and satiny? Would she be as drenched now as she'd been that night?

Gage couldn't wait to find out.

Inching forward, his knuckles brushed the silky hair at the juncture of her thighs, her body jerking in his arms. His finger dipped lower to skim the seam of her, and he grunted in pure male satisfaction at what he found there. She was hot, wet, and slick with arousal.

"I want to make you come again," he whispered, and bit into her earlobe, sucking it into the heat of his mouth as his finger made a second upward pass, catching the sensitive bundle of nerves at the top of her sex in the process. She whimpered and writhed, hips jerking.

"Vale," she gasped, working his cock as she rolled her hips forward begging for more.

He stilled and tapped her wet flesh. "Gage."

"Gage, please." The instant breathy capitulation pleased him more than the sound of his given name on her lips.

He obliged, brushing the pad of his pointer finger through her slippery folds, the slow slide making her squirm with need. When he lowered his palm and pressed that finger into her, she bucked and took him to the first knuckle. They both moaned at the sensation, the hot, greedy grip of her passage sublime. He could feel her walls pulsing around him, and his cock thickened.

"You feel so good, Evangeline," he said.

Her hips rocked, sucking at his finger. "I need more of that."

With a groan, Gage pushed farther in, wishing it were his aching cock buried in all that wet, slick heat. Apparently, she must have been wishing the same, because the fingers on his length squeezed *hard*. Lightning arced up his spine, the pressure of her fist and the tight clasp of her silken depths too much to take. His eyes nearly rolled back in his head at the pleasure coursing through him, and when it broke, his entire body seized. Gage let out a muffled shout as he erupted, the white-hot bursts of his release making him see stars.

His fingers didn't stop their work, even when blinding light obliterated everything in his brain. After a few frantic strokes, his thumb grazing over her clitoris in time with the finger edging in and out, she went rigid, head falling onto his shoulder as her body convulsed around him in slow, sweet undulations that had his cock pulsing in renewed release. With nothing short of reverence, Gage rode out the orgasm with her until the last delightful ripple.

"You are a fucking goddess," he whispered.

"Gage," she said, her palm falling to stop the slow movements of his. "Too much."

His tongue would not be. He had the urge to drop to his knees, revel in the delightful mess he'd made. But such urges would have to wait for when he could take his time and enjoy it, when they were in private with no fear of interruption.

Instead, Gage dropped her skirts and banded his arm about her waist to draw her close. He felt sticky and damp in his trousers, but not even that could take away from the exquisite weight of her in his arms, sated and boneless.

"This is madness," she whispered after a beat, still breathless.

"What is?"

"This thing between us, admit it," she told him. "Have you ever felt anything like it with anyone else?" She shook her head, her chest rising and falling with each shallow breath. "It's like I can't control myself when I'm around you. Earlier...with the glove. Nothing like that has ever happened to me before. Is that normal?"

"No. I've never experienced anything like this either."

She turned to face him, her lovely face flush with the afterglow of her release. "Why do you think that is?"

"I don't know," he answered honestly.

He didn't have an answer that made sense. They were attracted to each other, but even attraction didn't always translate into explosive pleasure for all couples. The truth was they *connected* in a way that made any physical touch between them something more...something much too real. Something that felt *right*. But the rightness of what was growing between them was a perilous slope. Gage knew that as well as he knew his own weaknesses when it came to gambling. Because this was him gambling with so much more than just his body.

She did not want marriage or a husband. She fiercely valued her independence. He planned to return to Scotland. Their agreement was supposed to be a pleasurable interlude, but they hadn't even done the full deed, and already it was more complicated than he'd ever expected it to be. Evangeline Raine was fast becoming a delectable addiction.

One that might have the power to ruin him.

Chapter Sixteen

Evangeline arched her back and rolled the remaining kinks out of her neck as she mounted her horse with the help of her groom. She gave Ares a pat, glad that her favorite stallion had finally arrived to the mews in London. She hadn't been sure that she would be staying long enough to need him, but things had...changed. Not only because of her arrangement with Vale, but she was starting to view London in a different way.

A dangerously *enthralling* way.

Last evening was a prime example. She could not fathom that scandalous parties such as the one she'd attended on the duke's arm even existed. In truth, a part of her still wondered if it was all some lust-induced fever dream. Evangeline could not have imagined any of the staid, buttoned-up gentlemen and demure, proper ladies of the ton engaged in such lascivious activity, but she'd certainly recognized some of the men from a distance, and Vale had told her that a few of the ladies, masked as they'd been, were ones she'd likely been introduced to over her many seasons.

Evangeline's body gave the tiniest quiver at the memory of Vale's hands stroking over her most intimate parts. The thought of his long, thick finger inside of her had tortured her for hours after he'd returned her home, and for the life of her, Evangeline had not been able to settle into sleep. Her body had thrashed in her sheets, over-heated and feverish, desperate for *more*.

She wanted Vale. The gnawing need had left her aching and empty, with a void that not even her preferred instrument of self-pleasure had been able to appease. She wanted *him* to fill her, not some pale, cold reproduction.

And so a brisk, hard ride was just what she needed after a rather sleepless night. She took Ares out to Hyde Park at the break of dawn, where she rode among the grooms exercising their masters' mounts, but she paid them no mind. If any of them balked at seeing a lady riding astride, she had not given it much thought.

Evangeline thundered down Rotten Row, letting her body align with the gait of the horse, trusting him even as her ironclad command of him never wavered. Horses were magnificent and well trained, but giving them their heads made them unpredictable. She had been thrown once by a horse spooked by a snake and had learned that vital lesson early on.

Idly, as she rode Ares back home, she wondered if Vale would ever let her have such control. She'd read in a novel that some men liked women riding them in such a manner during sexual congress. Her ears flamed at the deeply provocative image that rose in her brain, and she shoved it away.

"I've missed you, boy," she told Ares, running a hand down his velvety neck as they returned to the mews. Her muscles felt warm, her brain clear when she handed him over to the waiting groom. "I'm glad you're here."

She also missed the animals at her shelter, but she couldn't very well bring them all to London, and she knew they were all in good hands with Hannah. It was hard enough with Lucky, especially when Evangeline had to be out socially and couldn't devote all her time to her.

The caretaker's latest message had said that nearly all of the kittens were settling in well, including Beasty Buttercup. She'd also mentioned that someone had inquired about rehoming her. That news had lodged a spike of melancholy into Evangeline's breast—she cherished the little monster. For obvious reasons.

Not just those involving a tall, brawny, very attractive duke.

It was good that someone wanted to adopt the kitten. If Viola didn't erupt into violent sneezing whenever she was around cats, Evangeline would have kept Buttercup for herself. But alas, until Viola made her match and married someone who wasn't Huntington, Evangeline would have to content herself with feline companionship at her shelter.

Speaking of the foundling home, Sarah Major had been a font of information, and Evangeline hoped to expand her own operations and secure more funding. If she could persuade her father to let her have her dowry, she'd be in a much better place financially, but she wondered if, like most fathers, he was holding on to the hope that she might eventually marry. His edict to accompany Viola to London suggested that, along with his fears that she would not be settled after he was gone.

After instructing the groom to give Ares a good rubdown, Evangeline made her way back inside. Only to be accosted by her sister.

"Where have you been, Effie?" Viola demanded. "Have you had breakfast? We are going to be late!"

Evangeline blinked. Late for what? Why was her sister even awake? It wasn't yet noon, and normally, she slept well past the midday hour on any given day. "Slow down. What are you going on about?"

"The fitting!" Viola practically screeched.

Oh. The fitting. They were being measured for more gowns, which Evangeline had completely forgotten, given her mind was rather occupied by other deliciously provocative things. As expected, Viola had been named the season's diamond, and since Evangeline was now of a mind to stay in London, additional gowns had to be commissioned. Thankfully, Laila had volunteered her services.

"Very well," she said. "Let me bathe, change, and join you in the breakfasting room."

"Hurry up then! Lady Marsden is making an exception for us. She told me she would give me some tips on my design ideas."

Evangeline blinked. When her sister had been in France, she'd been passionate about fashion, but that interest had seemed to disappear the moment she returned and set her sights on marriage. Was the renewed interest because of William? Evangeline smiled. "Did she? I'm sure Laila's eager to talk fashion now that she no longer designs for anyone but her close friends. That's wonderful for you, Viola."

After a quick wash—in water so purposely cold she felt it frost her bones—she dressed and headed downstairs. Her father was seated at the breakfast table, hidden behind his favorite newspaper, while Lucky lounged at his feet, waiting patiently for scraps.

"Good morning, Papa," she said as the dog raced over to greet her and Evangeline bent to give her a scratch. "Hullo, sweeting."

Viola sniffed from where she sat munching on a bit of toast. The earl looked up from his newssheets, his wire-rimmed spectacles perched on his nose and hair askew as if he'd scrubbed a palm through it one too many times. "Morning, dear girl."

"You look perturbed," Evangeline said, filling her plate with some eggs and fried sausage from the still-steaming dishes on the sideboard. Her mouth watered. Riding always made her work up an appetite.

"The Duke of Vale is in the papers," he said.

She startled and nearly dropped her plate. "Oh?" she said, hoping her voice conveyed enough disinterest, though her pulse had started teeming in her veins.

"He seemed quite interested in you at the ball the other night," her father said with a twinkle in his eye, making her stomach sink. "Should I finally expect a happy announcement this season?"

"No, Papa. He's a friend." She cleared her throat and took her seat while Lucky disappeared under the table. "A patron of my shelter, in fact."

"Friends can make excellent spouses," her father remarked, peering down again at the paper.

And also, excellent lovers. Evangeline felt her face flush and pressed her hands to her cheeks. She kept her voice even. "I shall keep that in mind, Papa."

Thankfully he didn't press the issue.

"Looks like there's to be an exhibition match at Lushing's boxing club. Lethe or some such." The earl frowned. "I thought that boy was done with that nonsense."

Which boy? Evangeline wondered, the duke or the earl, though neither of them were boys.

"Is Vale a contender?"

"Yes."

A trill of excitement spun through her at the thought of seeing that magnificent, muscular body in action, but the notion of Vale getting hurt left her a little queasy.

"Ugh," Viola said with disdain. "Boxing is so plebeian. Doesn't he know he's a *duke*? Dukes shouldn't conduct themselves in such a barbaric, *common* manner."

"Says who?" Evangeline said with an eye roll. "The self-aggrandizing patronesses of the ton?"

Viola leveled a censorious look at her sister. "Lord Huntington, if you must know." Evangeline narrowed her eyes, disheartened that the pox of a man was still an influence. "Honestly, Effie, you should pay heed to those very patronesses and rethink how much time you're spending with Vale. Not even the title of duchess is worth *that* cost. Any wife of his will surely be shunned from civil drawing rooms."

As if she wasn't already unwelcomed in their illustrious circles. Evangeline bristled, but what Viola was saying wasn't far off the mark. The gossip about the uncultured, destitute duke had been the sensation of the ton and the *Times* for months. "Is that your own opinion, Viola? Or are you regurgitating what those empty-headed busybodies are spreading?"

Her sister blushed and had the decency to look abashed. "Vale has always been polite to me, but he's not the right kind of duke, is he?"

"And what is that? A man like your precious Huntington?"

Viola's eyes narrowed. "Don't you dare, Effie! Lord Huntington is a gentleman with impeccable breeding."

"I know," Evangeline shot back. "Just ask him."

Their father sighed and set down his newssheets, rubbing the bridge of his nose. "Girls, please."

"Who is Vale up against?" she asked her father, shoveling food into her mouth so her warring emotions wouldn't betray her: anger at her sister's heedlessness where Huntington was concerned, fear and excitement for the duke, and a general malaise that she could not place.

"Jem Mace. A prizefighter trained by Nat Langham himself at the Cambrian Stores."

"What's that?" Viola asked, wrinkling her nose.

"It was a renowned fighting house that got shut down when Mr. Langham lost his license," Evangeline replied and then avoided her father's raised eyebrow as she fed Lucky a bit of sausage. She didn't want to go into how she even knew of such a disreputable place frequented by London's lower classes.

She'd heard the name, of course, from Vesper, who had made it her business to eavesdrop on her brother's notorious business dealings. Lushing's own boxing social club was on Upper St. Martin's Lane and inherited most of the displaced clientele that had wanted a new place to patronize. He'd obliged and reaped the profits ever since.

Vesper had eagerly informed their little group about some of the stories she had heard about Langham's infamous Rum-Pum-Pas club that had pandered to the ton's debauched tastes, where pugilists fought exhibition bouts in the nude and one could pay to fight if one had enough coin. She couldn't help inserting Vale's face in such a scandalous scenario and found herself growing short of breath and then choking on a mouthful of egg.

Served her right!

Her throat tightened as she coughed violently into her napkin.

"Goodness, Effie, swallow and then you won't gag," Viola said.

An image of Vale, nude and imposing in the center of a fighting ring with Evangeline on her knees about to do just that, filled her brain, and she let out a demented giggle-snort. An efficient footman instantly brought her a glass of water, and she guzzled it after thanking him. It was official. Her good sense was officially on hiatus.

They fell back to eating in silence until Viola let out an unlady-like shriek, making both Evangeline and their father jump. Shuddering, Viola drew up her feet in horror, right as Lucky let out a sharp whine and raced out of the room. "How did *that* creature get in here? And what are those ugly things behind it?"

Evangeline peered under the table and grinned at the sight of the hedgehog she'd rescued from being trampled on Rotten Row last season. Given its usefulness in the scullery, the kitchen staff had kept an eye on it. Her eyes widened in delight at the two tiny hoglets trundling along behind their mother. Pushing off her chair, she sank to the ground, gently stroking one of the babies. "Hullo, Mrs. Speckles. Who have you got with you?"

"Effie, you're eating," Viola said with a wrinkled nose. "Don't touch them! They're pests."

"They *consume* pests," Evangeline corrected. "They're rather useful animals. Many households keep them in their kitchens to control insects."

"Well, fine, but they should not be in the dining room. We could catch something!"

Evangeline stifled her eye roll, considering the suddenly fastidious Viola had been knee-deep in animal fluids at the shelter without complaint, and gestured for the footmen to gently remove the animals back to the kitchen. She excused herself to wash her hands before returning to her place to finish the rest of her meal.

When she was done, she stood and glanced at her sister. "Come on then, hurry up or we will be late."

"I'm not the one who was gallivanting across London on her horse all morning," Viola grumbled, though she pushed back her chair and followed.

"You should try it sometime."

Viola reared back as if Evangeline had suggested she wander outside without a stitch of clothing. "And get all sweaty? I think not!"

Evangeline frowned at the sudden switch in her sister's temperament. This didn't seem like the girl who'd spent time with her and William at the shelter. This reeked of the self-centered version of Viola who had been Huntington's influence. Why was it always two steps forward, ten steps back with her? Evangeline didn't remember being so fickle at that age.

"Sweat does wonders for a lady's complexion. And besides, healthy exercise is good for everyone. Perhaps you should ask William to give you a lesson or two. He's absolutely marvelous on horseback." Evangeline glanced over her shoulder, expecting Viola to retort with some flippant comment that she wasn't interested in riding or the tutor in question, but to her surprise, Viola wore an intrigued look that she immediately tried to hide.

Evangeline hid her own smile. Perhaps all wasn't lost, after all.

Walking back toward the table, she gathered up her father's discarded newssheets. "Are you done with these, Papa?"

The earl nodded, and Evangeline let out a breath of relief that he hadn't interrogated her more on why she wanted them. It wasn't uncommon for her to read the papers when he was finished—she liked to keep herself abreast of world news—but she felt like her true intentions were written all over her. She wanted to learn more about the forthcoming match.

Her eyes scanned the sheets after she settled herself into the carriage on the way to Lady Marsden's residence. The article went on to list statistics and measurements of each man. At over a hundred and sixty pounds, Jem Mace was about three stone lighter than the duke as well as several inches shorter. And from the glowing account in the piece, Mace was fast, flexible, and lethal. She let out a soft noise of concern.

Viola, who was more perceptive than their father, glared at her through narrowed eyes from across the coach. "Are you planning to go to that match? Is that why you pilfered those?"

"What's it to you if I did or not?" she replied.

Viola's mouth turned down. "I'll tell Papa."

Evangeline met her sister's eyes and lifted her brows. "Will you?" she said softly. "And what do you think will happen when he forbids me from going, sister dear? Or sends me back to Chichester because London is simply too much for my poor, delicate constitution? What will happen to your precious season then?"

"You wouldn't!"

"Charity goes both ways, Viola." With a wink, Evangeline shook out the edges of the folded paper and opened it wide. "If I'm to stay in London, then it will be on my terms. If I choose to go to a public house or even a brothel, then it is no one's business but mine." She speared her gawking sister with a meaningful look. "If you expect me to pander to your whims, Viola dear, then you must also do your part."

"Going to that match is unseemly! What will people think?"

Evangeline let out a small sigh though she, too, once upon a time, had obsessed over the ton's shallow opinions. "I suppose the same cruel things they have always said about my person. You cannot let yourself be ruled by what others say, Viola. You can only be true to yourself. Anything else leads to misery."

"Says the woman who is practically a social outcast."

Evangeline shrugged. "At least I live life on my own terms."

"By cavorting in seedy establishments?"

If her outraged sister only knew what kind of establishments she had recently frequented, she would have a fit of the vapors. "By pleasing myself."

Evangeline understood Viola's fears—it was ingrained in the female aristocrat from birth how and *who* she must be. Be demure. Be obedient. Be respectful. Don't veer from the path or risk outrage and ostracism. Follow the rules. Speak only when spoken to. Dance the requisite number of times. Never have an original opinion. And most of all, never *ever* demonstrate superiority to a man.

Unless he was a man like Vale. He *enjoyed* her opinions. He encouraged them. He valued her idiosyncrasies. He made *her* think highly of them. With Vale, her mind had no narrow boundaries to obey, no absurd directions to follow. She could speak her thoughts without fear of recrimination or without being labeled a shrew, a bluestocking, or *ghastly*.

That acceptance was more precious to her than any arrangement between them.

"It's simply not *done*, Effie," Viola protested.

Evangeline peered at her over the top edge of the newssheet, her voice soft. "Don't you ever get tired of doing everything you're told? We women have our own minds and our own dreams. Shouldn't we get a chance to follow those?"

Her sister did not answer, but Evangeline could see her brain working as she gave a dismissive huff and stared out the window.

Viola might be silly at times, but she wasn't stupid. Like many other young women of her station, she had been indoctrinated in how she should think, speak, and feel. Going against that ideology felt frightening.

Evangeline worried that her sister, despite being surrounded by admirers, did not have any true bosom friends, ones who would stick with her until the end. Without Vesper, Laila, Briar, and Nève, Evangeline would not have survived the cruel vagaries of the ton.

"Do you even like Huntington?" she asked her sister.

"He's the catch of the season," Viola said, gnawing her lip. "I'm its diamond, so naturally we're expected to pair off. I want the best."

She exhaled. "You do deserve the best, but is that man the best for *you*?" Evangeline lowered her voice when her sister didn't answer. "You don't have to do what they want, Viola," she said quietly. "Not Papa, not Huntington, not anyone else in the ton."

Her sister's response was nearly inaudible. "But what if they cut me?"

"What if they don't? What if you chart a new path? Being a diamond isn't all it's cracked up to be if you can't be your true self." She let out an exhale. "We can't live our lives in the land of negative conjecture. We'd never try anything new if that were the case. It's easy to be meek and follow. It's much harder to be bold and lead."

"Is that what you've been doing?"

Evangeline shook her head. "Not always, but I am trying."

She had always been different—a square peg that never quite fit in, and while she had learned to accept her differences, she'd begun to actually appreciate them of late. Perhaps because the Duke of Vale didn't see her as any less because of them. He saw her as so much *more*. She might not be a diamond, but she still had value.

Their conversation ended as they came to a stop outside the Marquess and Marchioness of Marsden's palatial residence. Just as they were about to exit the coach, her sister took hold of her hand and squeezed.

"If you do go to the match, promise me you'll be careful," Viola whispered before descending. "Not because of your reputation or mine, but it could be dangerous for a woman in your position."

Evangeline nodded, struck by her sister's concern. "I will."

"Effie?"

Perched in the doorway, she glanced down into Viola's brilliant blue eyes. "Yes?"

Viola gnawed on her lip, but then smiled. "You are an extraordinarily courageous woman. I might not always tell you so, and you are decidedly odd with your penchant to collect random animals, but I hope you know that."

Evangeline could only stare in dumbfounded silence after her sister.

Chapter Seventeen

The Earl of Lushing's club was packed. Gage could hear the bois-terous cheering from where he was warming up. He had only agreed to Lushing's request because he did owe the man a favor for offering up the invitation to the masked event with Evangeline, but fortunately, it was a friendly, amicable exhibition.

He shouldn't have been surprised by the turnout. A fight with Jem Mace, who'd won the title of heavyweight champion of En-gland a handful of years ago from Sam Hurst, would have drawn an enormous mob. The man was a bull in the ring, trained by Nat Langham himself. It would probably be a bloodbath, considering Gage was nowhere near fighting form.

Rolling out the knots in his neck and shoulders, Gage continued to loosen up his body in preparation. He needed this. He needed the challenge to get his mind clear. Recently, his goals had become muddled, especially with his growing feelings toward a certain beautiful and alluring heiress that weren't impartial in the least. Keeping her busy for six weeks had changed into him wanting to keep her for a good deal longer than that.

Some people could save their emotions from getting tangled up in purely physical liaisons, but Gage was evidently not one of them.

The more he had of her and the more Evangeline shared with him, the more he craved. He wanted her body, her beautiful brain, her smiles, her caustic wit, her generosity of spirit…all of her.

And that terrified him.

Because he had to stay focused on what he was here for: three more weeks to resolve Asher's debt. Huntington was sure to be here at the fight tonight. The man could not stay away from a chance to throw around his status like the privileged fop he was. Gage's fingers clenched. What he wouldn't give to be facing him in the ring instead!

"Are you ready?" Lushing asked, coming into the room on a roar of noise from the adjacent hall. "It is a madhouse in there." A wide grin stretched his face, and Gage rolled his eyes. The amount of money he would be earning was no doubt responsible for that shit-eating grin.

Gage snorted. "To be pummeled into meal, why, of course. It's my life goal to be a champion's punching bag."

"It's an exhibition match, Vale," Lushing replied with a careless wave of his hand. "You're a duke. Mace knows that."

"Only skill and strength matter once in the ring."

Lushing laughed and patted Gage on the shoulder. "Just don't get knocked out in the first round. I've a few thousand quid riding on you making it to ten."

"Only *ten*? You wound me, old friend." He'd be lucky if he lasted five rounds.

"Money is king."

Gage let out a laugh. In Lushing's world—and his as well—wealth was important. He needed it to clear Asher's debt as well as to take care of his estates and his tenants, but he wasn't doing this for the coin. Other than a favor to his friend, he had no stake in the fight. Win or lose, the outcome didn't matter to him.

Why not? a voice taunted.

It would be so easy to make his own bet and not have Huntington's agreement hanging over him. Then he could have Evangeline and be in the clear. Gage hissed out a tight breath. It would be only one time...

No. He swore to himself he'd never gamble, and that was one oath he refused to break.

When he walked out toward the ring, the roars were deafening. People were crammed in from corner to corner. Even the upper mezzanine was packed with standing room only. A man dressed in a florid waistcoat sauntered into his path.

"Ready to lose, Vale?" Huntington drawled with a pugnacious smile. "I've a fortune wagered on you getting knocked out in any of the first three rounds."

His fists balled. Punching a peer with no outward provocation was a crime. "Hope you brought a full purse."

"Lose the fight and I'll make it worth your while," the bastard said in a low voice.

Gage's lip curled. "As much as you think I can be bought by your filthy money, Huntington, I am not a cheat."

"You're just like your foolish brother." Huntington leered. "He never knew when to cut his losses either."

"What the fuck did you just say?" Gage growled, but Lushing's firm hand steered him toward the ring. He didn't have time to do anything but meet his opponent face-to-face, fury boiling over in his blood.

"Mace," he grunted in greeting to the waiting boxer.

The man nodded. "Vale."

As expected, once the fight started and the first round began, his rage at Huntington morphed into motivation, and his vision tunneled into intense focus. Jem Mace, despite knowing that Gage was a peer of the realm, would not go easy on him. Champion pugilists weren't built that way. Grunting, Gage took a deflected punch to his abdomen and then feinted right, ducking as he got in a strike of his own that glanced off Mace's arm.

Within seconds, Gage recognized Mace's superior skill. His adversary was also in peak physical condition. It made little difference that Mace was shorter and smaller. He was agile, skilled, and experienced, his fists snapping out with unerring accuracy and his feet in constant motion. But Gage had the advantage of muscle and brute force. One punch, delivered correctly, could be the end of the match. There was no way, however, he'd be that lucky.

Mace was too good.

Sparring, they circled each other, and the first round went into five, then six, and then seven. The thirty seconds of rest between each round were barely enough to catch his breath before going back to the scratch line in the middle of the ring for the next. Lushing would be happy, Gage thought idly, as he blinked blood out of one eye. They were in the tenth.

The noise was earsplitting, the crowd rowdy and sotted. Out of the corner of his eye, he could see money changing hands as the predictions of the match changed with each second, each punch, grapple, and tug. And then he caught a glimpse of a shard of moonlight that shouldn't be in such a place.

The left hook that Mace landed to his temple would have knocked him out, if it hadn't been for his sideways sway. Gage stumbled back, a blurry gaze scanning the crowd as if in defiance of the blow that would have felled a lesser man. *There!* His stare swiveled back to stop on a pale beauty, hidden in the deep cowls of a cloak, but Gage would recognize her anywhere.

What the devil was Evangeline doing here?

She and the lady beside her—Lady Briar, if he wasn't mistaken— were intent on the fight, unaware of the criminals and lowlifes surrounding them. The look on Evangeline's face was indescribable. Fascination warred with horror as that silver-blue gaze met his and fled when he roared in anger and frustration.

"Who's *that* bit of muslin?" Mace taunted, catching his stare.

"No one to you."

The man had the audacity to laugh. "Bet if I won the fight, she could be someone to me. Ladies of quality like a bit of rough in a champion."

Red filled his vision like a cloud. Gage knew it was a mistake as soon as he put himself in striking range of Mace's fists and took a teeth-shattering blow to the chin. Luckily, he landed an answering gut punch that made the other man wheeze. It was worth it to see Mace sucking wind, but fuck, his jaw was going to be sore. His head felt as though it'd been crushed beneath a boulder.

Gage tried to center on the fight, but throughout most of the sixteenth round, his concentration was half pulled toward the upper mezzanine. Lushing must have noticed his earlier distraction and was there now, thank God, and seemed to be in a ferocious argument with Lady Briar. Evangeline only had eyes for him, gloved hands gripping the railing. He ground his molars, his own fierce gaze promising retribution, but her chin only went higher.

That brazen little vixen.

In the next round, it was a miracle that Gage managed to avoid the next few rushes, shifting and bobbing, while he muddled through his own dwindling offense. His jabs were short and powerful when they landed. His opponent was bleeding from his lip, and one eye was swollen shut. Mace was quick and flexible, but he had a predictable fighting pattern, particularly a combination of a two-step feint, jab, weave, and hard punch with his left. That had to be his opening into the man's unbreachable defense.

In the eighteenth round, Mace grinned through a mouthful of bloody teeth, dancing from one foot to the other. "Want to throw in the sponge and go rescue your ladybird?"

"You wish."

"Or is she the earl's jade? Looks like Lushing's got her good."

His glance up to where he'd seen her last—*nowhere near Lushing*—was automatic and indubitably stupid. Mace's fist crashed hard into his ribs, sending him stumbling back into the ropes. Dimly, he heard a female scream amid the roar of noise, but a jab to the cheek had him reeling. Gage saw stars, black spots dancing in his vision, as he lunged toward Mace. The man dodged, and then started the combination that Gage had noticed before. Two steps, feint. Gage bobbed away from the jab, waited, and once Mace weaved, he struck as hard as he could.

The clip with his right to the side of Mace's nose had a spray of blood flying across the worn mat. It also dropped his opponent to the ground. It wasn't a knockout as he'd hoped. Within seconds, Mace wobbled to his feet, blinking to get his bearings. Twenty fucking rounds and still going. Gage blew out an exhausted breath. There wasn't much more left in him, and Mace had been known to go to forty-three rounds before. Perhaps Gage *should* throw in the sponge.

Suddenly a whistle blew, and pandemonium erupted. "Police!"

In a panic, his blurry eyes scanned the maddened crowd as they rushed around in a frenzy trying to escape arrest. Hadn't Lushing put measures in place with the Metropolitan Police? And where in the hell was Evangeline?

"Fucking capital, mate!" the earl roared, suddenly at his side as the throng went wild.

"Where's she?" he mumbled, shoving past him.

Lushing's grin vanished. He knew exactly who Gage meant. "Safe. Trust me, she and that reckless brat, Briar, are in a world of trouble for coming here. Follow me. My men are already stalling the police. I'll get a doctor to see to your injuries."

Blood pounding, he followed Lushing through several tunnels and ended up in a ladies' salon filled with agitated women. The earl had created the retiring area for his female members, and with a wild gaze Gage scanned the room, looking for that distinct head of moonlit hair.

Where *was* she?

"She's not here, Vale," Lady Briar said, coming to his side. Her eyes were wide as she took in his bare and bloodied chest. His state of undress was outrageous, especially among gently bred, unmarried ladies, but Gage did not care. If they were *here*, in Lushing's enterprise, they were most likely not the swooning sort.

"Where then?" he grunted.

"Upstairs, second room on the right," she replied without hesitation.

He took the stairs three at a time, ignoring the ache in his cracked ribs, and smashed open the door that Lady Briar had indicated. Relief poured through him when he caught sight of his quarry standing near the window. She turned, her beautiful face filled with concern. A maid hovered in one corner.

"Get out," he told the young woman, watching as she scurried from the room with an alarmed squeak.

"Vale, she has to stay," Evangeline began, but he cut her off with another irate look.

"Give me one good reason," he bit out and kicked the door shut behind him, "why you've put yourself in this kind of danger?"

Evangeline gulped.

She had no idea why his growled demands made her core tremble. Her brain was going haywire at the look of him, feral and bruised and so sodding attractive she couldn't find enough air to fill her lungs if she tried. Blood, sweat, and grime streaked him, and she'd never found him more seductive.

Watching him in that ring—the ease and primal power with which he'd faced his opponent—had both shocked and thrilled her. She had winced each time he'd taken a blow, but watching his huge body in action had made parts of her ache with unfulfilled want.

"I've had a bath drawn for you and the doctor will be by soon," she croaked.

He prowled toward her, and her breath snagged in her throat. "I do not want a bath."

Lord, the gravelly burr had her knees quaking beneath her skirts. She resisted the urge to flee, standing her ground when he stalked closer. The musky male scent of his sweat assailed her senses. She should be repulsed, but instead she was aroused. A strangled breath left her lips. Vale looked unhinged as though the slightest movement on her part would cause him to pounce. Was he still in fight mode?

And if he was, why did that excite her so?

"Why did you come?" he demanded, and it jolted her into action. Rounding the armchair, she stepped out of his reach. "Do you think that chair will save you?"

She bit her lip, having seen his strength in action and knowing he could lift the furniture with one hand if he wanted. "No, but perhaps you will be in a better mood once you've had some time to think."

"You still haven't answered me, Evangeline."

This time, her shudder was full body at the dark resonance of her name on his tongue. What was *wrong* with her? She was a strong woman with her own will who did *not* tremble at the sinful tone of a man's voice. "I do not need to give you a reason, Your Grace. I wanted to see the match, so here I am."

Wrong answer.

His green eyes darkened to the hue of a roiling ocean, as if Poseidon himself were about to rise from its murky depths. "Do you know the kind of danger you were in?"

"I was positively safe, I assure you."

Stormy eyes slitted. "In a den full of ruffians and thugs?"

"Don't be so dramatic," she said with a dismissive sniff that belied her churning insides. "It's Lushing's club, Vale, and I was surrounded by other gentlemen and ladies. Besides, I can protect myself."

With one swift move, he lifted the chair to one side, leaving her open to him. That chair had to weigh a considerable amount, and he'd just moved it as though it were a feather. And from the way he carried himself, she knew he had to be injured.

"Dramatic?" he echoed softly.

Oh, hellfire.

He was a coiled beast getting ready to spring, and she was his target.

But Evangeline was saved from enduring the brunt of his displeasure when the door opened and Lushing strolled in with both the ousted maid and the doctor. His eyes widened at the fraught scene, a low chortle leaving him.

"You two are lucky I'm not a stickler for the rules of the ton, or I'd have the good doctor here perform marriage rites instead." They both leveled him with identical glares, and he threw his hands into the air. "I'm being practical here."

The duke turned that turbulent stare back to her. "This isn't finished."

Reaching for patience, Evangeline walked over to where the earl stood as the doctor took her place to evaluate Gage's condition. She probably should have gathered her wits and left when she had the chance—for modesty's sake, at least—but for some reason, she didn't want him out of her sight, even if he was being insufferable. From what she could overhear while facing the window, he was as much of a grouchy bear to the poor doctor as he'd been to her, answering in monosyllabic grunts and growling when prodded too hard.

After a lengthy examination, the doctor cleared his throat and beckoned Lushing. "Apart from the cut on his brow, which I've cleaned and disinfected, he has three bruised ribs as well as a possible concussion," he said. "All in all, I'd say he was lucky it wasn't much worse. I would suggest some laudanum for the pain, but His Grace has refused." Evangeline knew the duke would decline. Laudanum was as bad as spirits. "Rest would be a good alternative," the doctor said.

"Minthe," Lushing addressed the maid. "Can you show the good doctor out?"

She bobbed a curtsy. "Yes, my lord."

"You, too, Lushing," Vale ground out. When Evangeline moved to leave with the earl, an ominous growl stopped her in her tracks. "Not you."

"Vale, this is not proper," Lushing said, pausing.

"Fuck what's proper. Get out. She stays."

Evangeline met the earl's eyes. "I'll be fine," she assured him.

"Effie—" he began, clearly uneasy at leaving her and an unmarried and *underdressed* gentleman together, but she lifted a palm.

"Lord Lushing, I appreciate your concern, but what I do with my own person is my business. I am safe with him, as you well know."

"But your reputation—"

"Is *my* affair." Her tone was gentle but firm.

With a fulminating look in Vale's direction that promised retribution if he did step out of line, the earl bowed and exited the room, but left the door open a crack. Evangeline rolled her eyes and kicked it shut with her heel. Her eyes met Vale's, who was watching her with an unreadable expression.

She made her way across the room and into the connected bathing chamber, adding more hot water to the bath she'd had drawn, and returned to the bedroom. Vale had not moved, but she caught a wince as he cradled his bruised ribs.

"Bathe now," she said softly. "I'll get you something to eat."

She braced for argument, but after a labored exhale, he pushed upright and moved past her into the chamber. What she wouldn't give to follow, knowing exactly what lay hidden beneath those snug fawn-colored breeches. *He's injured, you half-wit!*

Shaking her head at her utterly untimely thoughts, she opened the door and conveyed instructions to the nearby footman for food to be sent to the room. She had half expected the earl to still be lurking, ready to defend her precious virtue, but Lushing was nowhere to be seen.

Evangeline glanced down the quiet, thickly carpeted corridor and wondered what this level of the club was for, and then blushed at her own stupidity. Privacy? Elegantly furnished bedrooms? Of course it had to be for intimate liaisons.

Heavens, was the Earl of Lushing running a brothel above his club?

A frown creased her brow. Craning her ears, she didn't hear nary a moan that might accompany such a place. The floor didn't seem to be occupied, but that could have been because of the police raid. She blew out a breath. She was lucky that she and Briar hadn't been crushed in the mass exodus, but clearly Briar knew more about this secret club than she'd been letting on, which was curious in itself.

When the food came—swiftly, steaming hot, and ferried by the maid from earlier—she thanked the young woman as she settled the dishes onto the table near the window. For the first time, Evangeline noticed Minthe's dress, likely because she was not bamboozled by Vale's presence. It was expensive, low-cut, and not at all the kind of clothes a servant would wear. Perhaps Evangeline had been mistaken about the girl's position. "In what capacity do you work here, Minthe?"

The girl's smile was coquettish. "In whatever capacity my lord requires, my lady."

Evangeline blinked. Well, *that* was illuminating. Minthe's polished speech suggested that she was educated, and Evangeline's mind swiftly considered the significance. Pretty, refined, and obviously not ill-treated. Thanks to Briar, she'd read quite a lot about the plight of women who were forced into terrible circumstances. This woman, however, did not seem to be unhappy or forced into anything. "Are you compensated well?"

"Very well."

Minthe's throaty innuendo was not missed.

"And you're here by choice?"

A smiling Minthe nodded. "Her ladyship is an excellent employer."

Evangeline blinked. Her *ladyship*? Didn't Lushing own the place? "Did you mean his lordship?"

"There's a lady *and* a lord, but it's nice working for a female who runs her own business and cares about the lot of us. Lord Lushing doesn't really have a say. He's more of the face of the place, while the lady is its spine."

Well, that was curious. Who on earth was Lushing in partnership with? Perhaps Minthe had used *lady* loosely and the true owner wasn't an aristocrat. But if she was...how scandalous!

"Thank you, Minthe."

The girl bobbed. "Let me know if His Grace requires assistance with the bath."

A sound that resembled an actual growl slid from her chest, prompting Minthe to back away with a wide grin. Mortified,

Evangeline turned to the delivered dishes, only relaxing when she heard the soft click of the door. Goodness, one moment she was respecting Minthe for her choices, and the next, she was ready to drag the woman out by her hair for doing what she was probably paid well to do. Was Vale a regular here? Just because he was a virgin didn't mean he wasn't experienced.

Oh, button it, you needy twit!

What did it matter if he was a member or not? His habits and proclivities were not her concern.

When the duke emerged with damp hair and a scrubbed face, wearing nothing but a gold and black banyan that spawned a hundred more wicked fantasies in her head, Evangeline felt her cheeks flame. Pinning her lips, she prepared him a plate in silence, a bit of game pie, spiced beef, and toasted mushrooms. "Eat," she told him.

"You seem to enjoy giving me orders," he said, pulling out a chair for her before taking his own.

"What's not to like?" she said. "Having a celebrated pugilist biddable, compliant, and entirely at my mercy is any lady's dream."

Green eyes flared, a dark flush tinting his freshly scrubbed cheekbones. "I am not of the mind to be at anyone's mercy. I am still furious with you for putting yourself in danger."

"And yet, you have no grounds for that, Your Grace." She smiled to soften the blow of her words. "You are neither my father nor my husband."

He finished his mouthful. "I'm not allowed to care what happens to you?"

The unguarded response made her falter. She sucked in a breath, ruthlessly squashing the breathless feelings expanding in her chest. "Veering down that path would be an irredeemable mistake, Your

Grace. For both of us. We agreed that this would be a platonic adventure."

Vale stared at her, so many unsaid things in that single glance, but they were feelings that neither of them could express...or perhaps *should* express.

"Speaking of adventure," he said eventually. "Are you free next week?"

She blinked, mind going to the mountain of invitations that her sister had insisted they accept. The last fortnight had become a blur of balls, soirees, musicales, endless garden parties, and tedious operas. On occasion, she was saved from boredom by her friends as well as the occasional escape to Mary Tealby's shelter home, where she volunteered whenever they needed extra help.

But her friends had their own, full lives. Vesper, who had just announced she was with child, seemed to be casting up her accounts at every turn; Nève was constantly back and forth in Paris, assisting with her sister's ballet school; Laila was busy being a mother; and Briar was off on her marches condemning the patriarchy and scoffing at any event celebrating the archaic marriage mart.

"I was thinking of going back to Chichester soon," Evangeline admitted, though she didn't reveal the full reason behind it—that she was petrified of what consummation with Vale meant to her heart. Already, it seemed to be unreasonably possessive, and that was alarming in the extreme. Vale wasn't *hers*. "I'll ask the girls to chaperone Viola or pay someone if they can't. I'm not needed here, and well, my shelter is important to me."

Was that a sheen of panic in those green eyes? "You can't leave. Not yet. And besides, we have to fulfill our...er...agreement."

Her cheeks heated. "You're injured, so I assume that might be a challenge."

"Barely bruised," he replied. "Please don't go. Stay until next week, at least."

She started to shake her head and then stopped. Everything inside of her felt needlessly jumbled. The astonishing spike of possessiveness with Minthe had troubled her, and the duke's soft words about being allowed to care had burrowed under her skin and arrowed directly to the yearning organ in her chest. She *should* say no and leave...save herself before she sank too deep.

"Why? What's next week?" she asked instead.

"The Henley Royal Regatta." With the slightest wince, the duke propped his arm on one bent knee. "I'm racing on the first day with Lushing, Marsden, and Greydon for sport. It would be...nice if you were there to cheer us on."

Pleasure filled her at the request, and Evangeline warmed at the dull flush that deepened his cheekbones. This did not seem like an offer bound by the nature of their arrangement. It felt like a sentimental invitation. As though perhaps, just maybe, he *wanted* her there.

Her good sense told her to refuse, to keep it impersonal, but her silly, foolish heart bullied its way forward. "I would love to."

CHAPTER EIGHTEEN

It was revoltingly hot for July, and not even the slight breeze off the Thames made the stifling air any cooler. His broad-striped blue-and-white jersey and flannel trousers clung to his skin, but thankfully, Gage wasn't the only one suffering, as Greydon wore a disgusted face while yanking at his own snug neckline, and Marsden swiped a damp handkerchief over his head, soaking up the beads of sweat on his brow. Lushing, of course, looked as collected and dapper as ever as he sipped from a hip flask with no sign of discomfort whatsoever.

Gage raised a brow.

"Mother's milk," the earl replied, holding it out in offering, but Gage shook his head. Even if he did drink, alcohol in sweltering weather was a terrible idea. "If my blood's hotter than the air, then I feel nothing," Lushing explained.

"That makes no sense," Marsden said before accepting the flask and taking a deep draft. He groaned immediately as if regretting the sip. "Your theory better work. When's the first heat for our challenge?"

"We go at half past two, which is in an hour," Lushing said, snorting as Greydon refused the flask as well and passed it back to him. "Never thought I'd see the day when my best friend was henpecked by my sister."

The duke scowled. "Not henpecked. She's pregnant. I'd rather not have her spew on me at the smallest hint of whisky. Learned that lesson the hard way the other night. I'll pass, thank you."

"Well pulled, London!" Lushing bellowed when two vessels rounded the bend.

Gage watched as the boats raced past them nearly neck and neck for the Diamonds, the watermen moving in tandem, their oars cutting into the water with precision. Cheers and screams filled the air from the motley crowd on the banks. Smaller boats clogged the waterline but left the main pathway for the contest clear.

The regatta had been Lushing's idea. He'd somehow been roped into a bullish wager with Huntington, of all people. Both members of the London Rowing Club, they had managed to secure a time for the friendly competition, and honestly, Gage had his doubts about their chances of winning. They had not trained together, so the race was going to be either a massive surprise or a colossal disaster.

"Where have the ladies gone, do you know? My marchioness was rather excited to see us win today." Marsden cupped a hand over his brow, looking out toward the crowded banks of the Thames.

Gage forced himself not to follow the man's gaze, although he was desperate to know whether Evangeline had kept her promise to attend. He'd seen her sister Viola earlier fawning over Huntington, so he knew Evangeline might not be far behind. He ignored the thump of his heart in his chest and the urge to search for her.

"They are headed to the grandstand near the Red Lion, I believe, so they can see the end of the race." Greydon pointed to the spectator marquee that had been erected on the lower bank. It was much too crowded for him to distinguish any singular person, and Gage couldn't depend on seeing Evangeline's distinctive hair, as most of the ladies were wearing enormous bonnets and carrying parasols.

Maybe she hadn't come. Squashing the disappointment he felt, he rolled his neck and cracked his fingers. "Tell me again why we're doing this?" he groused.

"For the glory!" Lushing lifted his flask and winked. "And maybe two thousand quid. That sniveling jackanapes, Huntington, better be good for it."

Gage frowned at the number. It could hardly be a coincidence, considering that was the exact amount Asher had owed Huntington. Was it some sort of message? No, Huntington was not that clever. His thoughts were interrupted by the arrival of the clerk of the course, who'd come to review the rules for the friendly amateur club race. He went over the starting place, downstream at Temple Island, and the end goal, which was just in front of the Red Lion Hotel, nearly a mile and a third of distance.

Gage hoped they had the stamina for it. Not that any of them were men of excess or indulgence, but sculling required experience not to crash into the booms that separated the competing boats, listening to the coxswains, and aiming to keep the same rhythm. Thank God they had all done it at university, albeit for different teams. Rowing was like riding a horse—one never truly forgot how.

At least, that was the hope.

Needing to clear his head, Gage walked the short distance from his crew to the area where the boats were being readied in the water, one on the Buckinghamshire side and the other on the Berkshire, known as Bucks and Berks respectively. What looked like a man swimming away from the bow of their craft caught his attention, but before he could call out, the swimmer disappeared behind another boat.

Gage blinked. Perhaps someone had fallen in from one of the

surrounding craft. It was a wonder more people didn't drown from the copious amount of alcohol that was flowing, causing them to do stupid things. Striding past a group of drunken onlookers, he squinted as the blond, drenched man climbed from the water some distance away and melted into the crowd.

"*You're* racing?" a sneering voice asked.

He turned to see Huntington, dressed in a light blue jersey and flanked by some of his mates all wearing the same toffee-nosed expressions. Gage lifted a brow at Huntington's surprise. Maybe the two thousand was simply a coincidence. "Scared?"

Huntington laughed. "Of you? I shall take great pleasure in trouncing your crew and fattening my pockets while I'm at it."

"You'll need more than luck to win."

The man did not even flinch, though a smile curled his lips. "Haven't you heard, Vale? I am unbeatable even against the worst odds. I'm a man who makes my own luck." He sniffed and beckoned to Viola, who was standing behind him. "Come away, Viola. I've heard misery and misfortune are catching." He sauntered away, but not before Gage caught a look of revulsion crossing Viola's face just as it was smoothed away by a false smile.

When the umpire gave the call for the start of the race, Gage tried to shake off his worry about the swimmer and joined the rest of the crew, but the bad feeling remained. He took his spot at the center seat and grabbed hold of the oars.

"Something doesn't feel right," he said, having long learned to trust his instincts.

Two seats ahead, Lushing craned his neck over his shoulder. "It's nerves. You'll get into your stride once we get going. Let's crush these nurslings."

Gage didn't have time to voice any more concerns, as the race began, and all he could hear and feel were the brutal splash of the water and the answering burn of his lungs. The bruises on his ribs ached dully with each movement of his arms, but he'd taken some willow bark tea that morning to lessen the pain. Thankfully, his concussion was gone. His muscles stretched from the exertion as the skiff pulled forward and then inched back with each effort. Lushing was right; Gage's brain fell into an instinctive mode, following the rhythmic calls of the steersman.

"Pull, lads, pull!" he shouted. "Coming up to Barrier!"

It was one of the first progress markers, and Huntington's team had already gained some yards on them.

"We're taking on the drink!" one of the oarsmen yelled behind him. Marsden, it sounded like. "There's a nail or stud loose!"

The disturbance caused them to flounder in rhythm, leaving them to lag even farther behind while the mistake was corrected by the frantic coxswain. "Pick her up, Brightley! Stroke, lads! We're gaining, up, up!"

They weren't gaining. They were slowing.

The man in the water from earlier niggled at him.

"Marsden," Gage shouted over his shoulder. "Pull your oars up and reach down to where you see the water." He felt the slack when Marsden's oars retracted and the rightward drag when his hand plunged into the river.

"Fawley," the steersman shouted, indicating the second progress marker.

"By God, there's something down here," the marquess barked, grunting as he yanked upward from the underside of the boat. "Metal piling tied to a rope! Someone's trying to bloody sink us."

That no-good sodding cheat! Gage knew it had to be Huntington. The extra weight would have been enough to give the opposing
team a slender margin of a lead, but the loss of Marsden while he
detached the line had cost them dearly.

"Throw it out and plug the goddamned hole, if you can, then
pull, men, pull!" Lushing roared. "No way we're giving up now!"

The boat pressed forward with renewed force, closing the distance to the rear of Huntington's boat. They were still more than
a full length behind. Gage gritted his teeth, redoubling his efforts
despite the now excruciating throb in his injured ribs. The bridge—
and the finish line—loomed in the distance. Their vessel pulled
alongside Huntington's team, the boats lurching forward and then
surging back. The opposing team's faces were grim, mouths open
and nostrils flared, their boat only a yard ahead.

"Pull, Vale! Pull!" a woman screamed.

The roar of the crowd above him at the bridge where carriages
lined its surface narrowed to a single voice that sounded like music
to his ears, and Gage looked up to catch a flicker of bright hair
beneath a wide-brimmed bonnet and a smile so broad, he felt it
echo on his own face.

She'd come!

Hell if his arms didn't feel like noodles and his ribs like an elephant
had decided to park its arse upon his chest, but he gave everything
he had, and when the bang of a cannon shot across the river past the
bridge over the howls and the hollers, they were ahead by a nose.

They had bloody won!

"Well done, gents!" Lushing panted as they rowed slowly to the
bank and disembarked.

But Gage was intent on one man. Ignoring his cramping upper

body, he stalked across the way to where Huntington was standing with his own crew, a rancid look on his face at the loss.

"I know what you did, you louse of a man," he snarled. "With the weight and the hole in our hull."

"Careful, Vale," Huntington sneered, eyes darting around. "Don't forget who's paying your bills."

Gage didn't care who heard. His fingers curled at his sides. He wanted to pound the cheating sack of shit into the earth, but he settled for a different kind of blow...one to the man's ego. "You've barely made inroads into your so-called suit, considering all the time you spend in darkened arbors with other women. Ticktock, Huntington. Your six-week marker is coming up fast." It gave him great satisfaction to see the cad lose his smile. "You are nothing but a disgraceful cheat, and the truth will come out sooner or later."

"Where's your proof?"

Gage scowled. He had none. It was only his word about the man he'd seen in the river, and anyone could have planted the weight, which Marsden had tossed into the river for the sake of the race. Any evidence of wrongdoing was at the bottom of the Thames.

"Is everything all right?" a female voice asked, making them both turn.

Lady Viola was followed by her sister, who had asked the question. Evangeline had brought Lucky, he noticed, as the small dog stayed close to her on a short leash. To Gage's surprise, Viola did not rush forward to console Huntington but seemed intent on remaining at Evangeline's side. Curious.

"Fine," Huntington snapped. "Don't you know better than to have your blade of a nose in everything?"

Gage bristled at his tone toward Evangeline, but to her credit, Evangeline only arched a silver-blond brow in amusement. "Don't *you* know better than to be such a sore loser, my lord? I'm sure the duke and his crew will give you a rematch and a chance to earn back your pride soon."

Huntington's nostrils flared, rage snapping across his face, but with an avid audience close, he could not say anything that would land him in poor light. "Viola, come!"

While Evangeline had kept her composure when he'd talked down to her, Evangeline's jaw went hard at his attitude toward her sister. Her cool expression went positively glacial after Huntington slammed a hand onto Viola's arm, yanking her toward him. Lucky gave a loud growl, the dog's fur practically standing on end at the man's aggression. Gage stepped in front of Evangeline as she moved toward Huntington, her face a mask of fury.

"Release the lady, sir," he snapped.

A muscle flexed in the man's jaw, his fingers tightening, and Gage felt his own muscles coil in readiness when Viola's pained hiss cut through the air. Fuck, he was going to put that bastard on his arse. How dare he manhandle a woman? Gage stepped forward, and in that instant, Huntington released his grip. "No harm done."

No harm done? Gage stared incredulously at Huntington as Viola rubbed her sore arm. "I should teach you a fucking lesson in manners."

Huntington gave a dismissive laugh, though it was obvious he was simmering with rage...and something else. Fear? Dread? "I'd hardly take lessons from a Highland bumpkin like you, Vale, but keep thinking you're on the same level as the rest of us. You're nothing, just like your brother." He sniffed pompously and crooked a finger. "Viola, I said *come*!"

Viola shook her head. "I'm not a dog. Take care not to speak to me that way. No, I think I'm staying here with Effie."

Huntington looked taken aback at the rebuff, but his face hardened, then went devoid of all emotion before he stalked away.

"Are you hurt?" Evangeline asked her sister. "God, Viola, has he treated you like that before?"

Viola looked discomfited, sending Gage a sidelong glance. Did she not wish to speak in front of him? "No, I'm not hurt. And he's never been like this, at least not physically. But he's overbearing when he doesn't get his way, and I've a feeling he will be untenable with this loss." Her voice went low. "He had a fortune wagered on them to win."

Evangeline frowned but then nodded, though her brows remained pleated when her sister wandered off to congratulate Lushing and the others as they were being met by their wives and friends. Gage wondered what such a loss meant if Huntington was still plagued with money troubles. Not that it was Gage's problem; he just wanted Asher's debt gone.

Huntington was a cheat... but a desperate cheat was a whole different beast.

Gage clenched his jaw; two more weeks and this would all be over.

Out of the corner of his eye, Gage saw Marsden's marchioness launch herself into his arms, followed by a cherub of a little boy dressed in a smart seersucker striped suit. Vesper also joined her duke but looked a little green to the gills. He thought she might have remained at home, given what Greydon said about her pregnancy at the start of the race, but he suspected Vesper was as stubborn as Evangeline. No wonder they were such close friends.

"Brilliant win, Your Grace," Evangeline said, once they were alone. Lucky deigned to give him a small lick when he reached down to let her sniff his hand in greeting. "I saw it from the bridge. Well done."

"Thank you. I'm glad you came."

"You asked me to," she said and then pinned her lips, a wary gaze darting to the side to her friends as if she didn't quite know how to conduct herself with them watching. It was perplexing, considering the playful, assertive version of her he was used to. Was she nervous?

"You're right, I did," he said. "I'm glad nonetheless."

"It was my pleasure," she murmured.

In a summery cream-colored embroidered gown, she was lovely. Pink roses that matched the color of her lips were gathered on her bonnet, a bit of lace netting hanging over the brim, making her look entirely too delectable. He had the sudden urge to wrap his arms around her as his friends were doing with their wives.

Christ, would he ever get enough of her?

"Oy!" Lushing shouted in their direction. "Where did that cowardly little miscreant get off to? I intend to collect my wager." He stalked down the hill toward the refreshments tent. "Huntington, where the devil are you?"

Evangeline stared after the earl, opening her fan for a modicum of privacy and keeping her voice low. "What happened with Huntington just before? You looked ready to kill the man. In fact, I was certain I would have to shove him into the river to save his useless life. I wouldn't want you to go to prison for murdering a peer."

Gage felt his face break into a smile at her tone. "You would do that for me?"

"Lord Cuntington will get what's coming to him one day, but not at your expense."

Gage couldn't help it. He burst out laughing, the sound drawing the stares of most of his crew, but he could not find it in himself to bother with them. It drew the attention of her friends, too, and he didn't miss their speculative looks. "That's quite a creative insult, my lady. One would never expect to hear such filth from such pretty lips."

She smiled back, her beautiful face half-shadowed in the sunlight, and lowered her voice even more. "I am sure you know by now, Your Grace, that I never hold back."

"I'm well aware."

"In fact, these lips are capable of many things." His mouth went dry at the hint of hunger glinting in her eyes as she rose onto her tiptoes, said lips nearly brushing his ear, just out of sight of prying eyes. With a throaty chuckle, she bit down on his lobe before whirling out of reach.

There was no earthly way a sad piece of flannel was going to contain the trajectory of his cock, which had decided to shoot to violent and painful attention at the sultry bite. His hands shot down to hide the evidence even as a wicked giggle reached his ears. "Evangeline, what the hell?" he ground out. "You cannot do such things to me in broad daylight!"

"Everything is fair play in this little game of ours, Your Grace," she said, tugging Lucky and skipping backward like the minx she was, silvery blue eyes alight with mischief and desire. "One pair of sodden drawers in exchange for one"—her eyes dipped down—"pair of ruined trousers seems a reasonable exchange, don't you think? I must admit that seeing you all sweaty and flushed is enough to get a lady hot and bothered."

Sodden drawers? He goggled at her, his brain on fire at the bald admission of her arousal beneath those layers of pale muslin that he suddenly wanted to tear off with his teeth. He was so hard it hurt…and his friends were much too close for comfort. They would never let him live it down if he sported a raging erection in the middle of a royal regatta. He swallowed and cursed, keeping his body carefully angled toward the river.

"Everything well, Your Grace?" she teased. "You seem over-wrought."

His eyes met hers in a dark stare he knew she felt to her bones, especially when her pupils eclipsed the silver of her irises. "I hope you realize what you've started," he said.

"I look forward to it, leannan."

Leannan. Murmured in the sweetest, sultriest voice imaginable. It was the ultimate coup de grace. The proverbial match in the powder barrel. Immolated by lust, Gage did the only thing he could. He took his flaming body and walked it right into the bloody Thames.

"Vale, what on earth are you doing?" Greydon yelled when Lucky started barking, nearly breaking free from her mistress in a frantic attempt to save him. "That water's filthy."

"It's not so bad up here as it is in London proper." At least he hoped it wasn't, but it didn't matter if he was wading in sludge. His swollen body parts were finally getting the message that he wasn't playing around. "Besides, Lady Evangeline dropped her parasol. I thought to retrieve it, but it's lost now."

Greydon narrowed his eyes. "I don't see a parasol."

"Yes. Because she *dropped* it and it floated downriver."

He could sense Evangeline's glee from where she stood—that wicked little scamp was going to be put over his knee, and he was going to make her scream with pleasure until she was hoarse. He didn't have to look at her to know she was making those adorable, uncontrolled little snorts from behind her fan.

"Effie." Viola strode over to them and frowned with some concern. "I didn't think you brought a parasol. In fact, you distinctly told me that you were leaving it behind so that you could add to your freckle collection."

Those tiny snorts amplified in intensity as his impish and willful quarry collapsed in mirth to the grass in a froth of creamy skirts, not giving a whit that she was getting green stains on the fabric while being licked to death by a small dog, that she was the subject of dozens of stares, or that she was laughing quite openly at his expense. He'd never seen anything lovelier than Evangeline Raine in that moment—eyes crinkled, cheeks upturned and flushed, joy in every line of her body.

He would risk ridicule all day long to keep her thus.

Gage bit back his own grin and waded from the depths of the river, his lower half thoroughly soaked, but back to normal size, thank God.

"What a relief," he pronounced loudly, meaning it in more ways than one. "It must have been a walking cane or some such then, not a parasol. My mistake."

Evangeline was laughing so hard, her eyes were watering.

"My sister was not carrying a cane either." Viola frowned again, her eyes panning between her sister and him. "Are you quite all right, Your Grace? Perhaps you've had a bit too much sun and you're confused. Did you exert yourself overly in the race?"

He smirked. "I assure you, Lady Viola. I am quite well."

Even if he was quite at risk of falling head over heels in love with her sister.

But that was a problem for another day.

CHAPTER NINETEEN

Wasn't it the point of a sexual arrangement to be thoroughly *swived*?

Because by God, Evangeline was ready for it. Ready for *him*. A week had gone by since the regatta, and he hadn't so much as touched her or seen through on *any* of his erotic promises. She was nearing her wit's end.

Then again, it wasn't as though she and Vale had the time to get away or any opportunity for actual privacy. Between the fight, Vale's injury, the regatta, and visits with Edward and Sarah at the shelter as well as with the RSPCA, the time had passed eventfully. Evangeline had ended up staying in London much longer than she'd planned, but the truth was, she was enjoying the bloody season, despite all her initial worries. Notwithstanding her secret liaison with Vale, Evangeline quite liked seeing him interact with her friends, and for the first time since that very first dismal season, she looked forward to going to the events that she used to loathe.

Take this ball, for instance. Laila had thrown it in honor of the Henley win, and Evangeline hadn't even balked at being ordered to attend. Normally by now, she would have been lodged behind her favorite potted fern, sipping awful ratafia, while counting the minutes until she could leave. Instead she stood with Viola near the refreshments table, her eyes locked on the ballroom floor where

Vale was dancing with their hostess. She exhaled a breath and snapped open her fan.

Could a man get more handsome?

His dark auburn hair had grown longer, curling over his collar in thick waves, and his formal clothing fit his big body like a glove. Every step in the waltz was a study in grace, those long limbs of his moving with exceptional fluidity. Laila fairly floated in his arms. If Evangeline didn't know how besotted she was with the Marquess of Marsden, she would have felt jealous of how well they looked together. Green eyes met hers, catching her ogling, and a smirk that could melt undergarments broke over his sinful lips.

The man was driving her mad with his little flirtations and sultry stares, so much so that her body had become a coiled mess of want whenever he was near. Which was often. The Duke of Vale had been in attendance at nearly every event that she and Viola found themselves, including a musicale at Nève's before she'd departed for Paris, the opera, a garden party on the Serpentine, and this ball in his team's honor, yet he'd managed to stay a far step away.

Close enough to tease, far enough to make her lose her mind.

It was bloody torture.

What the devil was he up to?

She'd already broken two of her favorite fans from attempting to cool her overheated body. The delicate lace fabric of her newest splitting with a ripping sound when she snapped it open was the final straw. "Bloody hell!"

"Language, Effie. Fans are not meant to be wielded thus, you know," Viola scolded in an amused voice. "No wonder it's broken. You've been using that thing like a hammer."

"I'm hot," she groused.

Viola frowned, peering at her. "You do look feverish, though you appeared to be quite fine in the carriage on the way here."

"This. Ballroom. Is. Boiling." The words emerged in a panted staccato, as if the very air in her lungs were about to desert her.

Her sister sniffed. "Yes, I agree, but no need to be so aggressive about it. Go out onto the terrace for some fresh air then. I'm going to dance with William."

"He's here?" Evangeline asked in surprise. She didn't realize her friend was personally acquainted with the Marquess and Marchioness of Marsden. In hindsight, if her brain were in good working order and not besieged by thoughts of Vale, she probably should have invited him, but Evangeline was glad he was there nonetheless. For Viola's sake, at least. Perhaps Vesper had mentioned him to Laila. Evangeline would have to thank them later for being so considerate.

That was one thing to be pleased about at least. Viola seemed to have been avoiding Huntington since the regatta, much to his displeasure, but there wasn't a damned thing he could do about it. He pretended to be unaffected by her behavior, but Evangeline caught sight of a few thunderous glares in her sister's direction whenever Huntington thought he wasn't being watched. The man did not like being snubbed by the jewel of the season.

Too damned bad.

When she saw her sister safely in the arms of the veterinarian, Evangeline exhaled with a soft smile. Then her eyes panned to where the Duke of Vale was now paired with Briar in a country dance, the two of them laughing and clearly enjoying each other's company. Her smile faded, her stomach turning slightly sour. She wasn't jealous! Like Laila, Briar was one of her best friends.

But the conversation at their weekly tea several days ago at

Vesper's residence was seared into her brain. The three of them had been catching up when the ever-matchmaking Vesper had casually suggested the Duke of Vale as a potential match for Briar. If Evangeline hadn't seen the sly look that Vesper slid her way, she might have reacted quite differently. As it was, she'd barely been able to keep the possessiveness at bay.

Briar had stared at them, cup halfway to her lips, her eyes dancing with mischief. "You think Vale and *I* would make a good match?"

"Don't you?" Evangeline had replied coolly. "He's handsome, smart, and can handle someone as outspoken as you."

A devious Vesper had raised her brows. "You don't want to marry him, Effie dear?"

"I don't wish to wed, you both know that."

"And you think he and Briar would make a successful couple?" Vesper asked.

She had glared at her friends. "Why do you two keep asking me that?"

"Why are you keeping secrets from your best friends?" Briar tossed back. "Are you shagging the hot Scot or what?"

"What?! No!" Evangeline had spluttered, going crimson.

"I mean there's nothing wrong with a little fun, if both parties are consenting adults," she said with a wicked look at Vesper. "Just ask her. She and Greydon got quite naughty in the dovecote before they were wed."

"And the billiards room," a red-faced Vesper added with a chortle. "And at the Crystal Palace."

Evangeline's mouth dropped. "Vesper!"

"We won't judge you, that's what we mean to say," Vesper went on. "The Hellfire Kitties vault is a sanctum."

Evangeline had no idea why she hadn't confessed. Perhaps it was because she knew her friends would see right through her that she was starting to fall for the Duke of Vale. Or perhaps she'd already fallen so deeply that she was lying to herself that things were platonic. "No, Vale and I are just friends."

The girls had exchanged a knowing, amused look that had irritated Evangeline further, but it was by a miracle she'd kept her temper under wraps. After a beat, Briar had grinned. "Pity! Who wouldn't want a hot, ginger Highlander in their marriage bed?"

Evangeline positively *did* want a hot ginger Scot in her bed.

No marriage required!

She could not blame Briar for dancing with him, but watching them together was a hard pill to swallow. Her fists wound into her skirts, emotions curdling in her belly. She decided to take Viola's advice, because if she didn't get out of this ballroom, she was going to break more than a fan. But before she could do just that, she was stopped in her tracks.

"What is going on between you and Vale?" the Earl of Lushing demanded.

She blinked. "Nothing."

"He's not being untoward with you?"

Evangeline lifted a brow. "What do you mean?"

"You're a lady. I would not see you … dishonored."

"*Dishonored?* I am so sick of labels and the impractical expectations placed on women," she burst out. "We are quite capable of thinking sensibly without the constant surveillance of men, you do realize?" Vexation mounted, and her anger landed on an available target. "And I fail to see the difference between the two. You run a club of vice and sin, play at being a libertine, avoid the responsibilities of your future title and estate, and yet, you have the audacity to judge me?"

"I beg your pardon. You mistake me, Effie." He exhaled and spread his hands wide in supplication. "Surely you know that I only care about your welfare."

Seeing his regretful expression, she softened her voice. "While I appreciate your concern, my lord, I am a grown woman in full possession of all my wits and faculties. Trust that the Duke of Vale and I are not engaged in a sordid affair that will have the aristocracy's collective tongues wagging with the taste of gossip, if that is your worry."

Lie. She'd been well and truly in the altogether with His Grace, and the ton would absolutely salivate at a hint of such a scandal. Ruination would be the least of her worries. She would become completely and irrevocably shunned.

"And Lady Briar?" the earl asked, eyes flicking to the couple in question, a muscle flexing in his jaw as if it had pained him to ask.

She gave a small shrug. "I do not presume to know of Vale's intentions, my lord, when it comes to any woman in this hall or whom he seeks to court. Perhaps you should ask him."

With a forced smile, she moved past the earl, whose unguarded expression was painfully vulnerable, clearly at the sight of seeing a smiling, flirtatious Briar in Vale's embrace, only to be halted on her way out again. In a fit of frustration—*couldn't she escape this ballroom for one sodding minute?*—Evangeline opened her mouth and shut it when she realized who it was that had called her name.

"Huntington. What do you want?"

His dour face pinched at her waspish tone and the complete lack of the proper address. "What did you say to your sister about me?"

"I said nothing that hasn't already been said," she replied with narrowed eyes. She was *not* in the mood to deal with a scorned gentleman's childish tantrum over what he thought he deserved. "Viola is of her own mind."

Goodness, what was with men questioning women's abilities to think for themselves? If she had to listen to one more male denigrate female intelligence, she was going to punch them right in the nose!

"You had something to do with this change of heart, I know it."

She lifted a shoulder. "You give me too much credit, my lord. Is that legendary, self-professed charm failing you, perhaps?" Evangeline stared at him and then at her sister, who stood with William, a broad, genuine smile on her face as they conversed. "Or maybe you never had her heart to begin with."

"That mongrel is no one compared to me," he scoffed.

She laughed softly. "And yet he's the one waltzing with her. These are modern times, my lord. A man with a kind heart is superior to a selfish peer without one." Evangeline didn't hide one lick of her disdain. "Perhaps you should take a page from Mr. Dawson's book. Women are not playthings meant for cruel sport."

"Aren't they?" he asked with an unkind sneer. "I broke you, didn't I?"

"Alas, Lord Huntington, the only thing of mine you broke was the veil of ignorance I wore over my own eyes, so I thank you for that. You showed me the true nature of spoiled, indolent gentlemen who have little care for anyone beyond themselves. Viola was smart to finally see through you, and trust me, I had little to do with that. You did it all on your own." She drew in a breath, hands trembling with the force of her emotion. "But in case you did not get the message, stay away from my sister, you useless dunghill."

"How dare you insult me?" he spat. "Or give me orders? If I want her, I will *have* her. Your father would be a fool to refuse me."

"My father only wants for her happiness, and I doubt, sir, that you can ever provide that. Set your pitiful snares elsewhere and save yourself the trouble."

Evangeline left him spluttering and made her escape to the terrace, where she hauled great gulps of air into her aching lungs.

Finally.

Confronting Huntington had been long in coming. All of those emotions had been buried deep and brought close to the surface by one maddening duke whose motives she could not read.

A throat cleared behind her. Had Huntington followed her? Evangeline whirled, ready to give the odious lord another blistering setdown, and froze.

"Oh, it's you," she choked out.

"Indeed."

The Duke of Vale crowded the glass-paned door of the terrace, standing in a halo of light from the ballroom behind him. The glow made him seem like some warrior angel come down to earth to wreak vengeance. He wasn't an angel, however. He was a devil, toying with her like a dog's old chewed-up plaything, and she had had enough.

"Am I to be flattered that I seem to exist to you now?" she muttered.

"Absence makes the heart grow fonder—"

A snarl broke from her. "Fuck your platitudes, Vale."

Green eyes widened and then darkened, his tongue slipping out to moisten his lips. She hated seeing the sight of it, so pink and glistening, and wanting it on her body. Between her lips. Between her *legs*. Evangeline gritted her teeth and turned away.

"You're not enjoying our game?" he asked.

She blinked, whirling toward him and misjudging how close he was when she nearly crashed into his huge chest. "Game? You think this is a *game*?"

"Of course it is," he replied, a frown appearing on his broad brow. "You called it so yourself. I was simply playing along and following your lead after the regatta when you so sweetly sent me for an impromptu dousing in the very filthy Thames."

At a loss for words, she could only blink owlishly up at him. Devil take it, had she read things so incorrectly and let irrational jealousy ruin their whole tryst? Evangeline had no idea when it had ceased to be a game to her, only that it had. It was one thing to be possessive of Vale with a stranger like Minthe as she'd been at Lethe, but Evangeline *knew* he wasn't the sort to dally with others, much less her best friends. And yet...her illogical emotions had convinced her of his perfidy. What on earth was happening to her?

She glanced up, an ugly knot in her throat. "What about Briar?"

"What about her?" he asked, clearly confused by the question.

Evangeline sucked air through her teeth. "Do you...fancy her?"

His confusion vanished, and the twinkle that appeared in his eye was too much to bear. "You want to know what she said to me when I asked her to dance? She said she was happy to be the spare while her best friend got her head out of her *arse*."

"I do not have my—" she began and then broke off. She tried to step back, but one long arm banded her waist, plastering her to him. "Why did you come out here?"

"I was attempting to protect you from Huntington." A chuckle reverberated between them. "Though you were hardly in need of protection, were you? That tongue of yours is as sharp as the most lethal of blades. The poor man didn't know if he was coming or going after you sliced him to sad little ribbons."

She was confused. Why would he hurry out to protect her when he'd been in the midst of a dance? "Weren't you dancing? Vale, you can't just leave a woman on the ballroom floor."

"Of course I can. I don't care about Lady Briar or anyone else."

"So what was the last ten days then, Gage?" she asked. "You were avoiding me on purpose?"

His voice was pure smoky honey. "God, I love when you say my name. I wanted you liquid with desire, Evangeline." His nose grazed her temple, and her pulse tripled. "Tell me that your skin feels like it's on fire and that your heart is trying to pound its way out of your body." His fingers moved toward her ribs, grazing the side of one breast. "That my touch makes your nipples bead and ache for my tongue."

"You're a cruel man to do this here," she whimpered, knees going weak at his lewd talk.

"My carriage is ready to depart whenever you are," he whispered.

"Now. I'm ready now." She paused, reason filtering through the lust. "Just let me find one of the girls and see if they can make sure Viola gets home. I wouldn't want her to worry."

"It's already been arranged," the duke said. "With your friend, Mr. Dawson. I did invite him here, after all."

Evangeline faltered. It hadn't been Vesper or Laila?

"Wait," she said. "That was your doing?"

"Dawson is a good man, and he's in love with your sister," he said. "It doesn't hurt for him to be seen in powerful circles. He and Marsden have quite a lot in common as it turns out."

"You—" she broke off, unable to find the words. "Why?"

"Must you ask," he whispered softly. "I did it for you, Evangeline. Because her happiness is important to you, and yours is...important to me."

This *man*. She pushed up onto her toes and kissed him, right there outside the ballroom, reputation and discovery be damned. "Take me away, Your Grace, before I scandalize the denizens of the peerage and ruin us both."

Gage didn't waste any time sinking to his knees before her in the carriage. If she thought the last ten days had been torture, then she had no idea of what he'd put himself through. Cold baths had done little to reduce the excruciatingly keen edge of arousal, but he had refused to pleasure himself, refused to accept anything but her hands, mouth, and sex on him.

Now, he grasped her ankles, spreading her legs wide beneath her skirts. Her gasp was loud in the confined space. "Did you touch yourself, Evangeline?"

"Yes," she admitted.

"Like you showed me in your chamber?" he rumbled, both hands sliding up the backs of her stockinged calves to the bend of her knees. "With your toy?"

"No. I didn't use it. Only my fingers." She moaned when he flipped her skirts and petticoats upward to reveal the lace edges of her drawers. "I was waiting for you."

He skated his fingertips up her thighs, the heat of her almost scalding when he met the tops of her garters and a tantalizing sliver of bare skin. Palms outward, he parted her legs wider so that he could fit his broad shoulders between them. The brisk movement made the delicate seam of her silk drawers split farther apart, exposing her glistening sex, and he could not help himself. He leaned in for a hungry lick. And fuck if she wasn't as sweet as he'd imagined. Better, even. Salt and honey on his tongue, and his mouth watered for more.

She whimpered, a hand tangling in his hair. "Gage."

"Say it again," he ordered, peering up at her. Her cheeks were flushed, and her lips parted with pleasure. Evangeline in all her forms was beautiful, but like *this*, on the cusp of release, she was magnificent. A goddess of unguarded passion.

"Gage, Gage, Gage." Her head lolled back on the squabs. "Don't make me beg."

"What if I want you to?" He blew on her tender folds, feeling her thighs shiver beneath his palms.

A whisper of laughter on the heels of a moan met his ears. "Dreadful man."

He bent just as the carriage flew over a bump, lodging his mouth right where it needed to be, and Gage needed no more incentive. Hell, the flavor of her was beyond sublime. He went to work, lapping and sucking, memorizing what made her writhe, what made her whimper, and what made her pretty skin flush darkly with arousal.

"Gage, please," she begged willingly now.

Loving how responsive she was, he rewarded her and sucked hard, tongue sinking into her in a carnal way that had them both moaning. Her body locked and shivered as it undulated around his tongue, her sweet cries of release like music to his ears. He kissed her mound when her body finally settled. "You are beautiful."

A soft giggle erupted above him. "Are you talking to my vulva or to me?"

Gage grinned at the anatomical terminology. "Both. She's a needy little thing."

Evangeline laughed again, a beautiful flush filling her cheeks, eyes silvery and sated. "That is all your doing, Your Grace. You only have yourself to blame for any *neediness* you may find down there."

"It is part of my nefarious plan to keep you thus in a constant state of wanting." He pulled down her skirts with some regret, but he knew it wouldn't be long before they arrived at his residence. His coachman had taken the long way around at his instruction, and his carriage for the evening was plain and unmarked. It was a risk, but she would be cloaked and covered. He could not chance going to her home or visiting a public hotel. At least at his house, he could ensure discretion and safety.

"And you," she whispered. "What of your state?"

He rose, one hand braced on the velvet cushion behind her head, and took her palm to place it on his distended groin. "A constant burden, I'm afraid."

Her lip disappeared between her teeth. "I'm sorry."

"Don't be. I've ached for you from the first moment we met."

Something indefinable flickered in her eyes, a mirrored sentiment perhaps, but then her gaze shifted to amusement. "Covered in kittens in the middle of my shelter? I hardly see how that was any inducement for seduction." She ran her knuckles along his abdomen, his muscles flexing at her light touch. "Though I must confess, I was intrigued by what I grasped."

One finger teased over his hard groin, and the corner of his mouth kicked up, as if he recalled her untimely handful. "Were you?"

She nodded. "In fact, I was also rather envious. Of Buttercup, in particular."

"Of poor Beasty?" he asked, incredulous.

Evangeline rolled her lips inward, hiding a smile. "She treated you like her own personal mountain. I suppose I wanted to do the same." Blushing, she cleared her throat. "Climb you, I mean."

"Why do you think I am stealing you away to my house, free of felines and canines for that matter? You can climb me to your heart's delight." He tucked a tendril of hair behind her ear and winked. "Besides, I'd rather not have any furry or feathery audiences undermine my performance this evening. I intend to dazzle you senseless."

"Come now, Your Grace." She giggled. "Surely you know that you have nothing to be ashamed of? My cats adore you."

He took her hand and grazed his lips over her knuckles. "I'm only interested in being esteemed by one beautiful creature, and she is sitting right in front of me. I expect to have your full and complete dedication this evening, my lady. *My* teeth and claws will be the only ones you have to worry about." He raked his fingers along the inside of her bare wrist, making her beautiful body quiver.

"Is that so?" she whispered.

"Yes," he promised with a grin that turned wolfish.

Gage did not miss the way her eyes dilated or the way her palms fisted into her skirts. It looked like Lady Evangeline was intensely curious about what that eroticism might be, especially if it involved *teeth* and *claws*.

He smiled. By the end of the evening, he would know exactly what made her scream.

CHAPTER TWENTY

As they entered the silent domicile and made their way up the stairs to the ducal bedchamber, Evangeline's thoughts were churning. She was determined not to give in too easily, but every part of her wanted to throw caution to the wind and just let herself feel. It was a slippery slope, giving in to the powerful emotions swirling inside, because beyond this chamber and their agreement, she had no claim on him.

This was about sexual congress, she reminded herself firmly.

Maybe if she said it enough, she would believe it. He was not someone she should esteem, or think of as charming, smart, kind, sweet, or funny. She should only be concerned about his prowess in the bedroom and his talents therein. She should *not* think of his touch as one she yearned for beyond physical desire. She should not equate it with what she saw in his expressive gaze either. The unguarded affection. The open regard. The fact that he liked being with her, and she liked being with him. Or the fact that he made her feel heard. Seen. *Valued.*

Because none of that mattered. This was an emotionless, fun, pleasurable diversion.

As they'd agreed. Because it categorically couldn't be anything more...

Dear God, *was* it more?

The sudden loss of control over her feelings and questionable motivations made her feel dizzy. Squashing down every other emotion but lust, Evangeline regarded her prize. She *wanted* him and she would have him, regardless of her unwelcome epiphany that despite all her efforts, she might have gone and lost her heart to this man after all.

Because by god, tonight he was hers.

"Strip, Your Grace," she told him, unable to wait a second longer. "Will we be interrupted by your valet?"

One reddish-bronze brow arched at her impatience. "No, Pierre has been dismissed for the evening." God, even that low rumble did things to her, scraping along her senses like those very claws he'd promised.

Vale prowled toward her, making her breath catch, until he'd crowded her against the door. "You seem to think that you are in charge here, my lady."

"I'm not?" she whispered.

His nose trailed along her cheek as he breathed her in, each fraught second making her skin tingle and burn. "Not at the moment, no." He reached her earlobe and bit gently. In truth, her useless knees nearly buckled as hot breath shivered over the sensitive whorls of her ear.

Huge and handsome, he peered down at her, all rugged angles and hard lines from his jutting cheekbones to his square jaw. Auburn hair fell into his brow, disordered from where she'd grabbed ahold in the coach to keep him lodged between her splayed thighs. She blushed at the recollection as she closed the bedroom door shut behind her. The Duke of Vale might not be experienced in the most literal sense of the word, but after his performance in the carriage, he certainly knew his way around a woman.

"You know what's the best thing about my quarters?" he asked with a mischievous expression.

She lifted her brow, wondering what wicked thing he was going to say that would reduce her to a mess. *More* of a mess. "What?"

"No cats."

Evangeline couldn't help it, she burst into laughter. What was it about this man that made her want to tear his clothes off *and* talk to him like a best friend for hours? He made her head spin while keeping her heart warm. He made her laugh, even when she wanted to scale him like a bloody tree. "You love my cats."

"There's only one kitty I'm interested in," he said with a wink. "And she's ferocious but oh, so sweet. Gives in with a single pat like putty in my hands. A complete pushover."

Her jaw dropped as his words sank in, heat curling through her at the hungry look on his face. "I am *not* a pushover."

"Feel like a friendly wager?" he asked, leaning to nuzzle her neck.

She suppressed a moan at the slight swipe of his tongue, arching to give him better access. He obliged, sucking and nibbling along the column of her throat, and making her knees shake beneath her skirts. "You don't gamble, remember? It's not good for you."

"I would risk it all for the right prize," he told her, voice low and raspy. He pulled back to stare at her, tucking a strand of hair behind her ear. His gaze traced her face. "You're so beautiful, Evangeline," he whispered, and she was completely mesmerized by the look in those limpid green eyes. Admiration, adoration even. He made her feel…like she was the only one he ever saw. Like she was everything.

"Gage."

"Go and hold the bedpost so I may unlace you," he rasped.

Had any other whispered command ever sounded so erotic? That rumbling Scottish burr sank into her bones and spread heat everywhere.

"Now, Evangeline," he said when she didn't move.

Devil take it, the way he said her name—the steel draped in silk—made her embarrassingly wet beneath her skirts. She licked dry lips, feeling his eyes drop there, a hiss escaping him as though he wanted to do debauched things to her mouth. He *would*. She knew it as well as she knew that she was never going to forget tonight for as long as she lived. Gulping past the lump in her throat, she moved toward the bedpost and did as he instructed.

"Good girl."

Hell and damnation, why did that growled approval make her wetter?

Take control, you daft chit!

Before she could lose her nerve and any more of her diminishing wits, she pressed the length of her forearms into the carved mahogany bedpost, pushed her arse out provocatively, and glanced at him over her shoulder, letting every ounce of her arousal show in her eyes.

"I'm not a girl." She drew her lower lip between her teeth, watching that telltale muscle jump to life in his cheek. "And I don't plan to be good."

His nostrils flared, eyes nearly black, only a sliver of green remaining, as if the beast beneath was about to burst through. It was intensely gratifying to see him holding on to his control by a thread. She wanted him undone, reduced to nothing but want. But when she felt the heat of his body and the fingers that traced along the laces at her spine, she was the one unraveling. She was the one reduced to whimpers.

"Done this before?" she asked, desperate to hold on to something besides the bedpost. Self-control was fast slipping away, like holding on to falling snow.

"Undressed a woman?" he said, lips grazing the inside of her gaping neckline at her back. Something wet and hot traced the upper indents of her spine. Her fingers curled into the wood, ribbons of need arrowing to her tender breasts and between her hips.

"Yes," she bit out.

"Not like this," he said in a thick voice. "Never like this. Every inch of your skin is a temptation." He slid his hands up her nape, long fingers wrapping around the front of her throat as he drew her head back, angling her chin upward. She felt so fragile in his arms, knowing the strength in those hands, and yet he was so gentle. He loomed over her, lips taking hers in the briefest of kisses. A hint of heat, a flick of his tongue, and he was gone, fingers delving in her hair and loosening the few pins he found there.

"Your hair is like liquid moonlight," he whispered in reverence, palms threading through the strands.

"It's a nuisance," she replied. "Gets tangled at the slightest breeze, won't be held by pins, never cooperates, does what it wants."

A muffled laugh. "Sounds exactly like the rest of you."

"I cooperate given the right incentive."

"Care to share?"

She shivered when fingertips danced down her spine. "Keep doing what you're doing."

The warmth of him at her back disappeared, and Evangeline turned at the same time that the bodice of her gown slid to her waist.

He loosened the ties holding her petticoats, and soon, they, too, fell in a crumpled pool on the floor. She was still covered by her corset, chemise, and stockings, but she could feel his stare burning through her remaining layers. The air grew heavy with anticipation and want.

"I have never seen anything like you, Evangeline, pure perfection," he said thickly, making quick work of the corset and undoing the ribbons of her chemise. Pleasure filled her at his soft words, undoing all of the flimsy barriers she'd erected against him. She was already helplessly, irrevocably lost.

Nothing on her person was safe from his dexterous hands. He knelt to remove her slippers and untie her garters, hands skimming over her skin as he rolled down her silk stockings, and she could barely breathe as his nose grazed the backs of her thighs. He inhaled deeply and she froze in mortification.

"Are you *sniffing* me?" Evangeline asked, a little horrified.

"Undressing you is an all-senses experience. Touch"—he dragged one palm over her buttocks to the crease where they met her upper leg, the soft touch making her shiver—"scent, sight, sound, taste." And with the last, he licked her right along that sensitive crease, his teeth closing over a fleshy mouthful of her behind.

"Gage!"

Evangeline almost buckled and had to hold herself upright with all her strength. One single thought remained in her head. There was no way she was ever going to survive this.

She smelled like lilies.

Gage filled his lungs with her scent. Forced himself to go slow. To take his time.

But he was a starving man faced with a banquet…a banquet of rose-tinted flesh spread out for his viewing and gorging pleasure. He wanted to breathe her in, taste her everywhere, mark every part of her as his. One bite and he was already done for. The circular, red imprint of his teeth on her pert bottom made his cock pulse.

Fuck if she wasn't the most stunning thing he had ever seen.

Evangeline Raine was a Botticelli painting in the flesh, but even the most famous Venus could not compare. Long and lithe, Evangeline's curves were spare but well-formed, her legs long, that moonlit hair spilling down her shoulders like a silken waterfall. Gage stored away the memory of her just like this. Sultry ice-blue irises edged in silver met his. Her bottom lip was red from biting it.

"Face me, Evangeline," he rasped. "Keep your hands where they are."

Slowly, she turned, wrists high above her head, and his breath fizzled. Small, round breasts rose high on her chest, their peaks topped with tight, luscious nipples that begged to be stroked, sucked, and bitten. A creamy torso curved into a soft belly, leading to deliciously flared hips and the white-blond tuft that shielded her mound at the apex of her thighs. Those long legs were crossed at the ankles.

"You are fucking perfect," he whispered.

"I'm glad you think so," she said, blushing and abusing her lower lip again. "No one could ever call me tiny and dainty."

"I could," he said, removing his coat and waistcoat, and tugging on his necktie.

"That's because you are a giant."

He sat in an armchair and tugged off his boots—thank God he'd thought ahead and worn his loosest pair, which did not require the assistance of his valet. Nothing was more of a mood killer than summoning one's very opinionated servant to help get undressed for pleasures of the flesh. "I'm of average size for a Scot," he said.

"Nothing about you, Your Grace, is average," she said, her cheeks going scarlet. "Especially your size."

He laughed at her expression and then felt his chest puff at her obvious meaning. Tearing his stockings off, he wiggled his toes for effect. "You know what they say about men with big feet."

"Big boots?" Her lips twitched.

Gage grinned. "Enormous."

"You don't have to convince me, Your Grace." She licked her lips and shifted against the bedpost, her sinuous body writhing in a way that had his cock twitching. Fantasies of her mouth around him had him dampening his fly. If he wasn't careful, he wasn't going to last, and then any boasting about foot size would become tragically irrelevant.

Impatient, he tugged his shirt over his head. Her breathless gasp pleased him. He liked that she appreciated his body—his physique had been earned from hard work, here in England and growing up in Scotland, and while he was not vain about his appearance, it gratified him to be attractive to her.

"Get on the bed," he told her in a hoarse voice.

"Is that an order?" she teased, a barely there shiver racking her frame, though her chin went high and her eyes glinted with delicious defiance.

Gage stilled, hands at his waistband. "Get on the bed, *please*?"

There was a beat before the bright tones of her laughter filled the room. "I do love a man with manners."

"Never let it ever be said that I am not a gentleman."

He held her gaze, his barely slitted open, as he unfastened his trousers and let them fall. That sassy mouth of hers parted on air, a swallow working her slender throat. Kicking his pants away, he closed the distance between them, noticing her pulse fluttering like a confined bird at the base of her neck. Despite her cheek, she was nervous, he realized. Nerves that she shrouded in bravado. She wanted this, but lovemaking was a momentous step.

For both of them.

Evangeline did not move a muscle until he was nearly upon her, craning her head to keep her eyes locked on his. God, he loved her fearlessness. Give him a strong, frustratingly independent woman over a simpering, timid miss any day. Even one who had no interest in giving up that independence, who was adamant that she'd never marry, and who would never, ever consider leaving England for good.

Fuck. The desolate thoughts shook him.

"We don't have to do this if you don't want," he whispered.

"Don't be daft, Vale. What girl in her right mind would want to waste that?" An arch glance slid down to the straining erection that was level with her belly. With a slow grin, she removed her arms from the bedpost and looped them around his neck. "Besides, I was promised I could climb to my heart's content. I did not think you so cruel to deny me, Your Grace."

Without warning, she jumped upward, and he caught her under her buttocks at the same time, both of them groaning in unison as she twined her legs around him. He could feel the heat at her core and her dampness, her breasts squashed against his chest. She moaned as her nipples tightened, abraded by the hair on his chest, then proceeded to rub them shamelessly into him.

"May I tell you a secret?" he whispered as he ferried them toward the bed, the high mattress bracing against the backs of his thighs. When she nodded, he smiled. "You're a much lovelier handful than Beasty Buttercup."

She laughed and he nuzzled her neck. "More than a handful, I wager."

"Much less furry, too."

She sifted her fingers through the bronze curls over his pectorals, grazing over his flat nipples and making him hiss. "Good thing you have enough for both of us. I like this." Her palms trailed up to cup his jaw and rub the stubble there. "And this. I want to feel it scratch against my thighs."

"God, that mouth of yours," he groaned.

Evangeline wrapped her arms around his neck and caught his lips with hers. "It's quite obsessed with you."

Her kisses were wet and messy, and they drove him wild. There was little finesse, only an insatiable, unpracticed hunger, and Gage wouldn't have it any other way. She was fucking perfect. He kissed her back, a palm tight against her spine to keep her flush, his mouth devouring hers with equal intensity. She tasted like summer days in the Highland dells.

She tasted like home.

Gage eased them both down so she was sitting upon him, legs still tight around his waist, but now his cock was wedged snugly into the damp cradle of her body. He wasn't even inside her and it felt like heaven. She adjusted her weight, and his eyes nearly rolled back in his head when her wet folds dragged against his length.

"How would you like to proceed, my lady?" he grunted in

strained, clipped tones, pleading desperately with himself to go the distance. "Would you prefer to ride or be ridden?"

"So formal, Your Grace," she said with a laugh and a gut-clenching undulation of her hips.

"Well, it is an official arrangement, so I am determined to leave my lady satisfied." Gage wanted to kick himself the moment he said the words when a flicker of what could only be *hurt* passed over her irises. "I only meant—"

"I know what you meant," she said softly. "And you're right. I asked for this."

"Evangeline."

"We both know the terms of our arrangement, Gage," she said, eyes searching his. "And perhaps we needed the reminder. You're meant to go back to Scotland after the season. We knew what this was, but that doesn't mean we can't live in this moment."

Her words were heavy, but she was right. A flush flooded his cheeks. "The truth is I've dreamed of being here with you for so long and I want so terribly to make this good for you." Overcome by his own admission and worried that he'd bungled it, he took her mouth in another heated kiss, his tongue finding hers with unerring speed and sweetness. It descended into blissful savagery soon thereafter, all heated licks and nips. When he pulled away, they were both panting, platitudes and arrangements forgotten.

There was only *them*.

Slowly, he unclasped her legs and lay back on the bedclothes so that she straddled him, knees on either sides of his hips. Pale ice-blue eyes met his, a shimmer of that same earlier pained emotion visible for a moment before it was hidden anew. When she leaned over him to take his lips in an open-mouthed kiss so hot it made him see stars, it was sublime.

"Touch me, Gage," she said, moving his hands to her breasts. He couldn't obey fast enough, filling his palms with her and then rearing up to fill his mouth, one succulent taste at a time. He licked and sucked until her head fell back and her hips were rocking uncontrollably over his. "I need you," she whispered.

"I need you, too," he said. He reached for the drawer near his bed and opened it to reveal a slim pouch.

"What's that?" she asked.

"A French letter. To prevent conception. I could withdraw, but better for us to be safe than sorry."

Her eyelashes dipped before he could see her expression, but she observed intently as he removed the nearly transparent covering and sheathed it over himself, adding a few drops of oil from the accompanying bottle for lubrication. While the thought of getting her with child made a pang take hold of his chest, children were no part of this arrangement. The only thing between them would be pleasure.

When he was ready, she lifted her hips and reached between them to position him at her entrance and then began the slow, exquisite slide. Her breath hissed as his crown breached her tight body and stalled. Bloody hell, he should have prepared her more. Cursing himself and his own greenness, he held himself still, letting her lead and hoping she knew what to do. He closed his eyes in self-disgust.

"What's the matter?" she whispered.

"I should be better at this for you."

She let out a breathless laugh. "You're wonderful as you are, but I'll tell you what—we can both be dreadful at our first time together, and then we will both become experts with copious amounts of practice. What say you?"

"I knew you were brilliant."

"Good, now caress my breasts and do that flicking thing with your tongue again. I liked that very much."

He did as she bade him, toying with her pretty, taut nipples, and she rolled her hips down, making them both gasp. With a moan, she arched as her delectable body commandeered more of his, one glorious inch at a time. "Yes, just like that," she panted. "Gage, you feel so damned good."

He huffed a laugh at her growled curse, groaning as pleasure streaked through him. Gage looked up, and the sight of her was too much. With her head thrown back, lips parted, hair tumbling in an erotic waterfall over her breasts and shoulders, he locked his gaze on where she worked him into her in small, careful pulses. "You feel like fucking paradise."

Eyes melting with desire, she leaned down to kiss him, her body rocking into his with each excruciatingly slow roll. He wanted to move, to thrust, to rut into her delicious heat, but this was about her. That was why he'd chosen this position. He would die before he rushed a single moment of this. Fucking hell, her body felt like the sweetest, hottest clamp, her walls squeezing him to delirium with each conquered inch while her mouth claimed his, hot and hungry.

With one last nibble on his lower lip, she shifted up onto her knees and sank back down, the slickness and gravity doing their work until he was wholly seated inside of her. They both groaned at the hedonistic fullness. Evangeline squirmed and canted her hips, inner walls rippling as if trying to adjust to his girth, and Gage felt lightning gather at the base of his spine.

Oh, hell no! He was going to...

His body twitched and froze, the orgasm taking him by storm. A kaleidoscope of lights burst across his vision, the release exploding through him like a molten crashing wave, fire and pleasure spiking through all his nerves until he could barely see. And still she rocked above him, chasing her own bliss on the heels of his, and wringing every last bit of pleasure from him like the beautiful goddess she was.

"Fuck, fuck, fuck," he whispered, his fingers clenching on her hips. "I'm sorry. I didn't mean to finish so quickly."

Whimpering, she stared down at him. "Are you done? Do you wish me to get off you?"

"No." He felt himself blush. He was still inside her, softened but nowhere near done. "Give me a moment. You have no idea what being inside of you felt like. *Feels* like."

She bit her lip with a small sideways smile, and a roll of her pelvis that had them both gasping anew. "I think I have some idea."

Evangeline felt the semihard length of him twitch inside her, and she marveled at the power of his body to be capable of such intense pleasure, as well as the ability of hers to drive him to such passionate extremes. She could have easily found her own release with a quick stroke of her fingers over her sensitive clitoris, but she'd wanted to watch him...to savor each second of bliss breaking over his beautiful face.

And Gage had come *beautifully* undone in the throes of pleasure.

She wanted to see it again and again.

"I'll be right back," he told her, easing from within her and making them both moan at the slippery friction. He gave her a quick kiss then left the bed, striding purposefully toward the connected bathing chamber.

Body still humming with energy, Evangeline boldly admired the tight curves of his buttocks and the thick strength of his muscled legs until he disappeared from view. When he returned, she stared quizzically at him, trying not to stare at the long but partially flaccid length of his spent phallus that was now bare of its temporary covering. It was truly a fascinating organ—angry and hard one minute, and soft and inconspicuous the next. Though Vale's could scarcely be called *inconspicuous*.

He held up the newly clean contraceptive sheath. "One of the disadvantages of using such devices."

"I'd say it outweighs the negatives if it prevents pregnancy."

He nodded. "Though it disrupts the romance."

"Good thing ours is a scientific study then."

She kept her voice calm but felt the lie echo in her heart.

He frowned but then rejoined her on the bed. She pulled him to lie on top of her, and he lifted to his elbows so he didn't crush her with his weight. Evangeline didn't mind. She liked the solid feel of his body on hers, of being pressed into the mattress. In truth, she hadn't minded being on top and controlling the pace, but she liked this way, too.

"I'm sorry," he murmured, lips brushing the tip of her nose.

"What for?" she asked.

He hesitated, a dull flush deepening over his cheekbones. "I wanted you to get there first or at least make sure you reached your peak at the same time."

"You made me come in the carriage," she pointed out. "So now we're even."

He flexed his hips, drawing a hiss from her as the ridge of his staff rubbed over her mound. "Is it a competition?"

Undaunted, she flexed back. "The best kind."

Gage stared down at her, amusement in his eyes. "So how does one win? Do we bring each other pleasure until we pass out? I seem to recall your saying something about copious amounts of practice, and while I am up for the challenge, I do not want to hurt you, if you are too tender."

His face was earnest, worry flickering in those gorgeous green eyes as he stared down at her. Evangeline was in fact a bit sore, but she grinned and wrapped her legs over his hips. "Practice makes perfect."

Calloused fingertips stroked over her cheek. "Are you sure? There are many other ways I can bring you pleasure."

"I want it all, Gage."

It didn't take him long to get back into fighting form, after a few gentle touches and impassioned kisses, his cock hardening between her legs in record time. He lifted to his knees to retie the sheath, and she assisted him, once more marveling at the thickness of him and the fact that she'd had all of *that* buried deep inside of her.

"This time," he whispered, "I'm going to take you to the stars."

"Bold boast," she told him with a laugh.

"It's not a boast, it's a vow."

Evangeline did not reply, because when he slid into her, pinning her to the mattress, her faithful tongue went on vacation. She was so wet that she took him all the way to the hilt on the first thrust. And as he stroked all the right spots inside her body and fingered the bundle of nerves at the apex of her swollen sex, the stars seemed to arrive rather too quickly.

She clawed at his back, fingers digging into the hardness of his muscles, sweat building between them as her body softened to the pliability of honey. And still he worked her. Relentlessly. His huge body grinding down, driving her to the precipice that loomed bigger and bigger until it was all she could see.

"Gage!"

He took her lips, tongue claiming her as deeply as his cock did. Above and below, she was his. When the spark he was stoking ignited, detonating inside with a shock she felt along every inch of her body, Evangeline's mouth fell open in a soundless scream as pleasure blasted her over the edge of the cliff into bliss. The orgasm roared through her core, scorching her veins, the feel of it almost too intense to bear. Gage joined her there with a pleasured growl of his own, gathering her in his arms and taking them to their sides.

Evangeline blinked, lucidity returning in flickers of light and sound. "I definitely saw *something* for a moment there. You win."

"The stars?" he asked, his lip curling in a very satisfied grin.

She heaved out a breath, relishing the little quivers that still rocked her insides. "The moon, Your Grace. I saw the moon."

CHAPTER TWENTY-ONE

Evangeline was done for. Well and truly so.

It'd been two days since she'd been with Gage, and she was still sore. Despite the duke's protestations to the contrary, he was not a man of average size, and she had the tender lady bits to prove it. She'd moved gingerly around the house and had to lie to Viola that she'd injured herself riding. Though not *technically* a lie. She had just ridden an uncommonly large mount with a very large...pommel.

She let out a mortified giggle-snort.

To top things off, as she'd discovered in such an untimely manner when they'd arrived in his bedchamber, she was ninety-nine percent sure she was falling in love with him. The remaining one percent was the only actual part of her brain that seemed to still be in working order and was painfully aware that falling for the man was a guaranteed trip to heartbreak. Gage was returning to Scotland; she was going to be focused on her shelter. On the future she wanted.

The one she'd *always* wanted.

But no matter what she did, Evangeline couldn't stop thinking about him. Fantasizing about him and some alternate version of what could be, in which their liaison was something real. Wondering if he hadn't worn a protective sheath what their children would look like. Why on earth was she thinking about *children*? Especially bright-eyed, red-haired offspring with cheeky grins? Maybe they would have ice-blue eyes like hers. Or green eyes with blond hair.

Stop.

She had to stop. She *couldn't* stop.

Which was why she found herself in a hackney at midnight, dressed in a dark cloak that covered her from head to toe and en route to the duke's residence.

You will be caught.

No, she was being extra careful.

You are wearing nothing under this cloak.

That was indeed a fact.

You are a desperate, besotted fool.

This was also true.

"Is your master at home?" she asked when she was deposited at the duke's home and greeted by a handsome young man who wasn't the duke. She faltered and almost turned back around. He didn't look like a liveried servant either. "Who are you?"

"Jenkins, my lady, the footman, er, the butler," he stammered, going red. "And I'm sorry, but His Grace is not home to callers."

Evangeline frowned, wondering if she'd made a horrible mistake by showing up so boldly without invitation. She did not need the gossip to spread of anyone knowing that a lady of quality had visited the duke *unaccompanied* in the middle of the night. "I'm not a lady and he will be at home to me." She fought back a semi-hysterical snicker. "Please inform him that Miss Philergood is here."

"I beg your pardon, miss? Fila-who?"

"Phil-er-good," she enunciated with half a snicker that threatened to spawn more snorts, only to catch sight of a very rumpled-looking duke himself at the top of the staircase. He was staring at her with an unreadable expression on his handsome face.

He descended, and every step he took made her breath catch. He was, indeed, not dressed for callers, in a linen shirt and trousers with a banyan thrown carelessly over the top of it, and scandalously bare feet. He looked *delicious*.

"Thank you, Jenkins," he rumbled. "That will be all."

"Yes, Your Grace." The butler nodded and disappeared, not seeming to care that his master wasn't dressed or was breaking all kinds of rules by welcoming her. It was decidedly odd, but then again, the Duke of Vale wasn't the usual kind of duke.

Nor are you the usual kind of lady, the dreadfully annoying voice in her head reminded her. It wasn't wrong. She made for a rather terrible lady, truth be told.

"I didn't quite get your name," he said softly when he reached the foyer. "Miss Philergood?"

"Miss Philer*now*."

His lips twitched, and his eyes went wide at the patently obvious double entendre. Blushing at her flagrancy, Evangeline cleared her throat and walked into the nearest private room she could find, which happened to be empty. "Where's all your furniture?" she asked, knowing the duke had followed her when she heard the snick of the door.

"Renovations," he said. "Is something amiss?"

With a bone-deep shiver at what she was about to do, she shook her head and turned, heart hammering to see him in touching distance. Her hands itched to pull him closer. He was so beautifully disheveled, her sinful mountain of a duke. Instead her fingers went to the ties of her cloak.

She let it fall. "I needed to see you."

Nude, except for her shoes and a pair of black gloves, she cataloged every heartbeat of his reaction, watching him blink in disbelief, those sensuous lips parting on a ragged breath as he took her in, desire flooding those angular cheekbones with a ruddy flush. That telltale muscle flexed to life in his cheek.

"I want you, Gage."

Her voice broke the spell over him. "Dear God, Evangeline, did anyone see you?"

"I took a hansom."

Green eyes glinted with a flash of ire as they swept down her naked body. "Like *that*? What were you thinking? What if something had happened? What if the coach wheel had cracked on a cobblestone and you were forced to disembark?"

She slanted him a look. "Contrary to what you might assume about my sex, Duke, I am not an idiot and I do have a pair of working hands to keep my cloak tightly closed." She bit her lip, embarrassment filling her. "This was a bad idea. I shouldn't have come."

"Wait," he said, reaching for her elbow when she knelt to retrieve her belongings. "Yes, you should have. I'm not thinking straight at the moment. That happens when a beautiful woman in the altogether makes all reason fly out the window."

"I wasn't thinking either," she admitted. "I haven't been able to. I cannot even function. I volunteered at the Temporary Home for Lost and Starving Dogs in Holloway yesterday and was sent home because I fed the wrong food to the animals and made quite a mess of things because I was distracted. Me! Distracted!" Evangeline poked at his very firm chest and winced. "And it's…all. Your. Fault." She punctuated the last three words with more poking that turned into a lewd sort of rubbing.

God, he was so *hard* and muscled everywhere.

"My fault?" he murmured.

She nodded furiously. "We need to get this out of our systems, whatever this is. We need to"—she choked on her own tongue—"fuck it out."

Russet brows shot high, that thick throat of his working. "*Fuck* it out?"

"Did I stutter, Your Grace?" she asked, and placed a hand directly on him. He was hard as a brick there, too, confirming her suspicion that the Duke of Vale was in as bad a state as she was. "Since you have no furniture, the wall will have to do."

"I've created a monster," he muttered as she unfastened his fly with trembling fingers, freeing him from the confines of his trousers.

"There are worse monsters in the world than me," she replied on a gasp when he positioned himself right where he needed to be. "People who abandon animals. Murderers. Thieves. Philanderers."

"True, though one could argue that giving in to an addiction is monstrous."

"I am not addicted to you." She yanked on his hair, fingernails scraping against his scalp. "Are you planning to moralize all night, Duke? Or will you take me up against that wall?"

"So imperious," he said, one palm banding across the globes of her arse and squeezing. She bit back a moan when the blunt tips of those thick digits ventured perilously close to her damp, aching sex.

"I go after what I want," she whispered. "And I want you. Now, Gage."

Eyes hooded and dark with lust, her obedient duke bent his knees, notched himself at her wet entrance, and slid into her with one powerful upward thrust. They both gasped at the too-tight sensation as she went to her toes. She was more than ready for him, but her body still had to adjust to his girth. The noises that wanted to climb out of her felt obscene when he angled his hips, hoisting her up in one effortless movement, and walked them backward to the wainscoting.

He braced one hand against it for purchase. It didn't take long— a handful of deep, frantic strokes—before pressure began to build in her already oversensitive core, and Evangeline exploded with a muffled cry. The duke wasn't too long after her, holding her up against the wall with one hand while pulling out of her with the other to spend on the polished floor with a groan.

"That was...too quick," he said on a jagged exhale.

"Perfect," she panted. "Hard and fast."

He let her down gently, one leg at a time, eyes searching hers. Heat flooded her face at how wanton she'd been by showing up as she had. What if he'd had company? She hated to think of him entertaining anyone else, especially of the female variety, but he was a man. Now that he'd experienced copulation, perhaps he'd want more of it...from others. And it wasn't as though she had any claim on him. Their arrangement had served its purpose.

Once or twice, she'd told him, if she recalled, and this was the second.

More would only complicate matters.

Keeping her eyes downcast, she moved around him to gather her cloak, a wave of sadness choking her.

"Evangeline?"

Shrugging into the cloak that felt cold on her damp skin, she blew out a breath. "I'm sorry. This was beyond foolish to do this to myself. We're done, Vale."

Before he could even form a reply, she scurried from the room and out the front door, grateful that the hansom she'd paid a small fortune and promised more to wait was still there. The driver snapped to attention the minute she descended the staircase and opened the coach door.

"Thank you for waiting," she said, eyes stinging. Hell, she would *not* cry.

"Shall I deliver you where I picked you up, miss?" he asked, eyes brightening when she handed him a fat coin purse with the promised remainder.

Evangeline nodded, her throat tight. When she glanced up through the narrow, grimy window, she could make out the huge frame of the duke crowding the doorway, his face grim. A frown marred his brow, his lips pulled tight in displeasure, but he made no move to stop the coach or come after her. He wouldn't. Vale knew too well that she was a woman of her own mind. She *hated* being coddled, though at the moment some comfort wouldn't go amiss.

It was her own damned fault.

She was the one who had created a monster, not him. And now she was wrecked because of it. In truth, she wanted nothing more than for him to come after her. To hold her. To show her everything would be well, that she wasn't alone in the vulnerability she felt...that letting him in and letting herself love was what he wanted as well.

She wanted…*God*, she didn't bloody know what she wanted anymore.

By the time she made it back to her residence, slipping in via the quiet kitchens, tears were running down her cheeks. After a quick wash to scrub away the evidence of her folly, she changed into a night rail and gathered Lucky close. She buried her tearstained face into the pup's fur.

"Oh, Lucky, I've made such a terrible mistake," she whispered. "I thought I could keep my mind clear, but it's gone so muddled. I don't know what I want anymore."

You want Vale.

The dog licked her cheek, huge eyes shining with the unconditional love only an animal could offer. Evangeline bit her lip, her heart aching with the brutal realization of what she could never have—Vale to be hers for good.

Heavens, she was a hundred times the fool.

Gage stared at the beauty in blue across the ballroom, his breath hitching in his lungs. He had no idea why he'd even come, perhaps to punish himself with a glimpse of her. After Evangeline's impromptu visit nine days ago—now well past the six-week period of the agreement he'd made and yet he was still here—she hadn't so much as looked at him even though they'd seen each other several times in public since then.

It was as though she was going out of her way to deliberately ignore and evade him, much like he'd done before, only with a very different motive. She wasn't avoiding him in a ploy to make the heart grow fonder. She was running scared.

We're done, Vale.

He understood her last visit for what it was—one last interlude to say goodbye. She'd been in control until the very last. No strings, no entanglements. No unnecessary feelings.

Gage had convinced himself that the ache in his gut wasn't anything more than fleeting sentiment to a loss. He would get over it. Over *her*.

Someone sidled up to him, and he looked over, half expecting it to be Lushing. To his surprise, it was the earl's sister, the Duchess of Greydon. "Your Grace," he greeted her.

"Vesper," she said. "I've been *Your Graced* to death tonight already."

He chuckled. He knew the feeling. One of the consequences of being in town for the season, even if he wasn't actively looking for a wife, was the attention. Too much of it, in fact. Evangeline had been a bit of a buffer from the deadly focus of the many matchmaking mothers, though they had taken notice. Even as an infamous wallflower, she was still the daughter of a respected peer, and Gage held one of the most coveted titles in England. The ton thrived on competition, and he'd become a subject of considerable interest, despite his paltry coffers.

He didn't want their interest.

Gage wanted *hers*.

"Where's Lushing?" he asked the duchess. "Haven't seen him tonight." Gage frowned. He hadn't seen the earl in a week or so actually, and it wasn't like Lushing to miss a party.

"Our father has taken a turn for the worse," Vesper said, grief thickening her voice. "He and his solicitor have called Jasper in to discuss provisions."

"I'm so sorry."

The duchess gave a sad shrug. "Papa's been sick for a long while. We have been prepared, though my brother has taken it harder than expected." She sighed. "You know how he is. Pretending life is this brilliant, unending bash so he doesn't have to think about reality and the fact that he will be duke when our father dies."

Gage understood that motivation. It was how Asher had been and probably why he and Lushing had become friends in the first place. Free spirits who avoided responsibility at any cost, even at the expense of their own selves. Grief and duty took their pounds of flesh in different ways. Gage made a mental note to call upon his friend sooner rather than later.

"What's going on with you and Effie?" the duchess asked bluntly.

Taken aback, he huffed a breath. "Nothing."

"It doesn't look like nothing," Vesper pointed out and sipped from her glass. "You're like two wolves, circling each other."

It was an apt description. Evangeline would never be prey, his fierce vixen. Gage shrugged, unable to give an answer that wouldn't expose them both. He had no idea whether she had confided in her friend, but he was thinking not.

"I've never seen her like this," Vesper went on. "Withdrawn and fractious. Normally, she's quite even-tempered, even when faced with impossible provocation." Gage glanced at her, but she seemed lost in her thoughts. "Case in point, Lord Huntington approached her earlier with his usual Lady Ghastly fare, and she growled at him to take his puny, sniveling arse back to the hole he crawled from."

A laugh burst from him. "She did?"

"The Effie I know would have smiled, flayed him with her eyes, and walked away." The duchess narrowed her gaze on him. "What have you done to her?"

"Me?" He laughed harder. "How is her standing up for herself my doing? That woman has a backbone of pure, unyielding steel. Trust me, Lady Evangeline doesn't need anyone's help, least of all mine." His voice softened, pride filling him. "She is a force beyond anyone I have ever met."

The look Vesper shot him made his skin itch. A knowing, contemplative look. "She is, isn't she? Then why haven't you asked her to dance?"

"If I could, I would. But she's been avoiding me all evening."

She looped her arm in his. "Then come with me."

Gage could barely resist, and although she was a slip of a thing, and pregnant, she was strong and resolute. He did not want to accost Evangeline if she had been making every effort to elude him, but he could not shrug Greydon's duchess off, either, without causing a scene.

People were already staring at the determined duchess dragging a duke that wasn't her own in her wake. The Duke of Greydon lifted an amused brow as they stalked past, and shook his head when Gage shot him a beseeching look.

Powerless, he let himself be led, watching Evangeline's pale blue eyes widen the closer they got. He saw the scowl just as she shifted right behind a small crowd. Instead of following, Vesper yanked him to the left.

"Oh, no you don't, you sneaky little imp," she muttered to herself.

"Vesper," Gage protested. "She doesn't want—"

Vesper shushed him. "She doesn't know what she wants. I, however, her best friend in the world, am well aware of how stubborn Effie can be."

Stubborn was an understatement. Gage blinked just as they

cornered a flustered, red-cheeked Evangeline in a cerulean dress that brought out the bluer flecks in her eyes. Pink lips parted in shock, guilt flashing across her face as she pinned the bottom one between her teeth. God, she was lovely. Her elegant throat worked, even as she strangled her fan between gloved fingers.

"Got you, wench!" the duchess pronounced in a gratified tone.

"*Vesper*," Evangeline hissed. "What are you doing?"

"Saving a duke from pining himself to death."

Gage startled. "I was doing nothing of the sort."

Vesper speared him with a stare worthy of the queen herself. "So you weren't holding up a pillar across the ballroom and devouring Effie with your eyes? Much the same as she was doing whenever she thought you weren't looking. You could fill a pond with all the combined drool."

"I was not!" Evangeline blurted, her cheeks scarlet. "And you're being ridiculous. There was no drool."

Vesper shook her head. "I swear, just watching you two and I'm in an agitated *state*! And I'm already pregnant!" She lowered her voice. "If I weren't, I'd be suffering from hypertension of the pelvis."

"Vesper!" Evangeline shrieked, even as Gage gaped. He didn't know whether to guffaw or remove himself from a potentially explosive situation between the two friends. "That's not a thing, and shouldn't you be in your confinement at *home*, being a dutiful wife and mother-to-be? Haven't you been casting up your accounts willy-nilly over your poor husband?"

The duchess gave an airy shake of her head. "Oh, that was temporary nausea. The doctor says I'm fine now. And don't try to change the subject. What's going on between you two?"

Crystalline eyes met his and slid away. "Nothing."

"That's what he said, but if it's nothing, then why are you trying to run away from each other?" she countered, hands on her hips. Gage moved to shift away, and the duchess's eyes pierced him. "Don't even think about it, you. Something's going on, and I hate being out of the loop. I swear on the baby currently treating my body like its own sporting ground that I will get to the bottom of this."

"Darling," the Duke of Greydon said, finally coming to collect his wife. "Why don't we get you a cool drink?"

Both Gage and Evangeline let out a breath as the duke led his disgruntled duchess away. Craning around her husband, Vesper lifted two fingers to her eyes and then pointed at them in turn, and Gage couldn't help releasing a chuckle.

"She's relentless," he murmured.

Evangeline nodded. "Worse now that she's with child."

He cleared his throat when they stood there after a beat in awkward silence. "How have you been?"

"Good."

"That's good," he said. A smile touched her lips, and he followed her stare to see her younger sister twirling past with Dawson, all smiles. "Things look good there, too."

Dear God, did he have any other word other than *good* in his vocabulary? He felt unnaturally tongue-tied in her company, as if the wrong word would send her fleeing from him, and heaven help him if he didn't want to keep her close for as long as he could. Her sweet scent curled around him, and he forced himself not to audibly inhale.

"He approached my father last week for Viola's hand," Evangeline said. "Their engagement will be announced in the *Times* tomorrow."

"That's"—*don't say good*—"excellent."

Her shoulder lifted in his peripheral vision. His heart trembled at the difficulty of speech—ease of conversation had never been a problem between them. He'd always been able to tell her everything. Well, *almost* everything. Lately, Huntington had been off licking his wounds, but Gage didn't care. His failure to woo Viola wasn't part of their deal, thank goodness.

Gage couldn't be held responsible for the man's inadequacies, and if the cad chose to renege on their agreement, Gage had no problem taking the matter to court. Not that he would, for Evangeline's sake, but he suspected that Huntington, or better yet the man's father, would not appreciate any of that kind of scandal.

But he did intend to confess everything to Evangeline. Now wasn't the time, but she deserved the whole truth.

He cleared his throat. "Would you like to dance?"

Evangeline turned to him, her heart in her eyes for a moment before it was hidden from view. "Vale—"

"Gage," he corrected, needing to hear her say it, even if this was the last time he might hold her in his arms.

"Gage then."

"I want to start over," he said softly. "If our arrangement has made me realize anything, it's that I've never felt this way about anyone. You make me laugh, Evangeline. You make me see the world in a way I never had before. You make me want to dance at balls, to let the world know I'm with you and only with you." He breathed out, watching her expressions—the desire, the need, the helpless yearning—all echoed by him. "Please. Let me court you properly."

"You wish to court me?" she asked, voice shaky.

I wish to love you as boldly as you deserve. But it was much too soon to confess that.

Gage's heart swelled so much his chest felt a hundred sizes too small. "If you'll let me, I promise to do it right. Dinners, more than three dances, all my evenings, every one of my hours. No secrets, no more furtive meetings."

"Don't sell yourself too short, Your Grace. Perhaps one or two furtive meetings," she said, a hint of a smile hovering on her lips.

Hope bloomed. "You're it for me, Evangeline. And I'm sorry I was too afraid to make my feelings clear. I was scared you wouldn't want more." He paused, his breath stuttering. "But you do, don't you? Because it's all I desire."

Light glimmered in her gaze as she moistened her lips, but before she could reply, a loud, obnoxious voice cut between them.

"You thought you could make a fool of me, did you, Vale?" Huntington bellowed. "Everyone's talking about Lady Viola's rejection and *I'm* a laughingstock!"

Evangeline turned her head with curiosity. Cold slipped through Gage's ribs in anticipation of a blow that he knew would be catastrophic, should it fall…once the sotted lord revealed his secrets. *Gage's* darkest secrets. "You're in your cups, Huntington," he said, attempting to steer him away and avoid disaster. "Let's take this outside."

The fop scowled, shrugging his arm off. "I didn't pay you to seduce Lady Ghastly so that her sister could get herself betrothed to someone else."

Huntington's misleading words were deliberately insulting and incendiary, and there was no defense when the utter silence in the wake of that statement was damning. Gage opened his mouth and closed it. He didn't have a single breath in his lungs to combat the instant feeling of suffocation. His gaze slid to Evangeline.

An enraged, ice-blue gaze met his. "He *paid* you to *seduce* me?"

"No, it wasn't like that," he bit out, feeling every bit of the trust and rapport he'd built with her, and all of the precious ground he'd gained moments before slipping through his grasp. "He didn't pay me to do anything of the sort."

"So you didn't accept money from him?"

"No. Yes. I mean, it was an agreement to resolve my brother's debt at first. It was only supposed to be six weeks." From the affronted, *pained* look on her face, he was failing abominably. "It was before I knew you, Evangeline. Before I discovered how compassionate you were or how very much you loved your shelter animals, and how that heart of yours is so extraordinarily large that a lowly rat might deserve as much care as any other." He exhaled, tripping over his words, horribly aware of their audience but not stopping. "I learned how brave you were, and so deeply intelligent that your beautiful brain could rival the greatest thinkers of our time. Your devotion to your family and friends alone are testament to your strength of character." Gage sucked in a shallow sip of air, feeling her slip away with each second. "You inspire me, Evangeline, every single day that I am lucky to know you to be a better man. To be worthy of you." Her eyes fluttered shut, agony tightening her features. God, he was losing her. "I meant what I said, you're it for me."

Her hurt was tangible, obvious in her clenched jaw and too-pale cheeks, but her chin jerked high. She opened her eyes and regarded him down the length of her nose, irises like chips of ice, a winter queen in all her regal, glacial glory. "Then I'm delighted to be of service, Your Grace. I hope you got your money's worth."

Desperation bled through him, even as hope fled. "Evangeline, please. Wait. I fell in love with you."

She flinched as though he'd struck her a fatal blow, fingers fisting at her sides. Eyes blazing, she wavered on her feet as if she was fighting with herself before she stepped tantalizingly close, rose to her toes, and whispered in his ear, "No, Your Grace. You *fucked* me. Don't confuse that with love. I won't."

With that, she turned and left, taking everything that meant anything at all with her.

CHAPTER TWENTY-TWO

The only thing that could fix a shattered heart was time. One simply had to prepare for weeks and months of agony while one's heart mended at its own interminable pace. Thank God their season was over. Evangeline had spent the last week in her bedchamber, listening to the sounds of the servants packing up the residence in preparation for their return to Chichester, unable to drag herself out of her melancholy. Heartbreak was why love wasn't worth the cost.

It left a person numb. Hollow. *Wrecked.*

Evangeline, please. Wait. I fell in love with you.

Her heart flinched at the memory. He didn't love her.

No man who loved a woman would hurt her so.

Only now did Evangeline understand why her father had broken to pieces after her mother had left. She'd always wondered how he could give up one of his daughters, and now she knew. It wasn't because he'd wanted to. It was because he'd *had* to. At sixteen, she had been old enough to take care of herself, but Viola had been on the cusp of womanhood and in need of an effective parent. Something her father could not be in his grief. In those early days, he hadn't even been able to care for himself. It was how she felt now.

Absent of care. Of feeling. Of anything.

It had taken immense willpower just to drag herself out of bed to the window seat, where for the first time in days, she stared out at an overcast sky. Even the weather reflected her mood of eternal doom and gloom. Evangeline had thought that she could survive anything after Huntington. Lady Ghastly? What a laugh in comparison.

Because this had been soul destroying. The gossip had flown faster than a murder of crows, and now the entire ton knew that someone had to be paid to want her. He'd lied to her from the start.

Oh, she hated him!

"Effie, are you awake?" a soft voice called, drawing her attention from where she sat curled up on the window bench in her bedchamber. Lucky gave a happy yelp, recognizing the owner of the voice. Evangeline hadn't left her room in days, not even to walk Lucky, who had remained at her side like the faithful friend she was. Thankfully, the servants made sure she was taken outside a few times during the day.

Evangeline debated not answering, but Viola was not the most patient of people, nor would she take the obvious hint that Evangeline wanted to be alone. "Yes, I'm up."

The door pushed open and her sister's head appeared. "Goodness, Effie, you look frightful."

A puff of laughter passed through her cracked lips. "Thank you."

"I'm not jesting. You look like you've been trampled by a runaway horse, left for dead on the side of the road, and then pecked within an inch of your life by vultures." Her sister wrinkled her nose. "And you smell like sweaty dog."

"That bad?" Her earlier laugh turned into a tragic snort.

Despite the stench—which, in her pathetic defense, was probably more a stinky Lucky who *was* in desperate need of a bath—Viola joined her where she sat and took hold of her hand. "You need to pull yourself together, Effie. No man is worth letting yourself fall to bits. You of all people should know that. *You* taught me that."

Hurt loomed. "He made a fool of me, Viola. In front of everyone. It was worse than a silly name invented by an even sillier fop. That didn't hurt me. *Vale* did."

Viola squeezed Evangeline's hand comfortingly. "If it makes you feel any better, he's been shunned by half the ton. Vesper, Briar, Nève, and Laila have made it clear that they will cut anyone who supports him."

It did make her feel better. Marginally. But then it was followed by a rush of guilt. "He won't find a wife, if he has no one to choose from."

"Who'd want to marry that overgrown cod's head?" Viola said loyally.

Evangeline felt her wounded heart quake in her chest. They'd never discussed marriage, but she'd trusted him with her body . . . with her heart. Until she'd learned she had been the butt of some stupid, inconsequential agreement, and that he'd meant none of it at all. It cheapened what they'd shared, made everything seem utterly meaningless.

"Let's get you cleaned up," her sister said brightly. "You have guests."

Evangeline blinked. "Who?"

"Your friends are downstairs. Even Nève rushed back from Paris. They have refused to leave, and Papa has sent me to retrieve you."

Realizing that she could not put them off, Evangeline allowed Viola to usher her into the bathing chamber, where she washed. Admittedly, afterward, she felt better. Her hair was still damp, so she left it loose, knowing her friends would not care, and made her way downstairs. In the foyer, she was stopped by her father, clearly in the middle of a frantic escape from her visitors. He pulled her into an unexpected embrace.

"How are you?" he asked.

"Wretched. Trusting someone who turned out to be a liar is the worst kind of shock." She let out a sigh. "But I suppose you know all about that, Papa. How did you survive after what Mama did, after she left? How did you..." *Put together your smashed heart.*

"One foot in front of the other and one day at a time. It will pass, dear girl," he said softly. "Love isn't always easy."

She swallowed a sob. "It wasn't love, Papa. Love shouldn't feel like this."

The earl patted her back, his eyes kindly and filled with so much compassion that her eyes stung. "If it wasn't, then it wouldn't hurt so much, but you will get through it, my resilient daughter, one day at a time. There are people who need you. I need you, Viola needs you. That gaggle of geese waiting down there, too." She let out a snicker at his harrowed expression. "And your animals need you." He released a breath. "I know this is probably not the right time, but I have decided you may use your dowry for whatever you want. Expand your shelter, do as you see fit."

Evangeline sniffed in a state of shock. "Truly?"

"Truly."

She flung her arms around him, tears forming anew. "Oh, Papa! You are one of a kind, I swear."

He smiled and wiped the wetness from her cheek. "Yes, well. Don't tell anyone, but I do believe that most women can do anything they put their minds to, even better, ahem, I daresay than the men. Down with the patriarchy!"

Evangeline giggled. "You are the patriarchy."

"We all play our parts, dear."

A screech from the nearest salon had his eyes widening as he retreated toward the safety of his study to avoid being trampled by a herd of women. Evangeline turned as her friends swarmed her, their arms holding her close. She'd never felt so treasured. They walked, arms interlinked, back into the morning salon, and sat.

"So, how shall we do it?" Laila asked with a hard look.

Evangeline blinked. "Do what?"

"Do away with a duke," Briar answered with vicious glee. "I've heard arsenic is quiet and deadly. That's how Madeleine Smith allegedly did it even though she wasn't found guilty. Remember that scandalous murder trial nearly a decade ago? He wouldn't feel a thing."

"No one is murdering anyone," Evangeline said. "And how do you even know of these obscure murders?"

"I like to be prepared," Briar said with an evil wiggle of her brows.

Vesper grinned, showing all her teeth. "Moreover, it would be so fun."

"Prison would not be."

Nève pounded her fist. "Worth it!"

"Hellfire Kitties for life!" Laila yelled.

Vesper let out a victorious shout. "Indeed! I knew you'd come around to the name." Grinning, she stuck her hand out to Nève. "Pay up, you owe me five quid."

Evangeline nearly laughed out loud at her friends' antics and their utter devotion.

"We could kidnap him," Briar offered gamely. "Rough him up a little. Some of those ladies in Seven Dials who can lift me with one finger would be up for the task."

It would take at least half a dozen women to handle a man of Vale's size, even if the idea held any appeal at all. The notion of making him suffer brought some gratification, but it wasn't wholly his fault. Evangeline was also to blame. She had approached him with her proposal, after all, and she had to be accountable for that. He might have lied by omission, which was dreadful and even unforgivable, but he hadn't forced her hand.

"I adore you all for being on my side, but no death or abduction or putting yourselves in danger for my sake."

"How are you feeling?" Laila asked softly.

Evangeline swallowed, looking at her friends in turn. "I've been better, I'll admit. It's not every day you find out that someone has been spending time with you because they've been paid by a scoundrel to do so."

Vesper bit her lip. "I feel awful for my part in what happened at the ball. I forced you to speak to him."

"It's not your fault. The truth would have come out sooner or later."

Her friend frowned. "What happened exactly between you and Vale? I wasn't wrong in assuming there was something between you two, was I? The way he looked at you, well, it's the way Greydon looks at me. Like you're everything in his whole universe."

"I'm sure you were mistaken," Evangeline whispered. "Any affection you may have thought he had for me, it was fake. We were simply acquaintances."

But even as she said the words, Evangeline knew it wasn't true.

They'd been more than acquaintances. She had no reason—and no desire—to keep the secret of her arrangement with Vale from her friends any longer. She took a deep breath, then blurted out the story in its sordid entirety. When she was finished, the four of them wore equally fascinated expressions on their faces. There was not one hint of judgment, however, not from her friends.

"Wait." Briar broke the hushed silence. "How was the bed sport?" Nève thumped a cushion onto her head, and Briar threw up her hands with feigned innocence. "What? It's not as though we're all not thinking it. Effie doing the blanket hornpipe? *Our* Effie?"

Evangeline snorted. "Bloody hell, I'm hardly some sort of ice maiden prude."

"You loathe all gentlemen," Briar said and then wrinkled her nose. "*Loathed*, obviously past tense now, since you let the Dastardly Duke into your drawers. Didn't you tell Vesper you kicked him out of your animal shelter?" She brightened. "Oh, wait. Was it hot poking with your enemy? Like he let you ride the rantipole all night while trading insults?"

"Something is wrong with you, Briar," Laila pronounced though her cheeks were on fire at the crude mention of the sexual position.

"It was by mutual agreement, as I explained," Evangeline said, blushing hard at the recollection of said act, though she left out the part about Vale being a virgin, too. That was his private business. "And everything about it was perfect…until it ended because agreements of this nature have to end or someone gets hurt. And then I found out that Vale had been paid to get me to London for six weeks by Huntington of all people, so it was a windfall for him at my expense."

She lifted her shoulders, everything aching inside. "He found a way to have his cake and eat it. Screw the spinster, pay off his debts." Evangeline put her head in her hands and peered up at her friends. Their expressions were full of pity. "Don't look at me like that. I know what I'm responsible for here, but I trusted him, and he lied by omission. And, dear God, I almost believed he cared for me and agreed to let him court me properly. How stupid am I?"

"You're not stupid," Nève said loyally.

Briar nodded. "You have a soft heart, that's all."

Vesper frowned and cleared her throat. "Not that I want to pour oil on fire here, and I am on *your* side, but what did you think your arrangement was going to be? You both used each other for... er... carnal enjoyment, and you got what you wanted."

"He was paid to keep me in London, Vesper! By Huntington, the man I despise most in the world. There's no excuse for that. Vale lied to me! He let me believe..." She trailed off, gasping for breath.

"Believe *what*?" Nève asked, a compassionate look on her face.

"That I was more than the awkward, opinionated, odd-looking, eccentric spinster everyone knew me to be. That I was worthy of being desired. That I wasn't unwanted." She pushed the heels of her palms into her eyes. "That I was *more*."

"You *are* more!" Laila said.

"You're not awkward or odd-looking," Briar put in. "You're unique, and beautiful, and we love you as you are."

"I know *you* think that." She sniffed. "But no one else ever has, and it was all a despicable lie at my expense. Poor Lady Ghastly... can't even get the attention of a gentleman without his being compensated for his time. What a bloody joke!"

Evangeline covered her face with her hands.

Gently, Vesper drew Evangeline's palms down, away from her face. "What if it wasn't the joke you think it was?" When the others scoffed, Evangeline lifted her head in disbelief that her best friend would even consider defending him. "Lushing told me that Vale's brother owed Huntington two thousand pounds. Money Vale needed to repay."

"What does that have to do with Effie?" Briar demanded.

Vesper lifted a palm in Briar's direction, keeping her eyes on Evangeline. "When Vale inherited a rather destitute dukedom, he also inherited his brother's debt, which he has been paying off. But coupled with some misfortune at Vale Ridge Park, his finances worsened considerably. Lushing said that Huntington agreed to forgive the marker if Vale convinced you to come to town for the season." She expelled a breath. "I'm not excusing Vale. He did lie to you, and that was wrong, but perhaps you should give the duke a chance to explain before you decide that you are unworthy or undeserving of love and happiness, Effie."

"He does not love me," she blurted.

"But you love him, don't you?" her friend asked gently. "You don't owe him anything, but you owe it to yourself to know the whole truth, and that's something that you can only get from Vale." She smiled, a hand going to the barely there bump of her stomach. "Love is worth fighting for even when the odds are insurmountable."

"I don't know if I *want* to fight for it. I was happy alone. I could be happy again."

Vesper nodded. "That's true. But happiness isn't a stagnant target. It's always moving. Perhaps what you had before might not be enough, but only you will know."

Gage stared at the tumbler cradled between his palms in one of the private salons at Lethe. He hated the flavor of whisky—it tasted too much like failure—and yet it was the only thing that kept him from rushing off to Mayfair, his hat in his hand and begging Evangeline's forgiveness. Even though there was nothing he could say or do to change his actions.

Would he have changed his actions?

He was sorry he'd hurt her, but he could not regret taking Huntington's offer in order to square away Asher's debt and be able to support the tenants and staff. He had lied to Evangeline by withholding the truth, and he regretted that. Despite his oath, he had gambled...with the one precious thing that had meant anything to him.

Her esteem. Her affection. *Her.*

And he'd lost.

"Are you just going to sit here and mope?" Lushing demanded, taking the seat across from him. "I should cut you off."

Gage laughed humorlessly. "This is the same drink I started with hours ago."

"Cut you off from wasting my best whisky," the earl amended. "It's not meant to be nursed like a mother's teat, man."

"Oh dear God, I shall have to use the rest of this to scour my ears out and pretend I never heard that comparison from you," he replied. Lushing stared at him, face unusually somber as Gage regarded him over the rim. "Why are you looking at me like that?"

The earl let out a breath and crossed his booted ankle over his knee. "I know it's not important to you right at this moment, but we found the man."

"The man," he echoed in confusion.

"Huntington's man," Lushing said, making him sit up straighter in his seat. "The one you saw in the water during the regatta. He's confessed to foul play after some persuasion. Greydon is currently keeping an eye on him in my office, and he has agreed to be a witness. I haven't taken my seat in the Lords in years. If this requires proof from a peer, Greydon's a better backer than me."

Placing the glass down, Gage stood. "Take me to him."

Lushing nodded and led him up the stairs of Lethe to his office, where a man—a badly bruised man with one eye swollen shut— sat, his wrists restrained to the armrests of the chair. Greydon was propped against the desk. The duke sent them an apologetic look.

"He fought and injured two of my men. Refused to come quietly until we mentioned his association with one Lord Evan Huntington. Became as docile as a lamb then. Said he wasn't going down with a sinking ship."

Gage eyed the captive. Indeed, it was the same man with the sleek cap of blond hair he'd seen bobbing in the river that day, and in truth, the man seemed familiar to him...a face he'd seen somewhere in his memory. "Who are you?" he asked. "What is your name?"

"Horace Blunt, milord."

The pieces clicked. "You were Asher's groom." The man had the decency to flush, his cheeks reddening with shame even as he ducked his head. "He trusted you more than he ever trusted another, and he loved those horses, you know he did. He would have never ridden that pair in an intoxicated state." He took in a ragged breath. "What happened that night?"

"His Grace, your brother, was confident he would win," the man said. "His pair was unmatched, and they knew the track."

"But he didn't win," Gage said.

Horace shook his head. "Lord Huntington proposed a toast in good faith to the competitors right before the race. I did not know what had been agreed or discussed, only that the duke seemed enthused for the first time in months."

"Do you know what they drank for the toast?" Gage asked.

Horace nodded. "They called it Vin Mariani, a brain and nerve restorative tonic. I remember them talking about it because I wanted a dram of that coca wine myself."

Gage exchanged a heavy look with Lushing and Greydon. Worse than morphine and laudanum, cocaine deadened the nerves and one's ability to feel pain, or anything at all. His gut clenched. Asher would not have felt a thing when he was thrown from the curricle, that was a blessing at least. Gage's voice hardened. "And the loosened bolt on the wheel?"

The man blanched. "I don't know what you are talking about, I swear."

"I think you do," Gage continued. "If you don't tell me the truth, I will see that you face the same fate as your master. Life will not be kind in Newgate, I promise you."

"My wife and child," he stammered. "The lord threatened them. I *had* to."

Gage felt sick. "My brother died because of you."

"Please, Yer Grace," the man blubbered, tears coursing down his cheeks. "I had no choice. I didn't loosen the bolt all the way, I swear. Only enough for His Grace to realize something was wrong. He was too much of a good driver to not notice. You have to believe me."

Gage wanted to believe him, but even the most honest person could be coerced to lie with the right incentive. Horace could be lying about a wife and child to save his own skin. He needed to dig deeper.

"And the boats at the royal regatta?"

Horace's face fell. "He made me do that, too."

Lushing scowled and Greydon let out a noise of disdain. Gage was no fool. This man might have been coerced to betray a foolish duke who had treated him like kin, but he was in it for the money now. It was obvious from the man's tailored garments and well-soled boots that he was not lacking in coin. Working for an unscrupulous man like Huntington would undoubtedly be lucrative.

"Does Huntington owe any money?" he asked, remembering that Lushing had mentioned money troubles a while ago.

Horace blinked, relief crossing his features. "Aye. To the Covent Garden lads. The money from the boat race would have covered some of the sum owed, but he's supposed to be coming into a large dowry."

Gage exchanged looks with Greydon and Lushing. *Viola's* dowry. No wonder Huntington had been in his cups the night he'd revealed everything to Evangeline. The Covent Garden lads were some of the hardest, roughest men in London, and they took their lending very seriously.

"You swear this account is true?" Gage asked.

A fervent nod. "Aye, Yer Grace."

"Pray that it is, for your sake."

Chapter Twenty-Three

"Hullo, Jenkins," Evangeline said to the butler, who went a brilliant shade of red. She wasn't wearing a cloak to hide her features or going by a fictional name this time. No, she'd arrived in her father's coach with his coat of arms, and she was dressed in a new traveling costume and fashionable bonnet. Viola had accompanied her and waited in the carriage.

"Miss Philergood?" he stammered.

"Lady Evangeline, actually."

Philergood. The audacity. She felt her cheeks heat at the memory of the brazen moniker. She'd been driven by other pressing needs at the time, and the Duke of Vale had risen to the challenge remarkably well.

Breath fizzling, she bit her lip and brought her wandering mind back into focus. "Is the duke at home?"

"Er, he's not here, my lady."

Evangeline felt her face fall, her reply lost. It was much too early for Vale to be up and about. Perhaps he did not want to see her. She fought the regret that churned in her gut. Perhaps this was fate's way of saying let sleeping dogs lie. A blessing in disguise.

She gave a nod. "Will you tell him that Lady Evangeline Raine called?"

The young man fidgeted, and Evangeline suppressed a smile. He was not cut out to be a stoic London butler who let nothing show on his face. "He's been arrested, my lady."

Her smiled slipped. "Arrested?"

"This morning, the chief inspector came. Said the duke owed a man named Huntington money and refused to pay. They took him for questions."

Evangeline blinked in shock and surprise. She couldn't very well leave town now. The thought of Vale being held in police custody because of a scheming liar like Huntington didn't sit well with her. Redirecting her coachman, she gave her sister an apologetic look as she climbed back into the conveyance. Viola shot her an inquiring glance.

"We need to make a stop," she told her. "Number Four Whitehall Place."

"Scotland Yard?" her sister asked.

Evangeline nodded. "One and the same. Your former suitor has made up some cock-and-bull story about the duke. I intend to clear his name."

"He is a wretched man," Viola muttered. "I cannot believe I ever fell for his lies. He asked me for pin money once, did I tell you? To cover him for a bet one evening. The man is a scapegrace." She shuddered. "Not to mention a bully with a rotten temper."

Glowering, Evangeline stared at her younger sister. "Did he harm you after the regatta?"

"Oh, no. He was much too cowardly to do anything after his public outburst, and he became quite solicitous. If he hadn't shown his true colors, or if I were more of a fool, I would have fallen for his act. Then I overheard him crowing to his friends about how he planned to spend my dowry. I was a golden goose to him, you see. The answer to all his considerable money troubles." She swallowed and looked out the window. "I decided to be like my older sister and put my fortune to a more useful purpose. Since William doesn't need it, I'm going to use it to start a fashion line. Lady Marsden was impressed with my ideas."

Evangeline choked up. "That's amazing. But you do know that William loves you. He always has."

"I know," her sister replied softly. "And in time, I will love him, too. Love isn't always about fireworks or parties and diversions. It can be quiet and unhurried. And sometimes, it takes patience and work to nurture the smallest seed into germination."

"How did you get so wise?"

Tears glimmered in her sister's eyes, but she tossed her golden-brown curls. "I was always wise, Effie, considering I had such an excellent role model. You were simply too busy with your menagerie to notice."

"Shelter animals," she corrected with her own watery smile.

When they arrived at Scotland Yard, Evangeline was surprised at the commotion outside the building. She recognized three of the flashy coaches, one belonging to the Duke of Vale, and the other two with Greydon's and Montcroix's coats of arms. Three dukes at the Metropolitan Police had to be some kind of record.

"Wait here," she told Viola. "I won't be long."

She descended the coach and was crossing the yard when Vale came strolling into view, flanked by Vesper's and Nève's husbands. She faltered, seeing that he was obviously unharmed and *not* interned. Upon seeing her, he came to a halt, russet brows pulling together in a frown. The men at his sides grinned and made themselves scarce as he closed the distance between them.

"Evangeline? What are you doing here?"

The knot in her throat doubled. "Your butler said that men came and you had been arrested. I came ... to save you, I suppose."

"You thought I was in trouble?" Those clover-green eyes of his sparkled, making her desperately want to smile.

Embarrassment was swift, but she quickly regained her equilibrium. "Yes, well, you seem to require constant supervision at all times, like a wayward child. Rescue from kittens, burning buildings, and nefarious forces. You are a walking calamity, Your Grace."

His crooked half grin made a slew of butterflies erupt in her chest. "You thought I was in trouble."

"Repeating it does not make it hold more relevance, sir."

Evangeline drank him in as he stood there, watching her, letting her hungry gaze wander over his features. There were dark circles beneath his eyes and lines of strain at the corners of his mouth, but otherwise, he looked as compellingly beautiful as always. It wasn't a word that others would use to describe him—he was much too big and rugged—but beauty was ever held in the eyes of the beholder.

"I've missed you, Evangeline," he said at the same time that she asked, "What happened then?"

He cleared his throat. "I wasn't arrested. Huntington owed money to some very bad people and coerced my brother's groom to damage his curricle, causing his death during that dreadful race, and then tried to have him sink our vessel at Henley to throw the race. The groom was giving his account to the police. I came at the request of the chief inspector to bear witness."

"Oh." She put her hand on his arm and squeezed. He stared down at it, her palm tiny on his wide forearm, but Evangeline had no desire to remove it. "I am so sorry about your brother."

"At least the truth is out."

They both turned as a scowling Huntington emerged from the building with his very livid father. He looked like a sullen little boy who had been caught red-handed. Sometimes too much power and influence corrupted people, making them feel they could do anything without consequence. That had obviously been the case with Huntington for years. He'd been a spoiled rotten young man who had grown into an even worse adult.

"What will happen to him?" she asked.

"Nothing formal, I suspect," Vale said. "There's no real proof, other than the groom's account. He's a peer and his father is a respected man, despite his son's dishonest nature. We'll let his father handle him."

"That's it?" Viola asked from behind them. Rage suffused her pretty face as she stalked across the courtyard toward her former paramour. "That's not enough for me."

"Viola, what are you doing?" Evangeline muttered, hurrying after her.

Viola stopped in front of Huntington, who, despite his predicament, still had the ballocks to sneer down at her. "You are a sorry excuse for a man. What kind of gentleman maligns a woman for having a voice or puts their hands on them with intent to harm?" She got right in his face, making him back up a step. "You are a pathetic coward with an insecure disposition who couldn't handle that a woman was more than you could ever be."

"Lady Ghastly and Lady Featherhead, what a pair," he drawled, though his face was pinched at her insults. "Enjoy your life of insignificance."

"Better than a life of pettifoggery. I know a few big words too, you prickless weasel."

Huntington snatched her left wrist in a pincerlike grip, and Viola froze. Then she did what no one expected. She pulled back her free arm and walloped him right in the face, making him drop his hold instantly. "That's for my sister!"

Evangeline's mouth fell open, because her valiant sibling didn't stop there. With a roar, Viola lifted her hem, pulled her foot back, and kneed him right in the groin. "And that's for me! Don't ever touch me again!"

"Viola!" Evangeline burst out, eyes rounding in utter shock.

"What?" her sister asked when Huntington let out a high-pitched scream and fell to the dusty ground, clutching his spurting nose and cupping his crotch.

There was dead silence, and then Greydon and Montcroix burst into laughter from across the yard. Huntington's father shot his son a disgusted look and climbed into the coach, but Evangeline swore she saw a smile pulling at the older man's lips. It looked like Huntington would get his just deserts, after all.

"Where did you learn that?" she asked Viola.

Her sister eyed her with a grin. "William showed me." Her grin widened. "He doesn't condone violence, but he said that if Huntington or any man ever put his hands on me, I was to defend myself thus. No one tells you how much a punch bloody hurts though," her sister complained, wiggling her bruised fist. "Ow!"

"Next time, go for the fleshy part of the throat," the Duke of Vale suggested.

Evangeline was still staring at her baby sister in wonder. "Remind me to thank William. I must admit seeing Huntington go down like a sack of rocks was more entertaining than expected." She winked at Viola. "Don't make a habit of it, will you? Papa will not approve."

"I'm not the one keeping habits that will shock our father, sister." Face going hot, Evangeline sputtered, her eyes darting to the duke in mortification. Had Viola been eavesdropping during her confession to her friends? She suppressed a groan. Of course she had. Her sister was a master of artifice. She opened her mouth and closed it. Viola winked and clasped her hands behind her back as she strolled to the carriage.

"I never noticed that she's quite terrifying," Vale murmured.

"Me either."

They stood there, the awkwardness between them unspooling. There was too much left unsaid, too much betrayal and injury. Too much heartache. She understood why he'd done what he did—she also would have done whatever she had to in order to protect Viola. That didn't mean the trickery didn't hurt, even if his intentions had changed. Even if he'd fallen as hard as she had.

"You never did tell me why you went to my residence," he said softly.

She bit her lip, the lump in her throat enormous. "To say goodbye."

"You're leaving?"

"It is customary if the season is finished to head back to one's country homes, Your Grace." She blew out a breath. "My animals need me. Papa has agreed to give me my dowry for expansions. That's my purpose. It's what I always wanted."

Until you.

She shoved that away. That chapter of her life was now closed.

"That is wonderful, Evangeline. You deserve to be happy." He watched her, so many emotions swirling in his green gaze that she could hardly separate them all. One hand rose to rub at his nape. "For what it's worth, I'm sorry I hurt you. I know now that I was wrong to take Huntington's offer, even if I hoped to dig myself out of debt, but then things went from bad to worse at the manse, and I felt as though I had no other choice." He exhaled, swallowing hard. "It's no excuse, but I'm sorry I lied to you. You must know that everything else was real."

Oh God, her rib cage felt like it was cracking down the middle. "Nothing good can come of a million truths built on a lie."

His expression crumpled. "I know and I'm sorry."

"But I forgive you, Your Grace," she went on softly, knowing letting go was the only real way she could start to heal.

"Thank you." He nodded, his handsome face so somber she could hardly bear it. "Goodbye then."

Evangeline wanted nothing more than to run into his arms, wrap them about her, and demand a different end. But how could she ever trust him again? Her lungs seized, tears pricking the backs of her eyes. That was the thing about truth. It was hard, swift, and relentless, and in the end, it was the only thing that mattered.

She paused and let him see every emotion in her eyes—her regret, her love, her hopeless yearnings. "Goodbye, Gage. I hope you can be happy, too."

Was this how things were supposed to end?

How could he be happy without *her*?

Gage, too, had returned to Chichester shortly after the Raines left, though he hadn't ventured far from his estate. Without the weight of Asher's vowel looming over his head, he'd been able to hire workers to begin repairing the manse. He was also able to put Evangeline's drainage plans in place for his fields. In a year, the crops would be as abundant as Oberton's and his tenants would have farms that actually flourished.

In a year, you won't be here to see it.

Gage rubbed a fist against his chest. Now that his business was concluded, it was time to return to Scotland, just as he'd planned. Boone had agreed to stay on and manage the estate, and fortunately, Gage finally had the funds to make sure the man was well compensated.

To his surprise, he'd received a letter from Huntington's father, who had sent him a considerable fortune from his son's trust. The note had simply said—*No amount of money can be enough to make up for the loss of your brother. Thank you for not prosecuting my son.* The sum had been too generous, but Gage had never been one to look a gift horse in the mouth. He'd paid off his few remaining creditors, hired Boone, and earmarked the rest into a special trust.

Scotland Yard had exonerated Huntington, which was expected, but Gage had let go of any lingering anger surrounding the man. He had no wish to condemn Huntington to a life in prison or his family to the pain of watching their son wither away behind bars. Sometimes, compassion took more courage than punishment.

Gage stood and surveyed the entrance. Everything at Vale Ridge Park was nearly in place.

"Your Grace," Pierre chided. "You need to get ready posthaste. I heard that even Prince Bertie will make an appearance."

"What's wrong with this?" Grinning at his valet's fastidious nature, Gage glanced down at his worn, paint-stained trousers, the threadbare shirt that was threatening to unravel at any moment, and his scuffed boots. He rubbed the three days' growth of beard on his chin and grinned. "I could be a swashbuckling pirate duke."

"Absolutely not, or I'll quit," Pierre threatened.

Gage laughed at the man's theatrics. "I pay you too much for you to quit, and besides, no one else will put up with you, and you well know it." He blew out a hard breath, doing one last check that everything was in place. "Very well, good sir. I leave myself in your excellent hands."

His valet sniffed. "That's what I'm here for, Your Grace."

And he was worth every penny. Gage shook away the nerves as he followed a much-too-agitated Pierre to his dressing room inside the manse. He supposed the presence of the regent would do that, though his mind was on other things. Another *person*, in fact. Tonight could go any which way. He'd planned for weeks, but anything could happen.

Evangeline could refuse to come, for one.

Gage could not unravel the knot in his belly even as his diligent valet groomed, shaved, and trimmed him to a man of more ducal persuasion. He preferred the workman, truth be told, but tonight Evangeline deserved the best version of him.

Once he had dressed, he moved to the balustrade of the grand ballroom, now restored to its former glory and elegance. A beautiful woman with dark red hair who was garbed in a stunning emerald gown smiled at him from where she stood a half step away. "It looks exactly as I imagined it could be," she said in a low voice, coming forward to embrace him. "Whatever happens this evening, I'm proud of you, and I'm happy to be here with you."

Gage nodded at his mother, the resemblance between them strong. Lady Catriona Croft dazzled, whether she was in a ball gown holding a fan or in a tartan brandishing a broadsword. "I am glad you could come. I trust your journey was not too tiring."

"It was not," she said. She had gained a few more laugh lines at the corners of her eyes and bracketing her lips, but the dowager looked good. She peered up at him, eyes seeing through him as they always had. "So this woman? She's the reason for all of this?"

He folded his arms. "The party, yes. The restoration, no."

"You know that's not what I mean," she chided and waved a hand at his person, eyes perusing the immaculate clan tartan. "I must admit I've never seen you quite so...debonair. It suits you."

"Mostly thanks to my valet, who insists it was time to embrace my full heritage." Gage stifled his grin. Pierre was now obsessed with kilts.

"Well, you look the part." She narrowed her eyes. "Is she worth it?"

The smile bloomed from the depths of his heart. "She is worth it all."

With a soft smile, his mother nodded and patted him on the shoulder before moving back to the balustrade. Gage glanced down at the guests already filling the room. Relief filled him that people had accepted his invitation, but his guest of honor wasn't there yet. He would know. He would *feel* it.

His eyes caught on the Duke of Greydon and his extremely pregnant duchess as well as the Marquess and Marchioness of Marsden as they were announced. They made their way over to where the Earl of Lushing was in conversation with the Duke and Duchess of Montcroix and Lady Briar. They had been apprised of his plans.

Lushing had laughed and remarked that it was the epic grovel and that Evangeline was smart enough to see right through it.

Still, gratitude filled him that his friend and the others had all come.

"The Earl of Oberton, Lady Evangeline, Lady Viola, and Mr. William Dawson," the majordomo intoned. His heart stuttered in his chest, eyes flying to the woman who occupied his every thought. His breath caught. Dressed in a deep amethyst gown, those moonlight tresses wound through with sapphires, she had never looked more majestic. She was so incandescent, she glowed.

"Oh my," he heard his mother murmur.

Oh my, indeed.

Everything faded as he descended the staircase, stopping himself from running like a lummox. He ignored everyone else but her. He might be dressed to the nines, the epitome of ducal elegance, but propriety had never been his strong suit. He nodded mutely to her father as words deserted him completely. Viola gave a knowing chuckle and dragged her fiancé away.

"You're spectacular," he blurted on a ragged rasp.

Silvery-blue eyes widening, she took him in. "You're wearing a kilt."

He glanced down. "Yes, well, I am a Scot."

Mischief brightened those crystalline eyes as she leaned in, her voice a whisper of a caress against his cheek. "Is it true what they say about Scotsmen and their kilts?"

God, he wanted to laugh, grab her in his arms, and kiss that sassy mouth right there in front of the entire room. But there would be time for that later. He hoped. For now, everything about the evening was for her. "Ask me later," he whispered back, and then bowed, adding more loudly, "Thank you for coming, Lady Evangeline."

She stared down the length of her pert nose, though her eyes twinkled. "Well, I couldn't very well refuse, considering you were calling in the favor I owed you for your coat."

Said coat and the mud pit she'd been stuck in seemed like an eternity away. The handwritten note he'd added to the invitation had been a last-minute indulgence on his part. "I knew you were much too honorable to say no." He lifted her hand to his lips and kissed her knuckles, permitting himself that small act. "Though I was still afraid you would not come."

Uncertainty shone in her eyes for a moment before her usual cool mask eclipsed it. "Viola insisted, and you know how she gets. And besides, I did not want to miss the unveiling of Vale Ridge Park." She looked up at the gleaming columns and the polished floors, taking in the floral boughs hanging from the ceiling and the gilded accents of understated opulence. "You've outdone yourself, Your Grace."

"Thank you," he said. "I want to introduce you to someone very important to me."

Her gaze flicked curiously to his, and he smiled. Evangeline might not know it yet, but he'd never introduced a woman to his mother. No one had ever measured up before, and if he was going to go all out to win the love of his life back, no stone would be left unturned, no grand gesture uncompleted.

"Oh?"

Her pretty eyes went wide when he beckoned his mother to his side. "Lady Evangeline, may I present Her Grace, Lady Catriona Croft, the Dowager Duchess of Vale and my mother."

Evangeline sank into a curtsy. "A pleasure, Your Grace."

"And you as well, Lady Evangeline," the duchess replied.

"Effie, please," she said with a laugh. "Vale is the only one who insists on my given name."

"It suits you," he said.

"Both are lovely," his mother said and then took Evangeline's hands in hers. "I would love to get to know you later, if you find it in your heart to indulge me."

"It would be my pleasure, Your Grace."

Evangeline seemed quite perplexed as to why his mother would single her out, but then she blinked, her attention falling on some of the guests who had traveled from London as well as other parts of England, and her brows pleated with more confusion.

"What on earth are Sarah Major and Reverend Bates doing here? Are you acquainted?" Her voice fell to a whisper. "Is that the writer Mr. Dickens with them?"

Gage inhaled a deep breath. He supposed it was time to tell her the full truth and explain why her latest mentor and two of the trustees of the Temporary Home for Lost and Starving Dogs were here in Chichester at his home, and in the company of the celebrated writer to boot. He signaled the orchestra, and the music faded away.

Gage cleared his throat, eyes spanning the packed ballroom. "Thank you, everyone, for coming. As you know, the Raine Animal Foundling Shelter is a near and dear project, independently manned by one of our own, Lady Evangeline Raine, right here in Chichester."

He didn't dare look at her, but he heard her soft intake of breath. "Many of these poor creatures have been abandoned and left for dead, and Lady Evangeline has cared for them out of her own pocket and charitable nature. I have a particular affinity to this shelter because if it wasn't for a litter of mischievous kittens assaulting my person, I would never have encountered the most selfless, the strongest, and the most erudite person I've ever met. So please, eat, drink, and dance, and be sure to peruse the animals available for adoption in the next room. We also won't say no to your contributions either."

A laugh filled the ballroom, followed by clapping as he held up a water goblet and lifted it in toast. "To Lady Evangeline!"

"Lady Evangeline!" everyone chorused.

"Gage," she stammered. "What is this?"

Eyes filled with secret pleasure that she'd used his given name in her bewilderment, he peered down at her. "A fundraiser." He handed her a promissory note. "And your first donation."

She stared dumbly at the tremendous sum, eyes goggling at the number. "I can't accept this."

"You can and you will." Gage glanced at the group heading in their direction. "By my guess, you will be receiving a lot more after tonight."

She shook her head as though she could not make sense of what was happening. "I cannot believe this. How did you *do* all of this? When did you? Wait, did you say there were *animals* in the next room?"

"Most, except Beasty. He's already been adopted."

"Hannah said," she murmured, still dazed. "I wish I knew who."

"I thought Lucky would like a friend when she comes to visit us."

She was utterly adorable in her confusion, eyes so wide and blue, they were nearly translucent. "I thought you wanted to go back to Scotland."

"How could I?" he whispered. "You're here."

"Gage." Her expression was full of uncertainty...and so much hope his heart squeezed.

His smile was soft. "A categorically foolish fop paid me to convince a rather extraordinary woman to go to London for six weeks, and I didn't count on falling irrevocably and wildly in love with her. I belong wherever you are, Evangeline, and I'll wait, for as long as you need me to. Forever, if that's what it takes."

Her eyes filled with tears, but then she and Gage were thronged by her friends and neighbors who wanted to congratulate and wish her well. There was no more to say, no more Gage *could* say.

His future was tied to hers, whatever she decided.

CHAPTER TWENTY-FOUR

For once in her life, Evangeline was speechless.

The Duke of Vale had done all of this for *her*.

"Did you know about this?" she whispered to Viola and her friends, who had joined her in the salon reserved for all manner of pens, holding the animals she had rescued. Nearly all of them had been claimed. Not the rats, of course, or the fox kit and owl. Thanks to Hannah, they had already been released back into the wild where they belonged.

"Of course we knew," Laila said. "It was a surprise."

She breathed out. "He's..."

"Senselessly infatuated with you," Vesper supplied with a crafty look. "After all, what gentleman would go through all this trouble just to convince a woman of his devotion?" She answered her own question. "A besotted one, that's what."

"He loves me," she whispered.

Viola rolled her eyes. "You know, for an allegedly older and wiser sister, you're quite dense. Do *you* love *him*?"

"I suppose I do."

The little imp let out an exasperated sound. "Then why are you in here talking to us?"

She glanced at the others. "What she said," they cried in unison.

Laila grinned. "Go before Briar gets it in her head to lure you into one of the upper rooms with secret notes or some such. Her last story hinged on a snowed-in cottage with a single bed."

"Trust me, it works!" Briar enthused. "One bed, two lonely, horny souls."

"Briar!" Evangeline exclaimed, glancing around to see if her irreverent friend had been overheard.

"Maybe you and Lushing should find out," Nève said slyly to Briar.

"Bite your tongue, you wench! Should I ever end up in such a situation with that miscreant, no offense, Vesper, I will sleep on the filthy floor. On the windowsill if I have to."

Vesper's eyebrows rose. "No offense taken, but I think thou dost protest too much."

Evangeline chuckled at her friends. They were truly the best.

Just one bed sounded rather good at the moment, though she was nervous. She had little reason to be, yet still she felt on edge.

"Why are you still here?" her sister demanded, making her jump.

"Yes, well, I'm contemplating my approach."

A snort. "You think too much." Viola giggled. "Just tell him you want to take a turn in Cock Lane. Or perhaps that you *miss* his co—"

"Don't you dare finish that sentence, or so help me!"

Heat flooding her face, Evangeline walked away from her sister and the ensuing cackles of her devious friends. She changed her mind. They were the worst.

But perhaps her sister was right. She was thinking too much. Sometimes, courage took action, rather than thoughts or words. And she and Vale had always been quite good at nonverbal communication. Knowing the duke's eyes were on her, she strolled the perimeter of the ballroom, taking in all the work he had done. It really was remarkable. Most of it he'd accomplished on his own, she knew, with his bare hands.

His strong, beautiful, talented hands.

Crossing the hallway, she went out onto the terrace that looked over the duke's landscaped gardens. He'd made changes here, too, most of the overgrowth neatly trimmed and pruned. A few guests had come outside for fresh air, but not many. Evangeline relished the soft breeze that cooled her hot cheeks, and waited. She knew he'd find her eventually.

"Running away?" a deep voice inquired, and goose bumps broke over her skin.

"I do not run, Your Grace," she replied and turned to face him.

"No, you face everything like a queen."

She swallowed. "Not everything."

God, he was so big and unbearably handsome. And that dress kilt! It did things to her, the red of the tartan catching the bright copper notes in his hair. A sporran hung low on his hips, the flash of his bare knees visible over the folded stockings. Her mouth dried at the bronze hair dusting his skin there, making her think of the hair that covered him elsewhere. His thighs, his chest, his...She gulped and corralled her wayward, deliciously filthy thoughts.

He was quick to pounce. "What were you thinking just then?"

"That kilt is indecent," she blurted.

A wicked grin split his face, lighting those green eyes from the inside out. He let out a measured breath and moved ever so slowly, watching to see if she would make any effort to escape. Evangeline held her ground. The distance between them closed to a sliver, and her breath caught. "If you think that's bad, you should see what's under it."

She bit back a snort. "Let me guess. You're smuggling cabers again?"

"Dare to find out?"

It was the question he'd asked her during their first time together, when she'd put on a sensual show for him, and she grinned. Her blood warmed at the challenge, and before she could change her mind, she reached under and found herself with a handful of hard, plump ducal arse. Her face flamed, but the duke just laughed. "Caber's on the other side, leannan."

"You are insufferable!" she said, though she warmed at the endearment.

"Ah, but what will all those people say when they see the guest of honor with her hand up a Scot's kilt?"

She drew her hand back as if it were on fire, but he only laughed again. No one was paying them any mind. "They'll say, 'There's that penniless Scottish duke, snatching up our innocent English maidens and leading them astray.'"

"Innocent?" He held a hand up to shade his brow as if peering into the distance. "Where? I must corrupt her forthwith!"

Evangeline couldn't help it, she started giggling interspersed with snicker-snorts.

"I've missed those," he said. His fingers moved to caress her jaw, and she leaned into the tender touch. "I've missed you."

"I missed you, too," she whispered. There was no overthinking this. She wanted him. She wanted him without any rules or agreements. Evangeline turned her cheek to brush his knuckles with her mouth and met his stare head-on. "Kiss me, Gage."

He didn't hesitate. He swept her into his arms and took her lips in the sweetest, softest kiss, which she felt from her crown to the tips of her toes. It was unhurried, as if he wanted to take his time to savor her in the moment no matter the cost. And yet, she felt his need simmering beneath the surface, palpable in the hands that wound into her hair and kneaded her hip. His tongue teased hers, pliant but demanding, delving deep in imitation of what they both craved.

"I can't get enough of you," he muttered against her lips.

A moan escaped her as his mouth slid down the column of her throat in wet nudges and nibbles, pleasure arcing through her when one palm covered her aching breast and pinched gently. Hissing softly at the exquisite pressure, she rolled her pelvis into his, nearly groaning when she felt the hot brand of him against her abdomen. She wanted to be bare beneath him. For the first time in her life, she wanted to be *loved*.

"Gage?"

"Yes, mo chridhe." His voice was husky, filled with raw need as he licked across her collarbone.

She blinked out of her impassioned daze. "What does that mean?"

"My heart." His lips grazed over the swell of her left breast as he said it, resting his cheek there for a second as though treasuring her heartbeat. Dear God, if it were possible to melt, she would be nothing but a puddle on the floor at his feet.

"Please tell me you have since furnished your bedchamber," she whispered.

He broke from her body, lips swollen and eyes dilated with passion. "Alas, I still only have one bed."

Evangeline had never heard sweeter, more sinful words in her life.

Only. One. Bed.

Grinning, she bit her lip and wrapped her arms around his neck. "That'll do nicely."

Upstairs in his chamber—how they'd managed to remain unseen, he would never know—Gage pulled her into his arms. She was here at last. They had abandoned their guests below. No doubt, some of them would guess what they were up to, but Gage was beyond caring what the ton thought about him.

"I don't think I realized last time I was in here how big your bed is," Evangeline said throatily when he closed the door behind them.

"I'm a big man."

Crimson crested her already rosy cheeks, eyes darkening at the innuendo. He loved that he could make her react so splendidly to him, and he especially loved that she didn't hide it.

She shot him a coquettish look over her shoulder. "Shall I hold the bedpost again, Your Grace?"

"No," he said. "This is going to be hard and fast. I'll take my time with you later, I promise, but right now, I'm not going to last. I need to be inside you." Air hissed through her teeth at the raw hunger of his words. A dark shudder ran through her as he approached, her chest rising and falling with anticipation. "On the bed, on your hands and knees, Evangeline."

Without argument, she complied. "Like so?"

"Yes." He took hold of himself beneath his kilt, nearly growling at the exquisite sensitivity of his shaft. "Now lift your skirts and show me that lovely arse of yours."

She trembled again at his command, then shifted to flip her skirts and petticoats to her waist. Fuck his life if she wasn't wearing a stitch beneath her dress, and the sultry look she shot him over her shoulder nearly drove him to his knees.

"Surprise," she purred.

Surprise, indeed. He'd never seen a more gorgeous spectacle in his life, her pretty sex exposed and glistening with excitement. He fisted his cock with some intensity, forcing back his spiking arousal. If he wasn't careful, this was going to be *too* hard and *too* fast. He bit back a groaned laugh at his own weakness where she was concerned.

He narrowed his eyes at her playfully. "Did you *plan* this, my lady?"

"A lady always comes prepared."

Gage went still. "Prepared?"

Evangeline bit her lip, cheeks red as she flipped to a sitting position. "I'm not ashamed to admit I was ready to do anything to get your attention. I had an audacious plan to get you alone and have my wicked way with you." She smiled. "Your plan was much better. Seduction through my passions."

He approached the bed, desire choking him. "Trust me, leannan, I've no complaints about your plan whatsoever." He paused at the edge. "So you wanted me back?"

"I'd already forgiven you," she said. "But I needed to figure out whether I could trust you again."

"And can you?" he asked quietly, not moving an inch. This moment—her answer—was worth more than anything between them.

"I'd rather try than not know," she whispered. "Just please don't lie to me again."

He planted one palm flat on the bed and cupped her jaw with the other, wiping away the single tear that had slid down the curve of her cheek with his thumb and reviling the fact that he was the cause of her hurt. "I won't, I swear it."

He kissed her then, slowly, softly, letting his vow sink in. He would prove to her every day that he was worthy of that promise... with his words, with his actions, with his *love*. The embrace turned ardent as she nipped at his lips, her tongue dancing hungrily with his, until they were both panting.

She clutched at him, tearing at his kilt, and twisting back to her hands and knees. "Gage, now! I need you."

"I'm yours," he growled, running his palm over her hip and making her spine arch with want. He arranged himself at her entrance.

And then he impaled her in one slick thrust.

They both moaned at the sublime, impossibly snug fit. Fuck, this woman was made for him. The pulsating, hot clasp of her nearly made him see stars, and he hadn't even done anything but enter the harbor of her body. He could stay there forever quite happily.

Drowning in pleasure, he eased out slowly, eyes rolling back in his head at the exquisite drag, making sure that the soft sounds she made weren't ones of discomfort. They were both highly aroused, but that didn't mean he couldn't hurt her. He was too big not to take care.

Don't spend. Don't spend. Don't spend. It was a litany in his head.

"Gage..." His name was a pleading whimper.

Did she want him to stop or to keep going? He wanted to please her so badly, to make this so good for her that she would never leave again, but every roll, every gasp, and every needy pulse undermined his intention. Her walls quivered around him in answer, but he needed her words. "Evangeline?" he gritted out.

"Move," she growled, and shoved back against him, prodding him into action. "I need you to move."

He grinned. There she was. Demanding, vocal little thing. The truth was he would not have it any other way. He would never want her to change, not for him and not for anyone, and certainly not between them in private. He liked her wild and untamed. His fairy queen knelt for no one in the real world, and yet, here she was, kneeling for him. Willingly.

"As you wish, my love." He thrust back in.

"Say the last part in Gaelic," she gasped.

"Mo ghràdh."

She began to quake, more as he whispered it again, folding his big body over hers while his hips drove ruthlessly into hers. He sank his teeth into the flesh at her shoulder, not enough to hurt but enough for her to feel it and whimper. It didn't take long to push them both to the brink of ecstasy, and when he slung a hand around her torso to bring her spine flush with his chest, she moaned at the erotic shift in position. He slid his fingers between her legs, heard her cry out and then break around him in beautiful, erratic waves.

"Look at me, Evangeline," he commanded. Her chin angled up, those silvery-blue eyes half-lidded and glimmering with passion, cheeks flushed with pleasure. "I love you."

She exhaled, eyes burning brighter. "I love you, too."

"You're mine," he grunted, punctuating each word with a thrust.

A breathless whine left her. "Yours."

On that admission, her lithe body undulated anew, forcing him to chase his own release. God, she felt so good. Like utter perfection. Withdrawing, even though all Gage wanted to do was stay and spend inside her, his lips took hers in a tender, open-mouthed kiss, pleasure billowing between them like a gentle fog as he rode out the last spurts of his orgasm to the bedclothes below.

He nuzzled her damp neck when her head lolled back lazily against his shoulder. The sweet perfume of her sweaty skin surrounded him. "You're so agreeable like this," he whispered. "I should keep you in this soft, compliant, sated state all the time."

Her laughter was a balm over him. "If you could promise me countless orgasms, Gage, I would be the most biddable, delightful, obedient lover ever."

"Obedient? You?"

She ground her buttocks against his pelvis for emphasis. "I would be the best behaved mistress of all time."

"How about wife?" She went still in his arms, and Gage cupped her chin, holding that lovely clear gaze with his. He didn't want to hide from her. He never wanted to hide a single thing from her ever again. "Marry me, Evangeline. Make me the happiest man in the world."

Tapping one finger against her jaw, she pretended to consider his proposal. "Does this arrangement come with countless orgasms *and* kilts?"

"It does."

Full of elation, he bent to kiss her, but the little minx evaded his lips. "Actually, Your Grace, I require more time to think about concessions," she said, but the start of those adorably awful snorts under her breath told him all he needed to know.

Evangeline was glowing. She did not need a mirror to see it. She felt it.

Trust her mouthy little sister to point it out in front of all their friends, too, when they returned to the ballroom—via separate entrances, she might add. "Found what you were looking for, sister dear?"

Evangeline faltered. "Yes, I required a pin."

"And did you get *pinned*?" her evil sister asked, her emphasis on the word obvious to anyone in possession of a pair of ears.

"Viola!"

The mortified warning made no difference. Her entire group of friends graced her with knowing smirks. Even Gage's mother, to Evangeline's utter dismay, hid a secret half smile beneath her fan.

Kill me now … the mother of my future husband knows I just did wicked things with her son.

Evangeline bit her lip, wincing at the soreness of their well-kissed state, and forced herself to embody serenity. It was difficult when all she wanted to do was grab her duke by those gorgeously disheveled auburn locks and drag him back upstairs for a good hour. Maybe two.

But first … she nodded happily to the mountain of a man she called hers as he, too, returned to the ballroom and strode directly to her, allowing him to tuck her into his side like a piece of baggage. What was the point of using two separate entrances if he was going to be so obviously possessive? Evangeline giggled. She wouldn't lie—she loved it. Loved *him*.

The Duke of Vale cleared his throat. "We have another announcement. Lady Evangeline has agreed to become my wife."

The cheers and whoops from the crowd, and especially her friends, were deafening.

"Oh, Effie!" Her sister burst into tears and threw her arms around her, separating her from the duke. "I'm so happy for you. I hoped you would get out of your own way. He's perfect for you. And when he came to ask Papa's permission last night, I could barely contain myself. I knew it. I *knew* it!"

Evangeline blinked. "Wait, he asked Papa for permission?"

She turned her gaze up to the man who was looking down at her with such love in his green eyes that she felt warmed as if by the sun itself. His lips stretched into a grin that promised mischief. It did not disappoint.

"I wanted to be prepared in case you demanded I marry you." He drew her into those big arms, uncaring of what anyone thought. She didn't care either. Let them stare and let them be envious. "One never knows with a woman of your impetuous nature."

Evangeline arched a brow. "Impetuous?"

"A hothead. Heedless? Precipitous? Any one of those will do."

She wrapped her arms around his waist and snorted. "I prefer conclusive."

"Speaking of, you never did say what your conclusions were on your carnal endeavors," he whispered as he gave a signal to the musicians and steered her toward the center of the ballroom. "Did you prove your hypothesis?"

She winked. "Alas, Your Grace, this august researcher will require more extensive study."

"How extensive?" he asked huskily.

"I have a scandalous idea for those unwanted cravats of yours as well as our faithful bedpost. Two of said bedposts, in fact." His green eyes darkened at the image she painted, hands flexing compulsively on hers.

"You are diabolical, woman."

"Too late to escape, Your Grace. I already said yes. You're mine forever." She sang the last word.

The Duke of Vale threw back his head and laughed. When the strains for a waltz began to play and they took to the dancing floor as a newly engaged couple, Evangeline's heart felt as though it was going to burst. Everything inside of her felt joyous and light.

This was how a future should feel—full of infinite, weightless hope. She knew the road ahead would not be easy. She and Vale weren't so different in temperament. They were both strong, stubborn, and assertive, with their own minds and opinions. He would not give in easily and neither would she, but Evangeline had no doubt that even when they bickered and disagreed, laughter would never be too far away. She would be well and wholly loved.

He was simply that kind of man.

And he was *hers*.

EPILOGUE

Gage held the thick, heavy caber with two hands and estimated the distance and velocity he had to throw the thing to beat both Marsden and Lushing as well as the strapping village lads *and* lasses he'd grown up with. The performance pressure was intense.

Across the sea of red tartans, bagpipes, and competitors, his radiant new duchess was watching from her nearby perch, eyes as blue as a winter loch in the Scottish sunshine. He liked seeing her in his clan colors. They had chosen to forgo the fanfare of a large London wedding and had gotten married over the anvil in Gretna Green instead. It had suited them quite well.

The wedding celebrations, however, at his mother's great hall involved the entire local community, which was another matter altogether. It encompassed four days of feasting, singing, dancing, and friendly competition, including a traditional caber toss. And after all his boasting to his new bride of his prowess, he knew he had to make good on his claims. That, or be ridiculed forever. His wicked little wife would not let him off the hook so easily.

He winked at her where she stood, and she waved, touching a finger to the intricate heart-and-crown-shaped brooch pinned to her bodice. Earlier that morning, he'd pinned it to the edge of her gown and pressed a kiss to the mouthwatering swell of her breast over it. That had led to his tongue doing other naughty things and exploring other parts of her too-delicious body. Said brooch *and* gown had ended up in a frantic heap on the floor.

"It's a Scottish tradition dating back centuries, a token of my affection and love," he'd whispered when they were both lying in a sweaty, satiated heap. "A luckenbooth. It's a lucky charm to keep you safe from fairies."

Her eyes had widened with delight. "Fairies?"

"They're all over the Scottish dells, waiting to snatch unsuspecting maidens away for their beauty."

Evangeline had laughed and wrapped her long legs around him. "Lucky for me, I was stolen by the king of the fair folk himself. They wouldn't dare snatch me."

"Or perhaps," he'd countered, "*you* are Titania incarnate, and I am but a poor smitten soul groveling at your queenly feet."

"Groveling," she'd replied with a lengthy kiss. "Let's have more of that."

He'd *groveled* so much the night before that she was a sobbing, writhing mess of need, and had slept for nearly a full day following. Male pride sluiced through him. Let it not be said that the Duke of Vale didn't commit to a project with every drop of strength he possessed. In bed and out of it.

Like said caber toss.

A commotion through the participants made him frown as his new duchess sauntered toward him, an impish grin on her face. Everyone cheered raucously when she lifted to her toes and pressed a demure kiss to his stubbled cheek. Her words *weren't* demure, however. "Win and I'll take you with my mouth later."

He about swallowed his tongue. Now he had to contend with *two* cabers.

Surely he was the default winner by that alone! Nobody else had to throw a hundred-pound log with an iron bar in their trews.

Muttering to himself, Gage lifted and cupped the whittled end of the twenty-foot sapling in both hands, grunting at the substantial weight, and braced the lower half against his shoulder. It wasn't about actual distance, though prowess was important, it was about the log going end over end and landing in a perfect twelve o'clock position directly opposite him.

He didn't dare look at his wife, but as always, his will failed him. Her tongue pressed into her cheek in a lewd gesture as she held a fist up to her mouth, and he bellowed a pained groan. Cursing his luck, he ran forward a few steps and tossed the log, air punching from him as it completed a full revolution, the thicker end hitting the dirt and then flipping forward to thwack the ground with a loud snap.

It was nowhere near twelve o'clock.

Later that night, his sweet, wicked wife rewarded him anyway.

A few days later following the end of the feast and after most of the guests had departed, Evangeline glanced at the letters that had been delivered and forgotten among all of the wedding correspondence. One was from Vesper, who she was delighted to see had written about her new baby girl. She and Greydon had not been able to attend the festivities because of a challenging birth, but their daughter was a warrior just like her mother and was now thriving.

Briar, too, had not been able to attend, much to Lushing's dismay, though the earl had stalwartly pretended otherwise. Apparently, she'd been detained by the Metropolitan Police for disturbing the peace at Lethe of all places, and her father had forbidden her to leave London. That reminded Evangeline about how familiar she'd been with the social club the night of the fight.

She peered at her husband. "Do you know if Briar is a member at Lethe?"

"I'm not sure. Why do you ask?" Gage replied, looking up from his seat across the thick oak breakfast table.

"She knew where all the rooms were, and the maid seemed especially polite. Minthe, I believe her name was," Evangeline said frowning. "But Briar has never mentioned it. And now Vesper said that she ran into some trouble there."

"People can have secrets, love," Gage said, lifting his brows, considering they'd had a rather large one of their own. He slathered butter on some toast and handed it to her. "And besides, isn't she always protesting women's rights and getting into scrapes with unsavory types? Perhaps she knows the women who work there."

Evangeline nodded absently and bit into the toast. "Maybe."

But it didn't seem like that. She chewed, recalling that night. Evangeline had been more concerned with Gage's injuries then, but now she recalled other details, like the fact that Briar had known exactly where to go once the police arrived. And not main hallways either. She'd taken special corridors and a staircase, one that had led to a well-appointed office where they had remained until Minthe had fetched them. Briar had walked those halls with the confidence of a woman who belonged there, not one who was a member.

It was decidedly odd.

As Evangeline continued to read the letter, a hand flew to her chest, her mouth falling open into silent shock as she skimmed the paragraph, making her forget Briar for a moment. "Oh," she exclaimed.

"What's the matter?" Gage asked.

"Vesper writes that Huntington has been arrested for stealing," she said, scanning the lines. "He crossed the wrong man at the tables at a gambling hell, and now he's in jail, awaiting sentencing."

"Good riddance," Gage said. "Despite wanting to take the high road and being compassionate, I must admit that I regretted being too lenient with that bastard."

Evangeline agreed. The cad had killed Gage's brother, after all, and he'd been unforgivably violent to her own sister. It didn't seem fair that he'd escaped with no real punishment for his dreadful actions, but clearly, he was paying for them now.

As she continued to read, sorrow replaced her shock. "Oh no. There's more news. Vesper's daughter is doing well, but she has written that her father has taken a turn for the worse. I'd heard he was ill, but didn't realize it was so bad. Gracious, she must be so devastated."

Gage nodded. "Lushing mentioned that he'd been quietly sick for years. A wasting illness of the lungs, he told me."

"Doesn't make it any easier, knowing it's coming, and right after her child's birth, too." A tear slipped down her cheek. Evangeline couldn't begin to imagine how bleak both Vesper and Jasper were feeling. She loved her own father dearly and couldn't fathom life without him.

"Come here, mo ghràdh," her husband commanded gently.

Evangeline lifted from her seat and walked around the table, crawling into the welcoming haven of his lap. He kissed her brow and held her tight. Taking comfort in his warm embrace, she twirled the gorgeous ruby and diamond ring with intricate thistle engravings on her hand, a gift from her mother-in-law.

"It will be all right," he told her, rubbing her back in slow, soothing circles.

She breathed out. "Lushing will need all the friends he can get, too. He's never been able to deal with painful things, and Vesper has confided many times that he doesn't wish to become the next Duke of Harwick." A small sigh left her. "As much as I've loved being here, we should head back to England soon. I want to be there for Vesper and Baby Audra."

"I agree."

Evangeline glanced up at him, at his strong, handsome face, those green eyes as always aglow with love. "You don't want to stay longer? I can go alone, if necessary."

"I love the Highlands, Evangeline. I always will, but our home is in England. Your shelter work is there, and all our friends are there. Mother can visit when she wants, and we are also free to come back whenever we like."

She stared at him. "Travel is long and costly." She didn't know why she was pushing the matter. Perhaps she hoped to be reassured that she wasn't keeping him from doing what he'd always planned to do—return to his home. If he wanted to remain here, she would never want to deny him. Family was important to both of them.

He scooped her up and turned her so she was facing him. "Good thing I am married to a very rich heiress who is infatuated with me and quite devoted to making me happy."

Making a scoffing noise, though she didn't deny it in the least, Evangeline melted against him happily, breathing in his delicious scent. "But your mother is getting older. We cannot expect her to make the journey so often."

"My mother is an indestructible battle-ax of a woman who will ride a stallion over Hadrian's Wall if she had to," he said with a chuckle. "And when we start having bairns, trust me, nothing will stop her from coming to smother them in a tartan or two."

Chest clenching at the thought of his babies, Evangeline drew a finger over his bronze-stubbled skin. Her breath faltered. It was his right as a husband and her duty as a wife. As duke, Gage would require an heir, but she wanted to work first. Make sure she expanded her shelter and followed those dreams before she was shut away behind closed doors like half the women of the ton. "Do you want children immediately?"

His big hands traced over her spine, making her shiver when they rounded the curves of her hips. "Well, I suppose I do someday, when the time comes, but for now, these exhaustive experiments of yours are keeping me rather busy."

"Complaints, Your Grace?"

He smirked. "Never."

Evangeline couldn't help but feel relief. She wanted to be a mother, but later. Her expression must have been transparent, because he grasped her chin and cradled her cheeks in his palms. "We're in this together, leannan. Every decision we make, about children or our lives or where we live, we do together."

"How did I get so lucky?" she whispered. His green eyes shone with so much love that her heart felt absurdly full.

"No, *mo ghràdh*. I'm the lucky one because I get to love you." Gage took her lips then, in an unhurried, slow kiss as though she was something precious to be savored. "Every day until forever."

Acknowledgments

Gratitude time! To my editor Amy Pierpont, who saw this book through to the end before our paths diverged, thank you so much for everything. It was wonderful to work with you over the course of this series.

Huge thanks to Junessa Viloria, who took the proverbial baton and kept us running to the finish line!

To my agent, Thao Le, I will never stop screaming my undying love for you! You're a superstar and I'm so ridiculously grateful to have you in my corner.

Big thanks to Sam Brody and Sabrina Flemming! Thank you to the production, editing, design, sales, and publicity teams at Forever for all your efforts behind the scenes, especially my PR geniuses, Dana Cuadrado and Caroline Green.

A profound thank-you to the amazing ladies in my writing circles who are legit the most awesome friends a girl could ask for—Katie McGarry, Angie Frazier, Brigid Kemmerer, Wendy Higgins, Vonetta Young, Aliza Mann, and Suzanne Hammers (my fierce kickboxing queen)—I have so much love for you.

To my fabulous assistant, Karen Delabar—you are truly a shining star—I am beyond grateful for everything do.

To all the readers, reviewers, influencers, booksellers, librarians, educators, close family and extended family, as well as friends who support me and spread the word about my books, my very sincere thanks. I wouldn't be here without you.

Finally, to my family, Cameron, Connor, Noah, and Olivia, thanks for always making a girl feel loved every single day.

YOUR
BOOK
CLUB
RESOURCE

READING GROUP GUIDE

Author's Note

Dear Reader,

Thank you so much for reading *The Worst Duke in London* and joining Effie and Gage on their very (ahem) sex-educational journey to their happily ever after. Inspired by *10 Things I Hate About You*, which is one of my favorite '90s films, I had so much fun with this story. As with all my historical fiction novels, I truly enjoy the research. It is my hope to always make my books an immersive experience, especially when history is involved. As a diverse writer in this genre, balancing historical authenticity with relatability through a modern lens as well as challenging noncanonical concepts such as diversity and sexuality are important to me. Again, just because something has been said or written about in the past doesn't necessarily mean it's true. People of color existed, LGBTQ+ people existed, and certainly, pleasure and agency were not anachronistic concepts.

Since sensual lessons, pleasure, and self-pleasure are important themes in this book, let's get right to the data. While for the most part history records Victorians as being prudish, many of them were most decidedly not. There was a gap between the puritanical ideology put forward and what was actually performed in practice by both women and men, regardless of class. One of the interesting things I discovered when reading about Victorian sexuality was the work of Dr. Clelia

Mosher, who did an unpublished sex survey of women in the 1800s. This study was eye-opening! It asked questions about Victorian women's sexual habits, proclivities, appetites, pleasure, and partners, and what it showed was that Victorian women knew what they wanted and how they wanted it...and were vexed when they didn't get it! In this survey, a woman born in 1844 said sex was "a normal desire" and "a rational use of it tends to keep people healthier." Another claimed that if she didn't orgasm, it was "bad, even disastrous" along with "nerve-racking-unbalancing if such conditions continue for any length of time." One of the women surveyed claimed, "when no orgasm, took days to recover" while another attested, "men have not been properly trained." So, despite conjecture, Victorian women enjoyed sex, felt desire, and sought personal pleasure...with and without sex toys.

Consequently (or perhaps not), female hysteria was one of the most frequently and commonly diagnosed illnesses in the eighteenth and nineteenth centuries. Hysteria comes from the Greek word *hystera*, which means *uterus*. Several French physicians in the late 1700s had theories that hysteria was an ailment that led to emotional instability and that women were predisposed to it. Playwright Henry Fielding wrote in 1752 that women were subject to extreme emotions: "A Disorder very common among the Ladies...Some call it Fever on the Spirits, some a nervous Fever, some the Vapours, and some the hysterics." When Victorian women complained of restlessness, erotic dreams, irritability, sleeplessness, and cramping in lower abdomen, they were diagnosed with hysteria.

Some of my research pointed to pelvic massage as a physical treatment, to release a "paroxysm" or orgasm, which then led to different types of inventions in the service of medical therapy. Some historians dispute this as myth, however. In 1880, Dr. Joseph Mortimer Granville invented the first "percusser," or electromechanical vibrator. Stone, leather, and wooden dildos have been around forever in ancient Egypt and ancient Greece. A 28,000-year-old stone penis was discovered in Germany and touted as the oldest sex aid ever discovered! The word *dildo* was first used in AD 1400 but didn't appear in England until the sixteenth century. William Shakespeare used it in *The Winter's Tale*—"with such delicate burthens of dildos and fadings, 'jump her and thump her'"—with a very obvious sexual meaning.

My hero is half-Scottish, and he often says that Evangeline reminds him of a fairy queen. Scotland is full of awesome stories of the "fair folk," or the sìth as they're called. One of the cool things I read about was the Schiehallion mountain, or in Gaelic, Sìth Chailleann, which means "the Fairy Hill of the Caledonians," and it's the source of so many mythical stories. Apparently at the southwest side of it, there's a famous giant cave that is rumored to be a portal to the underworld! On the west side, fairies are rumored to live. Another legend says that it's a series of caves, and if you go through it, a door closes and you can never get out! The last I read was that it's haunted by Cailleach Bheur, an old witch of the winter who appears from Samhain to Beltane: "Her face was blue with cold, her hair white with frost and the plaid that wrapped her bony shoulders was grey as the winter fields."

However, most interestingly of all and more scientific in nature than mystical, in 1774 Schiehallion was used by the Astronomer Royal Nevil Maskelyne in an experiment to calculate the density and weight of the Earth, using the mountain's own mass, the rock it was made of, and a pendulum to calculate the gravitational force of the mountain. That sounds very complicated to me—I'll take the fairy myths over gravitational calculations any day.

Animal welfare is an important plot point in the novel. My heroine runs an animal shelter, and her character was inspired by real-life animal lover and activist Mary Tealby, who was a longtime supporter of the RSPCA and in 1860 founded the Temporary Home for Lost and Starving Dogs, which became the very well-known Battersea Dogs and Cats Home in 1871. The original home was housed in Mary's scullery, after she found a sick and starving dog in the gutter, but was then moved to rented stables on Hollingsworth Street. Mary herself described the home as a "temporary refuge to which humane persons may send only lost dogs so constantly seen in the streets." Not only was she a divorcée and independent but Mary was also not a wealthy woman, so she depended on charitable funding for the shelter.

Her efforts were frequently mocked by the *Times*, because her behavior and marital status was not consistent with the moral values of upstanding Victorian women, but author Charles Dickens fiercely defended her as well as the home and turned around support in her favor. He called her efforts an "extraordinary monument of the remarkable affection with which the English people regard the race of dogs." She also received the patronage of Queen Victoria, who was a notorious dog lover. Mary died in 1865 from cancer, and the leadership of the committee was taken over by her brother, Reverend Edward Bates, and her friend Sarah Major, who appears in this novel as a side character. Not a lot was recorded about Sarah Major, so I had to take quite a bit of creative liberty in my descriptions. She was instrumental in what eventually became the Battersea Dogs and Cats Home.

Speaking of the queen, when she was coronated in 1837 at eighteen, her dog Dash was her devoted companion. She loved many different breeds (Pomeranians, pugs, collies, dachshunds, and terriers, to name a few) and entered many dog shows during her reign. The Victorians in general were noted for their devotion to sporting breeds such as foxhounds, deerhounds, and bloodhounds. The Victorian period, 1837–1901, also saw a shift in the thinking toward animal welfare.

The Society for the Prevention of Cruelty to Animals (SPCA) was founded in 1824 in a coffee shop, led by Reverend Arthur Broome and, despite many financial challenges, was instrumental early on in banning cruelty to dogs and domestic animals. Richard Martin, also known as Humanity Dick, was behind the first law (Martin's Law) to protect animals in England in 1822, and the society worked hard to enforce this law. In 1835, the then Princess Victoria officially became a Lady Patroness of the society; a letter from Kensington Palace arrived to the SPCA that read: "Her Royal Highness very readily acceded to your request that her name and that of the Princess Victoria be placed on the list of Lady Patronesses." Her support completely changed how the society was received . . . and also funded. In 1840, as queen, she gave her permission to add "royal" to the name, making it the RSPCA.

Tangentially, in my research about common Victorian-era pets, apart from the usual feline and canine persuasions, I discovered some very interesting things. While pedigree dogs were very fashionable for the upper classes as noted above, some unusual pets of the period included hedgehogs, wombats, zebras, Eurasian badgers, parrots, monkeys, and wild squirrels. In *Domestic Pets: Their Habits and Management*, written in 1851, the author Jane Loudon stated squirrels should be housed in "little ornamental kennels, with a platform for the squirrel to sit on, and a little chain to fasten a collar round the squirrel's neck." Charles Dickens had a pet raven, and indeed, ravens and jackdaws became popular as pets, especially if caught as fledglings in the wild, but were otherwise sourced through a bird dealer. They could be taught tricks and words.

The Henley Royal Regatta, in which my hero and his friends raced in this novel, has been a British rowing tradition since 1839 and occurs in the summer for five days, Wednesday to Sunday, at Henley Reach, a straight part of the river that's just about a mile and a third long. In 1851, the "Royal" was added to the title, under Prince Albert's patronage. Each race occurs with two teams, and a new race starts every five minutes, with racers competing for the Grand Challenge Cup. The racecourse, beginning at Temple Island and heading upstream to Henley Bridge, is marked with floating booms—one course is known as "Bucks" on the Buckinghamshire side, and the other is the "Becks" on the Berkshire side of the river. The regatta was definitely an event where wealthy people went to be seen, with women wearing expensive and fashionable clothes, and carrying parasols, while cheering on the racers.

As for athletic events, with regards to cabers and caber tossing, my research into the Scottish Highland Games was fascinating. Tossing the caber is part of a series of traditional athletic games held in Scotland from May through September between the clans that started in the sixteenth century. A few speculative theories abound that the idea originated from lumberjacks using tree trunks as bridges to cross rivers, while another claims they were used by soldiers to break down gates or to cross moats in order to storm castles, though there isn't much historical proof of either. Cut from local trees, caber sizes can range between sixteen to twenty-two feet and anywhere from 100 to 180 pounds. One end is whittled smaller so the thrower can vertically cup it in their hands before the toss. After a small run, the caber is thrown and must complete one full revolution before hitting the ground on the thicker end so that the smaller ends falls away from the thrower. It's not about distance but about position. In the epilogue, Gage's whole goal is to make sure the caber lands squarely at 12, if you can imagine a clock, while he's standing at 6. It takes strength, control, and a lot of stamina as well as an excellent grasp of the hip thrust (heh … sorry, not sorry). Admittedly, I had way too much "kilty" fun looking at caber tossing videos.

Hope you enjoyed the story and learning some more about Victorian England and Scotland! Thank you for reading about Gage and Effie, and accompanying them to their happy-ever-after!

xo,
Amalie

THE WORST DUKE IN LONDON
DISCUSSION QUESTIONS

1) *The Worst Duke in London* takes inspiration from the '90s rom-com *10 Things I Hate About You*, which is a loose retelling of *The Taming of the Shrew*, written by Shakespeare in the late sixteenth century. Both considered comedies, *The Taming of the Shrew* and *10 Things I Hate About You* follow the courtship of two sisters, one biddable and one shrewish, and their respective love interests. While the play has been criticized for being misogynistic, the film is definitely more feminist forward, although some critics have argued that the play is a definitive satire on marriage and gender roles. Both, however, try to address the concept of toxic masculinity and the idea that a woman has to conform to be "acceptable" or "marriageable" or "dateable." How do the men in *The Worst Duke in London* (Vale, Huntington, Lushing, and Evangeline's father) react to powerful women? Consider the themes of power, social hierarchy, and patriarchal systems, and discuss their impact on my characters, both male and female.

2) My heroine is considered a shrew because she's opinionated and isn't afraid of sharing her opinions. While Evangeline has characteristics of both Kat in *10 Things I Hate About*

You and Katherina in *The Taming of the Shrew*, would you say one or the other is more prevalent in Evangeline's overall characterization? One example is that Evangeline has more control over her own choices, which is closer to Kat than Katherina. Another is that both she and Katherina suffered psychological abuse that informs their identities and responses to the world. What other parallels or notable differences do you see, if any, between Evangeline and Kat or Evangeline and Katherina?

3) Animal welfare is a huge plot point in this book. There are many parallels between Evangeline's treatment of her animals and the interactions of people. Gage admits that the way to Evangeline's heart is through her passion, namely her devotion to her shelter and her furry friends. In *The Taming of the Shrew*, the hero "tames" the heroine with cruelty, while in *10 Things I Hate About You*, the "taming" is more about real connection. Discuss how respect, kindness, and care can be better motivators not only with animals but also with people. Do you see Lucky or Beasty Buttercup represented in any of the characters? Evangeline also says that animals are an excellent judge of character. Do you agree?

4) In the Taming of the Dukes series, my heroines are unconventional in that they are driven by their own personal goals and agency. Feminism is not an anachronistic concept, especially for women in historical times who refused to toe the line of social expectation and rules of decorum. Similar to

my previous heroines from the other two books in the series, Effie's choices are certainly not typical of the period, especially when she makes an arrangement with an unmarried gentleman for "sensual lessons." Do you think that Effie was taking unnecessary risks for a woman of her station in her position? Or do you agree that she was within her rights to choose her path for herself? Women's rights have come a long way since the Victorian era—discuss limitations back then versus ones that might still exist today.

5) The pursuit of pleasure for an aristocratic woman who doesn't expect to fulfill society's expectations and decides to seek a lover is a controversial topic, especially as it will undoubtedly lead to a ruined reputation, if discovered. Discuss the double standards that existed in Victorian times and how they impacted women. Do you see any parallels today? Can a man still do things that aren't considered acceptable for a woman? Is a woman still defined by her actions and her behaviors?

6) The hero, the Duke of Vale, makes an untoward agreement to square away his brother's debt by convincing Evangeline to go to London. In the beginning, it's simply a means to an end, but as the story progresses, his motives become conflicted. If you found yourself in a similar situation to clear a debt or earn a significant amount of money, would you consider doing it? What are the moral implications, if any? Even though the relationship started out on a lie, do you think it can be salvaged in a satisfactory manner? What would it take?

7) Female agency and self-actualization are important themes in this novel, especially for my heroine Evangeline, who doesn't feel as if she fits into aristocratic society. Because she was shunned from society by a self-important gentleman for having an opinion, she decided not to fade quietly into obscurity. Instead, she lives quite unapologetically and doesn't give in to her tormenter's abuse. Do you think this was an admirable choice by Evangeline? What does it say about her strength of character? Discuss how her characterization is influenced by her friend group as well as how it influences the growth of her sister's arc.

8) The story is set in the Victorian era and references specific philanthropical and social structures. Real historical figures such as the champion prizefighter Jem Mace, Mary Tealby, founder of the Temporary Home for Lost and Starving Dogs, as well as her brother, Reverend Edward Bates, and friend Sarah Major, were interwoven with my fictional characters to make the story experience more authentic, especially in terms of what kinds of movements were important during the period. Do you feel these historical people enriched the reading experience, or do you prefer all characters to be fictional?

9) In Regency and Victorian times, the aristocracy was very elitist and aloof. Most peeresses would support charities from afar and not devote their personal efforts to the betterment of the less fortunate by getting their proverbial hems dirty. However, Evangeline uses her time to help her animals

without care for her reputation. Do you think this was an unwise choice, considering what she had to lose, or is this an admirable characteristic? What could she have done differently?

10) Bonus round: Which plot/character elements are similar to *10 Things I Hate About You* and which ones are different?

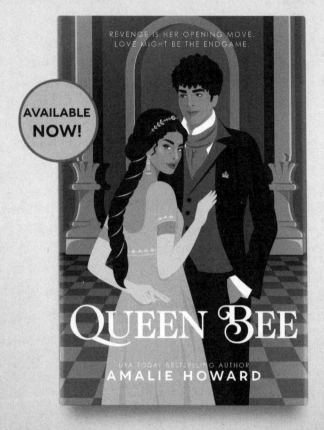

About the Author

Amalie Howard is the *USA Today* bestselling author of *Never Met a Duke Like You* and *The Beast of Beswick*, one of *Oprah Daily*'s "Top 24 Best Historical Romance Novels to Read." Her books have been featured in the *Hollywood Reporter*, *Entertainment Weekly*, *Cosmopolitan*, and *Seventeen*. She is also the author of several critically acclaimed, award-winning young adult novels, including *Queen Bee*, which *Booklist* called "a true diamond of the first water." When she's not writing, she can usually be found reading, being the president of her one-woman Harley-Davidson motorcycle club, or power napping. She lives in Colorado with her family.

You can learn more at:
AmalieHoward.com
X @AmalieHoward
Facebook.com/AmalieHowardAuthor
Instagram @AmalieHoward
Pinterest.com/AmalieHoward
TikTok @AmalieHowardAuthor